Kingston

Anya Mamaeva

KINGSTON

Paperback ISBN: 979-8-9925239-0-4
Digital ISBN: 979-8-9925239-1-1

To my parents, for believing in my creativity and pushing to achieve.
To my sister, for convincing me to express my work without limitations.
For my best friend, Jacky, for supporting my crazy flight of ideas.

If this sucks, at least I tried lmao

Content Warning

This novel is not a dark romance, but it does have explicit and mature subjects, such as child marriage, child abuse, self-harm, mentions of rape/non-consent, sexual assault, physical abuse, verbal abuse, detailed sexual content, misogynistic behavior/power imbalance, and detailed gore/violence.

Please be advised of the mature and sensitive themes.

It is essential to take care of yourself.

The name, **Kingston**, is typically thought to mean "king's town" or "royal town." However, it could also mean "king's meadow" or "royal meadow." Regardless of the interpretation, Kingston conveys a sense of royalty and power.

l Ocean

Zuiphate

Cinderhaven

Onyx Falls

Map

Marana Forest

Gentle Meadows

Hartfelt

Baysor Groove

Great Plains

Neemere Forest

orningstar

Ironwood

Silent Trees

Callous Hills

1

The Bride

As a highly sought-after princess, Lucia Morningstar attracted numerous suitors across the lands.

Her short, fluffy, and streaked blonde hair was constantly, perfectly styled and occasionally adorned with flowers. Her skin was flawless, free from any blemishes or marks. Striking blue, crystal eyes and thin, curvy physique further accentuated her allure. Moreover, as demonstrated by her diligent adherence to the king's commands, her exceptional obedience and housekeeping skills made her a desirable asset for kingdoms worldwide. And when she ripened and a line of outsiders began to form to eagerly get a chance to propose, King Johnathan knew it was time to pick her spouse.

King Johnathan sought a solid kingdom to help leverage his already large empire. He was picky, denying men of different statuses left and right. His daughter helplessly stood by his side for weeks on end, a visual trophy to show what these suitors missed by the king's refusal.

A gorgeous virgin with desirable traits and breathtaking beauty.

Oh, it drove these suitors mad, trying at everything to offer and please the king.

Everyone wanted a beautiful, obedient spouse to effortlessly accept their seed. When a rival prince, the youngest of three brothers, and his family dared to tread on Father's land with the best offer of a lifetime, it struck an everlasting impression.

Plentiful gold, sparkling jewels, brute horses, and fine literature by the stacks. Plus, a peace treaty and trade contract with new roads. The two realms had been at odds over territorial and toll disputes, but a truce, with exclusive offers, was promised for the exchange of King Johnathan's only daughter. The amount of power Father would gain for himself and the kingdom, he could not deny.

The arranged marriage was scheduled.

At age fourteen, Lucia was a wife, tasked with loving and caring for the neighboring royal family and her new husband. The newlywed bride was showered with luxurious silk and jewels by the king and queen-in-laws as she settled into her new home. Gift after gift, she thought she had settled in Heaven.

However, the in-laws' kindness was a way to conceal their son's vituperative nature—a dark secret behind closed doors, hidden deep from the public eye.

Lucia remained innocent and dutiful, fulfilling her role as a perfect wife as she flawlessly executed her wifely duties directly to her husband without defiance or stubbornness—the epitome of support and attentiveness. The royal family-in-laws admired and praised her impeccable work, being spoiled by the fruits of her labor, but it was not long before the prince began picking on his wife.

It hurt the princess, unaware of whether she had done something wrong to deserve this cruel bullying. She tried harder, morphing into more of a servant than a spouse, to better please her husband. There was hope it was the right move, but she was wrong.

The abuse only flared— minor insults turned to screaming, harsh words, and new physical shoves soon warped into beatings. Bruises and cuts decorated her small body. Sprained muscles and carpet burns from the forceful drags across floors. Even when things did not go as planned or did not go his way, he released that stress upon his wife, a scapegoat of his insecure masculinity.

No one came to help her. The servants were ordered not to interfere. The royal family-in-laws were aware of the cruelty and decided to turn a blind eye.

Their son was perfect. Whatever Lucia did, she deserved it under their son's judgment.

As time passed, Lucia yearned for freedom from her marriage. The unfortunate girl was confined and isolated from the world, her body concealed from head to toe by the cruel marks of abuse. She was never permitted to venture outside, much like a caged animal locked away in the darkness. She could not fathom how much longer she could endure this torment, confronting the harrowing possibility of being killed by the prince's hand, perpetually living in constant fear and anxiety.

To exacerbate the situation, the royal in-laws demanded a grandson.

The arranged couple did not indulge in lewd activities after the vows were exchanged. The prince viewed the marriage solely as a means to gain more power, so the two slept in separate bedchambers. He did not favor sharing. But to satisfy his family's request, the prince began pursuing his wife intimately.

The prince tried to touch her delicate frame inappropriately and force her to touch him against her will, but she consistently managed to escape these ghastly situations. No matter how often the prince attempted to seduce her, she would always have a way to evade and reject his advances.

This behavior contradicted the submissive, mute wife that King Johnathan had promised to the royal in-laws, and the prince's frustration only grew with each rejection. Not shy about expressing his dissatisfaction and eagerness to fulfill his marital duty, the prince detailed his wife's constant refusals to his family.

The king and queen-in-law were furious.

Refusal? How could she refuse?

Immediately, Lucia was ordered to meet with them in their private quarters.

Initially unaware of the couple's intentions, it was soon made clear to her of their plan as they coerced her into submission through a series of yelling. The king and queen threatened to brutally behead her and return her lifeless body to King Johnathan if she continued to deny their son's sexual advances. The royal in-laws were not ones to be trifled with, and their threats sent shudders of terror through the princess. Being rejected by such high-ranking nobility was a shame she could not bear to bring upon her family.

So, she was left to acquiesce to their demands.

That night, locked in the prince's bedroom, Lucia's husband satisfied himself with the disregard for her anguish. He was careless as he ignored the cries and pleas, repeatedly using her body as a mere toy for his discarded semen. Blood and sweat were smeared between her thighs.

And ever since that night, the prince continuously pursued his sexual desires.

He took every opportunity to force himself upon Lucia, whether his wife was busy with chores, preparing for the day, or even sleeping. If she were folding freshly dried clothes, the prince would lift her skirt and bury himself inside. If she were preparing food, he would be there to fondle her curvy body inappropriately and whisper humiliating, foul language. Even when she was asleep, he would sneak in and pound his wife into the mattress. And, with constant unwanted sex, resulted in conception.

The kingdom celebrated. The king and queen-in-laws were ecstatic.

Lucia had fallen pregnant.

Midwives attended the princess's side at every step of the way. They assisted her with her bodily changes throughout her first pregnancy. The prince could not care less about helping, especially since he found her physically unattractive.

However, it was a different story for the princess. She had never felt so attentive before, grateful for the appointed midwives who stayed by her side every day. There were now people to talk to, who cared for her welfare and her unborn child. She was so, so tired of being alone.

Friends.

The midwives felt like friends. It was pleasant, a change, especially from the vicious, abusive cycle she had with her husband.

The kingdom prayed for a boy. Despite already having grandsons from their other sons, the king and queen-in-laws wanted an army of boys. The prince picked a traditional name and was thrilled when his wife went into labor.

All members of the massive court held their breath for the arrival of another young prince. Screams echoed out of her bedchamber and throughout the halls. What felt like hours of agony all came to an end when the newborn was delivered.

Lucia delivered a girl.

The husband and grandparents were utterly disappointed.

A girl would mean having to work to break, be obedient, and be sent off to be another person's seedbearer. Gifts for future engagements would be thoughtful, but it was only a temporary resolution. It was more of a burden than a blessing to the family.

Although the kingdom was disheartened, Lucia was ecstatic—a little girl, her own daughter.

Motherhood swelled in her heart as she reached for her screaming infant into her arms, startled from the sudden introduction into the world. The midwives rushed to clean.

She was perfect, nestled in a soft blanket as she cried.

Charlotte.

A name Lucia picked.

A beautiful name for a beautiful girl, a mere replica of her own birth parent. Small, with the same yellow hair and ocean-blue eyes.

The midwives adored her newborn, aided in the princess's breast-feeding, and monitored her postpartum changes. But Lucia knew the worst was to come when the midwives were sent away. She tried to convince her husband to let them stay longer, but she was met by his harsh hand to her foolish idea and uninvited words.

As Charlotte grew, the prince paid no heed to his daughter. He had practically disowned her the moment she was born. Lucia took it upon herself to raise her daughter with love and compassion, teaching her to be kind and empathetic to others. Everyone should be treated equally, regardless of their role—courtesans, counts, barons, musicians, servants, and more.

Although Lucia did her utmost to shield her daughter from the abusive environment, young children cannot help but be pulled into harmful altercations. The most traumatic experience was when she experienced the prince grab her mother's neck, strangling her to death due to a significant political deal gone wrong. Her face quickly turned purple, with saliva foaming over her lips as her hands weakly clawed at his tight grip. The prince used his weight as a placeholder while he watched his wife slowly go limp underneath him with satisfaction. Pillows and blankets were rustled onto the floor from the struggle. It was too much for Charlotte to comprehend.

The little girl cried helplessly, and with a small glimpse of hope, the prince felt pity at the pathetic sight of his daughter sobbing and pulling on his pant leg. Eyes of uncertainty moved back and forth between the near-lifeless princess and the unwanted daughter. If he killed Lucia, he would be left with the responsibility of taking care of his offspring; the same offspring that was not a son.

The idea disgusted him, and with some luck of Lucia's chest still periodically heaving for survival, he let go. His wife gasped for oxygen as his daughter sobbed by her side. Her little hands grabbed onto her clothing in a plea for her well-being. He stomped out of the room without a care.

The same went for the sexual encounters. Lucia tried her best to protect her little girl from bearing witness to her father's filthy hands and needy prick. Whenever the prince came to satisfy himself on her, she would make a game for Charlotte to play hide-and-seek beforehand. It helped the little girl avoid being exposed to inappropriate encounters, as she ran excitedly to find a hiding spot away from them. And when it was over, her mother would come find her.

It was a harsh world, and Charlotte was too young to understand the complex realities. All she needed to focus on was her imaginary friends.

Lucia did not believe in miracles. It was a false belief that gave people the desired hope in reasoning random coincidences. Yet, on one cold morning, her faith in miracles changed.

The prince dropped dead.

The servant screamed out in horror. Lucia stared as his body hit the floor of his bedchamber. She did not react, simply thinking it was a new scare to gain sympathy through his series of manipulation tactics. Physicians were summoned immediately to try to save his life, and priests prayed by his bedside, but it was too late. There was no blood pumping through his heart. He had suffered a spontaneous cardiac arrest.

The shock of the youngest prince's death rattled the kingdom. The king and queen wailed in grief, as did the two older brothers.

By request, the body was autopsied. It was revealed that the prince had a misshapen heart, a defect at birth, the physicians stated, which had caused his heart to weaken over time. It led to muscle fatigue and, ultimately, his death. The constant abuse and exertion he forced upon his wife had only hastened the process.

As the kingdom mourned, Lucia did the opposite.

She secretly celebrated her newfound freedom. The widow had no grain of sympathy as she maintained her focus primarily on her daughter during the funeral. The idea of her husband rotting in the ground brought pleasant thoughts. He deserved no long, fulfilling life.

No more pressures on her duties, no more fear to watch over her back, no more painful intercourse. A prayer answered: she was alive, not killed by her husband's hand. Better yet, her daughter unharmed by him. She feared that once she aged, he, too, would start to attack her as well.

It took weeks for the royal family to decide what to do next. The king and queen-in-laws had no desire to keep Lucia and her daughter, as Charlotte was female and could not inherit the throne as an heir without marriage. Their other two sons are already married to their brides and have children of their own.

So, it was decided.

Lucia and Charlotte were set to be sent back to Kingdom Morningstar.

King Johnathan agreed to take his daughter and granddaughter back into his care if the other party kept the trade and treaty in place. The king and queen-in-laws agreed only to the trade.

Father grumbled his dissatisfaction, but ultimately accepted.

Despite the unique circumstances, the king hoped to marry his daughter again. She was still fruitful and young, with many years ahead of her for childbearing. However, there was one particular importance that the king failed to notice.

His daughter was no longer a virgin—a must-needed requirement in royal marriage.

2

The Uprising Knight

Alaric Hartfelt was born and raised on a poor commoner farm, nestled among rolling hills and lush greenery. His ginger family, humble and traditional, consisted of his mother, father, and younger sister. They lived simply, relying on the land for sustenance and survival.

His father was a seasoned farmer, teaching him the ropes of manual labor from a young age. The fields of crops required constant attention, from plowing the soil to tending the growing plants. The cows and chickens, too, needed daily care and feeding. Alaric's strong work ethic and unwavering willpower were traits his father sincerely appreciated about his son.

Together, they've spent countless hours working side by side, their days beginning at sunrise and ending only when they lie their heads down to rest. Despite the grueling work, Alaric never complained. He cherished his family and understood the importance of providing for them all. Moreso, it built his character.

The woman of the house, his mother, was incredibly proud of him, not only because of his charming demeanor but also because of his empathetic nature. She never had to ask him to assist with cooking dinner, as he was always willing to lend a helping hand. And when he was present, she always told stories. He listened eagerly.

With his endearing baby sister, they were a loving family. They relied on each other in a society with a strict hierarchical structure, fostering a strong sense of unity and mutual support. Greed and self-ishness could not be afforded.

From all the laughs and stories, embraces and head pats, happy moments tend not to last forever.

During a particularly harsh winter, when Alaric first hit his teenage years, his father fell gravely ill with a high fever and a rough cough. The old man's lungs rattled as he fought to breathe. The family was too impoverished to afford a physician, relying on homemade remedies to aid their father in his battle against the dreadful sickness. Alaric's mother stayed by her husband's side almost every hour, using her garden-grown herbs and prayers, leaving it up to Alaric to continue the work duties at the farm.

The young boy did his utmost to handle it all by himself, growing increasingly weary as nightfall approached. He herded the cows, cleaned chicken coops, and dragged firewood alone. His sister tried to help, but due to her petite stature and frail strength, it was difficult for her to keep up, especially in the harsh outdoor conditions of winter. Nonetheless, they both tried their hardest. It was all they could do.

As they clung to hope for their father's recovery, their wishes were left unanswered.

His father had succumbed to his sickness and passed away, his lungs failing from fluid overload. Body fluids seeped out of the sickly man's mouth and nose after he took his final breath. It was devastating, especially for his mother. She screamed and wept for days as the love of her life had passed in an unmerciful way by Mother Nature. Consumed by despair and sorrow, she isolated herself from reality.

Although grieving himself, Alaric continued with the household responsibilities, taking on his mother's and father's roles. First thing every morning, the boy went out to maintain the farm. He made sure the animals were cleaned and fed, as well as watering and tending the remaining crops, before he went inside to begin the household chores. He prepared the meals and cleaned the house.

Feeding his mother was a constant struggle. She fell into a depression, refusing to leave the comfort of the bedchamber as she mourned. He would spend an hour trying to make his mother swallow a few bites of every meal. Sometimes, his sister helped with the feeding and entertaining so their mother would not be alone while bedridden, a reminder that she still had two children who loved her.

Alaric persevered as much as he could and continued to do his best to shoulder two adults' worth of responsibilities. Gradually, day by day and week by week, he grew tired. It was hard, and the stress slowly pushed the boy closer and closer to his breaking point.

With weeks of pressure, the weight of it all became too much. He strolled into the house and to his sickly mother before he collapsed in tears. His little body was beyond exhausted as he wailed out his frustrations. That was when his mother blinked, shaken to her core.

Had she been gone so long that it had pushed him too far?

Did he manage to do everything on his own?

How long has it been? How long has she been lying here? Where was her daughter?

She threw herself to her son, cradling him in her arms. Alaric quickly melted into her. He needed her, needed her so much.

Finally, he could breathe.

With their father buried in a beautiful patch by a naked tree on the farmstead, Alaric's mother forced herself back to be present, helping her son with the farm duties and resuming the house duties. It was a fairly good distraction, aiding her to move on slowly with the acceptance that her husband had passed. Life moves on, and she could not allow herself to decay either.

As winter drew near an end, the first signs of spring appeared, with blossoms filling the air and warmer days to come. Grass began to flourish, and wildlife returned to the forest. It was the perfect time for Alaric to venture into town.

Every year, throughout spring and summer, Alaric's father would journey into the town to earn extra money for the farm. He would work and provide services for traveling merchants, priests, artisans, minstrels, and even high-class barons and counts in exchange for coins. This time, however, Alaric was stepping up into the role as he was deemed the breadwinner at his young age.

This newfound role required him to be resourceful and adaptable. He assisted merchants with loading and unloading their wagons, helped priests with various tasks around their temples, and even provided companionship for lonely artisans and minstrels passing through the town. The older boy allowed his sister to join him, letting her explore the town and meet new people. It was a valuable time for her to make new friends with children around her age group, rather than helping their mother around the house.

When Alaric allowed her to tag along, it was time for fun, as long as she was by his side, right?

While doing repair work on a merchant's wagon one day, his sister strayed a reasonably good distance, chasing bees and grasshoppers around the grassy fields outside the town border. Everything seemed fine as Alaric chatted with the merchant, gaining insight into the financial situation amongst the people.

He twisted a nut onto the wheel until a sudden, blood-curdling scream pierces the air, startling him to stop. Snapping his head around, frantically looking for her, Alaric felt his heart sink.

His sister was nowhere to be found; she was missing.

The boy excused himself and dashed towards the wails and cries, not knowing that his world would be crashing down before his very eyes as he approached the scene.

A pack of dogs gathered around, tearing into flesh. Bright, red blood spilled onto the soft grass as sharp teeth sank and broke into blood vessels. Pieces of tissues crunched under their powerful jaws.

Everything was happening too fast. Alaric called out her name as he ran. His sister was being mauled alive.

There was no time to cry. There was no time to think.

Alaric grabbed the furred pelts, shaking fingers trying their best to yank away. Dirt was being kicked up from the strength as he tried to pull. However, the dogs paid no attention and kept feasting.

Sadly, her screams stopped after a few seconds, the worst coming to mind for the boy. He called out for her again while he fought the ravenous animals.

To his luck, Alaric spotted two knights on their delicate purebred horses, slowly approaching in a slow trot. They were in iron armor, not showing interest in the murder happening in front of them. Alaric ran up to them with tears soaking his face.

He could not find the words to explain. All he could do was point at the scene of his sister getting eaten alive by the pack of dogs. His voice was strained from his panicked wails, but the knights did not express any concern. They watched the dogs for a few seconds before glancing back down at the boy, releasing a chuckle.

Alaric's world froze when he heard the snicker.

"Dogs have to eat, too."

Those were the only words he registered. Anything after that was mute.

How could knights, meant to protect the people of the kingdom, laugh at his face while his sister was being eaten alive?

It was their job. It was an oath they stood by. Then, how come?

How come they did not save his sister's life?

Why laugh and discard her as nothing?

How could they not care?

Seconds have passed.

Minutes.

An hour.

He tried gathering whatever remained of his deceased sister, barely managing to make it back home before collapsing to his knees by the house. He had failed to protect his sister.

The scream from his mother was one he would never forget.

He apologized repeatedly, tears blinding him while the remains stained his arms red. He was a despicable person. A failure. He was supposed to protect his family. How could he allow this to happen? What kind of brother was he?

She was buried beside their father.

Although his mother never personally blamed him for her death, Alaric self-reproached for months as they grieved. It broke something inside the boy, and he would never forgive himself for it.

It was all his fault.

Without his sister, the two barely scraped by. It became too hard to manage the farmstead, and with a lack of hands, there was less product. They had become poorer, even after selling half the land to a wealthy baron and the farm animals to other commoners.

To make life easier, Alaric signed up for knight citizenship for Kingdom Ironwood. He saw it as the only opportunity to protect and provide financial stability for his ailing mother and uphold an oath to protect others. No person should experience what he experienced that day he lost his sister, and he promised himself as a way to redeem his failure for her.

Fate smiled upon the boy as he was trained under the king's tutelage. His dedication to his training and his natural aptitude for combat allowed him to excel in his lessons, surpassing all his fellow trainees and, soon, the seniors. The hard labor he endured at a young age was an advantage in his skills.

As a result of his outstanding performance, the king noticed Alaric and offered him a position as his Knight of the Body. This prestigious contract, meant to be the king's personal knight and political secretary, granted him the protection and resources he needed for his mother, sending her most of his earnings weekly. It made him leave his dirty, shared bedchamber with other low-ranking knights and arrive at a luxurious, small confinement within the castle, surrounded by opulence and comfort.

In addition to being the king's favorite, Alaric's new position led to invitations. He worked with the king and his advisor to attend private political gatherings, serving as a personal messenger for kingdom affairs, giving him invaluable insights into the kingdom's inner workings. That was how the young knight learned to manipulate and speak with eloquence and sophistication. His charm made him a captivating figure, often drawing him to the center of attention during his presence.

The king began to trust him more, granting him more privileges and responsibilities. Alaric was appreciative as he utilized these advantages to explore his own interests.

On silent nights, Alaric took his unlimited freedom to hunt his prey. It was his hidden specialty, secretly killing dishonorable knights and political foes, who left a bad taste in his mouth. Being a knight meant serving his people, not abusing the system. And with his luck, the favored knight was able to track down two particularly deserving knights at the edge of an outpost.

Alaric was swift, never making a sound as he stalked the knights who feasted on their meal together. This outpost was hidden amongst the thick shrubs of the corner of the kingdom border. It was designed to be invisible and track uninviting individuals crossing onto guarded territory. Only the elite knights knew of its existence.

To Alaric's luck, it was the perfect moment to strike. Any loud noises and dead bodies would not be heard or found for days on end.

These knights weren't just ordinary men; they meant much more to him. They were the ones who had allowed his sister to be mauled alive years ago, snickering under their breaths while he cried out for their help. Even after all these years, that scene was still fresh in his mind. It felt like it happened just yesterday.

With one pounce, he began his revenge.

He made sure not to give these knights any form of mercy, killing them painfully and savagely. They begged for their lives, swearing they did not know him and the situation he referenced, but the haunting trauma could never be forgiven through lies. He tied them up with rope, cutting off all their fingers slowly as they cried out in agony. Then, using his sword, he slit their throats with gratification. He watched them with pleasure as they drowned in their own blood. It caked the grass underneath them.

After the massacre, the dead belonged to the birds and the maggots as an upcoming meal for Mother Nature. If they were found, no one would know what happened to them. The king would first believe that they had gone awol. No one else in the castle liked them anyway. They were nothing.

For once, Alaric felt peace wash over him. When he returned late that night, he rested his head, eager for sleep. His sister may disapprove of his crimes in the afterlife, but he needed to do it for himself. Those two crooked knights deserved no painless deaths, no mercy, no forgiveness.

By age twenty, Alaric was still an ambitious senior Knight of the Body. His irresistible cunning wit was his secret weapon, allowing him to navigate and climb to the top of the hierarchy. In his free time, he found solace in the company of the castle's servants, providing them with the affection and attention they craved. Pursuing companionship was strictly forbidden for servants, as it was believed to interfere with palace work. As long as it was done secretly, the knight was never caught. In exchange for his friendship or partnership, especially if the sex was fantastic, the servants provided buried kingdom secrets. He took the information and twisted it into use.

With all the mingling and information gathering, Alaric stumbled upon a particular servant girl. She was a small and quiet brunette who hid in the kitchen most days. Other palace members did not see her much since she attended to herself, but she had excellent skills when handling a knife. With her strength and individuality, they became close friends.

Her name was Nadia, and her unique spirit intrigued him. She wanted to break away from her role and become a knight herself, and so Alaric embraced her wishes and began teaching her the proper sword-fighting tactics. During their training, it opened his eyes.

Education and knowledge were the authentic sources of power, and he wanted women and low-status individuals to have the chance to be treated with equality. He learned how the unfortunate suffered under the weight of tyranny, and with the kingdom secrets he gathered, he began his journey as a political figure.

Alaric began by pointing and speaking out against the flaws of his own kingdom. His passionate and persuasive speeches resonated with the common people as he vocalized his criticism. As more and more people rallied behind him, his influence quickly grew, and he became a powerful force for change.

The king felt like a fool for not paying attention. Alaric had abused his unlimited privileges and used kingdom affairs against his status, becoming a threat to the throne as the king's grip on his people weakened from the knight's increasing popularity and influence.

Now, Alaric was a mere cockroach that was overdue to be exterminated.

Desperate to regain control, the king furiously ordered his remaining loyal knights to capture the criminal. It did not take long for the rogue knight to be subdued, his wrists bound with rope and a sword pressed against his neck. A newly-fresh, deep, jagged wound across his chest soaked blood into his uniform. It resulted from a fight against his seize, in which he killed two knights before getting tied up.

Alaric was sentenced to death by a sword, his head wanted off his body and hung on the king's wall. The king sat on his throne, amused by the prospect of watching his former knight's execution, and presided over the improper trial in the palace lobby. The crowd of other palace inhabitants eagerly participated in the spectacle.

Bloodshed was wanted.

The knight holding the sword firmly gripped Alaric's dark ginger hair, using the force to lift and expose his broad neck to the sharp blade. Alaric snarled at the king, calling out words of insult. His shoulders shifted, attempting to struggle free from the ropes.

But before the sword broke his skin, Nadia jumped into action.

She snuck through the crowd with a stolen blade of her own, cutting the opposing knight's limb clean off. The sword dropped to the floor with a loud clang. Crimson red sprayed, and screams of horror filled the air. Alaric smiled at the sight of his loyal friend coming to his rescue.

With a cut of the ropes, Alaric was freed.

Hands scurried for the sword on the floor, pulling himself up and lunging towards the king. There were howls and mixed reactions from the crowd as he pierced the sword into the king. It had happened so fast that no other knight could stop it.

The blade sank deeper and deeper. Rib bones cracked from the impact. Blood drooled from the lips.

The King of Ironwood had fallen.

Alaric and Nadia fled together, but not alone. Followers from different backgrounds chased them, and as a group, found solace in a broken-down, abandoned town far beyond the kingdom's territory.

A new community was born, and the town was rebuilt with new buildings and homes. Alaric's charismatic philosophies attracted people to his cause, and he remained true to every word he spoke. Under his leadership, the people were treated fairly and respectfully as they worked together to build a thriving society. It influenced other individuals to join his following from neighboring realms.

He had made a kingdom of his own. Nadia was appointed his Knight of the Body. Together, they oversaw the construction of his castle, which served as the centerpiece of their new home. Alaric moved his mother to his kingdom's land, ensuring she would live comfortably in the country. In exchange for her sacrifices for him, she received free food and necessities, allowing her to enjoy an easy life.

However, foul rumors spread like wildfire throughout the lands about Alaric's rise to power. His opponents painted him as ruthless and murderous, causing fear and trepidation—a monster, they said. But Alaric's ambition allowed him to transform himself from a simple farm boy into an powerful leader to a newly established fair kingdom.

Now, all that remained for Alaric to complete his transformation into a fully-fledged king was to find a suitable royal-blood bride to receive his official title and finalize his realm—Kingdom Hartfelt.

3

The Snake

Marrying his daughter again was initially believed to be easy, but it quickly became a challenge.

King Johnathan and Lucia spent countless days traveling across the lands, reaching suitable kingdoms in hopes they would accept his daughter as a bride for their royal children. There was no shortage of suitors, but these potential spouses and their families all had one thing in common: a need for a virgin, an untouched bride.

Father even went to great lengths to make Lucia more attractive, dressing her in the finest silk, applying makeup, and adorning her with exquisite jewelry. With Lucia's undeniable beauty, this effort drew more attention from suitors. Still, when the inevitable question of the princess's virginity arose, it was always met with a firm refusal.

A non-virgin bride was viewed as dirty and unfaithful, as they had already experienced intimacy. This fear stemmed from a rooted idea: What would stop a spouse from committing adultery?

Most would politely decline, but in one instance, Lucia faced pure embarrassment. When Father and Lucia visited the Kingdom Shadowmere, governed by the fourth-generation prince named Victor, they were warmly welcomed. The prince sought a wife, wanting the most beautiful female on Earth. So, once the blonde widow entered his castle grounds, Victor was instantly captivated by her beauty.

Victor's guards encircled the two visitors as they introduced themselves to the prince. A quick apology followed for their unannounced arrival. However, the prince was not bothered at all. The sight of Lucia presented before him felt like a blessing to the young ruler. An angel descended from Heaven just for him.

Lucia knelt before Victor's throne, her head bowed in respect to the prince. Father stood beside his daughter, giving a brief bow before he began demonstrating her abilities. She was dressed in intricate lace, accentuating her delicate skin's radiance.

Victor was astonished.

The words from Father's mouth seemed to flow in and out of his ears without leaving a trace, sipping from a cup of wine in one hand. His eyes were locked on Lucia, observing every detail, but it was not enough. He felt compelled to take a closer look.

Standing up with the cup still in hand, the prince stepped closer to ensure his eyes were not deceiving him. Lucia heard the upcoming footsteps but refused to look until a finger curled underneath her chin. Eager force lifted her head. Blue eyes catch Victor's brown ones. The prince had to think for a few seconds to develop the words.

This was the most fitting offering anyone had gifted yet. He had to take it while he could.

Victor chuckled. "Wow, you are absolutely stunning. I have always needed a gorgeous bride. You will make a perfect specimen for my seed."

"Yes, her name is Lucia. Alongside her beauty are also her skills. Trained and obedient, she will follow every command as you wish. She has also learned to hold her tongue and fill your needs without reason or doubt."

That made Victor smile. The prince's fingers brushed upwards, touching the princess's soft, sensitive lips. Arousal sparked inside him. Fantasies of destroying the presented pretty blonde came to mind. He needed a trophy, and he was sure this was the one.

"How old?"

"Ripe age of nineteen," Father answered.

"Not very young, but at the most fertile age. A lot of years available for childbearing."

"Yes, indeed. However—"

Victor glanced at Father, raising an eyebrow in question. Fingers maintained at creasing Lucia's face. She knew what Father was about to say. He was expected to be truthful.

Father continued, "Lucia is not a virgin. She was previously married, but due to unfortunate circumstances, her ex-spouse passed away. May you seek forgiveness and still consider her as your bride?"

Disgust flashed on the prince's face.

Although he wanted the most gorgeous bride, he also needed her to be a virgin. To think that the blonde princess had opened her legs previously to someone other than him was a horrendous thought.

Victor yanked his hand away from Lucia's face, wiping it on his attire. "This is a whore! I do not need an already-used bitch. I deserve a pure wife!"

Without a moment of hesitation, Victor threw his cup of wine at the princess. Red, sour liquid splashed onto her, and she flinched from the sudden coldness. The decorative, luxurious fabric she wore was now permanently stained red.

But instead of reacting, she leaned forward and bent her head to the floor in a resounding, deep, apologetic fashion. She did not mean to disgust the prince. It was rude of her to come to his domain and cause repugnance.

Victor resumed, "You are a snake! A trap! You will tempt an innocent man with your beauty and entrap him with your used sex!"

Lucia stayed quiet, still bent forward apologetically. The words were hurtful and stung deep. She did not mean to be a snake. She does not wish to entrap a husband. All she needed was to fulfill her purpose in life by being a wedded wife again. It was the only thing she was good for.

It was her fate.

It took a while for Victor's servants to soothe the young prince, providing the two with an opportunity to depart hastily. They retreated to their traveling carriage.

Drenched in wine, the princess expressed no discontent as she wiped her face with a handkerchief. Although she would have to bathe upon their return home, she was grateful that it was only alcohol and not a striking hand. Rough contact would cause her to foolishly react.

Meanwhile, Father sat across from his child, infuriated and disheartened by yet another failed attempt to marry off his daughter. All hope appeared gone, as most kingdoms had already rejected her.

The notion of it incited his blood to boil. Anger was mounting. And when the carriage hit a bump on the dusty road, it caused an eruption of fury. "Fuck! Why did you have to carry a child?!"

Lucia flinched from the tone. She did not expect the sudden outburst.

"I am not going to take care of you all my life! I did not sign up to house a useless child of mine until I pass!"

"I apologize, Father," she said, staring downwards at her lap. It was not her intention to burden her only parent. It was the last thing she ever wanted to do.

"An apology will not fix this, you understand? You are so useless that you were sent back to me by your ex-royal-in-laws because they did not have a purpose for you after your husband died! It's utterly embarrassing!"

Her eyes brimmed with tears as she struggled to maintain her strict composure. To keep her hands from shaking, she clasped them tightly together, knuckles turning white. Father had provided a roof over her head, food, and clothing, even allowing her to stay for the past few years. She felt a deep sense of shame.

"If you did not have a child, then I could have bribed the physicians to examine your cunt and lie that you were still a virgin. That would have been a much easier solution." Rumors had already begun against his rule due to his daughter's return. It was starting to get out of hand. He took a deep breath to calm his nerves. "Lucia, you have to fix this, one way or another."

She quickly wiped away any tears that threatened to escape her eyes. The guilt was almost suffocating, and she felt like she was drowning in it.

"If I cannot find a suitor for you within the next month, I will have you publicly hanged to fix my honor," Father said. His eyes stared intently at his child. Waiting, watching for a response. "Do you accept that consequence? To exchange your failed life to fix your kingdom's reputation?"

The weight of her existence was too much. A failure, that was what she was. No matter what happened in her life, she was always set to end up as a failure.

Failure to obey.

Failure to bear a son.

Failure to marry.

She nodded, knowing well that this was the only way she could do right by her parent. "Yes, Father. I accept my death if I fail to marry."

Father rolled his shoulders and relaxed on the cushioned carriage seats. "Good. Now, do not weep. I do not need you to embarrass me more once we return to the castle," he said sternly. A royal child returning to the palace with a red, swollen face would spark even more rumors. He had enough as it is.

"Yes, Father."

As silence enveloped them, only the sounds of the soft crunching dirt beneath the wheels of the carriage and the gentle snorting of the horses could be heard. Lucia's tiny fingers fidgeted nervously in her lap; her mind lost in deep contemplation.

She refused to allow shame to be imposed upon Father, and not just for his sake, but also for that of her twin brother, Michael. The status of the royal prince would be tarnished if more despicable whispers began to circulate beyond the lands. This responsibility weighed heavily on the king and the princess, and she knew she had to tread carefully to ensure their family's honor remained intact.

"Why couldn't you have been born a male? Then, we did not have to go through all this annoying courting. Imagine a kingdom where twins ruled together; the amount of power and respect it would bring once I stepped down," the king said. A dream he replayed in his head for years, a world where his twins would rule his kingdom side by side. It would be unique, as no kingdom had ever had twins rule by record. The power they would wield would be unprecedented, and their influence would be overwhelmingly positive. If only his deceased spouse had not failed to give him two sons instead of one son and one daughter.

He shook his head. "But no matter how much I dreamed, your mother's body had other plans. It is such a disappointment."

"I am sorry to disappoint you, Father," Lucia murmured, returning her attention to her fingers. The tension between them simmered throughout the remainder of the ride.

Once they arrived back in the safety of their territory, a flurry of activity ensued.

A handful of servants hastened to the grand, wooden doors as they opened. With swift efficiency, they divest Father of his outerwear, revealing his resplendent uniform underneath. The coat was carefully hung, but their focus was abruptly diverted as Lucia emerged from behind. The sight of the wine-soaked princess elicited a collective gasp from the servants, their faces in shock.

The servants rushed to the princess's side, arms encircling her in a supportive embrace. They guided her towards the royal washroom, their movements gentle yet firm. The air was thick with the scent of wine and the soft murmur of hushed whispers. Father frowned, watching his daughter be whisked away.

Michael stood nearby, awaiting their return. In his regal attire, he presented a vision of unadulterated masculinity. His long, lustrous blonde hair was pulled back into a half-up ponytail, accentuating his chiseled features. His striking resemblance to Lucia was undeniable, yet he stood a head taller, his physique more robust. It was clear that when his time came to take the throne, he would be the object of desire for many suitors.

"Father?" Michael questioned as he approached, boots clicking on the marble floor.

"No fucking luck!" Father howled. He was still outraged from the incident hours ago.

Michael watched with sadness as the servants led his sister away. The sight of Lucia, dripping wet with red-stained hair, upset him.

He always had a soft spot for his sibling. Life was unfair, and he hated witnessing the cruelty it inflicted upon his sister.

"I am utterly embarrassed! All the hard work I put into presenting my useless daughter, just to have a prince spit at me!"

Michael's lips thinned, not enjoying the tantrum his father was presenting. The king tried every way to get Lucia married again, tossing her around as pretty meat, begging for someone to take her. At this stage, royal children who were unable to be married were subjected to humiliation.

"Do you think Lucia would be better off revoking her royalty status and living a peaceful life among the people? The townsfolk would stop their bubbling rumors, and mercy will be placed upon Lucia's—"

"Never! I will not change royalty customs or allow mercy on the young I created. If I pardon, then my rules will seem weak to my people. It will risk defiance and mischief. I cannot allow that in my kingdom."

Michael frowned. "But Father, it is your child. You must have sympathy for your bloo—"

"Lucia's life is nothing more than a speck of dust. She is easily disposable. If I wish to have more children, I can remarry as I please."

"Does it mean my life is easily disposable as well?" Michael firmly challenged. He disliked how repulsive the conversation was.

"Do not compare yourself. You are worth much more. If I had more children born male, it would make my kingdom flourish more graciously."

Michael's heart was stabbed to hear those words. He hated knowing that his life was more valuable in royalty due to the male characteristics that he possessed. It was a harsh reality that he had to face, one that made him question the very nature of society and its absurd expectations. Lucia deserved kindness, but even in royalty, it was less achievable than a commoner's daughter.

"Enough discussion. I must rest from the journey. I am tired," Father stated, excusing himself. He brushed past his son, not having a thought of regret from the chosen words he had spilled.

Michael felt shame in his place.

While the servants undressed Lucia, she maintained a stoic expression, her blue eyes betraying no emotion as her naked body was revealed within the humid confines of the royal washroom. This place was reserved exclusively for the royals and upper class of society, such as barons, counts, and courtesans. It was considered highly improper for those of lower social standing to partake in such opulence.

On the other hand, the servants had their own bathing facilities, which were often crudely constructed from wood, plagued with mold, and in need of a reliable water supply. In stark contrast, the royal washroom was a marvel of clean luxury, its walls adorned with intricate tiles, its floors immaculately clean, and its water supply seemingly endless, with the ability to provide hot water at a moment's notice.

Lucia stared downwards at the water in the tub below her. The servants had already left, leaving her alone with a stash of towels and soap behind her. The deafening silence consumed her, and she began to tear up. Salty water droplets scrolled down her face, instantly absorbed by the hot water.

All her emotions escaped—frustration, anger, sadness, and hopelessness. They broke out of her all at once.

She was nothing; she knew that all too well. A pathetic creature devoid of any real power or influence. All she could do was cry, and she did so with a ferocity that belied her weakened state.

Her screams of sadness echoed through the washroom, each one more agonizing than the last. Her shaky hands gripped tightly onto the wine-stained hair, fingers digging in profoundly and threatening to pull out the strands.

She was much like of an animal in distress, having no healthy outlet to express conflicting emotions, constantly subjected to a cycle of despair and self-destruction, with no hope of escape. Luckily, she was young, and any hair yanked out grew back quickly within only a few days.

The servants outside the washroom door could hear the sobs and raw pain emanating from within, their hearts aching for the princess.

They knew Lucia was hurting.

If they could, they would provide the much-needed comfort in her time of need. Yet, the consequences of intervening resulted in the loss of life.

It was an order from Father, a decree that the servants were forbidden from meddling in the royal family's affairs. This mandate was explicitly aimed at Lucia, as the king feared that the princess's tumultuous emotions could disrupt the order of the palace and affect the servants' abilities. If the servants were to be swayed by her emotions, their skills could be compromised.

And so with that rule, the servants could only stand helplessly outside the doors, listening to her sobs and praying that she would find the strength to overcome her pain.

A few strands of hair floated on top of the water. An ugly sniffle erupted. Thoughts swarmed and consumed her mind.

What about Charlotte? Would her daughter be hanged, too, due to her failures as a wife? Or would she be sold to a kingdom as a maid? Worse yet, as a bride at only age four?

Whatever it came to be, it was all her fault, regardless.

4

Blue and Green

Refusal was on all royal tongues.

Due to his tainted, rogue reputation after ending a member of a royal bloodline, Alaric was matched with the reality of rejections. No kingdom offered their young in fear that he, too, would savagely kill. He was a menace to society, a curse that would inevitably bring chaos. People believed he shall not breed.

Undeterred, Alaric continued his search. Days turned into weeks, and the delay in achieving his ambition of becoming a king began to wear on him. His frustration grew with each failed lead, each dead end, and each fruitless search. But he refused to give up, driven by his unyielding determination.

Eventually, he stumbled upon a rumor about an unwanted bride. It spoke of a princess from Kingdom Morningstar, a blonde girl shunned by society due to her failure to marry. The townsfolk whispered about the troublesome princess, awaiting the day to view her public punishment. There was thrill and enthusiasm as it was approaching in only three days.

The gossip piqued Alaric's interest, and he was drawn to the prospect of this mysterious, unwanted bride. He was unsure what public punishment was, but he did not dig further. If the kingdom was willing to hand over the bride without any special circumstances, this could be his last opportunity to obtain his title. Otherwise, he would have to wait years for another princess to ripen and hope his foul image evaporated from commoners' minds.

Partnered and armed with his Knight of the Body, the two traveled through the treacherous terrains towards their destination. The sun had beaten them mercilessly, weaving past trees and prickly bushes, but they refused to stop for even a moment's rest. There was limited time, and Alaric could not afford to miss his introduction to the bride.

By the time they arrived at the kingdom's town on their steeds, a day had passed. The exhausted equines let out a series of loud neighs as they approached the gravel roads that led to the palace doors. Locals watched the two travelers with a mix of fascination and wariness, wondering about their purpose in seeking their king.

The town was enormous, with houses built side by side with brick and wood—stands filled with farmers, fishermen, dressmakers, and carvers selling their goods. Alaric was impressed by the sheer size of the castle ahead of them. Weather-stained stone towers stood tall, with massive, decorative flags waving in the subtle wind. It was a clear display of the kingdom's economic prosperity.

Standing pridefully in silver armor, the palace guards eyed them suspiciously before halting them amongst palace property. With a dazzling smile and quick introduction, Alaric stated his purposeful arrival to wed the king's daughter. It eased the knight's concerns right away.

The knights signaled to follow their lead, and Alaric and Nadia dismounted. Their legs wobbled from the strain of the long ride, and two farriers approached to care for their thirsty equines. Sweat was caked underneath the animal's saddles, and hunger was amidst. Alaric showed appreciation, but the farriers turned away with the reins in their hands. None took note of his thankful gesture.

"This is troublesome," Nadia mumbled. As Alaric's most loyal knight, she hated how poorly he was treated. He was one of the most kind-hearted individuals she knew, and due to his ruthless act for survival years ago, he was punished by tainted rumors. The only people who saw through the lies were Alaric's own kingdom.

The prince released a soft sigh. Nadia was the only person who understood the exasperating travels. "I know."

The two followed behind the knights as the large palace doors crept open. A long, decorative rug ran from the doors and across the throne room. Sleek furniture and paintings clung to the paneled walls, with pure gold designs marked within the materials. This was a presentation of wealth and luxury—a slap in esteem compared to Alaric's small yet growing castle.

King Johnathan, seated on his ornate throne, engaged in a hushed conversation with a group of influential courtiers, all of whom were discussing the prospect of renovating certain parts of the palace to better showcase the king's changing taste in architecture and design. It took a minute before the blonde king gazed upon the uninvited guests. A small smile curled his lips.

Guests who dared interrupt the king's schedule pleased him immensely. Many feared him and, when wishing to see him, scheduled appointments for his time to avoid backlash. Those who did not were more intriguing and brave. In this incident, the view of Alaric and Nadia did not anger him.

Father flicked his hand to halt the previous discussion with the individuals, signaling them to leave and provide privacy. They obeyed and rushed away quickly.

"Come forward," Father announced. The palace doors shut behind them.

Alaric studied the self-assured king, noting the sumptuous attire as they approached. It became apparent that this kingdom was prosperous. The vast expanse of land owned by this realm and its massive population dwarfed that of most other kingdoms he had visited, leading to the belief that he might hit a gold mine in wooing the bride. A powerful kingdom-in-law like this was a dream come true for outside royalty.

"Who do I have the pleasure of having in my presence? My knights have thought you both were worth my time for the unpresidential arrival. Please, introduce yourselves."

Alaric bowed apologetically for their unexpected arrival. Nadia, in turn, pulled out her sword and laid it on the floor, the metal glinting in the light. She then dropped to her knee, her posture demonstrating respect and passivity, clearly showing that she posed no threat. The sight of a female knight captivated the king, stirring a mix of questions and even a small hint of disgust, but he chose not to press for answers at this time.

"I am Alaric Hartfelt. This is my Knight of the Body, Nadia."

Father's eyes lit up with excitement. He had heard of the name. "Oh, you are the ex-knight who has been raving amongst people throughout the lands. You have brought so much honor and shame to your name, as well as obtained many followers and enemies, going as far as establishing a new kingdom under your rule. I can respect a man like that."

King Johnathan was truthful.

Most kingdoms were formed by royal members splitting off due to disagreements and establishing their own kingdoms based on their unique visions. It is highly unusual for a knight to possess the influence and followers necessary to create his own realm. Nonetheless, it was undeniably impressive.

Alaric did not expect the compliment. "Thank you."

"Hmmm, I wonder, why must you arrive? I do not see your purpose for being here before me, and I am sure you have more important matters to attend to with your tiny realm."

"Yes, but this meeting is just as important. I have heard you may offer me a bride."

The king's brown eyes were narrow, sharp, and deadly, signaling his keen interest in Alaric's words. This was the first time since Lucia's return that a suitor arrived and stated their interest in marrying.

It got his smile to widen with anticipation. With a spring in his step, he left his throne, landing on his boots. "Ah, yes! My daughter, Lucia! Allow my servants to prepare her for your display. And please, make yourselves comfortable. I cannot allow my potential in-laws not to be flattered in my castle."

Father loudly clapped, and servants scurried up with platters of beverages and finger meals. It startled Alaric, and even Nadia, as she stood back up with a conflicted expression. This was the first time a king had shown hospitality to their request for marriage.

No denial, no harsh words.

Showered with deliciousness.

The king made a hand signal, and another servant ran up to his side. He leaned in and whispered, "Scrub Lucia clean and dress her most beautifully. I need her to be breathtaking, including her cunt. It may be used, but make it look unused. Now, be quick."

The servant nodded and took off.

Lucia's fingers skillfully combed through Charlotte's golden locks as she hummed a soothing melody. The young girl relished the sensation, remaining motionless on the chair in their bedchamber. There was something incredibly satisfying about having her hair attended to by her mother, and she particularly enjoyed the intricate braids she would create. It was a bonding experience that left both of them feeling close.

It was nearing the month's end, and Lucia's time was running out. She only had one day left before she would be shackled and dragged to the castle dungeon. It was a dank, dark pit deep in the basement where the most ruthless criminals were kept. From there, she would be paraded through the streets, a spectacle for the masses, before meeting her end at the executioner's rope.

But the princess refused to let this bleak future taint her final moments with her daughter. She spent every waking moment with her, cherishing each laugh, each smile, and each tender touch. She could not bear the thought of burdening her with the truth of her upcoming execution. She deserved to be happy, not to be consumed by worry and fear. So she kept it secret, a heavyweight in her heart, as she savored the precious time they had left together.

Lucia had begged Father to exclude Charlotte from the event. She didn't want her to witness something so distressing. Father hesitated, wanting his granddaughter to see the consequences of her mother's failures, but he ultimately agreed. She would be locked away in their bedchamber while her execution was in action.

Without warning, a servant burst through the threshold, gasping hard for air. She ran through the palace hallways with a mission in mind. It spooked Lucia and Charlotte.

"Princess Lucia, you have a suitor. He came for you."

"Pardon me? A suitor?" Lucia gasped. She observed the additional servants squeeze in, hastily seizing hold and escorting her towards the royal baths. Charlotte was left bewildered, dismounting the chair. But before she could chase after her mother, a servant used an arm to block her. She was stopped in her tracks.

Charlotte looked at the servant anxiously. "Will she be all right?"

"Yes. She will get bathed, dressed, and then shown off."

"Shown off?"

"For marriage."

"Oh."

Charlotte was very young during Lucia's previous marriage, barely remembering her other parent, but the lingering emotions from the abusive treatment still haunted her. She was helpless in those past situations and could only hope her mother would not get severely hurt. She carried the weight of these traumatic memories.

Right away, Lucia was bathed by the servants with warm water and floral soap. It happened so fast that she could not comprehend the multiple hands nonconsensually touching every inch of her body. Despite her attempts to resist, the servants grew more and more aggressive, their voices barking out in anger as they continued their invasive cleaning. It only panicked her more, and she fought back tears as she felt violated and humiliated.

"Hurry!" a servant commanded. All their efforts were dedicated to her cleanliness. After the bath, Lucia was thoroughly dried, brushed, and dressed in an expensive, statement silk white dress with real gems sewn in. It gave the illusion of purity.

Live flowers were picked and pressed into her blonde hair. Although she liked flowers in her hair, she did not enjoy this—it was forced. Makeup was powdered on and jewelry clipped around her neck and ears. Completely surrendered to the servant's work, Lucia asked softly, "Who came to see me?"

"An ex-knight named Alaric Hartfelt," a servant replied, tugging the dress fabric to soothe the wrinkles.

"Alaric Hartfelt?!" another squealed. It shocked the other attending servants as they circled the dressed princess, trying their best to make her as gorgeous as possible.

"Who is he?"

A servant answered, "You have not heard? He is a savage ex-knight who killed those who opposed him. He betrayed his kingdom, killed his ruler, and fled with a handful of sinners to the outskirts to build his own brutal castle."

"What?!" another gasped.

"Yes, and as a leader, he probably wants to become king since he is not a prince by blood. He'll gain more power that way."

"He seems politically motivated."

"Yes, but the lands will be shaken with fear. He will probably conquer other kingdoms in the following years. He is really dangerous."

Lucia tuned out the servants' bickering conversation.

It all made sense now. No other kingdom would offer its children for Alaric's request for marriage. Lucia was the leftover pick, and Father desperately needed her gone.

Another brutal man? How ironic.

As the servants gossiped, Lucia stood still as the remaining products were placed on her. It was the best job the servants had ever completed.

"Lucia is ready," the servant declared, watching as all the attention of the lobby turned towards her. Anticipation quickly filled the room, particularly within the king. He was ecstatic to showcase his child to a suitor who wished to see her. And based on their brief exchange with Alaric and Nadia, he was convinced this would be a perfect match.

Father purred, "Bring her in."

The back doors opened as the princess emerged. Her tiny hands were clasped demurely in front of her as she walked gracefully. The hem of her silk dress trailed behind her, shimmering due to the gems in the light, accentuating her striking features and making her appear all the more captivating.

Father's massive court watched the princess's every move. There were more courtiers present than earlier, all crowded around to catch a glimpse of the ex-knight who murdered a tyrant, who stood right in front of King Johnathan.

The king was brave, they whispered. How heroic, others mumbled.

Lucia stopped beside Father, her eyes fixated on the floor, her posture straight. Not a single comment was made as the court studied the gorgeous creature standing beside their king. No words could fully describe the undeniable beauty.

Nadia leaned in and whispered, a cup of wine in her hand, "She is very pretty."

Alaric nodded in acknowledgment. He did not expect this from an unwanted bride. He had seen so many *desirable* brides; less than half were as beautiful as her.

The bride's eyes flickered upwards to catch a glimpse of him, and their eyes interlocked instantly. Alaric was struck by the intense blue hue, a color that seemed to hold a world of secrets and desires within it. But she quickly looked away.

Copper hair, stubble beard, subtle freckles, and strict green eyes. The intensity of his glare was enough to send shivers down her spine, and she could not shake off the feeling of dread that lingered in the air.

He was going to kill her, she was sure of it.

"Lucia here will be a wonderful, perfect bride for you. She had excelled through strict wifely teachings, as I had hired the best royal tutor to enforce these desirable traditions. She was approved by many kingdoms around." Father then touched his daughter's shoulder, and she obeyed silently to get on her knees. Her hands remained clasped together, displaying royal submission and respect. "My gorgeous daughter will care for you, do her duties, and bear fruitful children. Her beauty and fertility are a bonus in expanding a newly built kingdom. Every kingdom needs a starting point, and Lucia will be the best role model for future brides within your growing family."

Alaric was aware of whispers about the bride's multiple refusals. Rumors tend to spread like a plague, and he wondered what made this enchanting bride so undesirable. Was she a troublemaker, causing strife among previous suitors? Perhaps she was disabled in some form, making it difficult for her to fulfill her duties. Or, maybe, she was simply unintelligent, lacking wit and charm.

He questioned, "If she is so ideal, even approved by many, why must she be hard to marry? Surely, other kingdoms have better offers than I do. I have no riches or ancient luxuries to offer."

Father braced himself before exposing the truth. "That is because she is not a virgin, sent back to me due to her ex-spouse's unexpected passing, and with a child. No prince wants a child not of their blood."

"I do not care. I need a bride."

A sigh of relief from the king.

Alaric only wanted to marry for politics, needing the official title as king. Intimacy was not his priority.

Father was overjoyed nonetheless. "Excellent! Please, do not feel obligated to owe me later for Lucia's hand in marriage. Instead, allow me to do the honors to express my appreciation. I hope these please you."

With no reluctance in his spirit, Father clapped again, and within mere seconds, more servants rushed in with plates filled to the brim with stacked currency, glittering gold, shiny jewelry, rare and exotic goods, and classic, timeless works of literature. Courtiers wooed and awed.

"These should be enough to help your new kingdom grow and shoulder your new responsibility of my daughter and granddaughter."

The abundance was almost too much, Alaric's eyes scanning back and forth between the endless goods presented to him. This would do more than help his kingdom grow; he was going to flourish.

"And do not fear the transportation. It will be an honor for me to provide carriages for a more pleasant travel," Father added. The smile has not once left his lips.

It was done.

Lucia was promised to the man who stood in front of her. She tried her best to keep herself from trembling.

"I can arrange a quick ceremony here to make it official, if you like," Father offered.

That piqued Alaric's interest.

5

The New Kingdom

The wedding was quick.

No other attendees were present besides the priest and another family member, who joined the small, nontraditional ceremony in the private chapel within the castle walls. Since Lucia was not a virgin and had been married before, it would be inappropriate to orchestrate a lavish, kingdom-wide wedding.

The chapel was primarily used for personal events amongst high-class individuals and royals. The lower class was not permitted to set foot on the polished floors. It, too, was laced with gold trimmings and mesmerizing furniture that cost time and wealth to purchase. The rows of wooded benches were also pleasing to the eye. There is not a single flaw to be noted.

The family member who joined the short ceremony was Lucia's twin sibling, Michael. He, too, wore expensive fabrics that defined his status as the king's other child. He stood tall with his hands held behind his back for presentation, yet his manner was soft. He was the opposite of King Johnathan's ruthless nature. Human kindness and humanity could be found within his ice-blue pearls.

The sight of the twin took Alaric aback. They appeared identical, except for the fact that Michael was born male. It was fascinating to observe what Lucia might have looked like if she, too, had been born male.

Twins were a luxury and a blessing in a cruel world like this. It was believed to be a personal gift from the Heavenly angels themselves.

Father stood proudly beside Michael, observing Lucia's position before her upcoming husband. She still avoided all forms of eye contact, keeping her gaze fixed on her clasped hands instead. Nadia guarded her prince from behind, her eyes scanning their surroundings for any signs of disturbances. It was a precautionary measure, even within the confines of the fortified palace.

Dressed in the same dress as earlier, Lucia tensed once the pruned priest cleared his throat and opened his prized pages. There was no effort from the king's side to make the event memorable. It seemed unfair as it was Alaric's first marriage, yet he knew better than to push for more, since it was not socially acceptable to be gifted by the bride's king in a marriage proposal. King Johnathan must have been desperate.

"Lucia Morningstar, upon this marriage, you will uphold your wifely duties and respect your new husband, Alaric Hartfelt. You will follow every word of his without a statement of defiance, care for him, and sacrifice your life to keep him alive and well to maintain his kingdom properly," the priest preached, standing in the middle of the arranged couple. His voice echoed throughout the grand chapel, his eyes fixed on the bride and groom.

Lucia bowed her head forward, a silent acknowledgment. She does not speak a word.

The priest continued, "Any foul word or touch can result in a legal allowance of punishment or death. Do not do intentional harm and lend your body for his usage. He is the purpose for your life."

Alaric tried not to cringe. He was unprepared to listen to the misogynistic ideology.

"Now, be grateful, Lucia Morningstar. Submit your life to this man and be his property. Feel honored to achieve this milestone again."

Without warning, Lucia slowly dropped to her knees and bent forward until her nose touched the floor. It was a high royal practice of mute acceptance, giving her soul and bodily rights to the man before her. A sworn alliance and bond by marriage.

Father beamed to witness the gesture again. Like Lucia's previous wedding, the same flow of emotions threatened to overtake him. It made him proud of his daughter's obedience to royal traditions. Michael presented a face of sadness instead.

The priest mumbled and prayed, showering the power from Heaven to make the commerce official. The groom was not expected to dedicate or sacrifice for marriage similarly as the bride; it was purely for the male's gain. It only took a minute before the priest concluded Alaric's one-sentence commitment and final statement.

Now, they were husband and wife.

As the ceremony ended, Lucia inhaled deeply before she raised herself back onto her delicate feet. A variety of emotions swarmed inside her, but she refused to let them show.

This was her life now.

She had escaped death and was remarried to another unlovable man.

Michael quickly rushed by his sister's side, giving her a small hug before whispering good luck. All he could do for her was pray for the best.

Lucia nodded. She hated being separated from her twin brother again; besides her daughter, he was empathic and kind. Those two helped her maintain hope and happiness in her life. She depended on that deeply.

Before anything else moved forward, Father stepped up to join the two. A sharp glance at his son triggered him to step away. It was a signal to provide proximal privacy.

Alaric could not make out the words but watched as King Johnathan approached his daughter's ear. There was a low growl in his tone as he spoke a few sentences. Lucia responded with two words of her own before their exchange was complete.

Bells rang loudly throughout the streets. Townsfolk waved red-inked kingdom flags, threw flowers, and yelled joyful words toward the parading carriages. It was ecstatic, and the roads were filled wall to wall in celebration. Citizens, a mix of young and old, slowly parted to allow passage of the royal parade.

Alaric rode up front on his Friesian, a black horse dressed in colorful fabrics that draped down its sides—another gift added from Lucia's guardian. He cheered loudly and touched the hands of his loyal people as he led the parade to the palace. Nadia was right behind him on her own horse.

Large, muscled equines marched forward, pulling wagons of various goods, but more importantly, the new additions to the royal family. A closed carriage carried the new queen and young princess into Alaric's new realm. The people were eager to see.

A sense of happiness permeated the air. The kingdom was now blessed with a king and queen. However, Lucia, who sat silently across from Charlotte in the carriage, remained an exception. Her heart sank as she contemplated her new reality: a forced marriage to another horrifying, cruel man.

Lucia had long accepted that life had dealt her an unfair hand and that not everyone was entitled to privileges and happiness. Nonetheless, the thought of being bound to Alaric filled her with dread and despair, but she was determined to endure whatever came her way.

After all, what other choice did she have?

The little blonde girl gazed outward from the carriage window, clutching her raggy, old teddy bear tightly against her chest. Her eyes widened with delight at the unfamiliar surroundings teeming with enthusiastic admirers, unlike anything she had ever witnessed. She had been trapped within the castle walls alongside her mother and not permitted to venture outside, so this experience was entirely new.

Lucia could not bring herself to glance with her daughter, focusing on her hands resting idly on her lap. She had changed out of her luxurious dress and into something more comfortable: a simple, bold, brown dress. All of her possessions wield no value. Her treasured silks, pieces of jewelry, and bedroom furniture were left behind for Michael's future children, by Father's request.

As the parade progressed up the rough gravel path, it came to a halt in front of the small stoned castle. Lines of neatly trimmed bushes lead up to the doors. It was not as tall as the well-nourished kingdoms, yet it still had high cobblestone walls, tower seek-outs, and an expansive courtyard with several fruit trees dotting its landscape. It would more likely continue to grow in only a matter of years.

The wooden double doors opened, and the servants emerged fervently. They could not suppress their excitement. Riches were presented, shining with beauty upon their eyes, and the announcement of the new queen had them practically leaping with joy.

"Majesty!"

"Can we see her!?"

"Yes! I must see!"

"I feel so thrilled!"

The news traveled fast.

Alaric dismounted his horse, the gravel beneath him crackling under his heavy footfall. A middle-aged man, hair grayed with matted dirt and sweat from a long day of labor, emerged from the shadows. His plain clothes and work apron had ash and burns caked within the seams. As the lead farrier, he had spent hours shaping hot metal for the horses, only stopping when the commotion interrupted his work.

He extended his hand, grumbling softly under his breath. The man was known for his rough personality, but he spoke truth and did his work flawlessly. It was favorable for Alaric's growing kingdom.

"My queen has traveled far. Please, do not overwhelm. This is a new environment for her," Alaric answered, handing the farrier the leather reins to his Friesian stallion.

"And she must be exhausted," the head servant added, pushing herself through the crowd of servants. She walked gracefully, hands together. Her attire was more formal than the other servants' usual uniforms, demonstrating her status within the palace. Her name was Rose, and she was Alaric's most entrusted servant and chamberlain.

Rose diligently oversaw and disputed duties, planned the meals, and ensured that order was maintained within the castle's walls. She had left her previous kingdom to join Alaric's, drawn by his beliefs and unwavering respect for individuals of lower social standing. In return for her loyalty, dedication, and knowledge, Alaric provided her with a comfortable bed, private quarters, free linens and clothing of her choice, and even financial compensation for her services. The other servants had similar trades. Many kingdoms did not provide these basic necessities.

Alaric leaned in, closing the space between Rose and himself. He mumbled, "She has a child, and I do not want to separate them. Make sure they stay together at all times."

"A non-blood child?"

"Yes, a little girl."

"Your Majesty, that is the first I have ever heard of a royal wedding. You are bold," Rose commented. The young ex-knight always had a way to surprise her in multiple ways. This was added to the list.

"I know, but I do not mind. This marriage was for politics, not companionship."

Rose's frown deepened as she pondered the implications of the answer. She was all too aware that most royal suitors pursued diplomatic advantages by marrying ripened brides, but there was always the unfortunate catch of forced intimacy within the relationships. From all the opposing beliefs that Alaric had preached, she hoped he wouldn't succumb to the cruel cyclic traditions.

Her eyes glanced at the closed carriage. It awaited to be opened. Alaric continued, "Can you do me a favor and take them to the guest bedchamber on the fourth floor? I want to give them privacy and time to adjust away from the majority of the castle population."

The small castle was an architectural marvel, meticulously designed with four floors aboveground and two basement levels. The fourth floor, the highest level, was reserved for Alaric's bedchamber and a simple guest bedchamber for visiting dignitaries. The strategic placement of the ex-knight's quarters on the highest level was a testament to his importance, and, as a safety measure.

Rose bowed. "Yes, Your Majesty."

But, before Rose could even straighten up, the carriage door was thrown open by Valentino and his men.

Valentino was Alaric's notorious affair advisor, and he wasted no time reaching inside and roughly grasping the bride by the arm. He dragged her out into the outside world with a forceful yank, sending her tumbling onto the rough gravel below. Her plain dress began to stain and tear as it rubbed against the unforgiving ground. Lucia tried to regain her footing while confused and startled by the sudden turn of events.

Charlotte cried, "Mommy!"

The little girl's scream pierced the air. One of Valentino's men grabbed the child from the carriage's safety. Her toy dropped on the ground between them.

Alaric and Nadia reacted instantly to the sound of the unfolding scene. The servants followed after but kept their distance to avoid getting mingled in any physical violence.

"What a nasty pig!" Valentino hissed, his tight grip unforgiving on the soft skin.

The pain becomes unbearable, her skin turning red and purple from the force of the advisor's hold. It triggered a painful and vivid memory of her abusive ex-spouse, remembering how roughly and harshly the spouse would handle her. At times, it would happen so fast that her fragile body could not keep up, and she was basically dragged around like a rag doll across the floor.

"Valentino!" Alaric shouted as he ran. But his call was ignored.

Lucia's heart raced as she instinctively tried to tug her arm away from the restricting hold. Tears threatened to swell. But the more she struggled, the angrier Valentino became. "Stop squirming, you whore!"

The bride did not listen. She pulled again, and with no hope, she was met with Valentino's raised hand. He delivered a devastating blow to her face.

Lucia yelped and sprawled to the ground, her face contorted in pain. Her small hands reached out to catch her fall onto the rough, gravelly surface beneath her. It painfully poked and pricked the skin. Blood started to drool down from her nose, and a few drops stained the rocks. She wasted no time covering her nose, attempting to stop the bleeding quickly.

"What the hell are you doing?!" Alaric yelled, confronting his advisor with a shove. Nadia was behind him, ready to defend her king. She only needed one word of direction, and the man would be slain before them.

Charlotte continued to cry while held captive by the man. She felt helpless, and Valentino was annoyed by her pathetic sobs.

He stumbled a few steps, fury engraved on his wrinkled features. From years of traveling outdoors, writing lengthy papers, and managing political affairs, his skin had aged beyond his proper age. Long streaks of grey mix with his slick, black hair. He was a respectable man who had a talent for specializing in growing kingdom matters. "I cannot believe you went off and married a used slut without consulting me!"

"I wanted to do this alone!"

"Alone?! My— Your standards are to the dirt when you're alone!"

Nadia scoffed, her hand gripping onto her sword handle. She was ready to unsheath her weapon.

"No kingdom would accept me and offer their children! I had to take what I could get, and in exchange, I was gifted and blessed by this bride's kingdom."

"But the other kingdoms will taunt your name more! This is a whore; a worthless bitch that opened her legs for another! Have you heard the rumors!?" Valentino questioned.

Alaric snarled in response. He wasn't clueless on the matter.

He quickly glanced at his newlywed wife and noted her trembling body on the ground. The right side of her face was beginning to swell from the harsh slap. Her hands were now stained with the liquid crimson. She looked humiliated.

"M-Mommy!" The little girl's cries were heart-wrenching, and the bride could not help but feel the urge to comfort her child. As she tried to crawl towards her, bloody hands painting the rumble, Valentino did not hesitate to grab the neckline of her dress. He pulled her back, preventing her from reaching for her scared daughter.

"Let them go," Alaric ordered.

"Why? I'm not hurting them."

An ironic lie.

The advisor continued, "I know you needed the title of king, but you can still keep it even if the queen *disappears*." His finger curled the bride's fabric to secure his grip. He had Lucia on her knees, at his mercy, by his feet.

"I do not like what you are suggesting."

"But it is simple."

Lucia continued to shake like a leaf. She was terrified to hear the man's response, but her gaze focused on her beloved daughter.

"Kill her and dump her body for the wild animals. You will then become a single man again for another, more proper virgin bride."

"Please, stop—"

"Claim that sickness took her, send your condolences to the whore's kingdom, and you will still keep your title as a widowed king. Then, this rotten girl can be used as a maid an—"

"Stop!" Alaric's voice boomed, his anger palpable as he silenced his advisor mid-sentence.

His word was the law in this territory.

Lucia's world seemed to blur as her mind raced with thoughts of her impending doom, the fear growing with the idea that she might meet her final demise before she even had a chance to settle into her new surroundings. It hadn't been over five minutes since the carriage stopped at its destination.

Is her life coming to an end now?

The advisor's suggestion revolted Alaric as he said, "Stop. No more. Let them go."

Valentino scrunched his eyes but muttered, "Yes, Your Majesty." He was disgusted, but he released Lucia from his hold. The bride immediately sprang forward. The man, who had been holding the girl back, slackened his grip and stepped away as well.

The two crashed, wrapping arms around each other. She immediately rubbed Charlotte's back in a calm and soothing rhythm. She could not express the words to comfort her, but her loving gestures were enough to lessen her sniffles.

As Valentino and his men left, the stunned servants wasted no time and ran to assist the shaking queen and her child. They murmured gentle words, attempting to coax Lucia back onto her feet. It took some persuasion to break her embrace and obey their instructions. Rose hastened over to join them, brandishing her handkerchief out of her uniform pockets and dabbing at the bride's bloody nose. She commanded Lucia to keep it in place, and she complied.

The servants worked diligently to restore Lucia's balance as she stumbled in place. Charlotte clung to the dirty fabric of her dress for comfort. She did not want to be separated like that again. She needed her mother.

With meticulous hands, the servants guided Lucia and her daughter towards the castle doors. Her arm began to ache, and she knew a bruise would soon embellish her skin. The swollen cheek stung her nerves. She was a mixed mess of snot, swollen skin, teary eyes, and a bloody nose.

As they passed the king, she refused to acknowledge him. Embarrassment arose.

He, in return, observed their every movement.

6

Hand in Hand

As they entered the small palace, Lucia's eyes were immediately drawn to the marvelous grand staircase, centered in the middle of the grand hall, adorned with a plush, red carpet that seemed to invite them upwards. Compared to her previous home, there was an absence of flourishing ceiling candlelights and furniture along the entrance. Polished, marbled stones echoed beneath their steps. The walls were unmarked and freshly painted. This castle was new and bare.

Despite her facial pain, Lucia noticed the simplified carved designs in the wood as she ascended the stairs with the servants. An array of thoughts consumed her mind while Charlotte matched her climb. The little girl's teddy bear was returned to her grasp as she silently walked alongside her mother.

The staircase seemed to stretch on forever. Her calves began to burn from the number of steps. The servants carried their bags of belongings as they directed them to the fourth floor.

Not a word was spoken. The air was too heavy with conflicting emotions. Luckily, the blood had stopped, and the handkerchief allowed Lucia to hide her crusted nose. She was appreciative of the servants' kindness.

Alaric stood at the doorway of his castle while Nadia was by his side. Her arms were held behind her in a formal stance. They maintained silence as they watched them ascend to the guest bedchamber.

The servants, the queen, and the princess had faded from their view in just a few minutes.

Then, the king released a deep sigh, catching Nadia off guard. She turned her head in question.

"I did not expect Valentino to spew such foul language and gestures. He has never done this before. It caught me off guard," he mumbled, catching Nadia's gaze.

The knight pressed her lips together in a thin line. She, too, was not expecting the sudden aggression. Although she did not favor the advisor, he was an asset to Alaric. The kingdom would not be flourishing so well without him. But it did not keep her from forming an opinion.

"With all due respect, Your Majesty, I never liked how pricky he is."

The comment made Alaric chuckle. "Prickly. That describes him well."

Another second of silence passes. Valentino may have importance, but the newly titled king's perspective could not dismiss his actions. It had to be addressed.

"I will talk to him privately. If I catch him doing this again, I will remove him from his position. That was way out of line."

"It will cause a fight. He is a stubborn man," Nadia pointed.

"I know. Be on standby for me. I'll do it tonight when he returns to rest."

The knight nodded. "Yes, Your Majesty."

The queen, her daughter, and the servants had finally reached the top floor. A servant, short in stature, excused herself as she stepped forward to open the door to the tiny guest bedroom.

The room was lit by a single candle, casting soft shadows across the simple furnishings and bland sheets. A decent-sized bed with a strong wooden headboard was positioned in the center of the room. A small table with two chairs was in the corner for the purpose of meals and conversation. On top of that, a six-door dresser with decorative metal handles sat beside the single window, covered by leftover curtains. Extra bed sheets were neatly folded on top, while a mirror hung above.

It was bland yet comfortable, more than Lucia could ask for. The servants followed in to gently lay their bags on the bed before excusing themselves. They intended to give Lucia and her daughter time to adjust and not be overwhelmed by their presence. This resulted in brittle silence.

Charlotte plopped her toy on the bed before walking to observe the furnishings, her mind still reeling from the aggressive confrontation and new environment. She was quiet and stressed, as she did not expect to find herself suddenly moving to a new home with her mother.

Her fingers ran through the smooth dresser wood before moving to the window, grabbing the edge of the fabric and pulling it out enough to peek through. She saw a forest of light-colored trees settled in the back of the property. The room faced the back end of the palace rather than towards the town filled with new people. On the left, she could see the horse stables. Low-class workers tended to feed and groom the equines. Stacks of hay were settled up against the building. She wondered if there were other animals on the castle's property.

While Charlotte observed the view, Lucia busied herself with unpacking their belongings. She dropped the stained cloth on the bed and unbuttoned the first luggage bag, revealing a pile of folded commoner clothes— plain and unpresentable. It was the opposite of her closet back at Father's palace, but it did not bother her one bit.

She began to disassociate.

The fear of the unknown was suffocating. Instability was all too familiar, a sensation the queen had grown accustomed to. She hated living a strict life in Father's kingdom, but there was at least stability. Now, the undetermined possibilities increased her anxiety, growing by the second.

Would the king come in and take advantage of her?

Would he take her daughter away and make her a maid? Or worse, dispose of her due to being another man's child?

Or would he change his mind and follow his advisor's words?

"Mommy? Are you all right?"

Charlotte's voice pierced through Lucia's haze of thoughts. Her small hands tugged on the dirty dress as her big, blue eyes looked for an answer. Her concern was noticeable, especially as her mother stared at their clothes silently, frozen in place.

Lucia's gaze dropped to meet hers. Her daughter was brave, and her unwavering empathy for her was something she cherished deeply. It was a quality she admired, and she felt a pang of guilt for putting her through this unstable turmoil. The queen did not need to add more worry to her little girl.

She forced a smile onto her face. "Yes, princess," she replied, her voice low and gentle as she threaded her fingers through Charlotte's long, blonde hair. "I will be all right. This is a new place, and I don't know what to expect."

Charlotte's nerves shiver with pleasure. She loved it when her mother did that. However, the calm words did not ease her troubled thoughts, so she had to ask. "Are you scared?"

Lucia hesitated, halting her fingers. Charlotte was too perceptive to fall for her fake smile. They had just been through a lot. At least she deserved the truth, no matter how painful it might be.

So, the newly titled queen crouched down, meeting her daughter at eye level, her hands grabbing and holding the smaller ones. It was warm to touch her daughter's soft skin. She still had a lot of growing to do.

"I am. I am terrified," Lucia answered. Every possible fear was soaked in her mind.

Charlotte studied her mother up close, now getting a proper view of her battered face. She whispered, "I am terrified, too."

"You are?"

Charlotte nodded. "And... I hope they don't hurt you too much." She hated seeing her mother get hurt, and it was even more unbearable to see her so vulnerable. She was kind and passive; she did not deserve to be picked on.

It stabbed Lucia's heart. "Princess, as long as we have each other, we can make it through anything."

"Really? You think so?"

"I know so." She leaned in to press her lips on her daughter's forehead. "We'll stick together."

"You promise?"

Lucia's gaze softened. "I promise."

As the day wore on, Lucia and Charlotte refused to leave the room, content to stay in their sanctuary and reorganize their space to their liking. They worked together as they unpacked and placed their small personal items in the proper areas. The clothes were stacked neatly in each drawer, hair brushes lined up on top of the dresser, and shoes arranged by the threshold. It was too soon to call home, but their efforts made it less barren.

Alaric made his way to the fourth floor, beginning his preparations for the upcoming slumber. Yet, his thoughts turned towards his newly wedded queen and child once his eyes fell on the closed door of the spare bedchamber. It was stationed across the floor, and he could not help but wonder how they were faring.

He found himself standing in front of the closed bedchamber door, his curiosity getting the better of him. A hand hovered over the door handle, inches from the metal. He knew better not to intrude, especially unannounced, but rationality was not on his mind. His fingers twitched with the urge to turn it; however, he hesitated.

What if they did not wish to see him? What if they hated him? Would he only be stressing them out for infringing on their only private area? What if they needed something? Does the room meet their requirements?

Though with all the questions rummaging in his head, why should he care?

With a heavy sigh, Alaric slowly backed away from the door, his hand dropping to his side. He knew he should not be standing there, frozen in indecision. He needed to rest, clear his head, and be prepared for tomorrow.

But his body refused to move.

He could not deny that Lucia was beautiful, but he had no reason to pursue her if they weren't married for intimacy. Marriage should be between two participating parties; indeed, Lucia did not participate. Alaric wondered if there was a way to make the best of this situation.

Perhaps once Lucia settled into her new life, she could be appointed to a job in the court. It would be a way for her to make use of the situation and to find some purpose and meaning in this forced union, but it was too soon to know.

Several servants settled into their quarters for the night, though they whispered among themselves, their voices hushed and conspiratorial. Their rooms were on the second floor, alongside the hall's storage spaces. The walls were dark and imposing, the only light provided by the flickering candles held by the undressing servants. Despite having private rooms, the servants preferred to gather in the common area to relax and chat before retiring for the night.

The common area was a cozy space, with chairs and a large, round table set in the center. The servants often gathered here to share stories, gossip, and news, their laughter and conversation filling the room. Tonight, however, the atmosphere was subdued, the servants' minds still filled from the day's events. The candles crackled on the table with clothes laid out.

Although servanthood was a woman's job, one individual stood out from the rest. Born male, Axel was the tallest of the group, and his slender frame and long legs made him a striking figure. He had been an orphan, raised by a group of servants from a wealthy baron's household, where he learned daily living skills, proficient in cooking and cleaning. The simple life brought him joy, and the gossip was his luxury, a rare indulgence in a world where he was often misunderstood.

It was unusual for a male to be a servant within palace walls, but Alaric was an unorthodox individual who had taken Axel under his wing. The king had no issue allowing a male to take on female duties if he wished, and that made Axel grow appreciative of the freedom and acceptance he found in the castle. "She's so beautiful. Small, slim, and has such an innocent face," Axel gossiped, sliding on his white nightgown. A brush lay in front of him, and he grabbed it to fix his almost-white strands. He was blonde, but it was so light it often came across nearly bleach-white under the sun. It was an interesting trait he carried.

Mia, the shortest servant, could not hold in her excitement. She threatened to squeal. "And that girl of hers is so cute!"

"Their blue eyes were stunning," Victoria added. She was the newly appointed servant, having stumbled upon Alaric when she needed work. The girl was still wearing her servant uniform, currently emptying her pockets. Many items, such as pins, dirty cloths, and sewing supplies, were forgotten throughout the day whenever dropped inside the fabric folds.

Caroline joined in with the pocket emptying, her red hair a fiery contrast to the dimly lit room. She was known for her wild nature and sharp tongue. Her previous kingdom had been repeatedly disappointed by her mountain of failures, and her ex-king had given her a choice: either cut out her tongue and retrain with traditional servant values or be banished from the territory. She decided to keep her snarky words.

"It's so sad that she got hurt. She did not deserve that," Caroline said. She empathized with the new queen.

Victoria replied, "I know. I cannot imagine coming to a new place, being stressed from sudden travel, and then getting tossed around immediately. She must have been so scared."

"That is what happens to brides," Rose commented, startling the group with her sudden appearance. The older servant had snuck up on them, her hands full with first aid supplies, a plate of food, and a pitcher of fresh water. She went to bed last, her final duty being a final check of the palace, ensuring the walls were secure and quiet for the night, before resting herself.

Victoria questioned. "Pardon?"

Rose continued, "Brides may be royalty, but their lives are worth much less than a maid's at the end of the day. They are expected to be hidden underneath the king's shadow and bear as many of his children as he pleases."

They were silent, unsure how to reply. Uneasy thoughts consumed them. Rose could sense it. "Now, do not dread. Alaric is unlike other kings, so we can only hope he will be fair to our new queen."

Victoria nodded in agreement. She knew well that the older woman spoke truth, and only time would tell how the new couple would react to each other. The others looked down at their hands nervously.

Rose did not say more as she turned to leave, her hands still full, on her way to the stairs. Her footsteps were quiet on the creaking steps, steadily reaching the fourth floor. The guest bedchamber door was shut, with no light peeking underneath, but there stood the king.

He was still, staring at the door.

"Your Majesty?" Rose whispered.

He turned. "You startled me."

"Go rest, I will attend to their well-being. I am certain they do not wish to see you."

"You are right," Alaric said, lips thinned. "It is foolish for me even to try."

"Now, now, I know you had good intentions. They had a rough day. Open the door for me, please?"

Alaric did what he was asked before he retired to his bedchamber, the door closing softly behind him.

The head servant assumed the queen and her child were asleep, but she was wrong. Lucia sat in a chair beside the bed, petting her daughter's head while she slept under the covers. The silence was comfortable, and when their eyes met, she noted the exhaustion underneath her queen's eyes.

Before Rose could move, Lucia jumped to her feet. She turned around the corner of the bed to properly get down on her knees. She then bowed her head, presenting a royal apologetic gesture.

This was also a sign of submission. Rose was all too familiar with it from her years of experience.

"I apologize for my troublesome arrival. I hope I did not distress you and the other servants," Lucia sincerely whispered, not wanting to wake up her daughter.

A pang of sympathy hits the head servant. "None of that."

She walked over to the table and gently set down her items. Since the queen and her child did not leave the room once they arrived, she assumed they must be hungry, thirsty, and sore. This was the least she could do. "Here are some supplies for you and your daughter if needed. Food and water, too."

Lucia looked up. The plate of food was too big of a portion, but she was still grateful. Plus, she could finally wash out the clogged blood inside her nostrils. "Thank you."

The head servant doesn't say another word, studying the queen for several seconds before she headed to the door. But before she stepped out, Lucia's small voice stopped her in her tracks. "Please tell my new husband that I am grateful for his acceptance of me. I am appreciative of this room and the bed sheets, pillows, dresser, and table. I will make myself useful and not be a burden here."

Rose allowed the words to sink in momentarily, trying to formulate a response, but she could not think of one. So, she left, shutting the door behind her. Her heart was heavy with the memories of her old, abusive kingdom that she escaped from. Seeing another brainwashed, helpless queen and hearing those vulnerable words again shattered her heart.

7

Ambivalence

"Do not fuck up this time. If you are sent back, I will immediately hang you. No excuses," he lowly growled. It was a threat, and Lucia knew he was true to his word. The reality she was unable to deny.

"Yes, Father."

Those were the exact words exchanged at the wedding, which haunted her relentlessly throughout the night. She could not sleep.

Lying in bed, her ears tuned to the sound of her heartbeat through the pillows, watching Charlotte dream beside her. Her only toy, the teddy bear hanging on by its last threads, was snuggled up in her arms. Witnessing the tranquility engraved at the scene was perfect.

Once the sun arose, the queen slowly wiggled out of bed, trying her best not to disturb her sleeping daughter. She sat at the edge, thoughts clouding her mind.

She had to start the day for her new husband. Even with the improper sleep and new home, it was her responsibility to make sure he was adequately maintained.

Truthfully, she was scared. New fears raced, alongside previous ones, that had plagued her from the day before. In her first marriage, she had been hopeful to be happily wedded, manipulated into believing her purpose was to be a caretaker and seedbearer to a man who loved her, until the abuse occurred.

Now, what made this marriage any different?

Rumors of this newly titled king being ruthless were known throughout the land, and she could not help but wonder if she would suffer the same abusive fate as before. The danger led her fingers to dig into her blonde hair unknowingly, and the unwanted notions consumed her. She grabbed onto her messy strands. Without realizing it, she began pulling, the self-soothing pain distracting her from an upcoming panic settling deep in her brain. Her breath quickened.

Luckily, she only managed to pull out a few strands before returning to the present. It hadn't been a full day since they had arrived; maybe it was too early to judge her new life entirely. So, she quietly stood up, dressing in one of her plain dresses, brushing her hair, and putting on indoor shoes before heading towards the door. The queen tried to close it softly behind her to not stir her daughter.

Eyes studied the surroundings, taking in the unfamiliar layout of the castle. A large wooden door was closed on the other side of the floor, which intrigued Lucia. No other rooms were on this floor, but it was not the time to poke around. She needed to find the kitchen, which meant a need to explore.

Her tiny feet carried her down the dark stairwell, the silence oppressive and weighing heavily on her. On the third floor, she first noted two large glass doors, their panes made up of stained glass, promoting color and detail within the engraving. She did not need to open the doors to glance at the piled papers and books covering the rich wood table. Bookshelves crowded the back of the room, and she suspected it belonged as the king's personal office.

Other large rooms were located nearby, possibly used for political gatherings. Rounded tables and chairs were placed all about. The castle was vast, so she kept moving.

The second floor seemed to house private rooms and storage. She wondered if it was for the servants. There were too many rooms to be used primarily for guests, and if she was correct, then it was the first time she had ever known servants having their own private quarters.

This kingdom was already odd to her standards when she first noted the female knight by the king's side.

Resuming her journey, her steps were light before she met the cold marbled floor. Her eyes met the similar, open space known as the grand hall. More details caught her eye, missed by her shaken arrival from yesterday.

A variety of oil landscape paintings hung on the walls. She admired the beauty of the different atmospheres and scenery before coming across a particular picture. It was Alaric, standing tall in red and gold fabric, tailored to his muscled body handsomely in a statement of leadership. An older woman sat by his side, hands neatly lying on her lap. Grey hairs painted on her ginger hair as the strands were pulled into a lazy bun. They looked similar, having the same soft eyes on their freckled faces. It made Lucia wonder: Was she a family member? An older sister? Mother? Aunt?

Lucia had plentiful days ahead of her to wonder who the woman was in Alaric's life, so she couldn't allow herself to get distracted now. She continued to walk, her feet carrying her through the halls. Each hallway had its own interesting features, so it was impossible to get lost.

She then stumbled upon a community bath and a small private bath nearby. She guessed the latter was for the king's use.

Next, the queen discovered a spine-chilling hallway that seemed to stretch on endlessly. Its darkness was only interrupted by the faint outline of a single, ominous door at its far end. If she were a child, she would have been convinced it was haunted, especially given the conspicuous absence of any flickering candlelight to dispel the daunting shadows.

With a brave inhale and cautious walk, her hand reached out towards the cold metal handle of the door. Fingers barely grazed its icy surface. She mustered all her courage and gave it a firm tug, only to be met with resistance.

The door was locked. A large, foreboding keyhole yawned beneath the metal handle, a silent invitation to secrets long hidden and dangerous yet unknown. It was a journey for another day.

Lucia hadn't finished exploring the entire floor before entering the kitchen. It was decently sized, the walls adorned with an array of pots and pans, their iron surfaces gleaming dully from the rising sunlight peeking through. Stone countertops provided ample workspace with a hearth nearby, its embers still faintly glowing. Closed-door cabinets, their contents hidden inside, held ingredients and kitchen tools. An island, its surface cluttered with neatly stacked steel plates and woolen napkins, served as a focal point in the room, where meals were prepared and served.

Two servants were engaged in a hushed conversation, their voices barely audible as their hands moved with practiced ease. They were pulling out supplies for the upcoming morning meal when the blonde queen suddenly made her unexpected appearance.

The servants were stunned into silence, their eyes wide with surprise. The queen's presence was an interruption they had not anticipated, a break from their routine. They turned to face her.

"Good morning, Queen Lucia," Victoria bowed, her hands clasped together. "Why must the queen be up so early?"

Lucia was shy. She did not know these servants. Everyone she knew was gone from her life again, except her daughter. She softly replied, a hint of uncertainty in her voice, "I have to start the day for the king."

"Queen Lucia, that is our job, and you have just arrived. Please, take this day to settle in with your child."

Lucia's eyes gazed around the kitchen, immediately drawn to the rack hanging on the wall, laden with a row of neatly hung aprons. The aprons were a riot of colors and patterns. Without a second thought, she plucked one from the racks, wrapping the apron around her small waist. "That is no excuse for me to be lazy. I must take direct care of King Alaric, as it is my duty. I will cook and clean for him."

"My Queen—"

"Please, allow me to do this. I have to do this," Lucia sternly pleaded. She feared punishment if she failed to comply with the tasks she had been taught.

Victoria turned to glance at Rose, confusion read on her face. She did not know what to say. Lucia was adamant.

"Where can I find the king's sleeping chamber?" Lucia asked. She began opening the wooden cabinets around her in search of particular items she needed.

"On the same floor as your bedchamber, My Queen," Rose answered with a frown.

"Thank you."

Rose's face was a mask of disapproval, her brows furrowed. She was familiar with the traditions of a royal bride, but not to this extent. This meant that they would see their queen more often than expected.

With a sigh, Rose gestured to Victoria to follow her, excusing themselves out of the kitchen. They left Lucia alone, giving her the most needed space for the morning. The queen paid no attention to their departure while finding the item she was looking desperately for: a tea kettle, its metal surface cool to the touch.

Fingers danced over the rows of spices and tea leaves stored in clay jars in the corner of the open room. She wasted no time creating one of her personal blends as she poured and mixed the ingredients by memory. The blend was tangy, contrasting the sweetness from the dried berries she had added. It was a flavor uniquely hers, a taste that Father's servants and her twin brother enjoyed.

As she waited for the tea to boil, her gaze was drawn to a partially hidden latch door nestled behind the stained stones of the hearth. The door was old and worn, its wooden surface darkened with age and use. Curiosity, that insatiable itch that drives exploration and discovery, got the better of her.

With a soft click, she lifted the latch, the door swinging open to reveal a set of narrow stone steps leading down into darkness. The air that wafted up from the basement was cool and dry, carrying with it the scent of Earth.

Descending the steps, she found herself in a large, underground room. The walls were lined with shelves filled with preserved food and supplies. A section of drying meat hung by the legs of the dead animal. The hunted creatures were probably gutted and skinned outdoors before being stored here. She made a mental note of its existence and its contents. This was a space to use in the future.

The scent of the tea quickly filled the kitchen. That was the cue that it was ready to be served.

She carefully lifted the hot kettle, grabbing a clean cup while navigating the grand staircase.

Steady and slow.

The last thing she needed was to accidentally burn herself, which would make her tasks more challenging to manage.

Reaching the fourth floor, the unknown closed door was untouched. It was Alaric's room, according to the servant's instructions.

As she brought her hand over the door handle, she hesitated. Her heart was pounding hard within her chest. She was afraid, a fear born of past experiences and lessons from her previous kingdom. Awakening her ex-husband had been akin to signing her own death warrant, a transgression that had been met with swift and brutal retribution.

But she was no longer in that kingdom, no longer bound by those rules. She was in a new place, with a new husband and new barriers to face. Though she felt like she still needed to deliver the luxurious refreshment to her spouse, no matter the excuse.

So, she forced herself to take a deep breath, calming her haywire nerves before softly knocking on the door. She waited, listening for any sound from the other side, for a response that did not come. The silence was a heavy blanket, a shroud that seemed to smother any hope of a reply. She doesn't dare to knock again.

With a sigh, Lucia turned her hand to open the door. Immediately greeted by soft snores, she saw Alaric buried beneath a mountain of red, thick, padded blankets. The room was warm and inviting, a personal sanctuary that reflected the king's tastes and preferences. A fancy, patterned rug with textile flowers and birds sat in the center of the room, its vibrant colors and intricate design starkly contrasting the stone floor beneath.

Alaric's bed was large and imposing, its tall bedposts reaching the ceiling and meeting above. Silk curtains draped down from the posts like silhouette shadows. His fireplace, made of lighter stone and lacking the much-needed polish, barely cracked from the burnt wood. Grey ash was collecting on the sides. It needed to be swept.

A small table set, complete with two cushioned chairs, sat in the corner of the room. It was a perfect, quiet nook for conversation. Another chair, this one positioned by the dying fireplace, offered a solitary spot for contemplation and relaxation. A cherry wood-carved dresser with a mirror was located on the other side, and there were two bedside tables on each side of the bed.

She thought the room was beautiful, much better-looking than the small bedroom she currently shared with her daughter. Maybe in the future, if things went well, she could request an ornamental rug or bed drapes. But that sounded more like a dream rather than an option.

Lucia moved with the grace and silence of a phantom, tiptoeing across the room with the hot tea kettle and tea cup balanced carefully in her hands. She placed the items on the bedside table, the porcelain cup clinking softly against the wooden surface. With a final glance towards the still-sleeping king, she quietly slipped out of the room, closing the door with a soft click. It was a successful task.

She made her way back to the kitchen to resume breakfast. Her hands moved nonstop, covered in flour, as she kneaded the bread dough until it was smooth and elastic. She had also washed and cut up fresh fruits.

By the time she had finished, other servants had joined her in the kitchen. They worked around her, their eyes occasionally straying towards the hardworking queen. They were amazed at her capabilities and how she had taken charge of the kitchen. It was the last thing they expected from outside royalty.

Breakfast was ready when the king awoke.

Lucia quickly and efficiently set up the dining area, arranging the dishes in a manner that was pleasing to the eye. The dining room consisted of a large wooden polished table with rows of cushioned chairs on both sides, able to accommodate twelve guests. Credenzas were displayed along the walls. By asking for more advice from the servants, Lucia learned that the king sat at the end.

"Good morning."

"Good morning, King Alaric," Rose greeted.

"It feels odd to call you king. It will take some time to get used to," Axel chuckled.

Alaric smiled in response.

The servants sparked conversation as they followed the king to the dining area, a complete difference from the life she was previously accustomed to. Servants held their tongues and awaited the king against the walls in a row in proper royal palaces, not freely conversing as they pleased.

She remained by the king's favored seat, anxiously waiting with a hot kettle in her hands as the voices grew louder. She had to be sure he had his morning meal. The servants ate earlier on.

Alaric stopped in his tracks when he saw Lucia. The servants had attended to him, so seeing the queen present instead left him confused. He wondered how she felt, how she slept, and how her child slept, but the smell of the food prepared made him forget quickly.

Once he sat, she poured a new cup of tea and set it down by the dish. He was silently impressed and surprised by the hot tea awaiting him when he woke up this morning. It was splendid: rich, sweet, and complex. He could not help but wonder who had been responsible for the tea, but his thoughts immediately turned to his new wife. No servant had made such a gesture before, and once she arrived, it had magically appeared.

Lucia waited on him like a personal servant, a role familiar to her but strange to the king. There was a tinged sense of awkwardness and uncertainty, and Alaric was not used to such personal attention.

He shifted uncomfortably in his seat, trying not to glance at Lucia for fear of making the situation even more tense while he savored his meal. No servant stood by him this close. They weren't even present while he ate alone, leaving once he settled.

She moved to pour more tea. She was careful not to make eye contact; her piercing blue eyes focused on the kettle. As several minutes passed while he chewed, the king could no longer take it. He dared himself to look up at her.

His wife was in a plain dress, nothing compared to the first time he saw her yesterday. Her flawless skin was glowing under the sunlight. He could not get over how stunning she was, though he wondered again: Had she taken the time to have her own morning meal? And was the hot kettle burning her small fingers?

He did not press to ask; his discomfort with the current situation prevented him from doing so. Lucia did not return the glance even though she felt it. He was observing, making her feel small under the new power that reeked from him. She hoped he wasn't displeased with the meal she presented for him.

Just as he looked away, the silence of the room was shattered by the sound of footsteps. The advisor entered, his smile as bright as the sunlight that streamed in through the windows. He was waving a paper in his hands. "Your Majesty, I bear good news!"

"Yes, Valentino?"

Valentino's eyes flickered toward Lucia, taking in the details of the new queen shadowing behind Alaric. But his gaze did not linger, his attention quickly shifting back to the king. He was not a man to apologize, and he was not planning to change for yesterday's encounter.

"Kingdom Cinderhaven would like to arrange a meeting with you," he announced, his voice hopeful. "They have sent their messenger to deliver this request. They would like to meet right away."

The news was unexpected, but it brought a big grin to the king's face. "What is it in regard to?"

"In regard to new trade arrangements between borders. This will boost the economy on our end and provide more opportunities to the people. You must attend."

The letter was placed in front of Alaric. He grabbed the crinkled paper and studied its contents, furrowing his brows in concentration.

Lucia's eyes drifted to the page. Unlike other brides, she knew how to read and write. It was a skill that her twin brother had taught her in secret. She read a few sentences before forcing herself to tear her eyes away. It was not in her place to be involved in political affairs, and she did not need to get in trouble on her first day.

As the king continued to read the letter, his smile grew bigger and bigger, his eyes shining with delight as his cheeks ached. Kingdom Cinderhaven was a well-proclaimed kingdom ruled by a timid king and queen with two heirs, both still at the tender age of toddlers. It was a kingdom ripe for alliances and partnerships. It could prove to be a valuable ally in the tumultuous world of politics, located past the Baysor Grove, a dense forest of birch trees that stretched between the territories. It was a half-day journey on horseback. The only challenge would be the small river, which was nearly labeled as a creek.

Building relationships with other kingdoms had proven challenging for Alaric, particularly due to the rumors that swirled around him. This letter, this unexpected request for a meeting, was a miracle. It was a chance for him to prove that he was more than his reputation, that he was a king capable of diplomacy and peace.

"A chance like this isn't handed over on a silver platter daily."

"Absolutely not."

"Then, we must get ready. This is important," Alaric declared, pushing back his chair and rising to his feet. He was done with his meal.

As soon as he stood up, Lucia jumped into action. She quickly cleared the table. It made the king glance from her sudden, swift movements, but he returned his attention to his advisor. He needed to focus on new plans and strategies for the future of his kingdom.

8

Timorousness

Lucia finished tidying up the kitchen and prepared a plate for her daughter. She attentively walked up the grand stairs and headed to the guest bedchambers, where her little one was getting ready for the day. She was delighted to see her four-year-old daughter dressing herself without assistance as she entered. It was a remarkable display of independence, and Lucia felt a surge of pride.

The click of the plate on the table grabbed Charlotte's attention. She squealed, "Mommy!"

The queen's heart swelled warmly, helping her daughter up into one of the chairs in the room. Standing from behind, she worked thoroughly with her daughter's hair knots and sang a comforting melody. Charlotte's legs swung back and forth excitedly while she savored each bite.

A figure remained concealed beside the threshold, unnoticed by the mother-daughter duo. He quietly pushed the door open—just a crack—and listened to the sweet song.

Memorizing. Notes as sweet as honey.

Alaric stumbled across the enchanting voice when he left his private bedchamber after a quick change of formal clothing. Never hearing her words, let alone singing them, he had to stand there for a few minutes, listening—hypnotized.

As much as he wanted to continue lingering, he could not allow his court to wait on him any longer. He had a meeting with Kingdom Cinderhaven to attend.

He pushed himself to leave with a heavy heart and jogged down the staircase.

Lucia finished, unaware, as she placed the brush on the table. The bristles were recently cleaned. "You look so beautiful."

"You always say that," Charlotte giggled, swallowing a bite of bread.

"But it is true. Do not allow anyone to tell you otherwise."

"I won't," she replied. Her eyes sparkled as she finished her meal before placing her silverware on the plate.

"Are you done with your breakfast?"

She nodded before jumping off the chair to retrieve her beloved teddy bear from the bed. Lucia smiled as she watched, her voice soft and soothing as she praised. "Good, you ate well."

She then sat down, eating the unfinished portion of bread and left-over bites of oats.

This was Lucia's breakfast, a meager portion designed to maintain her slender physique. As a royal princess, she had been trained from a young age to be as thin as possible, with a small waist, hip dips, and a thigh gap considered the epitome of physical attractiveness. The memory of her royal bride tutor's scornful gaze during monthly measurements, where she was forced to stand naked with a measuring tape wrapped around her body, still stained her mind. She was constantly underweight and in need of nutrients, yet her portions were deliberately kept restricted. It continued into her adult years.

Truthfully, she feared Charlotte's future. The thought of her daughter following the same fate of being appointed a royal bride tutor burned sorrow deep within her. No child should be forced through such torment.

However, having only spent a day in the new castle, Lucia could not help but feel a glimmer of hope. The king was unusual and progressive, and she wondered if he would actually follow authentic traditional customs regarding royal females. Charlotte may have had a merciful upbringing.

"This castle is not as fancy as the last one," Charlotte plainly stated. She stood by her mother's side, clutching her toy. The teddy bear was a gift from a past servant, a token of kindness in her ex-marriage. It was loved, even having a name, and despite its old treads, age, and lack of fabric fur, Charlotte still loved it like new.

The queen was not allowed to have money under her name, so she relied heavily on her ex-spouse for her daughter's and her own needs, such as clothes, blankets, and hygiene accessories. Toys were not part of his agenda to provide.

"Be grateful, my child. At least we have a roof over our heads," Lucia purred, brushing a hair strand behind Charlotte's ear.

"It's just not pretty."

Lucia swallowed a bite. "It may not be pretty, but it serves its purpose."

The room fell silent briefly, but Charlotte's young mind quickly shifted gears. Now that her stomach was full, she had energy to burn. She asked, "Can I go play?"

"As long as you behave."

"I will."

"And be kind and polite to the servants, use your inside voice, and do not make a mess while you play. We do not own this home, so treat it with respect."

"I know, mommy, you always tell me this."

Lucia softly smiled, swallowing her last bite. "You are a good girl."

"I try to be," Charlotte chuckled, now impatiently swaying on her feet. Her teddy bear is still pressed tightly against her chest, eagerness consuming her as she watched her mother stand up with the empty plate in her hands. She was about to start bouncing up and down.

"All right, go have fun."

Charlotte did not need to be told twice as she dashed out of the room. She was an extrovert, always eager to explore and meet new people. It was her most extraordinary charm.

As she ran through the hallways, she mentally mapped out every room, her confidence growing with each step. Soon, she got bold enough to open each door and peek inside, even the king's bedchamber. She admired the rugs, paintings, and furniture, even seeking out potential hiding spots for future games.

It took her some time to explore the whole castle, except for the locked doors. There were a few, but one in particular was too eerie for her to step close to. She swore it was haunted.

Quickly, she introduced herself and made friends with all the servants while they worked around her. Sometimes, she joined in and lent a hand.

"I'm Charlotte; meeting all of you is a pleasure."

Axel smiled. "How polite."

"Nice to meet you, sweetheart," Caroline replied.

Victoria greeted, "Hello."

"You are a charming lady," Rose remarked, even offering a bow of greeting to the little girl. It made Charlotte fill to the brim with joy.

Despite the friendliness of the servants, there was one that was the total opposite. She was determined to befriend him.

Hank, the lead horse farrier, was known for his gruff and unfriendly personality. The servants only acknowledged his presence with a nod, knowing that a conversation was not ideal for the older man. So, when he came in for a break, covered in hay and dirt, he was taken aback by the little girl standing right before him, eager to initiate a conversation.

Hank had a particular disdain for children, and the sight of Charlotte's bright smile and outstretched hand only made him uncomfortable. He refused to shake hands. "Go away."

"Why?"

"I do not wish to be in the presence of a child."

"Why?"

"Because I want to be alone."

"Why?"

Hank groaned. He did not expect her to be so persistent. "Because I was working hard, therefore I have every right to request alone time on my break."

"What were you working on?" Charlotte asked, ignoring his demands.

"I work with horses."

"Oh, those are enormous animals."

Hank frowned, crossed his arms, and silently studied the little girl, not caring that she was the new princess. A child is a child—messy, loud, and careless.

Charlotte continued, "I wish to pet a horse someday. I heard their manes are like hair. It's so funny when it's braided."

"You have never touched a horse?" Hank questioned, raising a brow. Most children by her age had at least ridden on a horse with their parents. It was a common ordeal among the people, and he wondered what had made her miss out on that experience.

Charlotte's fingers nervously fiddled with the bald ear of her teddy bear, her big eyes pleading for no criticism. It was not her fault that she had been confined in her previous palaces. Animals roamed outside, and strict royal rules prohibited her from setting foot outside unless it was related to political actions with her mother.

A moment of realization, an idea running through the older man's mind before he groaned to a conclusion. He had never allowed himself to commit such acts of kindness, but the girl's character captivated him. "You are lucky you are annoying."

"What do you mean?"

Hank sighed, lending down a hand. The palm was calloused, presenting years of hard work. "Come on, let's go pet a horse."

Charlotte gasped. "Wait, really!?"

Hank grunted in response, his face threatening to flush with embarrassment at his cheerful idea. Charlotte giggled and threw her arms around him without warning, nearly knocking him off balance before grabbing his hand. She tried to contain her enthusiasm, her feet barely touching the ground as she bounced. Hank could not believe he made himself agreed to this, but he could not deny the infectious joy radiating from the little girl as he began leading her to the stables.

Lucia had spent the day working tirelessly throughout the castle, a sight that left the servants in awe of a queen doing hard labor. She knelt on her hands and knees, taking time to scrub the stone-tiled floors, wipe down furniture, and change the sheets on every bed she encountered. She even cleaned Alaric's master bedchamber, starting with the fireplace. She swept with a broom and collected the dust from the crevices and cracks, her sweat evident on her face. Sometimes, the particles would tickle her nose, triggering her senses to sneeze.

As noon approached, Alaric returned to the castle, and Lucia hurried to undress his outer garments. "Oh, thank you," he said, not expecting the gesture. Lucia remained silent, her hands moving swiftly as she gathered the clothes for a later chore.

The meeting with Kingdom Cinderhaven had been a resounding success, with a new trading agreement established and implemented, focusing on exchanging fabric materials and wood. This would allow Alaric's people more access to building materials and textiles to sew into other goods. With this small victory, the king took a moment to rest, his mind at ease.

The small solar room was filled with comfortable, decorative woodwork and wool tapestries hung on the only wood-planked wall. Glass panes encased the room, offering a picturesque view of the birch trees, where wild animals, such as birds, raccoons, and deer, occasionally passed by. This serene room was perfect for indulging in reading, and Alaric was doing just that.

A book lay on his lap as he quietly turned the pages. He was at peace, lost in the printed words, until Lucia unexpectedly entered. A small plate of hot, sweet dough buns, drizzled with honey, was in one hand, and a cup of tea was in the other. The sweet aroma immediately filled his nostrils. "What is this?"

Lucia did not respond; instead, she placed the baked goods onto a small, wooden table beside the cushioned chair where Alaric sat. He closed his book, his eyes drawn to the food. He had never seen such a dessert before. "Is this for me?"

She nodded before quickly exiting the room and returning to her duties. He watched her depart without finding the words to stop her. She was too quick.

Left speechless, his eyes fixed on the plate. He studied the buns for another minute before getting the courage to pick one up and take a bite. Soft and sweet, the honey coating the top layer. The flavors danced on his taste buds, and he was amazed. He had never tasted anything like this before.

Lucia continued relentlessly cleaning and meal prepping, her dedication to her duties unwavering. She stepped outside beside the castle's back door with a pail to clean and scrub Alaric's dirty clothes. She rolled up her sleeves, preparing for the grueling task ahead. Despite her exhaustion, with no sleep and no breaks, she pushed on.

"Your wife is a busy bee. She won't stop cleaning," Caroline commented. Alaric walked down the castle halls, making mental plans to focus on local affairs with the people tomorrow after his break in the solar room. The only way to provide acknowledgment and improvement within the town is to listen directly from the source and communicate on a solution. His people held the power in expansion, not him.

Caroline happened to encounter the king and joined him on his walk. He did not mind. "I noted."

"She is scrubbing your clothes right now."

"Is she?"

"Absolutely, I saw it with my own eyes through the windows. Have you tried talking to her?"

Alaric's lips pressed together into a thin line. "I tried, but she does not respond to my words. If I am lucky, she'll do a head gesture."

"Victoria told me she's shy."

"I do not doubt. When I slept on it, thinking about the events that went down yesterday, it felt like I kidnapped her from her family."

"You intended to marry."

Alaric sighed. "I did, but I did not think I would feel guilt afterward."

They approached the grand staircase. The king gripped the wooden, carved railing and took his first step. But before taking a second, he halted, turning his back to share again with the servant.

"What is on your mind, big guy?" Caroline improperly addressed. It was a miracle in her life that Alaric enjoyed her vulgar tongue.

"I told Nadia how I felt, but she thinks I did Lucia a favor."

"How so?"

"I did not want to eavesdrop on family matters, but she told me that the familial exchange, after the priest commenced our status as husband and wife, was hostile; like, she was whispered a threat by King Johnathan, her own father." There was a short pause before he continued. "And she was scheduled for a public punishment before I arrived."

Caroline frowned. She wasn't aware of this information.

Alaric dropped his tone down to a whisper as he embarrassingly asked, "Do you think her family would purposely hurt her?"

The servant opened her mouth, but she could not form a proper reply. She was not sure herself. Lucia was still a mysterious woman with a hidden past. "I am not sure."

Alaric expected that answer. Caroline knew less than he did.

He thought about it for an additional second before giving a simple nod to end the conversation, followed by a smile of appreciation for

Caroline's company during his walk before turning and resuming his journey up the stairs.

After more cleaning was completed, Lucia began cooking the king's dinner. Just like this morning, she stood beside the king's side, another hot kettle in her hands as she served. It was a collection of tender meat and vegetables that melted in the mouth, flavorful to the tongue. He purred in delight while he ate.

The smell tickled her nose, but the fatigue overtaking her body was the challenge, not the food. Her eyelids grew heavy by the second, and her head slowly started to rock. Alaric took notice immediately, but every time her chin touched her chest, she yanked her head up with droopy eyes.

She looked so exhausted. The king pitied her.

Then, the queen dozed for a few peaceful seconds before she jerked so hard that it startled the king.

"Are you all right?"

Lucia quickly nodded. She could not allow herself to snooze like that again. It was entirely inappropriate for her position.

Alaric frowned at the all-too-similar head gesture. Not only did the king notice Lucia's struggle, but the servants did as well. Rose peeked over the kitchen threshold with a worried expression as she caught a glimpse of Lucia's drained stature. The queen had overdone herself on her first day living in the castle, and the head servant wished she had been more stern with their objections earlier in the morning, but it was too late now. Hopefully, Lucia would not push herself this hard again tomorrow.

As soon as Alaric finished his meal, Lucia sprang to clean again. Following the routine, she prepared a plate for Charlotte. The little girl waited for her mother in their bedchamber, engrossed in a picture book that Mia had kindly given her. The book had been stored for her nephews in the past, but since they were grown, she was delighted to see it find a new purpose with Charlotte.

The little girl described her day while she ate, delighting Lucia as she learned that her daughter had a good adventure. Lucia knew her daughter would adjust quickly, and this palace seemed kinder than her father's and ex-spouses'.

There was no yelling, no harsh glares, no mean gestures. Instead, the servants offered smiles and nods around her presence. And from what she gathered from her daughter, they adored her.

As usual, her daughter left some leftover bites for her to finish. Then, they prepared for their slumber, snuggling under the covers together. Warmth was exchanged, and all Lucia could hope for was rest. She struggled for a few hours, watching Charlotte peacefully rest in her arms while her thoughts swirled uncontrollably.

She hoped she proved her worth today, but doubt remained.

Eventually, her mind ceased, and she succumbed to her exhaustion. Dreams took over.

Buried deep into one of the meeting rooms on the third floor, a man quietly wrote with a single candlelight at his side. It was late at night, darkness enveloping him. All were sleeping except for the standby knights guarding the outside castle walls during their rounds. He focused as he reprinted all the words onto new pages. It was the trade agreement from earlier, and he was copying it.

Once he was finally done, a grin formed on his face. The copying processes took a long time, but it needed to be done. He dropped the white quill pen onto the table, relief washing over his fingers.

"My wrist cramps keep getting worse," Valentino murmured, rubbing his right wrist. He gave the bony structure a few rubs before picking up the pages. He then reorganized the papers, planning on returning the original documents to their proper storage. He was finally done for the night.

9

Mysterious

Lucia still did not speak a word to the king. It frustrated him, but he refrained from displaying his displeasure. Even when he asked the servants about his wife, whether they had heard anything or if she had confided in them, they merely shook their heads to his questions.

Rose had attempted to broach the subject in private, assuring Lucia that it was safe to share about herself with the court members, but Lucia dismissed the conversation with a shake of her head. She did not have much to share anyway.

A woman of mystery, even to herself.

She was never granted the opportunity to explore, express, or truly learn about herself, unsure of her interests, hobbies, or passions, as her existence was confined to being a mold of pleasing others since birth. Her worth was measured by her ability to perform her wifely duties, not her individuality. It was frowned upon by Father as it went against the traditions of a bride.

However, at times, especially in her dreams at night, she wondered what activities she would excel in. Maybe she would have liked painting with delicate brush strokes, gardening's verdant embrace, creating an allure of crafts, or playing the soulful melodies of music—calming activities that could bring more diversity into her life.

But she would never know.

Despite her aloofness, the servants still held a fondness for her. They viewed the queen as an enigmatic figure whom they could not quite figure out. She was kind and gentle to those around her. This made it easy for them to be around her, even though she was a silent presence in the castle.

Every morning, Lucia would begin her routine by concocting a unique tea blend. Alaric would awaken to find a freshly brewed pot at his bedside, the enticing aroma filling the air. Each day's tea offered a new and exciting flavor, keeping the king engaged and preventing him from growing tired of the same old refreshments. This delightful addition to his mornings was quickly becoming a favorite.

Just like the tea, Lucia ensured that each meal was a unique and novel experience for the king as well. The servants could not participate in the meal preparations, as Lucia objected to their involvement with an argument that it was her responsibility to provide direct care to her husband. However, some were stubborn and managed to sneak a hand after ignoring her protests, their efforts limited to mere stirring and cutting.

The queen even went as far as to aid Alaric in the bath. He attempted to resist her advances gently, but she persisted with a stern expression, arms full of wide towels, small rags, and musk-scented soap. Her piercing blue eyes held him captive, and he found himself easily defeated without her saying a word. No one had ever looked at him quite like that before, and the captivating blue hue left him breathless.

She wasted no time lathering Alaric's dark ginger hair with soap, using her fingers to delicately scratch his scalp as she washed. It felt nice to the king to have his body touched, each muscle quickly relaxing from the weight of her massaging maneuvers. The sensations tickled and radiated underneath his body.

Alaric was a sight to behold, his chiseled physique a testament to the hours spent honing his body from hours of unshy common labor. His skin was a canvas of taut muscles, with a generous sprinkle of chest hair and a pair of thick, bushy eyebrows. The freckles added a touch of charm to his rugged appearance. The only feature that piqued her interest was the large scar marked across his chest. She wondered about the story behind its appearance.

With a subtle shake of her head, Lucia maintained her composure, keeping her gaze averted and her demeanor professional as she bathed him. She had no intention of indulging in the voyeuristic pleasure of ogling her new spouse by his attractiveness. Her goal was to keep him clean.

On the other hand, Charlotte refused to acknowledge the king. She would steer clear of him and recoil in fear whenever he was in the vicinity, observing her frolic with the servants or her mother. The king could not fathom why the child was terrified of him. A frightened child is challenging to win over, particularly when her parent remains silent and unresponsive to his open-ended questions.

This left the king at a crossroads, uncertain of how to establish some connection with his new wife and stepdaughter.

Days turned into weeks as this continued. Everyone in the castle closely watched Lucia in hopes of uncovering more about her identity. Even the royal advisor, who still suspected her of being a royal prostitute, could not help but notice her impeccable manners and duties. He paid particular attention to her movements.

"I did not expect this from your leftover bitch. She is trained as a high-class wife," Valentino commented, standing proudly beside the king. He wore an elegant, neutral uniform bold enough to command attention to his rank. His hands were clasped together; his chest held high. The king frowned, already anticipating that the conversation was going to be unpleasant.

The two stood on the second-floor balcony, which overlooked the grand staircase with a railing in place. They gazed down at Lucia as she moved gracefully through the grand hall, aiding the servants as she swept with a broom. Alaric wondered what was going through her mind as she carried out her task. She moved quickly and precisely, never appearing to falter or slacken in her efforts.

"Breed her and get her pregnant with your heirs. You need blood-related children that have that kind of genetic work ethic. It's a desirable trait."

"No, I will not do that."

Valentino shook his head. "Why must you always disagree?"

"You first suggested that I should kill and dump her body in the woods. Now, you want me to have sex with her?" Alaric questioned, sending a sharp glare at his advisor. He was repulsed.

"I did not expect her to be a hardworking and high-standard bride. Beautiful, yes, but many others out there have that kind of beauty. But obtaining a hardworking bride is not easy; that's the catch."

Alaric furrowed his eyebrows. The subtle smile on Valentino's face disgusted him more. "This one's mute, attentive, and nurturing with excellent housekeeping skills—"

Alaric interrupted, "Please, stop." A flicker of agitation ignited within him. Although he barely knew her, she was not an object to be possessed; she was a human deserving of respect.

Valentino rolled his eyes, mumbling, "Suit yourself," under his breath before dismissing away from the king's presence. Alaric watched until the advisor was gone before returning his gaze to Lucia, watching as she moved on to her new task. She, too, wandered away from his view.

Later in the day, Alaric was drawn back to Lucia as she played with Charlotte. The scene was idyllic as the queen joined her daughter in a game of imaginative play using her tattered bear. They were nestled together on the floor of the solar room, their laughter and whispers breaking all silence around. The sunlight streamed through the windows, bathing the room in a warm glow while the birds sang.

He felt a sense of warmth and admiration. It was clear that Lucia was a devoted mother, and her love for her daughter was evident in every playful gesture. Charlotte giggled as she shared her fantasies.

Alaric continued to watch them for a few more minutes before the queen noticed his uninvited presence at the door's threshold. Immediately, she tensed up and scrambled onto her feet, bowing to him. Charlotte followed suit with a gasp but hid behind her mother's dress. His smile shifted to a frown.

Feeling dejected at their startled nature, he cleared his throat. "I apologize if I scared you both. I was merely being nosy."

There was no response; Lucia was still bowing. Her eyes remained closed. Alaric hoped they did not think they were in trouble. After all, they were just playing together, engaging in harmless fun.

Defeat washed over him. He released a deep sigh as he turned, his footsteps echoing distantly on his journey to the study room on the third floor. He does not bother looking back.

Hours have passed. Seconds ticked. The king was deeply engrossed in his work.

With renewed determination, he reread and wrote political letters with his quill, his mind consumed by the task at hand. Several books were opened around as he would take a few minutes to study the contents inside. A few candlelights danced to provide light in the darkened study room. The only sound that broke the silence was random ruffles of paper. The air felt thick.

A figure appeared shortly outside the colored glass doors. Alaric failed to notice from his unwavering focus. The figure had to knock to break his attention.

A jolt from the sudden noise. Through the hazy appearance, the king could discern the silhouette of his wife. She stood motionless like a statue, clutching contents in her hands. She seemed to be waiting for his approval to enter.

"Come in."

The door creaked softly as she pushed it open. She held a steaming hot kettle and a cup, which she carried with utmost care. Her eyes glanced at the scattered mess, avoiding any direct contact with his gaze as she walked to his desk. He must have been busy, and she hoped she didn't disturb him in his prime time.

"You made tea? What kind is this one?" Alaric asked, shuffling some documents to create space. This gave him an excuse for a break from his work.

Lucia did not respond as usual; instead, she studied around the room, taking in the vast array of ancient artifacts that filled the space. She had only been in this particular room a handful of times, and the sheer volume of totems, books, binders, and other miscellaneous items left her feeling overwhelmed. Half of the items had been gifted by Father. She could recognize the golden kingdom's signatures on the spines.

She wondered what secrets these items held. Her birth kingdom was steeped in history, and King Johnathan was the eighth heir to rule over that land. The realm had centuries to study, experiment, and discover wonders, the ancient information and secrets stored away in the vast library she had never had the chance to explore in her birth palace. Even if she wanted to, she was banned from doing so.

She waited until it was clear and safe to gently place the cup before pouring the tea and settling the kettle beside it. The fragrance was enticing, wafting towards Alaric's nostrils. He was eager to sample it.

With both hands, he grabbed the cup and brought it to his plush lips. He takes a daring, small sip.

The tea was unlike any he had tasted yet again. It had a delicate floral aroma with hints of honey and spice. The flavor was equally captivating, with a smooth, velvety texture that coated his tongue. It made the corners of his mouth curl up. "How do you do it?"

Lucia shifted her gaze, meeting his eyes. Her expression was one of confusion, and he could tell that she did not understand his question. He clarified, "The tea, Lucia. How do you make it different, yet perfect, each time? It's like you have a secret recipe book deep inside your brain."

Lucia's eyes blinked in surprise at his compliment, her fingers nervously rubbing against the cheap threads of her dress fabric. The king took notice.

He had seen queens from other realms donning exquisite garments embellished with precious stones and intricate embroidery. They stood tall and immaculate, as if every day was a grand spectacle that required them to look their best. Witnessing Lucia, who was starkly different, made him wonder if she was undervaluing herself by wearing simple, low-class clothing daily. Could there be a reason behind her preference for old, maid-like attire?

He pondered this question. He thought he would see her dressed in luxurious fabrics, similar to the way King Johnathan had presented her.

"I must ask," he said before he took another sip, warm steam brewing above the cup. "Your choice of clothing: Why?"

Lucia was unsure how to answer. The king leaned in, elbows on the desk, and placed the teacup on the unoccupied space. He rephrased, "I have seen the most flamboyant textiles on brides in the past. So, why must you wear unpleasant fabrics?"

Alaric's question, though genuine, came off a bit off-putting. It created a more significant wave of anxiety to wash over her as she looked down at the clothing she was wearing.

Her husband was right.

She was unattractive in her current attire. She wished she had flattering clothing, but regardless of her protests, Father was adamant about leaving her proper outfits for Michael's future heirs.

If she had the option to be dressed in elegant clothing, she would do it in a heartbeat. She needed to be appealing to Alaric, or else, he might disown her.

Regret instantly pinched the king. He could sense the self-conscious turmoil. He sighed. "Forget my question."

It was dumb of him to ask. He was well aware that newlywed brides typically arrived with no money.

The nervous queen bowed politely before retreating as quickly as she could, her delicate form disappearing from the king's view. The soft click of the glass door echoed through the room as she gently closed it behind her. And in that moment, Alaric was left alone with his thoughts with a hot kettle by his side.

Lucia moved to the base of the grand staircase, away from the colorful glass. Her little fingers continued to fidget nervously as she tried to calm her fragile mind. The king mustn't be alarmed and gawk at her.

Rose and Axel, who were nearby carrying baskets of supplies, noticed the queen's unease from across the floor. They exchanged concerned glances, sensing that something was amiss.

"My Queen, are you all right?" Rose asked, the two of them approaching. Lucia's obvious distress drew them in. Luckily, the interruption knocked her out of her spiraling thoughts.

She gave a fake smile. "I am all right, just a bit anxious. Nothing too concerning."

"Why must you feel bothered?"

Rose and Axel waited intently for the answer, their expressions filled with empathy. They watched for any clue, and when Lucia's eyes darted at the glass doors for a second, Rose caught it right away. She leaned in to whisper, "Did Alaric say something? If so, I will not hesitate to chew him out."

The head servant glanced at the glass doors. She was serious with her words. She was essentially the king's godmother, not afraid to voice her concerns or help guide him if he had done something remarkably foolish.

"No, no. He did not," Lucia quickly reassured. She did not want trouble.

Rose could already sense a sugar-coated lie within the queen's response, but it was not her place to probe further. With a nod and Axel's hum in agreement, she added, "All right, but if you ever need anything, let us know. Don't be shy to ask."

"Of course. I appreciate you all, truly."

The head servant could already see the relief in her queen's eyes. She was now family, and if anything troubled her, Rose needed to hear about it immediately.

"Now, if you could excuse us," Rose said, lifting her arms to show the basket of supplies she was still holding. Her arms were beginning to ache, and they needed to resume the chore. Lucia produced a small smile and nodded. Her fingers had ceased picking.

As the two servants stepped away, only a minute passed before a small figure came rushing up the stairs. Her legs burned from the effort, and her chest heaved as she labored to make each step. Despite the discomfort, she pressed on. She was in search of her mother.

"Mommy!"

Lucia's small smile formed into a large grin as she watched her. Charlotte panted, "I was wondering where you were. You were missing for a while."

"I am sorry, princess. But never worry, I will always be here," Lucia replied, getting down on her knees to be at eye level. Her hands warmly held her daughter's smaller ones.

"What were you doing?"

"I was giving tea to the king."

"Did he like it?"

"Absolutely. Everyone likes my tea."

Charlotte giggled. She was aware of the delightful faces others made when they sampled her mother's brewery.

Lucia asked, "It is almost time to make the king's dinner. Would you like to help me?"

The little girl nods enthusiastically, her eyes sparkling with excitement. She loved spending time in the kitchen and helping her mother prepare meals.

Lucia smiled warmly at her daughter's eagerness and stood up, carefully picking her up and cradling her in her arms. "Princess, you are getting big and heavy."

"No, I'm not," Charlotte chuckled.

"Yes, you are."

Their voices went faint as they descended the stairs. Clueless to the commotion outside, behind the closed glass doors, Alaric had begun writing a letter to his mother. He had already finished the brewed tea.

Hello momma,

I miss your nurturing warmth, but I hope you are doing well. The news from the kingdom may already have reached you, but I feel compelled to share the details nonetheless.

I have officially become king and married a bride from Kingdom Morningstar, blessed by King Johnathan. He did not wish to house and care for his daughter any longer. As part of our union, gifts are expected from me to shower upon the bride's royal family. Yet, surprisingly, the kingdom bestowed upon me instead of the other way around.

The reason for this is that my bride is not a virgin. I find this a trivial and childish concern, but it is considered highly inappropriate for spouseless royalty to be unchaste. This left no obligations or ties to uphold my half of the marriage other than a simple alliance.

As you know me well, I have always opposed the frivolous rules of royalty. I pay no attention to the concept of virginity. I will go on and on about the displeasures of the old country, but if I do not stop now, you know this would be pages long. Moving back to the topic, my new wife's name is Lucia, and she has a daughter named Charlotte.

Lucia is very quiet, sweet, and quick with the household chores. She makes splendid meals and refreshments. What will truly amaze you, however, is her striking beauty—golden hair, deep blue eyes, cherubic lips, flawless skin, and so forth. You will be left breathless when you see her. Even the servants are stunned, haha! It is said that her previous spouse had passed away years prior, but I did not detect any signs of grief from her. She may be hiding it well. I am in no place to judge.

Charlotte is nearly identical to her in appearance. During my visit to Lucia's birth kingdom, I noticed she also had a brother. He was present at our wedding, and he bore a striking resemblance to Lucia. Come to find out, they were born at the same time.

Twins!

Twin offspring are fruitful in her family tree. I did not catch his name, but he seemed to be strong and kind based on my observation alone. I hope to meet him properly in the future.

I would be overjoyed if you could visit us soon. I long to see you and introduce you to my wife and her daughter. Your presence will be welcomed, and I miss you dearly. I love you, momma.

Your son,
Alaric

10

Neemere Forest

An important order has come.

    Alaric's departure was imminent, and an urgent matter demanded his swift action. The courtyard was bustling with energy and movement as a battalion of knights clad in gleaming silver armor assembled in precise formation. Their swords, sharp and lethal, hung at their sides. Yet, in only a moment, the grass field would become deserted.

Among them were the archers, their attire a blend of earthy hues—greens, browns, and tans; designed to blend with their natural surroundings. Quivers brimming with arrows were slung across their backs while dried vines adorned their shoulders. Their goal was to blend into the shadows of the forest.

Nadia was tasked with maintaining the troop count and ensuring their preparedness. She was also responsible for distributing the necessary supplies, including canteens, unlit torches, and light medical supplies in case of unforeseen circumstances.

Magnificent horses rallied as the barn laborers saddled the animals, preparing for the ride. Hank was amongst them, grumbling under his breath as his stained hands adjusted straps and buckles. Some of the laborers were young, so the older man checked over their work as they practiced mastering the technique.

The sun was gleaming under the new day, casting its golden glow over the landscape and banishing the last vestiges of night. The sky was a blanket of blue, devoid of even a single cloud—a perfect day for the journey that lay ahead.

Alaric descended the grand staircase quickly, his grey cotton attire billowing slightly with each swift step. The tight cuffs hugged his wrists, the cotton tucked into the loose fabric of his black pants. It was a look of comfort.

A look of simple pristine.

Lucia was already standing by the double doors, her hands full of a garment. This was a ritual she had perfected with her previous spouse. She prepared him before he left and then greeted him when he returned. Alaric was taking notice.

The outerwear was a masterpiece of craftsmanship—a sleek, black garment bearing intricate red patterns starting from the backside, moving upwards to cover the shoulders, and extending down to the mid-arm. Gold-plated buttons aligned the frontier, with gold tassels eloping along the dark red shoulder cape attached by the black threads—a rich hue in dark fabric.

This was not an outfit designed for warmth or protection from the elements but for show, a statement piece intended to impress and intimidate.

Despite her uncertainty about Alaric's destination, Lucia made an educated guess based on the crowd outside the doors. She had not seen such a large gathering since her arrival, and it was clear that whatever event Alaric was going to, held importance. In such appearances, she had to make her husband look powerful, confident, and poised like a true leader.

Before Alaric could protest, Lucia had already begun dressing him. He usually didn't mind what she chose for him to wear, but he did not want it. There was a reason he did not want it today.

"You should have asked me first. I do not want this god-awful coat," he said coldly. His tone hung heavy in the air.

Lucia immediately removed the garment, the fabric pooling in her arms. She bowed her head apologetically, and a pang of shame overcame her. This was the first time Alaric had objected to her choice of clothing for him.

The king reached for the metal ring handle of the wooden doors, his fingers brushing against the cold iron, but he could not bring himself to pull them open. He instantly regretted his words. It was his fault anyway, with his fidgety attitude.

There was no reaction from her, no response. He glanced over at his wife.

Her head was still bowed, and her posture was patient and resigned. She was waiting for him to leave before returning to resume her duties. He needed to make amends; otherwise, he would be distracted by his own piss-poor behavior for the rest of the day.

Taking a deep breath, he steeled himself and spoke. "I apologize. I should not have snapped and been rude to you. There is no excuse for my behavior." His voice was steady, his words sincere. He meant every word, and he hoped that Lucia could see that. He was not a man who was harsh to others. He knew better to watch his words.

Lucia's head snapped up, her eyes wide. It was rare for Lucia to look at him directly, and in these brief moments when she did, it was enough to leave him stunned over and over again.

Her emotions were a tumultuous storm. She had never received an apology like that before and honestly did not know how to feel. She would have been fine without an apology; she was used to it. But before she could slip away, to hide and allow Alaric to leave, he spoke up again. "And please take a break; you seem exhausted."

Before elaborating, he was gone. The doors swung shut behind him, leaving Lucia standing alone. She was speechless, her mind racing with thoughts and questions. Had Alaric noticed her exhaustion? Was it the dark circles under her eyes from her relentless work and lack of rest, or had her energy levels dipped noticeably? Whatever it was, he had seen it, and it was clear that he cared.

Lucia shook her head, chiding herself for getting carried away. This was not the time for daydreams or flights of fancy. She had jobs to do, and she needed to focus. She started by planning a hearty meal upon Alaric's return. He would be hungry and need rest.

Valentino witnessed it all.

The older man was from his vantage point on the second balcony, his keen gaze following her from above as she slipped away. He was not just observing the queen but studying her, his attention bordering on obsession. This had been going on for the past few weeks.

He clutched a letter, the envelope crumpled from his frequent rough handling. It had been opened and read but not shown to the king. It was from another kingdom, proposing a new alliance alongside Kingdom Cinderhaven. It could change the course of their future.

But in this case, he could not bring himself to present it before Alaric left. He feared it would influence the upcoming meeting set up in the Neemere Forest.

Large equines whine to a grinding halt. Sweat soaked their short, patterned coats. The creaking of the leather saddles attests to the heavy burden of the knights perched upon them. The branches of the greenery bristled by their path, casting ominous shadows.

The small group had traversed through the grassfield before entering the Neemere Forest, a domain primarily composed of towering white oaks. Some other species of trees were also scattered among these majestic giants, such as walnut and hackberry trees. It provided the much-needed food and shelter for smaller creatures, as well as close proximity for birds to hop from branch to branch.

Half of this forest belonged to the Kingdom Ironwood, while the other half remained unclaimed territory, serving as a neutral ground for this noon's meeting. The trees brought a sense of nostalgia due to the closeness of Alaric's former home. By this time, it housed either another family or the wild. Regardless of its inhabitants, it was a shelter and refuge for all who sought it.

Alaric gracefully dismounted from his sleek Friesian steed, and Nadia followed suit. The archers had already ascended into the trees, leaving their knight companions behind with the shared horses. They remained silent and vigilant, poised to respond. This was a precautionary measure.

Eyes scanned their surroundings. All were on alert, frozen in time. The last thing Alaric wanted for his people was an ambush, and he was already taking the risk of a trap.

As wildlife continued with its music, it wasn't long before the knights from the opposing kingdom arrived. Steps crushed the leaves underneath their path, halting several feet before Alaric's entire group. Their armor, though formidable, appeared dull and worn from years of use, with some pieces even bearing the scars of past battles. The majority of these knights were new recruits. Alaric would know.

Among them, a slim figure emerged. He had chestnut hair and chiseled features, standing almost equal in height. He stepped forward in front of his horizontal line of knights. His attire was flattering, consisting of high-quality grey and black cloth and an elegant short-shoulder cape. A massive sword hung at his side, and he stood tall with his chest puffed out. With a slight resemblance to the previous king, this was Prince Alexander of Kingdom Ironwood, the youngest and last surviving son.

Prince Alexander had been absent during his father's tragic death. Upon learning during his traveling expedition, he returned immediately to his kingdom. His older brother, who was deemed the next heir, had fallen ill and passed years prior. Now, as the sole surviving son, Alexander had inherited the throne.

The atmosphere was heavily thick with tension, willing to strangle anyone who dared to pass by. The archers held their breath in anticipation. The knights stiffened their postures behind their king. Nadia's gaze locked onto the man in front of her, her eyes narrowing like those of a predator assessing its prey.

No one dared speak for the first couple of minutes. Both sides were observing, judging, and learning; details were being burned into their brains. This was the first time the newly titled king and crowned prince had ever laid eyes upon one another.

With a surprisingly calm face, Alexander was the first to break the silence. "King Alaric, it is such a pleasure to finally meet you. I have heard a lot of controversial things regarding your name."

"You as well," Alaric replied.

"Maybe, but my rumors are not labeled as crimes."

"Only the listener can make the final judgment."

The comment makes the prince bluntly roll his eyes. "Let's not get ahead of ourselves, shall we? The remainder of my kingdom only wants to settle the past. That is the goal of this meeting, is it not?"

The soft breeze playfully danced with the ends of Alexander's cape, catching Alaric's attention with the elegant fabric. He did not desire to stand out from his attire; he wanted to blend in. He believed that his simplistic outfit should reflect the support and loyalty of his people, without whom he wouldn't have achieved his current position.

Alaric chose his following words wisely. Another sour remark might flare into a fight. He cleared his throat. "What is it that you seek?"

"Compensation, nothing else," Alexander said with a wide grin.

A flick of annoyance crossed the king's face. "In what do you wish to compensate for? For a piece of my land? Cattle? Crops? My people?"

"Heavens, no. I only have a simple request that will last as long as I rein in my throne."

Alaric raised an eyebrow in question. The prince continued, "I request that half of your kingdom's income be sent to me until I either retire or expire, collected once a month in pounds of gold and delivered by your men. This will support my kingdom's economy since you've stolen half of my taxpayers."

"Pardon me?"

"My current population can barely hand in their share for my palace to function, and soon, it will decrease our trade production and increase social stress. If you have any mercy for my people and are willing to work with me in writing a physical agreement, then I will drop your crime and forbid my blood-related heirs from demanding your head. I may even help stop the falsified rumors of your tainted name and generously recognize your kingdom, despite it being composed of my citizens anyway."

"Are you mad?" Alaric hissed. A request like this would ruin his own economy.

Alexander frowned. "Were you mad when you killed my father?"

"His sacrifice was needed for the achievement of goals for the people and myself."

"Your selfish goals ended a monarch."

"Death is required to start anew."

"His death was a laugh due to you twisting his words and tainting his image!"

"That was his own doing from his frail leadership!" Alaric yelled.

A fierce snarl escaped Alexander's lips as he gripped the hilt of his massive sword and aimed. But Alaric remained unfazed, standing tall with his feet firmly planted on the ground and his hands clasped behind his back—a display of confidence and composure.

Nadia responded to protect her king, drawing her sword and positioning herself protectively in front. Two swords now pointed at each other, the tips of the sharpened metal inches apart. The hidden archers reacted and lifted their bows at the opposing king from their vantage point in the thick vegetation of the trees.

Everything was at a standstill; neither side dared move.

Long seconds passed in the quiet forest, only the melody of the birds echoing their tunes until a booming laugh broke out to silence the small creatures. Alexander's fury transformed into hysteria. "You are one of the biggest fools I have ever met! You have a *female* to be your lap dog!"

Alaric narrowed his eyes. Nadia was no lap dog. She was like a cougar, ready to pounce and release her claws. All he had to do was give the signal, and she would unleash upon their enemy.

"As you see," Alexander chuckled, his laughter slowly dying as he lowered his weapon, "I don't need a lap dog to be by my side. I am quite confident in myself, alongside my knights. I suggest you remove her from your court so you don't appear weak."

"I did not ask for your sour opinion."

The prince smirked. "Maybe you should if you want to be taken seriously."

"I am serious about finding an end goal for this."

"Are you? From what I have gathered from this meeting is a list of pathetic excuses. Then, without challenging me yourself, you allowed a *female* to shield you."

"Do not—"

"Admit it. Your new, rule-breaking kingdom would not survive against outside forces, including Kingdom Ironwood; I have the supplies and resources in the palm of my hand. If war were to happen, Kingdom Hartfelt would be demolished."

Alaric loudly barked, "Is that a threat!?"

Alexander brushed off his opponent's tone with a shrug. "No. War is not my favorable choice during this time."

"War should never be a favorable choice. Innocent lives are too precious and fragile to gamble with."

"So my father's life was not considered precious and fragile?"

Nadia kept her stance, her sword still pointed. Alaric replied, "He wasn't exactly innocent."

"He was innocent enough to trust you." A hint of pain crept into Alexander's voice as he spoke. Although he may not have met the ex-Knight of the Body prior, he had been informed by his father of the young knight's remarkable intelligence and prospering abilities through his letters. The fact that their relationship had come to such an unfortunate end brought hatred into his chest.

"I will not apologize for my actions, but I acknowledge your grief."

"That does not matter."

"It does. There was an uproar being planned by a group of rebels amongst his population, seeking to stone him alive. I brought mercy instead with a blade in exchange for my life."

Alexander huffed. "And yet, I can't help but wonder if these rebels were motivated by your talented speeches."

"Many were motivated. Some sought a more violent measure to achieve changes."

"It still does not justify what happened. This is written as a tragedy in the literature of my kingdom."

"Surely, and I seek for a resolution to move this behind us, but I cannot condemn of giving away my people's hard-earned income. It would make me a back-stabbing jester for going against my principles and serving the very kingdom my people fled in the first place."

Alexander shook his head, but before he could reply, Alaric continued, "If you conclude a better agreement, one that is fairer, I am willing to meet again."

"And if not?"

"Only the future will tell."

A prolonged silence enveloped as the two leaders locked eyes. Nadia finally lowered her weapon, and the Ironwood Prince breathed a deep sigh, exhaling forcefully through his nostrils. "You are hard and stale, much like sun-dried bread."

"I may be so, but neither of us will be fulfilled in the end; only partially satisfied in terms of keeping peace."

"Then, all I can say is to wish you luck. I am unsure how my people would respond to your refusal, and I am quite displeased."

"Me, too," Alaric agreed. "Me, too."

11

The Beast's Generosity

As the king and his armed people returned to the kingdom, Lucia had already brewed a fresh pot of tea. A large meal was in the middle of preparation. Although the queen was initially hesitant to accept help from the servants, she finally relented and enlisted their assistance in cooking.

Alaric and Valentino had retreated to the private study room to discuss the outcome of the meeting in detail, the glass doors securely shut to maintain confidentiality. The meeting had left Alaric feeling exasperated. Valentino tried to turn the mood by presenting him with the open letter from Kingdom Zuiphate.

It was a large but quiet kingdom, partially isolated by the thick pine tree forest and the bordering ocean from the west. The people embraced the treacherous cold winds, specializing in fish trading and wood. It was within a day's travel to reach, but an invitation was considered a compliment, as the kingdom was strictly selective. In return, they requested mainly textiles and crops for their needs.

This offered an advantage in trade and relations, but Alaric's mood remained sour for the remainder of the day. He knew that Kingdom Ironwood would pose a threat, but he thought he would have enough time to strengthen his position and grow his kingdom beforehand. Now, this made him worry more.

Lucia trotted up the grand staircase, carrying a steaming kettle and cup. She had finally developed the stamina and endurance necessary to navigate the hundreds of steps with ease. Yet, as she approached the third floor, the tip of her indoor shoe inadvertently struck the edge of the final step, causing her to stumble and fall onto her knees with a soft yelp.

The hot tea spilled onto the floor and her hands, burning her soft skin. The kettle rolled onto its side, and the porcelain cup shattered into numerous pieces. Shards of sharp clay now littered the rug. It was a complete disaster.

She ignored the growing pain and began sweeping the broken pieces with her fingers. She tried to clean as fast as possible, but the creaking of the glass doors and the sound of conversation left her momentarily paralyzed with fear.

The two men stepped out of the study room, eyes immediately drawn to the fallen queen on the floor. Their expressions were a show of frustration and lingering anger. She had screwed up.

Valentino scoffed. "What is this? Clumsy bitch, do you want the king to slip? To hurt himself?"

"Valenti—"

"Even the servants don't make mistakes like you. Why bother being alive when you can't do the job righ—"

"Enough Valentino!" Alaric snapped. His anger was about to hit its boiling point.

Lucia never intended to provoke a confrontation, let alone endanger her husband. Her actions were unintentional, but the consequences were still dire. Still on her knees, she humbly bowed her head, prepared to accept whatever punishment her husband deemed fit. Given the gravity of her mistake, she would not be surprised if Alaric decided to scorn her or even resort to physical discipline.

However, to her surprise, only the sound of porcelain pieces followed, clacking together in front of her. She looked up to see Alaric crouching, carefully gathering the shattered cup fragments and arranging them in a cluster. "Are you all right? Do you need to see a physician?"

Lucia only stared at her husband's unexpected act of kindness. Her hands were turning red, and she knew the burning sensation would linger for a few days, but she did not want to burden him further. A simple soak in water would suffice, and perhaps one of the servants had aloe vera. Therefore, she shook her head in response to his concerned inquiry.

The answer disappointed Alaric. She had every right to request assistance as needed, but he doubted she would change. Weirdly enough, she was a stubborn queen; she probably didn't even realize it herself.

The king does a slight nod in acknowledgment before standing up. "All right, but do not hesitate to ask if you change your mind." He turned, resuming his way down the floor hallway.

Valentino was appalled. "What was that?!"

He rushed after Alaric, but the king did not respond. It was ridiculous that he had to explain his actions to the older man.

"You have to punish her! As a king, you demand order! When your spouse acts up, you must put her in their place! Otherwise, she'll do it again!"

"It was an acciden—"

"Nobody will respect you as a king! You cannot allow yourself to be weak! This will allow the lower class to step on you!"

"You are walking on thin ice, Valentino. If you know your place, then I advise you to shut it!" Alaric threatened, abruptly halting his stride and confronting his advisor face to face. Their bodies were mere inches apart, and their breaths mingled. Alaric's eyes blazed with fury, but he restrained himself from going physical.

Valentino attempted to voice his objection, but quickly clamped his mouth shut. He felt mortified and embarrassed at being reprimanded by the young monarch. The king was becoming more fond of his wife every day, so he had to be careful not to push too far.

After a few tense seconds of confrontational staring, Alaric resumed his walk, not caring if he had left his advisor behind. Lucia maintained her attention to her mess, using a handkerchief she had stored in her strained dress pocket to soak up the tea. She felt Valentino's stern glare on her back before he followed suit, maintaining a deliberate foot distance from his king, their footsteps reverberating against the stone walls as they vanished from sight.

As she scooped the mess into her soaked handkerchief, a tumult of emotions and conflicting thoughts surged within her. Alaric did not appear to be the brutal beast that the rumors of the lands depicted. In fact, he was the complete opposite.

She descended the stairs to the first floor to dispose of the broken clay pieces before a body gently collided into her for a hug—an audible oof before the little girl burst out in laughter. Charlotte was in her yellow plain sundress, tending to herself in play until she saw her mother. She inhaled into the clothing to take in Lucia's distinct floral scent.

"Mommy!"

Lucia immediately broke into a smile. Despite the discomfort caused by her burning skin, she placed her hands on both sides of Charlotte's head. She took a sizable sniff. Playfully, she feigned disgust. "You stink!"

Charlotte looked up at her mother. "No, I don't!"

Lucia sniffed her daughter's head once more, this time with a dramatic flourish. Charlotte giggled at her mother's teasing. "I beg to differ."

It was time to bathe.

The two of them then made their way to the servant's washroom. Supplies were already gathered for use on the stacked shelves against the walls. Small stone steps descended down to the warm water. A carved marble rim encircled the basin. The community bath was simplistic but better maintained than Father's with his servants.

Although she was the queen, Lucia felt using Alaric's private bath was appropriate. She did not need permission anyway, as she was content with bathing in the servant washroom. Lucia leaned in to help

Charlotte out of her sundress and undergarments before undressing herself. They were all alone for their private bath.

As they entered together, the water only reached Lucia's waist. It felt pleasant to the skin, and soon, they began to wash.

Soap suds floated on the surface. Lucia was seated in the water, barely submerging her small breasts, as she lathered her daughter's golden hair. Charlotte sat on her mother's lap, finding great pleasure while her head was being scrubbed. Fingers buried and itched the scalp.

By the time Lucia was finished, she grabbed a small pail and poured warm water over her head. The princess giggled with delight.

"You like that, don't you?"

"It's like a waterfall," Charlotte exclaimed, wiping the water from her eyes. She turned to face her mother, and when she placed the pail down, she noticed the red marks on her mother's hands. "Mommy, did you hurt yourself?"

The queen looked down at her red hands, which were temporarily soothed by the warm water. "Yes, I did. I spilled tea on myself."

Charlotte's eyes widened with concern. "You have to be careful. I don't like it when you are hurt. It makes me sad."

Lucia smiled tenderly, feeling overwhelming pride for her perfect daughter. Charlotte had been a blessing in her life, helping her in ways she could never have imagined. "I will try to be extra careful from now on."

"You promise?"

"I promise," Lucia replied, and the two embraced each other in a warm hug.

Once they had finished bathing, they dried off. Lucia grabbed the largest towel she could find, wrapping it around and vigorously rubbing it all over her daughter's body. She even squished her cheeks as she dried her hair. This made Charlotte scream in happiness.

It was time to redress. The queen found a temporary robe to wrap herself in while Charlotte remained covered by the large towel. It trailed behind her as they headed to their bedchamber. Lucia found it adorable.

From the vast expanse of the grand hall, King Alaric was engaged in a conversation with a group of his servants. He took some time to collect himself from his interaction with Valentino, and he was now receiving updates on the palace's activities during his earlier absence. He was delighted to learn that a meal was nearly ready. His hunger grew with each passing moment.

But his attention was abruptly drawn to Lucia and her daughter as they unexpectedly appeared and ascended the stairs. He could tell they had just come from the bath, and his sudden silence in the conversation left the servants perplexed. They, too, turned their heads to watch the queen and her child disappear.

"I am stuck. She won't talk to me," Alaric suddenly declared. The previous conversation had dropped entirely. He was now fixated on his wife.

Victoria replied, "Your Majesty, she is shy."

The king sighed. "More like trained to hold her tongue."

"You think so?" Mia questioned.

"She has yet to speak a word to me. I have tasted high-class royalty standards when I stepped up as a leader, but I had never seen someone be so confined to it. It's so limiting."

"I have witnessed many things during my past experiences in other kingdoms," Rose added. "Destined brides are trained since childhood to be strict and obedient for a future marriage that is years ahead. Some teachings are more severe than others." Her words were met with admiration from the other two servants. She was filled with wisdom.

Alaric included, "And to be a personal maid. If I wanted a servant, I could have just hired another one."

"She works harder than all of us combined. She is five servants in one," Mia said.

Victoria frowned. "It does worry me. She must feel drained."

The king shook his head. "I know I selfishly sought marriage for my title gain, but she is still a living being. At the very least, we could be more than strangers, much like adjusted acquaintances. And, I've been considering offering her a palace position."

"I don't think that would work," Rose stated, drawing the attention of the two servants and King Alaric. The king was puzzled by her comment. She continued, "You are starting to like her. I have noticed you studying, fixated on her whenever she does things around you."

"She's gorgeous and attentive; how can I not? Plus, she's so sweet to her daughter. I want to see how loving and sweet she can be." His words were filled with a hint of genuine affection.

"I know you want to know more about her, but you can't."

"Pardon?"

"You have to make Lucia as comfortable as possible first," Rose clarified. "She may be living here for a month now, but she's in a constant state of fear. She's been taken from her home a second time, and everyone in this palace is a stranger. Be gentle and patient, and let her decide when it's a good time to open up."

Every word was valuable from the head servant, and he was grateful for her guidance. He nodded in agreement. "How long do you think till she opens up?"

"That cannot be answered."

"I see," Alaric concluded. "I understand now. Thank you. You all have helped me in more ways than you can imagine."

It put a soft smile on Rose's face.

One small step at a time. Alaric can do that.

A carefully arranged stack of blankets and pillows adorned the bed. These were not typical bedding items but rather sumptuous and high-quality, filled with baby bird feathers and sewn in delicate silk. Lucia stood, surprised at the doorway, a plate of food in her hands.

Charlotte was overjoyed. The little girl rushed to the bed and ran her fingers over the fine materials. Her happiness was infectious, and Lucia could not help but smile alongside her.

A tiny, folded note rested atop the blankets and pillows, but it could wait. Lucia wanted to touch the items first. Luckily, she could still trace the precise seams, touch the smooth fabrics, and push the plushness with her sensitive fingers. There was a sting of pain, but it was bearable. It was undoubtedly one of the finest-quality blankets and pillows she had ever encountered.

"It's so soft!" Charlotte exclaimed, her excitement evident as she leaped onto the bed and buried herself within the pile. The note drifted to the side, teetering on the edge of the bed. Lucia swiftly picked it up before it could fall to the floor.

"It is," she said, unfolding the note gently. She begins to read the contents inside.

I am unsure if you know how to read, but if you cannot, allow one of the servants to help you. I grant the reader permission. Anyway, please enjoy. This should provide better slumber for you and your daughter.

Alaric

A gift. The king had bestowed upon them a set of the finest bed attire. He must have snuck it in while she was cleaning up the kitchen after the meal, as she was completely unaware.

"Who is it from?"

"The king."

"Really?" Charlotte gasped.

Lucia nodded. "I am surprised myself."

It was a generous and thoughtful gesture, and she was grateful.

His actions spoke of his true self; he had a loving heart. She could sense it. He was nothing like the drama the servants gossiped about on their wedding day.

Tonight, the two of them would enjoy a peaceful and restful night's sleep. It was more than she could hope for.

The little girl slept soundly, snoring softly and more comfortably than ever before. She nestled beneath the new bed covers. Meanwhile, the queen continued to prepare herself for sleep, carefully brushing out any tangles from her fluffy bob haircut under the dim light of the remaining candles.

She studied herself in the mirror. A thin nightgown hugged her slender frame, extending from her shoulders all the way down to her ankles. Her mind raced with a blooming fantasy.

She envisioned herself in a stunning ball dress, intricately flower-patterned and adorned with sparkling jewels woven into the scarlet fabric. The gown featured lace sleeves that draped elegantly down to a V-shaped neckline. As she traced her fingertips along her collarbone, she also imagined a delicate lace necklace with teardrop-shaped polished quartz stone dangling gracefully around her neck. The dresser surface would be compiled with layers of makeup.

Oh, how she dreamed.

Lucia didn't like living in Father's palace, but she fondly remembered the luxurious fabrics and jewels that were at her disposal. She missed the flowers her servants would bring her. They would carefully arrange the blossoms into her hair for her.

She longed for those moments. But it would be too much to ask.

She and her daughter were treated much more kindly than ever in this castle. Charlotte had more freedom to play where she wished. Castle members were polite and selfless. She gladly traded her desires for material possessions for the warmth and kindness she was now experiencing. That is what she wanted most.

A gentle knock on the door pulled Lucia back to the present. She turned her head, curious as to who might be seeking her company at such an hour. She hastily approached the door eagerly.

Upon opening it, she found Victoria, dressed in her uniform and holding a kettle and two cups. A weary, soft smile graced her face. She asked politely, "May I come in?"

"Yes, please," Lucia replied, stepping aside. As the servant quietly entered, she noticed Charlotte sleeping in the bed, wrapped snugly in the blankets and pillows that Alaric had gifted them. The young girl looked so peaceful and content.

Victoria approached the small table and placed the kettle and cups on the wooden surface. She began pouring the hot liquid into the cups. Lucia was unsure what to say to her unannounced but pleasant appearance.

"It may not be as delectable as your blend," Victoria admitted, setting Lucia's cup down in front of her before pouring her own. The steam rose from the cups, filling the air with its warm aroma. "Yet it was the least we could do."

"That is very kind of you," Lucia said as she sat. "But you did not have to."

"My Queen, you have been shouldering more than half of our responsibilities since you arrived. Allow us to take care of you tonight."

The servant sat down in the other chair and sipped her tea. Lucia appreciated their thoughts and consideration.

"Thank you," she replied. As the queen reached for her cup, Victoria's eyes widened in alarm.

"My Queen, what happened?"

Lucia was confused by what she meant. Only then did it click when Victoria quickly placed her cup down and grabbed the undersides of her hands, careful not to touch the redness coating her palms. A few blisters were beginning to form. It looked so painful.

Victoria examined. "Your hands."

"I am a clumsy person," Lucia nervously chuckled, but her response did not address the pending question. Victoria raised an eyebrow, seeking further explanation.

Lucia quickly answered, "Hot tea."

Victoria began to stand up. "Rose has a nice remedy for burns. I'll let her know so she'll prepare some in the mornin—"

"Please, don't go."

"My Queen, the burns–"

"Not yet, please?" Lucia pleaded in a soft voice.

Victoria stopped her attempt and nodded. She did not inquire further, and the two women sat silently for several moments, lost in their thoughts. The servant were unsure of what to make of the situation.

Lucia broke the silence first in a whisper. "Thank you. Sometimes, it is nice to sit with someone."

"It's nothing."

They enjoyed their tea, the queen being careful with her blisters as she savored the drink. It was a pleasant way to wind down before bed.

"Is the blend all right?"

Lucia smiled with reassurance. "Do not worry, it is perfect."

"To be fair, we were a bit apprehensive since we've never had a tea master in our kitchen before," Victoria admitted. "How do you do it?"

Lucia pondered for a moment before responding. "I suppose it is due to my excessive experimentation in the kitchen. I was trained to cook for half of my childhood."

"Is that so?" Victoria inquired, intrigued.

Lucia nodded, recalling those memories. She remembered the countless days she spent cooking and perfecting her skills under the watchful eye of her wicked witch of a bride tutor Father hired into his court. She hated that woman to the core. Some days, she hoped that woman would trip and fall into the hearth, screaming out in agony as she burned alive from the years of cruelty at her hands.

"You know, Alaric is growing interested in you. We can tell by how he talks about you and keeps a keen eye on you," Victoria said.

This statement snapped Lucia out of her reminiscing trauma. She did not know what to say at first, taking a second to formulate her response. She assumed that Victoria's comment was in reference to her wifely duties. "I hope I am meeting his standards."

"I believe you are way above standards, even when compared to a servant."

Lucia felt pride. It meant she was proving her worth.

"You haven't set foot outside castle grounds since you arrived. Why don't you go out? See the town? Surely, the people would love to see you." Victoria poured herself another cup of tea.

The queen was still sipping on her first serving, much slower due to her hand injuries. "I am not allowed to."

"What makes you think that? Alaric would not put such restrictions on you."

"A queen stays here and takes care of the family and castle. I cannot go out and neglect my duties."

"But that's why you have servants, and even we go out occasionally to see the town. The people are very welcoming."

"No, I cannot."

Victoria pouted. It hurt to know the queen thought like that. "Well, if you were given that chance, would you take that opportunity and explore your new kingdom?"

That sounded like another dream for Lucia. She smiled instantly. "Absolutely. I would take my daughter as well. She would love it."

"You think so?"

"I know so. She will make so many friends. It comes so naturally to her." The queen's eyes softened as she turned her head to glance at her daughter, who was still sleeping soundly.

Victoria followed her gaze. "You love her so much."

"She is my everything," she said confidently. The queen was certain that she would have taken her own life long ago if Charlotte had never been born—the driving force to give her the will to live.

12

Thespian

The night was alive with the sounds of nature, punctuated by the occasional hoot of an owl and the soft rustling of leaves as Valentino crept through the dense foliage. Fireflies twinkled in the darkness, their ethereal dance illuminating the path ahead briefly before disappearing again into the shadows. The moon was covered by a blanket of clouds, not providing much light, so Valentino had to resort to the flickering light of a single candle-lit lantern to guide his way.

He moved cautiously, careful not to allow the sharp thorns of the prickly bushes to latch onto his dark cloak. His grip tightened around the metal lantern handle as he approached closer and closer to his destination, wrinkled knuckles turning white. He ducked under a low-hanging branch.

He was late.

He didn't mean to be, but with each passing encounter, it became harder and harder due to the increased population of recruited knights. He couldn't allow himself to be seen. Too much was on the line.

A sudden crunch of leaves.

The advisor froze, swinging his lantern around. The thought of encountering a wild animal like a wolf or black bear sent a shiver down his spine. These feral creatures were known to roam the

Neemere Forest at night, and he didn't relish the idea of facing one alone. This was their territory once the sun had set.

Another rustle of leaves, and he does a spin of his surroundings.

His heartbeat pounded hard in his chest, his satchel hitting up against his thigh. He was not one to carry a sword, but he had a small dagger tucked in his boot. If he needed it, the weapon was within reach.

Before his eyes could adjust, a prominent dark figure emerged behind a set of grouped trees. The sounds of its steps on the forest floor followed. Valentino instinctively slid his hand downwards, fingers brushing against the warm steel of his dragger. Breath caught in his throat and adrenaline pumping, he was ready to fight, until he heard an amazed hum in a gruff, rough tone.

He froze again.

"Calm down, it's only me," it answered, approaching the light. Valentino's heart rate slowed as he recognized the man's face. The lantern's hue glowed a warm yellow on his bronze skin, highlighting the dark circles under his eyes and the deep, menacing brown of his irises. His scruffy, dark-brown beard and high cheekbones made him appear menacing.

Dangerous. Lethal.

This man was not one to trifle with. Known for his directness and unwavering commitment to his missions, he had earned the prestigious title of Knight of the Body from Kingdom Ironwood.

Just like young Alaric. His replacement.

"It took you long enough," he growled.

Valentino scoffed. "This is not exactly easy. I have knights to look out for—"

"I do not care. Abandon the lantern next time."

"Cain, do you honestly want me to wander aimlessly in the darkness when the moon is not present?"

"If it is necessary. I could spot you from a distance," Cain said, clearly displeased. The light could have given away their positions. He was armed, his sword sheathed at his hip, hidden well under his black cape, but he wasn't in the mood to use it if they had been spotted.

"How did the negotiation go?" Valentino asked.

"Not too well."

"I take it. He was frustrated when he returned. He did not specifically go into detail, but now he's making a flurry of plans in case his kingdom is attacked or so forth. I did not have much input to offer. Conflict hasn't been on anybody's tongues for years."

"Hmm." Cain wasn't one for idle conversation.

"Do you think he is overreacting? He lacks the experience of ruling a realm; therefore, he has yet to understand the true disclosure of outside threats. If I were king, I would call it a fool's tease. But what do I know? I wasn't present. Were you accounted for earlier?"

Cain stared at him.

Valentino sighed. "I suppose it doesn't matter. I pray that nothing serious comes out of this and that some kind of resolution is proposed and agreed upon. I never wanted to be part of this anyway. Such unforeseen events can cause so many issues."

"Papers," Cain demanded.

"Oh, yes. Forgive me." Valentino reached into his satchel, the sound of rustling papers filling the air as he retrieved a neatly folded stack of documents. He handed them over.

"Copies of his recent deals and schedule. Kingdom Zuiphate had requested his attendance for an alliance, wanting access to his crops and establishing a new trade road, but he has yet to reply. He is building allies; if you aren't careful, he'll grow big."

"It is not a problem. We have our own contacts willing to participate in this. Your concerns are unnecessary."

Valentino frowned, watching Cain flip through the papers. He studied them for a moment, his eyes skimming over the handwriting. A slight, satisfied smirk briefly curled his lips before he tucked the papers away.

An issue still itched the advisor. "Well, there is one concern that I have that you might favor."

Cain looked up at the older man, his eyes piercing hard. "I said there's no nee—"

"He's growing soft," Valentino interrupted.

Cain furrowed his thick eyebrows. The blabbering advisor was lucky that he wasn't in a bad mood. "Soft?"

"By his new bride."

"Isn't she leftover scrap?"

"Yes, but this leftover scrap is touching his heartstrings. He's flashing his eyelashes at everything she does. At this point, I am convinced he dreams about her."

"So?" Cain shrugged, not seeing how this could be vital information. He was not a man who sought pleasure in drama and rumors. That was one thing he hated most about Valentino—he engulfed it.

"It is now a weakness. View her as an opportunity to burrow into it and use it against him. Fragile emotions are easy to manipulate," Valentino clarified.

A pause before a chuckle escaped from Cain. Now, he liked what Valentino thought. "I'll pass on the message."

Valentino glowed, but before he could reply, Cain added, "Same time next month."

"Next month?"

"Yes, they're starting to get rallied up," he said, his voice low and ominous. "And don't be late."

"I am not trying to on purpose."

Cain doesn't reply, licking his thumb and pointer fingers before opening the lantern latch and extinguishing the candle's flame. A big grin spread across his face as he turned and disappeared into the pitch black. Valentino was left in solid darkness, dumbfounded.

Sudden preparations were being made.

Servants bustled around as they gathered supplies and hurried to the guarded carriage outside—clothing to food, weaponry and other essentials were packed in the storage compartment of the wagon. Knights waited patiently by their steeds as they helped with the outside labor.

Lucia was not sure what was happening, but the hurried movements of the servants, both inside and outside, up and down the floors, stirred up a trail of leaves and dust. Although she wasn't participating in the unknown urgency of packing, the least she could do was start on the cleaning.

She began with the second floor, sweeping the stranded leaves close to the staircase to gather later. The queen was attuned to herself, her thoughts clouding her brain and keeping her unfamiliar with the pair of eyes watching her every move. It wasn't until she looked up that the tall figure of Alaric standing before her seized her movements. Their eyes locked instantly.

She stood near a carved, quaint table positioned against the staircase railing, a broom firmly clutched in her hands. Alaric was holding a kettle and a cup, the contents of which were currently unknown. They observed each other for a few silent seconds before the king cleared his throat.

"I tried my best," he said, placing the kettle and cup on the table. "It may not be as good as yours, though."

Alaric had taken note and was concerned for her well-being. He desired nothing more than to prevent her from becoming overly exhausted, even though she did not heed his words.

"Please allow yourself to sit down and rest. And," he took a moment to release a deep breath, "I come to tell you farewell. I apologize for the sudden note of my departure. I will be with Nadia for a political gathering in the west and may not return for a few days. I did not want you to worry."

Lucia was conflicted. She was still learning to adjust to his kindness and consideration for others.

His gaze looked down at her hands. "May I see?"

There was a pause as Lucia processed his request, but then she nodded slowly and propped the broom up against the railing. She opened her palms, revealing her healing injuries to Alaric.

Rose's remedy was a charm. In two days' time, Lucia's hands were almost back to normal. The painful burn blisters had nearly faded, only leaving behind a few lingering splotches of redness. She could touch mostly without wincing.

The king smiled at the sight as her burns appeared on the mend. He longed to reach out and hold her hands, to feel the warmth and softness of her skin, so different from his own rough and calloused hands. It was a curious thought he had for a while. But he restrained himself, not wanting to overstep boundaries or make her uneasy.

It might even push her away.

"It seems to be healing well. Rose told me how swollen they were."

Lucia kept her eyes on her palms. Alaric continued, "I may not have a physician in my court, but plenty live on this kingdom's lands. Never feel ashamed to request one."

She did not respond, but when she raised her eyes to meet the king's once again, it made him suck in a breath through his teeth. He felt like a puddle.

"Excuse me," he murmured as he turned away, circling the stairwell railings, descending the steps.

Left alone, Lucia focused on the kettle still steaming on the table. She pondered about the destination he was traveling to, but she was in no position to ask. It wasn't her business to know. Yet, she felt a comforting warmth in her heart.

Alaric had taken the time to inform her.

Such a small gesture spoke volumes. It made the corners of her mouth twitch upwards.

She was smiling.

The queen's gaze snapped to the resting broom. The notion of resuming her task flitted through her mind, but her fingers refused to obey, remaining stubbornly still. With a soft exhale, she surrendered, sinking into the chair before her.

She poured a cup, the scent of mint filling the air. As she took the first sip, her insides warmed. It was simple mint green tea, but she found solace in the delightful indulgence of the oldest blends. Her smile grew wider as she sank deeper into the comfort of her chair, allowing the moment's tranquility to envelop her.

"Your Majesty?"

"Hmm?" Alaric turned his head away from the carriage window. He was lost in a reverie, his mind wandering through the ethereal landscapes of dreams. His eyes were glassy and distant.

The royal entourage was surrounded by a battalion of armored knights, bristling with swords and other weaponry, ensuring the safety of their king. The horses, too, were a spectacle in their own right, their muscular bodies glistening with rain and sweat as they stomped the rocky road beneath them.

Nadia sat directly opposite of him, perched on the plush, luxuriously cushioned seats of the carriage. She was deeply engaged in a discourse about the fortification of the kingdom's borders, proposing the construction of additional outposts to bolster their defenses and ensure the security of their territory. Yet, the more she spoke, the more she noticed Alaric's attention was elsewhere.

"I sincerely apologize. Your ideas do not bore me; quite the opposite, actually. I simply cannot concentrate," Alaric said, rubbing his eyes with his perked hand. Exhaustion from traveling was creeping in.

"Do not worry. It is a cloudy day. The mind tends to be drowsy in this type of weather."

Alaric nodded. "You are not wrong."

He looked back out the window, the sight outside becoming less appealing as the sprinkling rain dampened the surroundings. The clouds thickly blanketed the sky, casting a gloomy air of sorrow. Soon, it was going to get dark.

Yet, a deeper, more personal concern was gnawing at the edges of Alaric's consciousness. His mind was a whirlwind of worry, a tempest of fear for the safety of his people, his friends, his mother, and his wife and stepdaughter. The thought of potential harm from Kingdom Ironwood was a dagger that pierced his heart.

Nadia noticed the shift. She knew him too well not to notice something was bothering him. She asked, "Are you worried about this summoning to Kingdom Zuiphate?"

Alaric shook his head. "No, it is something else."

"May I ask what it is, Your Majesty?"

Alaric leaned his elbow against the edge of the carriage window seal, propping his head in a physical manifestation of his mental exhaustion. He focused on Nadia. "It is my anxiety with Prince Alexander."

"He is a fool," Nadia spat, her voice dripping with venom.

She hated that man. The mere mention of his name was enough to ignite a fire within her, a burning hatred that consumed her from within.

"I agree, but he is an unpredictable fool. He has yet to return my letters requesting for another meeting."

"He could not have missed them. I've delivered the letters directly to his Knight of the Body."

"If he is discarding them and flaunting jokes, this will be messy."

"Are you referring to the doll?"

Alaric growled, "A pathetic excess of a stunt."

Spotted by one of Alaric's patrolling knights several nights ago, a doll was fashioned to resemble a human, dressed in weathered clothes and devoid of any facial features. Hay poked out of its fabric material as it swung gently in the wind by a noose. It was held by a tree outside the Neemere Forest.

The news of this terrifying discovery reached Alaric almost immediately, and he felt compelled to see it for himself. It was a macabre display of intimidation. Anger consumed him instantly. He drew his sword, the steel gleaming menacingly in the dappled forest light, and with a swift motion, he severed the rope that held the doll. It crashed onto the forest floor with a loud thud.

"Do you plan to do something in return?"

"Never. I will not stoop low for a petty man like that," the king answered.

Petty men do not deserve attention. They thrived from it.

"But, Your Majesty, your avoidance might be perceived as weakness," Nadia cautioned, her tone laced with concern. "We cannot afford to show any signs of weakness, especially since our realm is still growing."

Alaric sighed. "You are right, Nadia. I know you are right. But no childish games. It is beneath me, beneath us."

"Then we should respond differently. A way to show Prince Alexander that we are not to be played with, without the need to resort to his level."

"What do you propose?"

Nadia thought momentarily, her fingers tapping a rhythm against the carriage's wooden ledge. It does not take long for an answer to come to mind. "We send a message. Not a letter, but a display and action of strength."

"How so?"

"Invade and claim the other half of Neemere Forest."

Alaric jumped. He perked up immediately with a grin, his previous fatigue vanishing from his features as he sat up tall. "No room for him to play," he added confidently, his voice resonating with authority.

"Exactly!"

"And we'll have our knights keep a constant watch over his half."

"Security!"

"And we'll build a physical border, and the forest will be filled with our archers," Alaric continued.

Nadia could not help but smile at the sight of her king's renewed vigor. It reminded her of their early days when they had just met, the two both full of ambition and dreams. Excitement coursed through their veins.

Repercussions will occur, however.

Cutting off his rival's unlimited access between current territory borders would weaken his foe's control over the situation. It may be an advantage, but there could be a strain on his new alliances with other kingdoms, as they might see this move as aggressive and unprovoked. It might even frighten future relationships.

Undoubtedly, Alaric would gain more resources and defensive capabilities. The most satisfying aspect of this plan was that the king would eliminate the possibility of future taunts from his rival. It was a second-hand embarrassment to witness such foolery.

"When do you plan to move forward with this?" Nadia questioned. She was eager, having to hold her fingers together to keep the digits from visibly shaking.

"As soon as we return. It will be our priority."

Nadia was still grinning. "How do you think he'll react?"

Alaric shrugged. "Maybe he'll actually read my letters."

13

The Despised

Valentino was entrusted with safeguarding the castle while the king was away. He navigated the corridors and rooms with a stealthy gait. Although he attempted to converse with the castle's court when he encountered them, his presence was far from welcome.

The older man's duties only extended to overseeing the castle's upkeep, but it did not prevent him from unnecessarily watching the queen and her child. He steered clear of direct interactions with them, opting to shadow their every move from a safe distance instead. He would discreetly hide behind door frames and around hallway corners, much like a clandestine stalker.

His behavior was undeniably creepy.

Several servants made Lucia aware of the advisor's haunting gaze. They expressed their concerns, fearing for her safety, as the man was slithery and sour. No one could understand his intentions. Rose planned to have it addressed upon Alaric's return.

Lucia could not figure out if she had done something to offend him, but she was too afraid to question him directly.

Her status as a queen was akin to that of a servant, lacking any real power or authority. On the other hand, the advisor wielded significant influence, and Lucia feared that a confrontation could result in him exercising his power over her. So, despite noticing his presence behind hidden corners at times, she tried to ignore him.

Daily, the older man conducted castle rounds. Footsteps clicked on the marble tiles as he moved with arrogance, inspecting and ensuring areas were not neglected with cleanliness. The servants stepped away from his space. They wanted nothing to do with him.

As Valentino snuck into the servant washroom, he strutted around the basin rim to inspect the enclosed area. The water was to his standards, and the storage racks were packed with supplies. There was nothing to hold someone accountable for. Although Alaric's hired servants were a joke to his criterion, he couldn't help but acknowledge their capabilities to perform duties correctly.

Just as he finished inspecting the washroom, a door opened. He whipped around to the sound.

"Go play, princess. I will be done soon."

"Do you think Hank will let me pet the horses again?"

"Why don't you ask him?" Lucia said. She tenderly ran her fingers through Charlotte's hair, marveling at its silkiness.

During a lively game of hide-and-seek with Caroline and Mia yesterday, Charlotte inadvertently stumbled into a dusty, cobweb-filled corner of the palace. Dead bugs were stuck to her hair and clothes, but she paid no mind. Lucia, however, tried to hide her disgust.

So the queen took her daughter for a joyful and laughter-filled bath time. The entire palace seemed to reverberate with the echoes of her mirth, as everyone in the court was well aware of the good-natured fun she was having. The palace had never been so lively without the little girl.

"That is a good idea! Do you think he's outside?"

"Where else would he be?" Lucia softly chuckled. The queen was grateful to the horse farrier for allowing her daughter to interact with the animals. Charlotte never had previous experiences chasing chickens, brushing horses, and playing with outside felines. It is a blessing from this marriage.

The little girl took off in the direction of the castle's back doors, excitement blossoming with each little step. Lucia watched until she was gone from her sight.

Unbeknownst to her, Valentino was behind her, in a state of silent panic.

He shouldn't be in here.

Being caught in the servant's washroom would severely breach his position, and he could not afford to be seen. He would be made into a mockery.

In a hasty move, the advisor sought refuge in a concealed area, hiding behind a tall shelving unit that stored layers of clean robes. The disadvantage of his only hiding spot was that he was only a few feet away from the stone steps of the basin. Escape would be a challenge.

The door closed. Soft footsteps approached. Rustling was heard.

Valentino carefully controlled his breathing before peering over the wooden edge. From there, he spotted the queen placing her gathered supplies by the steps— floral soap, wash rags, and a hairbrush. Charlotte was nowhere in sight.

With her back turned, she was here to bathe.

Alone.

Her stressed-worn dress swiftly glided down her body, like a serpent shedding its overdue skin, unveiling her near-flawless figure hidden underneath the concealed fabrics. Her undergarments went next, dropping to her feet. The sight sent a shiver down Valentino's spine.

He should have looked away—he is expected to have—but his burning desire to continue observing this unexpected display of vulnerability consumed his rationality. He would be hanged if others discovered his shameful actions. But the fear of being caught was quickly replaced by the queen's hip dips and small, plump buttocks. It fueled his infatuation.

As she stepped into the water, slowly submerged, she turned to grab her soap and washcloth. She lathered and began to bathe. Her breasts were on full display.

His heart pounded hard in his ears. A tightness in his pants was impossible to ignore.

This woman, whom he disdained pureheartedly as a queen, had somehow managed to expose his own flaws by her body alone. She was a nobody, he reminded himself, but with each movement she made to clean her body, the harder he got.

His erection painfully strained against the fabric of his expensive trousers, and he reached down to adjust it, feeling a sense of embarrassment at his arousal.

Lucia was oblivious to his torment. She took her time cleaning her body and washing her blonde hair. When she dipped to rinse the suds, the man swore he was about to orgasm from the sight alone. He could not look away. His selfish and sinful desires had taken over his common logic.

By the time she was done, she began to step out. Water dripped off her hair, trails sliding down her skin. She reached for a towel to dry herself from the racks.

Next would be the temporary bathrobes. She would need a fabric to cover herself, and *luckily* for the advisor, the bathrobes were stacked in the shelving unit he was hiding behind. He knew she would be coming over to retrieve one at any minute.

He needed to escape.

Fast and now.

When—not if—she finds him.

Alaric would skin him alive and turn him into a coat before putting his head on a platter for his next meal. That man wasn't afraid to do horrible things if pushed to the limit.

Panicked again, an unreasonable plan smacked him. It was a weak diversion with plenty of flaws, but there was no time to wait for the consequences. Anything was better than nothing.

Cautiously, he began to round the corner and move towards the queen.

He hoped to slip past behind her without being noticed as she was currently using the towel to ruffle her hair dry, temporarily blinded from her surroundings. With each quiet foot placement, he got closer and closer and closer. He was mere inches behind her.

He took a step.

He held his breath.

Another step.

He refused to blink.

Another.

He was so close to the exit.

But then—

Lucia stopped drying her hair, the towel resting around her neck. He swore his heart stopped beating.

In a blinded terror and desperate attempt, Valentino pulled out his leg and side-swiped her own in a flash. It successfully knocked out her balance.

He seized this opportunity and ran.

The queen, dumbfounded by the situation, stumbled and fell onto her side. A yelp of pain escaped her lips. She was too startled to notice the fleeing advisor as the pain burned her nerves and shot up her spinal cord. Worst of all, she landed awkwardly on her hip and twisted her ankle.

It was like a ghost had purposely pushed her.

"Shit..," she cursed, looking down at her injured leg. "I must have slipped...".

She attempted to get up, but there was a struggle from the sharp sting of her hip and the throb of her ankle. She had to resort to the wall for support as she caught her breath.

The more oriented she became, the more pain she registered. The state of shock was fading, and she had to fight back the tears.

Frantically reaching out to grab a bathrobe off the shelf, she wrapped it around her like a towel. She did not have the patience to hassle it on correctly. It barely covered her body.

Leaving the previous towel behind, the queen limped slowly out of the washroom, each footstep causing more agonizing pain. The robe she clutched to her chest threatened to slip from her grasp, her breasts nearly spilling out with every step she took. If she were to bend down, her backside would be completely exposed.

But she did not care. She needed a place to sit and rest, and her mind was drawn to her bedchamber.

By a miracle, Axel passed by. He noticed her distress as she paused her journey and leaned against the wall. She did not make it very far.

Actually, she stopped right outside the king's washroom that was along the way to the grand staircase.

"Oh, My Queen, what happened?!"

He rushed towards her, his hands full of a basket of clean linens. He dropped his chore to quickly wrap an arm around her barely covered chest, taking her weight and providing stability. Water soaked into his uniform, but he did not care. The queen's safety was his priority.

Lucia sighed in immense relief. "I have somehow slipped after my bath."

"Then you must sit."

"That was my plan," she faintly chuckled, trying to brush away the severity of her injury. But Axel could read the pain etched on her face.

"Come, come," he instructed, slowly guiding her as she hopped to a hallway chair. He carefully lowered her body, and as she sat, she instantly hovered her leg above the floor. Weight exacerbated the pain.

"Let me grab Rose."

"It is not an issue. Only rest can fix this."

"Yes, but there is more to it. Your ankle is swollen twice its size and turning red. It may be broken."

The queen hesitated to voice any further objections. Axel might be correct. "I will be back," he said before he left.

Only a minute passed before she heard sets of hurried footsteps approaching her. The other servants must have been nearby.

"Oh, dear," Rose murmured, taking note of the trembling, wet queen and the leg she held elevated. She glanced at Victoria. "Grab a sun-warmed towel, a nightgown, and my bundled aid supplies. And you," she turned to Axel, "go make some hot tea."

Victoria and Axel hurried off to fetch the required items. Rose remained, bent down to examine and assess the queen's injury more closely. A bruise was beginning to form on her hip. Her ankle was still red.

"What happened to cause this injury, My Queen?"

"I slipped in the washroom," Lucia replied sheepishly.

"It must have been a nasty fall."

The head servant carefully performed a range of motion test on the ankle, which caused Lucia to groan loudly in pain. Fingers pressed hard on the bone. It was hot to the touch.

"Do you think it is broken?"

"No, I believe it is sprained," Rose reassured her, offering a comforting smile. Lucia shivered, the robe barely covering her wet skin. The cold was starting to set in, and thankfully, Axel had returned with a hot kettle wrapped with a cloth and a cup. He poured and gave it to Lucia to drink. It would help warm her up.

Upon Victoria's return, the two servants helped the queen to her feet while they dried her body and dressed her in a borrowed nightgown. Axel stepped away to provide privacy, in search of another chair. Even though they were all women, Lucia could not help but feel a sense of discomfort as they tended to her. She hated being exposed to others. It made her feel too vulnerable.

Rose, however, was more concerned with the queen's overall health. She was too thin to her liking—ribs threatening to poke through the pale skin. But before she could voice her concern, Axel had returned with a chair.

The head servant went to work right away. She sat and fashioned a makeshift splint for the queen's injured ankle. A piece of cloth was wrapped around the skin before a thick, rounded piece of wood aligned the joint from her aid bundle. It immobilized the extremity as she grabbed a thicker cloth to hug the ankle tightly. Meanwhile, Victoria attended to drying the queen's blonde hair completely dry.

Lucia sharply inhaled in pain, prompting Rose to apologize, "I am sorry, My Queen," as she neared the end of wrapping.

"Do not be sorry. I am grateful that you are helping me."

Rose smiled warmly as she completed the splint. Victoria brushed her hair back with her fingers as Axel handed her another cup of tea into her hands. The trio focused on the queen, touched by their care and concern.

However, a brief frown crossed her face before she forced a smile to cover up her internal turmoil.

"Thank you so much, Victoria, Axel, Rose. You all have helped me so much. I wouldn't have been able to do this alone," Lucia expressed, grateful for their assistance. Moved by her kind words, Axel and Victoria bowed before leaving, but Rose remained seated, sensing a change in the queen's demeanor. She noticed the frown the queen flashed seconds ago.

Leaning in and lowering her voice, she asked, "My Queen, what is the matter?"

"There is nothing wrong."

"But I can sense that you have something on your mind," Rose objected as she reached out and took hold of Lucia's hands into her own, offering a comforting and loving touch.

Lucia shook her head. "I only have an irrational mind. That is the curse of being a woman; that is all."

"No, that is an excuse that pathetic men use to validate their cruelty upon women. While I am alive within these castle walls, no one will be condemned for having an *irrational* mind."

A new frown crossed the queen's face.

She was scared—scared to be judged, scared of the repercussions, scared to be vulnerable. Rose had been a source of support for the past month, and while she felt a sense of safety around her, she also hated to burden the head servant.

"You can tell me," Rose nudged. Her thumb stroked her small knuckles.

Luckily, that was enough to for her to answer. "I am afraid this will slow me down."

"Slow you down from what?"

"My martial duties," Lucia replied, her voice cracking. She could not allow herself to be useless. She could not, for the sake of her daughter.

Rose disagreed. "Your unrealistic, servant-like duties can pause for some time. You need rest to heal your leg."

"No, I cannot allow myself to stop."

"Why so?"

"So I will remain purposeful. If I am not, I am afraid my daughter and I will be sent back to my kingdom, and I cannot go back," Lucia confessed.

Rose's concern grew as she listened to Lucia's words. "Why can't you go back?"

Lucia glanced down at the hands holding hers. A simple, loving touch from another that she secretively craved. It felt odd that it did not come from her daughter. But, she liked it.

Her voice barely above a whisper, she confessed, "I will be killed."

"Pardon me?" Rose questioned, shock consuming her face. But before she could say more, Lucia hiccuped, on the verge of shattering. "And my daughter... I fear what will happen to her. Will she also be killed because of me? Or worse, married to make up for my failure as a wife? She is too young for such reality."

Rose was not sure how to respond. She was speechless at the depth of Lucia's trepidation.

"You have seen how carefree she is. She does not deserve to be a child bride like I was," Lucia added, her lip quivering as she struggled to hold back her tears. Rose immediately reached up and gently placed her hands on the queen's face, meeting her saddened blue eyes with a look of comfort. That tender touch was enough to break the queen's walls. "I am so scared," she wept, her voice shaking with emotion. "I don't want to mess up my daughter's future."

Rose's heart ached much alike a throbbing stab. She pulled the crying queen into her body, hugging her tightly in her embrace. Tears soaked into her shoulder as she rubbed the queen's shuddering back.

The pressure and expectations placed upon the queen, combined with her selfless nature, have pushed her to her breaking point. The head servant initially assumed that Lucia might have been involved in a premarital pregnancy, which is why Alaric was able to obtain a bride with his tainted name.

But now, she could see a much deeper and more complex story at play.

There were levels of trauma.

Levels of strict expectations.

Levels of brainwashing and manipulation.

This only meant her marriage to Alaric was not her first.

Rose pulled away a little to ask a more sensitive question. "Were you previously married?"

Lucia sniffled. She could only manage to nod her head.

"What happened that ended your first marriage?" Rose whispered soothingly. She pulled out her handkerchief, wiping away the tears that ran down the queen's cheeks like raindrops on a cloudy day.

"My ex-husband passed away."

"Were all these duties expected when you lived with him?"

Lucia could not form the words, choking on another sob. The stress had taken a toll, and it was evident that she had never had someone to confide in the past.

She was so broken.

"My Queen, I am so sorry that you are expected to do so much," Rose said, acknowledging the pain. "The other servants and I do not judge you on your work nor your emotions. Do you understand?"

The queen nodded with more tears wetting her face.

"And do not persuade this as a fall of weakness." Rose did not hesitate to wipe again. Although Lucia's eyes were swollen and she could barely see, she could feel the soft fabric patting away her tears and the remnants of her breakdown. "This was a build of strength."

"Strength?"

Rose clarified, "Whoever or whatever tells you that expressing your shattered soul is a weakness, is a fool to life and its experiences. Each time you lean on somebody to share your pain, it is a step to overcoming." A sniffle from Lucia, intently listening. "And you are on the path of overcoming this. You might need a few more cries, or you may not, but soon, you will gain strength as a reward."

Lucia squeezed her eyes tightly to keep the tears from forming again.

"And strength is like power," Rose concluded.

Those words, with so much meaning behind them, made Lucia fall into mental silence.

To be heard.

To be understood.

To be attended to.

To be encouraged.

To learn.

She felt like she could finally breathe.

Rose was truly a woman of knowledge.

They sat quietly together during this tender moment. The head servant attended to her face as the queen tried to recollect herself. Her nerves had calmed. Her heart slowed. Her sniffles stopped.

Both were unsure how long they stayed, holding hands while deep in their thoughts, but that was not important to ponder.

Time was needed to digest. Time was needed to heal.

The void of nothingness to the ears was loud enough to mute their surroundings, easing their understanding of their new thoughts and emotions for each other. But that was when they missed the large wooden doors opening from the distance.

Alaric stepped inside, followed by Nadia. Old sweat caked their skin; clothes ruffled from days of travel. They had returned from their trade expedition. Rest was their priority.

The castle looked the same inside—clean and pristine. But there was an eerie silence, not a figure in sight. The servants may not have noticed their return yet, but he had grown used to his wife's sensitive hearing, usually running to greet him upon his arrival, silently. A sense of worry spiked within him when she was nowhere to be seen. His Knight of the Body also expected Lucia to be present.

"Where is she?" Nadia asked.

"I am not sure."

"Ah, King Alaric! How was your journey?" Valentino cheered, slowly descending the grand stairs. A big grin was on his face, pleased to see his political partner's safe return.

"Have you seen Lucia?"

The sudden question and his avoidance of presence stunned him. The king had just returned from a long journey, conversed with a secluded kingdom about trade possibilities, and only wondered about his worthless wife. He had indeed gone mad.

"I have not," Valentino answered slowly, approaching the two. His happy expression had gone sour.

"Hmmm. That won't do."

Alaric takes another quick glance around before calling out her name. "Lucia!"

His voice echoed throughout the halls. It reached the ears of the two sitting silently together.

"It sounds like he is back," Rose whispered. "Go back to your room and take the rest of the day off. Allow us to take full responsibility for the kitchen and chores."

Lucia barely heard Rose's words as she hastily rubbed her eyes and fixed her hair, not wanting to be a mess before her husband. She forced herself to do one final sniffle.

"Lucia!"

She jolted. It sounded near.

Just as the queen stood up from her chair, Alaric appeared around the corner like a spawned ghost, his expression one of surprise and concern as he took in her swollen, red face. It was unlike her to be in such a state. She had been crying.

"Are you all right? What happened?"

Lucia nodded to his question, making her usual greeting bow before she began helping Alaric remove his outer garments. As she did so, Alaric noticed that she was essentially hopping on one leg, without indoor footwear and in a wrinkled nightgown. Her hair was roughly brushed back.

Something was wrong.

"Lucia, what is wrong with your leg? Why are you barefoot?"

She shook her head, brushing off his concern as if it were nothing, before limping over to the hallway closet to hang up his clothing. Even though she attempted to downplay the injury, her limping made it clear that she was in pain. And the splint meant it was serious.

Alaric looked at Rose as she stood from her chair. "What happened to her?"

"Your Majesty, she sprained it," Rose answered.

"Is that the reason she cry?"

"No, it is for a different reason. Try to talk to her tonight. Be kind and only listen; she truly needs it."

"But you advised me to wait till she comes to me," Alaric reminded her.

"I realized that I was wrong. It will take more than that. She is hurting."

"Hurting?"

"Yes, hurting. And I am not referencing the physical pain."

Alaric did not know what to make of it. He glanced down the hallway, catching a glimpse of his wife before she disappeared from his view. This was unusual for her. What had happened while he was away that got her all worked up?

A beat of silence passed before a warning arose from Rose. "Watch your advisor."

That caught the king off guard. "What do you mean?"

"He is getting too comfortable around your wife. The servants and I noticed him lurking around her while you were away."

"How can he? He hates her."

"*Despise* is a complex and misunderstood emotion," she sighed. "Do not underestimate it."

14

Fallen from Grace

Alaric followed Rose's advice.

When night fell, he summoned for Lucia's presence, wanting to converse during the less distributive hours. He did not know what to say, where to start, how to begin. The most daunting challenge would be her silent responses. It had been over a month, nearing two, since her arrival, and she had yet to utter a single word to him.

Why should she?

This particular moment was not any different from all the other incidents where she could have chosen to speak.

Lucia and Charlotte were preparing for the night, with the little girl dressed in a bold blue, comfortable nightgown. As promised to the servants, the queen had rested in the bedchamber, catching up on much-needed sleep from past days of exhaustion. And when Charlotte learned of her mother's accident, she refused to leave her side.

Rose brought in their evening meals. The portions were still too big.

Charlotte jumped onto the bed. "You promised you would be extra careful!"

The soft recoil was felt by her mother, who sat on the edge of the bed. "I know, princess."

The girl frowned, crawling on all fours. The look made Lucia's lungs freeze, her chest sinking with guilt. "I am sorry to disappoint you again."

Charlotte sat down beside her. Her short legs hung off the furniture. "I am not disappointed. I am worried. Please, be extra, extra, extra careful from now on."

Her daughter's concern always moved Lucia. Although she hated to admit it, she knew that Charlotte did not like to see her hurt because of her ex-spouse's cruel actions. She wondered what she saw during the times she could not shield the abuse. But some things are better off forgotten over time.

"I will try to be extra, extra, extra careful," she promised, watching the little girl. Her legs began to move back and forth as she glanced down at her mother's swollen extremity.

The splint had to be readjusted earlier to allow the release of pressure around the ankle. A large bruise, deep in the shade of black, consumed the skin while redness seeped downward around the foot. Her hip, the one she had landed on, had turned blue, soon to be a color of musky green. Despite the pain, she was grateful that it was only a sprain and not a broken bone.

Suddenly, a knock on the door startled the two, causing them to snap their heads towards the sound. "My Queen?" A voice questioned.

The servant opened the door seconds later, peering over the edge. It was Mia.

"King Alaric would like to see you in his bedchamber. He has requested for you alone."

"His bedchamber?" she repeated, denial in her voice.

Mia only nodded solemnly before she closed the door. Her footsteps faded.

The horror on Lucia's face formed as she quickly realized what this could possibly mean. Dizziness settled in, and her stomach churned with dread. She had never been summoned by the king before, let alone at this late hour.

Only one conclusion could be made.

Sex.

Lucia's mind felt fuzzy. She could not concentrate on her surroundings. She thought that he would never be interested, since he had never initiated such lewd actions, but now she realized how naive she had been.

She did not want it. She *did not* want it.

She wanted to be useful, but not to the extent of sexual desires.

It always hurt. Sometimes, she would bleed. In the end, she always felt the same— ashamed, disrespected, devalued.

The queen planted her face into her hands, her elbows resting on her knees. She could not cry now.

Not now. Not with her daughter present, but Charlotte immediately noticed that shift in demeanor. "Mommy?"

She tugged on the nightgown sleeve that Lucia still wore from earlier. As she looked up, she forced a fake smile on her face. She knew her daughter could see through it, but it was better than letting her see her cry.

"I am all right," she lied reassuringly. "I will go see what King Alaric wants. In the meantime, see if you can fall asleep."

"I cannot sleep without you," Charlotte argued, a pout on her lips.

"I will come back. When you wake up, I will be in this bed with you."

"You promise?"

"I promise."

Lucia limped to Alaric's closed bedchamber door, trying to put as little weight as possible on her swollen ankle. She did not have the supplies to paint her face or the jewels to adorn her skin, but she had styled her hair nicely and wore a nicer, cleaner nightgown with nothing else underneath, hoping it was enough to please him. She hoped she was pretty enough.

She raised her hand, but she hesitated.

She could hide. The thought of running away and locking herself in her room crossed her mind. But she knew that in the morning, she might face his wrath.

Should she endure the forced act now or risk being beaten and then subjected to the same fate later? The decision was hers, yet no matter what, she would be powerless against his will. This was a sacrifice she had to endure if she wanted to stay here. It was the safest place her daughter had ever lived.

Anything. She would do anything for her daughter.

Taking a deep breath, she raised her fist again and knocked on the door. A soft rustling sound followed, and a voice beckoned. "Come in!"

Lucia pushed the door open, her gaze fixed on the floor, down at her slippers, as she entered the warm and partially-lit bedroom. She noticed the rug that she adored in the center of the room. She remembered her love for the colors and design. It was sad that this beautiful fabric would be in a place she would dread the most.

A fire crackled within the fireplace, its red flames leaping and dancing with fierce energy. The glow illuminated Alaric's frame, making him appear more imposing as he sat on the edge of his opulent bed. The silk curtains were parted, much like an invitation. He was swathed in a deep crimson bathrobe. The sight of him, soaked in the flickering light, filled her with fear.

She knew it. He had waited for her.

Sex.

He wanted sex.

It was the only thing she was good for.

As a wife, and as the queen, she must obey.

She knew to expect it. It is her responsibility to offer her body, her fragile soul, to pleasure her husband's wishes, bearing heirs in addition to the man who picked her as his bride. She could not afford to be defiant and risk being sent back to Father.

Without a second thought, she gripped onto the fabric that concealed her bare skin. She hoped the look of her body pleased Alaric's tastes.

"Lucia, may I ask what you are doing?" Alaric asked, dumbfounded by her actions. He was clueless to her internal strife.

But she doesn't respond. She couldn't.

Instead, she pulled the nightgown over herself, dropping it on the floor. Right there, coated by the light from the fire, she was in full view, her naked body on display.

She was a work of art, a perfectly sculpted masterpiece that seemed to have been crafted by the gods themselves. Her petite frame, every curve and contour a testament to her beauty. Alaric could not tear his eyes away. His gaze wandered over every part, from her slick shoulders to her tiny waist, her stretch marks of womanhood, her blonde, curled slit, and down to her little toes.

She was nothing short of breathtaking. An ethereal being in his eyes. He wasn't strong enough to look away from the woman before him.

She was an angel.

No, more than an angel.

Before he comprehended the situation, Lucia moved towards him with a sense of urgency. She positioned herself to sit on his lap; her body angled so that their intimate areas were mere inches apart, separated only by a layer of fabric. She was as light as a feather.

He stammered, "Lucia? W-What—"

His mind raced as she reached for the knot that held his robe together. She began to undo it, her fingers deftly working to free him from the confines of his lovely garment. Anticipation flared within him. The king could feel his body responding to her touch.

But this wasn't right.

"Lucia, please—"

Alaric leaned back, trying to create some distance between them. Yet her fingers were determined, undoing the knot and gripping onto the ends of the fabric. She began to pull. He panicked.

"Stop!"

In his haste to escape, he pushed her off his lap, but due to lousy balance and pain in her leg, she stumbled and fell on her unaffected side. The impact left her stunned.

What had just happened? What had caused him to react so violently? Was she not attractive enough? Did he not like her advances? Did she scare him?

Lucia looked up at Alaric and saw the horror etched on his face. He quickly rewrapped himself, securing it with a tighter knot. The expression on his face was enough to make her realize that she had misinterpreted his intentions.

She had screwed up.

Tears began to tickle from the corner of the queen's eyes as fear consumed her. Her small, naked body shook from the idea of offending her king, her husband, her purpose in life. This could have her publicly shamed, or worse, punished to what Alaric's heart desired, which included death.

She opened her mouth to speak, instantly shut it, but then decided to take that chance to apologize. "I-I... I am sorry. I am sorry, Your Majesty. Please forgive me."

Alaric stared at Lucia with wide, conflicted eyes, the expression on his face unchanging. She shifted onto her knees, her head bowed so low that her forehead touched the floor. Her hands lay before her, close enough to grip a few strands of hair. She began to pull and heave, her voice trembling as she pleaded to the man who could amusingly end her life. "Do not send me back to my kingdom. I-I... I will try harder. Please, forgive my terrible mistake."

She was now sobbing, tears streaming down her face and dotting the floor beneath her. Alaric felt pity, but he was unsure of what to say. Or what to do. He could only watch as she fell apart on his floor, naked and shaken.

"Let me try again, please? I-I am sorry. I misunderstood," she begged, her voice small and pathetic.

It took a full minute before Alaric slowly took a step. Lucia flinched slightly, expecting to be hit in some way. She clenched her fists and tugged harder on her hair, the pain not enough to distract her from the reality of her situation. She wept, "I-I will accept any punishment that your heart desires. Please, do not punish my daughter for my wrongdoing."

Those words struck a chord in Alaric's heart, and he could see the depth of Lucia's shame. He walked away, leaving the queen to sink deeper into her despair. She was not sure what he was up to. He hasn't said a word.

Yet he returned a moment later, hovering over her bent body. She braced herself.

He was going to hit her. She knew he would.

But instead, a soft fabric enveloped her body.

It was a bathrobe, warm and plush inside. The fabric against her skin caused her to hiccup.

This was unexpected.

Alaric crouched low; his dark scent wafted around her. A single finger brushed underneath her chin, gently lifting. She was confused by this tender touch. It was the last thing she could have guessed would happen.

"You talked to me," Alaric said with a soft smile. "I always wanted to hear your words."

She barely gazed into his green eyes, swollen and stained with salty wetness. A tear rolled down her cheek.

Thoughtless. Speechless.

She could not believe that he was showing her forgiveness.

He delicately helped her to her feet, cautious with her splinted leg. "I did not ask for you to come to seduce me," Alaric said. "I wanted you to arrive so we could talk. You have lived in my castle for over a month, yet I only know your name and your daughter's."

Alaric carefully tied the fabric ends together into a knot. The garment was much too large for her, the sleeves draping over her hands and extending down to her feet. Regardless of its oversized nature, Lucia looked adorable in it.

"Please, sit with me," Alaric urged, sitting back down on the edge of the bed. She did not move, unsure of how to react to his kindness.

Nevertheless, a few pats by his side were enough for her to follow through with his request. She did not want to disobey. With her hands clasped tightly together on her lap, she remained awkwardly silent, unsure of what to say or how to act in this unfamiliar situation.

The king bit his lip. He felt the tension. "Speak to me, please. I grant you permission to converse."

Although she could barely express it from her swollen face, his words took Lucia aback. He was so willing. So eager. He wanted more of her words.

"I have permission?" she said, her voice so soft, so weak. A sniffle followed.

Alaric replied, "I never asked for you to be mute in our marriage. Please, speak as you will."

A wave of relief washed over her, relaxing her shoulders. She was afraid he would punish her for her uninvited sentences earlier, yet he kept surprising her with his oddity. "Thank you, Your Majesty."

"You are a queen; you can call me by my first name."

A soft, humorous scoff escaped her lips, and Alaric raised an eyebrow. What could be so funny, especially for their first, proper conversation?

She must be a cheeky thing.

"You have called me by my first name like it rolls off your tongue so smoothly, like softened butter."

"You have a gorgeous name. How could I not?"

"My mother blessed me with this name."

A spark of interest. He wanted to know more about her, to peel back the layers and reveal the person buried beneath. "Did she teach you the notes of music?"

Lucia glanced at him, inflammation taking its leave. "Pardon?"

The king's lips curled into a smirk. "I have heard you sing before. I did not know you could sing so melodiously."

"I used to sing a lot as a small child, but no, my mother passed shortly after childbirth."

Alaric's chest clenched at her words. "Oh, I am terribly sorry to hear that," he said, his voice softening and his grin fading. He could not imagine a life without his mother. He was very close to her, and the thought of losing her was unbearable.

"It is all right. I have no memory of her, so it does not burden my heart."

"What about your kingdom? Does it burden you?"

"No, I am honored to be part of it."

"Then why must you be afraid to go back?" Alaric inquired, alluding to the moment when she had momentarily lost control during her emotional outburst. He noticed she began to pick at her fingers anxiously, her eyes staring down at her lap.

"If I am sent back, my father will have me hanged by a noose for being an undesirable wife."

Alaric's eyes widened in shock; his face flashed pale. Was this true? Maybe he had misheard her?

"Did I hear that correctly?" he spat, tone laced with repulse. "You are telling me that your own father would hang you if you were sent back home?"

Home.

That place was not her home.

"Yes," she whispered, "My ex-spouse's family already sent me back. It brought so much shame to my father's kingdom despite the ex-royal in-laws announcing the particular circumstances around his death. But it did not stop the rumors; it only slowed them."

Alaric was astonished. He could not believe what he was hearing.

A surge of anger grew inside him, but he fought to keep his fists from clenching. He did not need to scare her, especially during this moment of vulnerability.

How could a family member be so malicious, so devoid of empathy? Families were meant to be a foundation of solace and strength, a place where one could find comfort and support in times of need. Not to break down if one was not capable of fitting under familial standards.

The king wanted to reach out to her, to comfort her somehow, but he held back, uncertain of how she would respond. He knew his wife was under a great deal of stress, but he hadn't fully realized just how anxious and overwhelmed she was. It was as if she were a bird, instinctively tearing at her feathers to cope with the intense pressure.

"I never wanted to bring such shame to my father and brother. And, I never want to bring shame to you."

Lucia continued to fidget with her fingers, her eyes downcast. Alaric released a deep exhale to steady his raging nerves. "Why would you bring shame to me?"

"Because I am *dirty* and *used*."

Alaric's eyebrows pinched together in dismay as he contemplated the image of Lucia being seen as dirty, used, and unfaithful due to her past marriage, even though her constant efforts to please and care for others. It was an injustice to the woman, bound by double standards and looked down upon. After all, he had been in a similar situation himself when he mingled with servants for political gain, but had been placed on a pedestal due to his birth sex.

"However," Lucia added, breaking the king's train of thought, "I want to thank you for looking beyond my past and accepting me as your bride."

"I suppose you have heard a lot of harmful words?"

Lucia nodded. She was now picking on a hangnail.

"I apologize on their behalf. No person should be bullied and told how little their value is because of one mere thing. My life used to be that way when I was a farmer."

His words seemed to resonate with Lucia, and the corner of her lip curled. "No, these people do not deserve forgiveness by your words," she replied. "Cruel people should never be pardoned, as they fail to acknowledge their faults."

It would be a lie if Alaric admitted that her response did not surprise him. He was thoroughly impressed. She wasn't some easily swooned girl; she had context and depth hidden deep within her. It just needed to be pulled out.

"That is... very intriguing to say."

"Am I too harsh?"

"No, you are insightful."

"Oh." Lucia was not expecting the compliment. She kept her head down to hide any unnecessary and womanish emotions, though she had finally peeled off that hangnail she fiddled with. Now, she was in search of another.

"Your daughter; did you name her?"

"Yes, my ex-spouse and his family did not want anything to do with Charlotte. But, she is my everything since the moment she was born."

"You teach her well. She is very kind and polite to the servants. Many children play jokes and rough play with lower-class individuals."

Lucia purred, "Everyone has a purpose in this world. Some cannot decide like others can. So, I taught her that you must be appreciative and nice to the people you meet, regardless of status."

It was a lesson she learned herself when she was just a toddler. She never wanted to be a princess, to become a bride. Instead, she had dreamed of being free like the children she watched outside the palace gates. They were not bound by the strict rules and expectations that governed her life.

They were carefree, days filled with laughter and play.

Lucia had longed to be just like them, but as she grew older, she quickly realized the difference between their lives. While she had been born into privilege and had everything handed to her, the lower-class individuals were forced to work hard to survive. Their lives changed to labor and pain, and she understood that they held little value in the eyes of society.

They did not wish to follow this path, and neither did she.

So, she promised herself that every person, regardless of their born-gifted status, deserved to be treated with compassion. Her father's servants began to befriend her. Guests adored her. And when it came to suitors, they saw her as an ignorant, native seedbearer.

She religiously taught this to Charlotte, making the little girl the most polite and caring child anyone ever encountered. Her kindness and empathy were a testament to the values instilled in her, and they were a source of great pride for her mother.

Alaric admired that. He replied, "I wish I had taught my sister that."

"You had a sister?"

"Yes, she was quite the character. She had a knack for playing cruel jokes on others, which was initially entertaining. But sometimes, she would lose control and end up causing actual harm to the kids and adults she was playing with," Alaric recalled.

"What happened to her?"

The muscles in the king's jaw clenched and twitched. Her death had occurred so long ago, but it still pained his heart from time to time. It was her laughter that he missed the most. "Her life was cut short, unfortunately, in a brutal way."

"That is awful," Lucia muttered as her hand rose to her chest. "I surely hope she did not suffer for long."

He realized that he hadn't considered that possibility before. He hoped Lucia was right. Otherwise, the doubt would eat him away, even though he had avenged her years ago.

Alaric slowly churned his eyes, only to be met by the unexpected hue of her blue ones. They were like a vast expanse of sky. An ocean. A field of blue flowers. A secret world.

He was obsessed.

Several seconds passed with neither word spoken, as if both had fallen prey to the sudden trance of each other's eyes, until a rush of words tumbled out of the king's mouth. "Your eyes are like glittering sapphires. Ever since I gazed into them for the first time, I never wanted to look away. It is becoming my favorite color."

He really did not think before he spoke.

Lucia gasped, her face flushing as she turned away. She did not know what to think of the unexpected admiration. It got her heart fluttering. "You are too kind."

That made Alaric light up with glee.

"You aren't as mean and cruel as many rumors say you are," Lucia whispered, still refusing to show the king her embarrassment.

Alaric chuckled, "Rumors? You mean jealous townsmen who seek power and got overstaged by a farm boy? They dream for power, for wealth, for obedient people, but lack the ability, bravery, or intelligence to achieve those goals. I was so eager for change that those perks came naturally to me."

"I believe you. I thought I would be constantly scared of being here, but I think I may be wrong," she concluded, returning her eyes to her lap. Her flush had faded, her face no longer hot.

That was a small victory. Alaric had never intended to project fear.

"However, I have noticed you do not have a lot of titles in your court."

"What do you mean?"

"There are no chaplains, barons, courtesans—" she began, but was interrupted.

"Those are man's true downfall of whores. I do not condone the slavery of sex."

Lucia was baffled.

He continued, "And my kingdom has much growing to do. I do not allow others into my palace unless they can be trusted. A flea of a conspirator can easily make it fall."

The queen nodded. "That makes sense, but can I be truthful?"

"Please, do. I am eager to know your opinion."

Was she dreaming? This man was something else. "From what I have observed from the weeks my daughter and I have stayed in your home, I firmly believe your kingdom will triple in size in no time. You are a very respectful leader, and people seek respect. It is a simple luxury that is severely deprived in our society. You will rob people from other kingdoms in a positive manner."

"Have you been through teachings?"

"No, it is forbidden," she partially lied.

Alaric was astonished. She had spewed words that a political scholar would preach.

As their conversation soon came to an end, Alaric graciously escorted Lucia back to her room. The hallway was lit by a single light, casting long shadows across the walls and floor. The darkness beyond the light's reach was tangible, but Lucia was at ease. For the first time in her life, she did not fear a man who walked beside her.

She may even call herself foolish.

Rose's words swirled in her mind as they approached the closed door. She paused, turning to snag one last glance. She had a question on her mind. "Would you like your clothing back? I can change."

"Keep it. I have plenty more," Alaric replied, opening the bedchamber door. Darkness peered out. Soft snores escaped.

Lucia was appreciative. Such simple pleasures in life were the greatest. "Thank you. I will certainly use it."

"That pleases me very much to hear." The king wanted to say more, opening his mouth, but then, he decided not to. Lucia could sense it.

"I hope you have a peaceful rest," she said slowly. She was not one to prod. It was late at night. Sleep was needed.

The corner of the king's lips curled into a tired smile. He hadn't gotten to wish her the same before she walked inside.

The man sprinted with all the speed he could physically muster. With no light for aid, he was blinded by the darkness, nearly disorientated as he barely dodged tree limbs and protruding roots. His black cloak flapped wildly, threatening to snag on the foliage as he careened through the dense forest.

He was too old to be running, or so he thought. His breath came in ragged gasps as he neared the guarded border. Beads of sweat trickled down his forehead.

He did not care if he was being loud. He needed to be heard. He needed to draw attention. And he did so when he took a leap over the territory line and collided with a group of knights on their strong steeds. They were doing a nightly patrol.

"Halt!" one shouted while the others brandished their swords. The man came to a sudden stop, dizziness threatening to overcome him. Both parties stood frozen in place, the stranger unable to speak due to his labored breathing.

Fortunately, one of the knights had a lantern, so he kicked his horse forward to get a closer look. The others followed, tensed and ready to swing. The light illuminated the intruder's face, and immediately, they recognized his features. They lowered their weapons, realizing that he posed no threat.

"You are far from where you are supposed to be. Did you get lost?" a knight joked. The others chuckled.

"I need to speak with Cain!" Valentino panted, struggling to keep up with the demands of his physical exertion. "It is urgent!"

15

The Lady

The first rays of dawn pierced through the palace windows, casting a warm, golden glow across the small bedchamber. Lucia slowly opened her eyes, her daughter still nestled comfortably against her side. Soft snores continued to escape her lips.

Memories of the previous night flooded back—the discussion, the raw honesty, the sense of liberation that came with sharing each other's stories. She would never share so much about herself to anyone, but the eagerness in his eyes as he listened, hung on her every word, had been intoxicating. It felt almost too good to be true.

It was an experience.

Lucia carefully sat up, trying not to awaken Charlotte from her slumber. And as usual, she began her routine.

She limped down the grand staircase with cautious steps. A single day of recuperation sufficed for her, even though she anticipated the servants' protests when they awakened. Once she entered the kitchen, preparations began.

The queen picked out preserved cranberry jam from Kingdom Zuiphate, a rare and expensive delicacy gifted during Alaric's travels. She never had the pleasure of tasting the sweet dessert throughout her life, but from the delight it brought to others' faces, she knew it was savory. It would be the perfect addition to her husband's morning meal.

Along with the preserved berries, salted fish, and meat that had been skinned and marinated in vinegar, were also given to the king. Rows of the aged goods sat organized on the countertops prior to being placed in the underground storage. She had a creative plan for how she could incorporate these ingredients into the future.

It did not take long before Alaric descended the stairs and, as usual, was greeted by the familiar faces of the servants. He strode to the dining table. The houppelande he wore was a magnificent masterpiece, rich in burgundy color that matched his skin fairly well. The embroidery that adorned the sleeves and hem were intricate patterns of gold thread woven throughout. The sleeves themselves were long and flowing, billowing out like dark wings as Alaric moved. A gold metal belt cinched at his waist. It went with the black trousers.

An artist had crafted this clothing. It made the king look stunningly handsome, a true vision of masculinity and grace. Lucia wished for a piece of apparel similar to that. She would feel so gorgeous.

The queen, as always, stood present by his chair, a hot steaming kettle filled with a new blend of tea. She appeared more at ease than usual when she noticed his approach. A plate was set on the table.

"Good morning, Lucia."

He took his seat, his eyes drawn to the delightful spread before him: freshly baked slices of bread, still warm and emitting fragrant steam, with herbs interwoven into its crust. A generous layer of cranberry jam adorned the cooked wheat, accompanied by a dollop of whipped sweet cream and a medley of berries on the side.

This meal was going to be exquisite. Having grown up on barley and oat porridge, this simple fare was going to be delicious.

When Alaric surveyed the table, he noticed only one plate. Lucia bent down to pour him a cup of tea, but he spoke up before she could finish pouring. "Lucia, could you please bring me an empty plate and a cup?"

She promptly complied, setting the kettle aside on the table to retrieve the items he requested. She tried to move quickly despite the pain. She handed the steel plate to the king, but what happened next was the least she expected.

Alaric started to divide his meal. He transferred half of it onto the plate and placed it across an empty chair beside him. His intention was clear: he wanted Lucia to join him.

"Sit."

Lucia hesitated, her fingers squeezing hard on the clay cup. "Are you sure? It is not my place."

"Yes, sit with me," Alaric reassured.

Lucia slowly drew out the chair with one hand as she gazed at the meal before her. The sunlight streaming through the windows enlightened the food, making it even more alluring.

"Cup," Alaric commanded, reaching for the handle of the iron kettle. Lucia hadn't realized she was still gripping the empty cup until he spoke. She set it down on the table, and he poured the warm liquid. The fragrant aroma wafted up to her nostrils.

The king eagerly took a bite, his expression flourishing with bliss. Lucia, on the other hand, did not indulge. She anxiously lifted the cup to her lips, taking in a small sip. Sweets lead to weight gain—a fact taught at a young age.

Alaric swallowed a couple of bites before he made a request. "Bring Charlotte next time."

Lucia opened her mouth to object, but he interrupted her. "Before you say anything, I am certain to have her present."

She reluctantly closed her mouth and nodded in agreement. Charlotte would undoubtedly love the opportunity to dine in such an elegant setting. No more meals in a small bedchamber.

The king took another bite, but he could not help but notice his wife's hesitation at the meal.

"Why must you not eat? Is it not to your liking?" he inquired, his eyes fixed on her.

Lucia swallowed hard, reached for a utensil, and picked out a small bite of berries. Although she took a nibble, Alaric could sense the discomfort emanating from her. She did not want to eat. Did food disgust her? Is that why she was so skinny?

"Do you even eat?"

"I do, only after you are fed."

"That is ludicrous. If you are hungry, you eat."

Lucia shook her head. It went against the lessons she had been taught since she was a toddler. The king, her husband, was her priority, but Alaric would argue that.

"It seems that you disagree," he smirked, placing a piece of his bread down on his plate. "Then, I won't eat if you won't eat."

She gave him a wry look. "Don't be childish, Your Majesty."

"I remind you that you can call me by my name."

"I have to acknowledge you by your title gracefully, I remind you so," Lucia corrected. Her fingers picked at each other underneath the table.

The queen hadn't anticipated this side of him when he requested for her hand in marriage. He appeared to be a reserved man, compassionate towards others, but now she noticed a hint of sarcasm in his demeanor.

Alaric tsked. "That rather makes it unfair. I would rather call you by your name than your title, Your Majesty."

Lucia did not appreciate the mockery. She blindly found another hangnail and pulled. "I do not deserve the title. I am only merely your bride, your wife, your servant."

"I shall challenge King Johnathan for allowing such poisonous thoughts to be buried in your head."

"You are challenging years of royal traditions."

"Who declared I was a traditional man?" Alaric provoked, his tongue laced with amusement.

She was at a loss for words. It was clear that he was aware of his unconventional behavior and did not feel the need to apologize for it.

"Despite my earlier bites, I am still hungry. Why would you allow your husband to starve?"

"Pardon?" She frowned. She would be lying if she wasn't the slightest offended by those words, even if it was a tease. "You created this game."

"I did? I suddenly cannot recall this game that you accuse me of."

"I wish I had a witness to hear your previous absurd statement."

"But that would be cruel."

Lucia scoffed and looked down to hide her puny smile. A joke he is.

"Well, as I must teach you, I cannot allow myself to indulge in sweets. A queen must—"

Alaric objected, "Do not tell me you refuse to eat because of the sugar. You are already as small as a twig."

A faint blush of embarrassment crept on her cheeks. Last night, the king had seen her bare, and she wondered what he thought. He surely took note of her petite stature.

"How about we strike a bargain?" Alaric suggested. "You take a single bite, and then I will free myself to finish my meal."

"A bite?"

"Yes, so at least you taste it. It is really divine."

A pause of annoyance.

"Fine. Your Majesty." Her words were purposely sharp.

Fingers grazed the crusted corners as she took a bite. The tangy flavor of the cranberries stung her tongue. The sugar was overpoweringly sweet, melting in her saliva to create a dance of flavors within her cheeks. She savored the morsel.

With her eyes closed, her imagination ran wild. Alaric was true to his word that it was divine. She had never tasted anything like this before.

Alaric observed her as he sipped from his cup, feeling blessed to witness this simple pleasure be adored. And as promised, he finished his meal. He dabbed his mouth with a wool napkin, his eyes still locked on the queen as he did so.

Valentino entered the space. Circles darkened his eyes, and his mood was soiled. He stood tall, his hands behind his back, and cast a heated stare in the queen's direction. She recoiled, nearly dropping the bread on her plate.

It was a rude glare. Nasty with intent. She averted and held her breath, sensing the jealousy simmering within him.

"Yes, Valentino?"

The older man's stare shifted to the king. "Your men are ready for the initial stages of outpost construction."

"Already?" Alaric asked, surprised.

"You stated that you would like to begin as soon as possible. I only delivered what you have commanded," Valentino replied, maintaining a stern expression. Lucia stayed quiet and clueless.

"Very well," Alaric sighed as he stood up. "Let us go. We can not allow these men to wait. They have families to attend to."

"As you wish, Your Majesty."

The party departed. The queen was unsure where they were headed, but knew her curiosity could lead to trouble. She had only just begun to engage in conversation with him. She shouldn't push too far.

After Charlotte had eaten, dressed, and was off playing on her own, Lucia tidied up the king's bedchamber. He was a clean man, and she appreciated that.

She did his dirty clothing, patched a stitch on a pair of trousers, and then joined in her daughter's imaginative play. When noon struck, she allowed the servants to serve them at the dining table.

Charlotte absolutely loved it. Throughout the entire meal, her chubby-cheeked face was plastered with a big smile.

Her ankle and hip ached from the previous activities, so the queen sat in the solar room after the two ate. She found solace in the soothing melodies of the birds outside, falling into a trance and nearly into slumber.

But just as her eyelids drooped nearly wholly closed, a sudden commotion erupted at the palace entrance. There were squeals of happiness.

A guest had arrived, and the servants swarmed and greeted her warmly.

"My Lady, your son is out," Rose informed the woman.

"I assumed. He shall always be busy," she said, but her tone was devoid of disappointment. Victoria removed her outer garment, revealing a lovely bell-sleeve blouse dress in a romantic olive-green color. The fabric was of high quality, suitable for a woman of her stature.

"Why have you come to visit?" Axel inquired, wrapping his arms around her. She returned the embrace.

"I received a letter from my son about some news. I had to visit and meet my daughter and granddaughter-in-law."

Lucia had already begun her journey down the hallway. She was eager to discover the source of the rapturous joy. But before she made it to the front of the palace, Rose appeared around the corner, accompanied by a woman who wore a cheerful grin. Their eyes met.

The woman's appearance was familiar. Ginger hair with grey streaks tied into a bun and freckles scattered across her skin. Wrinkles were buried in the creases of her eyes, but despite her advanced age, she exuded a lively energy.

"My, well, hello," the woman said as she rushed to greet Lucia. She grabbed the queen's hands and took them into her own. It was warm and comforting, a motherly instinct emanating from within. Rose stepped to the side.

"I am Elizabeth Hartfelt, Alaric's mother. He had told me so much about you in his letter. I must say, he was right to describe how pretty you are, Lucia."

It was the woman from the grand hall oil painting.

Her mother-in-law.

Lucia blushed at the compliment, assuming that Alaric had spoken pleasant things about her. His mother was already familiar with her name. "And small," she continued, "but that is all right. For the next future visits, I will bring my cooking."

Lucia politely bowed, offering a small smile that did not quite reach her eyes, and moved slowly, careful not to cause herself any pain. "It is a true blessing to meet you, Lady Hartfelt."

Elizabeth immediately noticed the injury. "Oh my, what happened to your ankle? You are only putting half your weight on it."

"I am all right," Lucia replied. "I was just being clumsy and hurt myself."

Elizabeth's eyes softened with sympathy. "My, you must be more careful. You cannot be going and hurting yourself."

"I know. My daughter has given me the same advice."

Just as the queen mentioned, her daughter, Charlotte, appeared from behind, her extroverted nature shining through. Wearing a white dress with worn-out lace, she enthusiastically waved hello. "Greetings!" she exclaimed.

Elizabeth gaped, then grinned, carefully bending down to meet her at eye level. Her old knees cracked. "You must be Charlotte," she said warmly. "I was told you were a lovely girl."

Charlotte nodded politely in response, her eyes sparkling.

"My, you look just like your mother," Elizabeth remarked.

Charlotte asked, "Is that a good thing?"

"Yes, it means you are as beautiful as your mother."

Charlotte giggled in response, clearly pleased by the compliment.

"Now, may we sit? My hips are sore from travel, and I would love to talk to you both more."

———————◆✳◆———————

The two women and child settled into the solar room, having moved the wooden side table to the center to accommodate the tea kettle. Charlotte was too small for the chair, her legs swinging back and forth as she tried her best to participate. But she was beaming to be included. The older woman was a new person, and she could not pass up making a new friend.

"My, this is a wonderful blend," Elizabeth praised.

"Mommy makes the best tea in the world. Everyone who tries it always has a smile on their face," Charlotte chimed. She, too, had a small cup for herself on the table.

"I can agree with that."

Lucia was confused about how to respond or act. She was not used to the shower of compliments. Elizabeth took another slow sip before she asked a question. "Tell me, has my son been treating you well?"

Compared to her past experiences, Lucia felt... comfortable? She hadn't been subjected to any verbal abuse, physical violence, or sexual assault. In fact, her new husband was the complete opposite. She favored this marriage, a blessing in disguise.

"Yes, My Lady. He is very kind and considerate," she sincerely replied.

Elizabeth let out a sigh of relief. "I am pleased to hear that. I was worried that he might get washed away by the customs of royalty and change as a person. But, it seems that it's just my anxiety overshadowing my logic."

Lucia softly smiled.

"He has strong morals," the older woman continued. "And it makes me proud to have him as my son. He has grown so much."

The queen was a bit shy, though it helped that the older woman charmed her like an old friend. She asked, "What was he like? Growing up?"

"He was, and still is, a sweet and hardworking boy. He took care of his family, took care of me. I would never imagine living the life I have today, surrounded by my lush land and spoiled gardens," Elizabeth replied, her mature eyes twinkling with fond memories.

"His Majesty accomplished so much."

"My son has, but do not let that frighten you. Even the most noble men have their foolish moments."

"Do tell!" Charlotte ejected. She struggled to grab her cup from her shortened height.

Elizabeth chuckled at the girl's enthusiasm. "Absolutely. One of my favorite recollections was when he was little. It was such a lovely morning, barely old enough to walk. I took him outside to take in the fresh morning crisp air. Anyway, he got confident and decided to challenge the rooster of the chicken flock. And that big, mean ol' bird—oof—jumped on him and got him screaming. Then, to make matters worse, he got his ass handed to him by wasps when he trampled their nest during his escape."

Charlotte laughed. "Really?"

"Really. He was bawling for days, too scared even to go outside again."

Lucia tried not to snort into her cup as she sipped. She could envision the king, known now as a rogue and feared leader, being attacked by the smallest forces of nature all at once. She surely would have laughed during the event.

"My, that sure taught that boy a lesson."

"There was a wasp in the castle a few days ago."

"Did it get you?" Elizabeth pounced, doing a quick tickle on the little girl's side. She shrieked with laughter, squirming in the chair.

Lucia sipped her second taste, and a memory from last night's discussion came to mind. She placed her cup down. She said lightly, "He had mentioned he had a sister."

The older woman froze and stopped ticking. Slowly, she recollected herself. Her eyes misted over as she remembered her lost daughter, like silken waves of a dead sea.

Lucia did not mean to strike such a tender part of the past. She only wanted to learn more. "I apologize."

"No," Elizabeth sighed, "you are fine. She was a rascal, causing mischief when she could. But she sure loved her older brother. Those two were a duo."

"I can't imagine losing a child."

"It was hard. It is still hard."

Charlotte frowned, unable to relate to the topic.

"I won't ask for more. Again, I apologize."

"My, as I said, do not take fault. You had no part in her death."

"I know," the queen whispered.

Elizabeth quickly tried to save the mood. "Anyway, enough about me. I am curious to learn about you."

"Me?" Lucia gawked.

"Yes, you," Elizabeth queried. "How was your childhood?"

Unfair. Hell.

It took her a moment to think up her reply, contemplating. She did not want to inadvertently alarm the older woman. It was much different from most commoner families, and she was unsure if she would even understand.

The queen cleared her throat. "Well, I——"

The door suddenly opened. Alaric stepped inside.

Upon his return from his arduous work at the outpost and the new territory construction, the king was utterly exhausted. He had stripped down to his basic clothing. Instead of Lucia, he was greeted by Rose. He asked where she was and was notified of his mother's presence. He hastened as fast as he could.

Alaric broke out into a broad smile. "Momma."

"Oh, my boy," his mother replied, rising to hug her child. They lovingly embraced.

Lucia quickly stood and excused herself. She did not want to interfere in their reunion and was partially thankful for the interruption. Trending on the past would conflict with her thoughts, so she picked up Charlotte in her arms and left the room, content to know they were together.

"How are you?"

"Stressed. Too many demands, too little time."

"I know. You got a lot on your plate," his mother said before breaking away. "But know that I am always so proud of you."

"I know."

"And Lucia, she is so lovely. We had a nice talk together, but it seems she ran off." Elizabeth was alone with her son, not noticing when the queen and daughter took their leave. She sat back down, and Alaric did the same.

"She does that a lot, unfortunately. One second, she's there, gone the next," Alaric replied.

"My, are you scaring her?"

"She told me her fear is fading, but I still somehow startle her little girl."

"Charlotte? You are scaring Charlotte? She seems so eager to meet anyone who comes across her."

Defeat was engraved on Alaric's face. "She runs to her mother when I try to get close. I do not know why."

"Maybe she needs more time. You are one big, powerful man who just suddenly appeared in her life."

"I understand."

"And," Elizabeth rose, "go buy Lucia and her daughter some clothing."

"Hmm?"

"No wife should wear such tattered rags, even her child. I do not care if she protests; get them a few dresses," the older woman said, giving him a gentle but firm thump on the head. Her displeasure was evident.

"I am unsure what to purchase. I have never searched for garments for a lady and a child before."

"Then we shall go to the market together."

Alaric abruptly stood up. "Now?"

"Now."

16

Blue

It was long hours of the night before Alaric returned back to the palace. He had already taken his mother home. She rode on her own horse, but he felt more comfortable being by her side to ensure her safety, holding a lantern to light their path. Freshly purchased clothes were folded on his lap, alongside a new stuffed toy, before he dismounted his horse.

The double doors opened, and the king was greeted by the quiet atmosphere of his residence. But he was startled by his discovery of Lucia, clad in a nightgown, slumped in a chair by the entrance in a deep sleep. Her fragile hands rested on her lap, her head tilted precariously to the side, resting on her own shoulder as if she had dozed off while waiting for his return. She looked so peaceful.

Alaric broke out a warm smile at the endearing scene. Axel approached, equally surprised by the unexpected sight. "Your Majesty?"

"How long has she been in that chair?" Alaric whispered.

"I am unsure. Charlotte had already gone to bed hours ago," he softly remarked. "She must have left her chambers to wait for your arrival, but fell asleep. Poor thing."

The king contemplated. He would feel guilty if he woke her now, but he needed to lay her to rest. "I hate to leave her here. Her neck will be sore tomorrow."

Axel sighed. "I do not doubt."

"Hold these and follow me, please."

"Yes, King Alaric," Axel said as he reached for the folded fabrics.

Hesitant at first, the king carefully wrapped his arms around her back and under her knees, slowly pulling her upwards into his hold. Lucia did not stir; instead, her head rested against her husband's broad trunk. From there, they began to climb the stairs.

Alaric attentively watched his wife as he took cautious steps. Her chest rose and fell with each breath, her lips slightly parted. His gaze lingered on her face, his heart blossoming with undigested emotions. He was unsure what the future held. The endless possibilities.

This marriage was for his political gain. The woman held tenderly in his arms is his wife by law. But could he be smitten with her?

He figured to have a mark of a passing fancy. Those come and go. But he had not had a young woman in his court, specifically married to him, in any part of his lifetime. The other female members of his court felt similarly to siblings in a tight-knit family. Could his deprived attraction be the only reason to take an interest in her?

Once they reached the bedroom, Alaric laid Lucia down on the bed. His mind was heavy like wet sand, sopping with unnerved reasoning and emotions.

Axel left the clothing and toy neatly on the dresser, and the two swiftly exited the room. Alaric wondered what Lucia and Charlotte would think in the morning. He would be lying to himself if he thought he wasn't excited.

Alaric reached his bedchamber, greeted by a small plate of cut fruit on his bedside table. He instantly smiled. "Bless her soul."

By dawn's first light, Lucia awoke with nary a recollection of how she had drifted off to sleep, but the morning's revelation brought a smile to her lips. There, laid out before her on the dresser, were not one but two exquisite dresses, and a nightgown, all tailored for her frame. Her heart raced as she eagerly spread the fabrics out, touching and savoring every stitch and seam. Charlotte received the same items in her size, along with a new stuffed toy resembling a horse.

Her gaze was drawn to a stately, deep blue dress that shimmered like the night sky. She wasted no time to dress herself.

The bell sleeves were adorned with intricate celestial embroidery, while the flowing hemline skirt danced around her ankles. A square neckline framed her face, and the corset-style top hugged her curves. It was a dress fit for a queen, and its hue nearly matched the color of her eyes.

She felt so beautiful, twirling around to watch the skirt swirl. This was more than just a dress; it was a phenomenal art piece. Simply breathtaking.

"You look so pretty, mommy!"

Lucia turned, unaware she had awoken her daughter. She got too carried away to notice, but she was beaming. "There are dresses for you too. And look," she said as she grabbed the horse.

Charlotte gasped and wiggled out of bed as fast as possible.

As the two emerged from their bedchamber, they were greeted by the jubilant servants who had already lit the hearth fire and prepared the morning meal. The queen and her daughter were complimented on their new attire, their eyes sparkling with delight from the servants' sweet words.

Alaric soon approached. Once his eyes landed on his wife, he was captivated and could not look away. He made a mental note to procure more such dresses for her in the future.

The servants parted, allowing Alaric space, and then resumed their duties. He leaned in, his voice low and sincere—nearly a vibrant growl. "Lucia, you look exquisite. It is as if it were made for you alone."

Lucia blushed at the praise, feeling a warmth spread through her chest. She tried to ignore it. "Did you purchase these dresses?"

A corner of his lip curled. "My mother has great taste, so I will not take the credit."

"Thank you, and please, send her our gratitude," she replied, placing a gentle hand on Charlotte's shoulder. Though not cowering behind her mother this time, the little girl still avoided direct eye contact with the towering man before her.

Alaric took a risk.

The king slowly bent down to his knees, unable to bear seeing the girl fear him any longer. He softly asked, "Was the horse to your liking? I can get something else if you inquire. I have noticed the bear you often carried may have needed a friend."

The kindness made Charlotte look at him for the first time. "I like the horse. Thank you, Your Majesty."

"You are very welcome," said the king, pausing for a few seconds, "and, I do not believe we have properly met. You can call me Alaric."

"Charlotte," the little girl replied, doing a slight bow in a polite introduction. A grin was plastered on the king's face. His stepdaughter finally spoke to him.

From afar, Valentino and Nadia stood observing. The advisor's eyes were fixed intently on Lucia, lingering a bit too long, which Nadia noticed from her peripheral view. She squinted her eyes, her skepticism growing as she quietly watched him.

A letter fidgeted in the older man's hands, the paper crumbling with numerous indents. He was in mental turmoil.

Nadia wondered why the advisor's thoughts were consumed so much at the woman in the deep blue dress.

"This is it?" Cain spat, clearly disappointed by the two pages in his hands. It was much less than he expected to receive.

Valentino frowned, annoyance read on his face. The two had met up in a new location, west of the Neemere Forest, in uncharted and unclaimed territory. It may be easier for Cain's travel from the new border changes, but it was safer to avoid the newly built outposts. It was suggested in the letter the advisor received.

Cain flung the papers up and down. "What happened? You were perfectly executing your job well before."

The advisor did not reply. Cain could not care less for an answer anyway. "I can tell you are distracted."

"No."

"Then get your head out of your ass and get to work. Prince Alexander will be after me for this piss poor handout," Cain snarled, shoving the papers into trouser pockets.

"Was my unannounced warning deficient in compensating for the lack of copied paperwork?"

"No, but it proved your loyalty. You should have tried harder to convince your king not to move forward in overtaking half the forest."

Valentino's patience had worn thin, and he was tired of the criticism. He snapped, "I tried! I told him it's an act towards war!"

"You didn't try hard enough!" Cain barked, taking a step forward to try and intimidate. The two stared hard at each other, the sounds of the night overtaking the sudden silence that followed. The new conflict induced by King Alaric had them both on edge, as Kingdom Ironwood had doubled their knights and implemented tightly scheduled patrols. This had kept Cain busy to the point of mental exhaustion.

Breaking the silence, Cain spoke, "Whatever it is, it caught Prince Alexander's attention. He wants another meeting."

"King Alaric already tried to reach out prior to the forest invasion."

"Well, he wants to see what is pissing off this prick. Maybe chop off his balls while he's at it, too, to help calm him down."

Valentino swore he could feel his scrotum tighten from the thought. He sighed. "It might help, actually. He still flashes his bedroom eyes at his wife."

Cain huffed in amusement. "I am surprised a child has not been conceived yet."

"If she gets pregnant, it would make King Alaric more hostile and erratic."

"You reminded me; we have an appointment set up with Kingdom Morningstar," Cain stated, crossing his arms. "Prince Alexander proposes an alliance to secure his support."

"What good would that do? He is already bound to Kingdom Hartfelt by his daughter's marriage. King Alaric was a simpleton for marrying her without even consulting me," Valentino hissed. He still seethed about the political move the king pulled, kept in the dark while he searched for a bride. "And now, your prince suggests this ludicrous move? It will only worsen the mess between these realms."

"I know King Alaric is a pathetic simpleton, how unfortunate for the man, but Prince Alexander is aware of the bride's," he makes a hand gesture to think up the proper words, "complicated circumstances, and from information gathered from a little birdie within King Johnathan's palace walls, we learned he was planning to execute his daughter because of it."

"What good would that do? She's already married."

"It means that she is worthless to even her own father. The marriage between your king and his leftover scrap was not condemned for King Johnathan's favor. He could probably care less about his bound allegiance to Kingdom Hartfelt."

Valentino thought on this. Cain could be right.

Cain continued, "It is worth a try. At this time, the details are still being sorted out. It is about a month's wait before the meeting takes place."

"What should I do during the wait?" Valentino asked.

"The same as before. Copy all reports and keep your king on a leash. Kingdom Ironwood does not want any more stunts like these in the meantime. Meet me here in a month. If something unexpected happens to this new meeting arrangement, as it did before, try not to take any rash action. Wait for a letter from me."

And just like the previous meetings, the man vanishes into the darkness before Valentino's response. The advisor stood there alone.

17

Man's Toy

The two leaders stood face-to-face, their armies arrayed behind them, locked in a fierce stare. The trees of the Neermere forest provided a canopy of shade from the scorching sun. Only a foot's distance separated them, not daring to cross the border that divided their realms.

Nadia, her sword sheathed but her hand gripping the hilt, stood steadfast by Alaric's side, her demeanor exuding a sense of menace. In contrast, Cain seemed utterly unbothered, even picking at his fingers out of pure boredom.

Prince Alexander rolled his neck, stretching his muscles. He and his army of knights had arrived a few minutes ago, curious but not daring to ask how long King Alaric had been waiting. He muttered, "I am here. You got my attention."

"We have agreed to meet again if a better agreement was introduced, have we not?"

The prince sighed. "Yes, but do you think conquering land up to my borders would fall in your favor?"

"I believe it would," Alaric replied confidently. "You ignored my letters."

"I bluntly ignored them because I did not think a better deal could be struck," Alexander retorted. "My people still stand with the previous arrangement."

"I gave you my reasons why my kingdom can not agree to your terms, and as previously discussed, I have brought a new proposition."

Alaric opened his satchel and pulled out a neatly tied parchment, but before he could hand it to his foe, Alexander raised his hand. "I do not care. I could see through your ulterior motives when you decided to take over the remainder of the forest."

"Are you joking?" the king asked, his brow furrowing.

"No, I assure you, I am entirely serious."

"How absurd of you to think otherwise. I have devised a plan that could bring balance and peace between our lands, and instead, you choose to engage in your childish pastimes."

"Games?" Alexander scoffed derisively.

"Yes, and you are deliberately attempting to provoke conflict."

"You encroached upon our borders, and you have the audacity to claim that you are not playing games?"

Alaric glared. Nadia was fuming. The prince was playing smugly.

"Anyhow, if you are not here to follow through on the initial compensation, I believe we are done here," Alexander said. A corner of Cain's lip curled. He knew this was a waste of time.

Alaric's eyes narrowed as he stuffed the papers back into his satchel. "You are underestimating me, Prince Alexander. I have worked with my people and the court to figure out a solution, yet you are flaunting your pride in favor of your treaty without giving a read to this one?"

"Like you mentioned, I enjoy participating in my *childish pastimes*," the prince replied as he turned. Kingdom Ironwood took their leave.

Since the day was bright and sunny, the queen decided to sew up a few torn stitches in Alaric's garments in the solar room. She sang a soft but cheerful song to herself while she did so, wearing a stunning red velvet gown with gold trim and a tie-back. The fabric was smooth and silky to the touch, and she absolutely adored it.

Lucia's ankle was now a shade of green, which had improved significantly. She could now bear most of her weight and walk almost normally. She was offered to join the servants on their trip into town to mingle with the townsfolk, but she declined. She did not want to overexert herself.

Valentino followed the servants shortly after their leave on his own list to purchase at the market. Rose and Charlotte were outdoors, playing with the farm animals. Alaric and Nadia were attending a political gathering. The queen was all alone.

Moments passed when only her notes filled her ears. It was momentarily peaceful in her whole little world as she focused on the needle in hand.

Then, a set of footsteps approached. She wondered if she had missed Alaric's return. It was still quite early for him to be back, so she assumed it was the servants.

But to her surprise, Valentino stood on the threshold, his eyes scanning her up and down with a predatory gaze. Lucia felt uneasy, unsure of how to react to his sudden presence.

What should she say? What should she do? This was the first time Valentino had sought her out alone, which made her uncomfortable.

"Queen Lucia, what an intriguing woman you are. You have no qualms in *shared* lovers."

Lucia stood up, folding the trousers she had been working on, and placing them on the side table. She spoke softly, barely audible to the naked ear, "I do not follow."

Valentino let out a frustrated sigh. "Of course not, you are ignorant."

The queen tried to process his words, but more confusion crept onto her face. However, she did not appreciate the insult. It was not her fault that education was denied due to her birth sex.

"Excuse me." She gave a short bow and walked past him with a cold shoulder. She did not want to be alone with this man.

Valentino followed closely behind her as she walked down the hall, matching her stride. She aimed for the palace front doors, but the advisor hovered his whole body over her. Panic was settling in her mind. Would he lash out at her for trying for the doors? Would he block her? Grab her and drag her away?

She only needed distance. Perhaps being locked alone in a room would be beneficial.

He continued to speak, "Please, do not take my words as an insult. It is blissful to be ignorant in this world. All you need in life is to be pregnant to achieve happiness. It is simple and straightforward."

Lucia ignored him, feeling increasingly uncomfortable as he stayed by her side. Reaching the stairs, the queen turned to ascend, grabbing her skirt as she went. Valentino followed her up. "I wish for a wife like you. Truly, I admire you."

She stopped on the second floor, her heart pounding in her chest. "To your definition, I thought I was a whore."

Valentino scoffed. "You are, but your strong need to care for your young is very attractive. It means you are meant to be bred. Not many women have that nurturing trait, and the only way that desire can be filled is to be a man's whore."

The queen resumed climbing the stairs, her mind reeling from his words. She was truly baffled, unable to comprehend how someone could view her in such a foul, animalistic way. Those thoughts were the worst she had ever been told.

The man followed her to the third floor, where she finally turned to face him. "Stop following me," she said firmly, her voice steady despite her fear.

"Why so? Isn't a man following you something you find pleasure in?" Valentino asked.

Lucia snapped, "No!"

The man slapped her. "Do not yell at me."

Her head had flipped to the side, cheek burning.

She did not argue. She did not glare. She did not even look up. She simply turned and continued moving, her steps quick and small. She knew it was wrong to shout at a man, but the more the advisor followed, the more she kicked into survival mode.

"I was, somewhat agreeable, to the king to allow you to speak, but do not raise your voice," he said, trailing her like a little dog excited for its upcoming meal. "As I may add, you should take pride in having a man follow you unconditionally. And, you should be grateful that a nobleman, like myself, is attracted, and not a poor commoner, like the king."

She was getting close to her bedchamber, where she could finally lock the door and create the much-desired distance. He continued, "Did you know that? King Alaric was born an impoverished man in a destitute family. He has no noble bloodline, no historical familial accomplishments, no generational wealth. He is nothing in the royal hierarchy."

Lucia did not respond.

"I came from a line of honorable familial advisors and generational wealth. I can provide as a true nobleman."

Finally, the queen reached the last step and took off as fast as possible.

Her trembling fingers gripped the handle and yanked the bedchamber door open. She tried to slam it shut, but Valentino was too quick. He had already anticipated this.

He barged in and closed the door from behind. Frantic hands grabbed the chair, and he used it to prop up against the door handle, blocking any chance of escape. He laughed as if this were a child's game. The queen froze like an alert deer.

"Lucia." Valentino took a step towards her, his eyes locked on hers. "Run away with me. Have my offspring," he said softly, his voice filled with urgency.

Lucia stared at him in disbelief, taking a step back in sync.

"This kingdom is going to fall soon," Valentino continued. "And to have you murdered for the failures of your unnoble husband would bring waste to your uterus."

A chill ran down her back. She knew the advisor was an awkward man, but she never thought he would go to such extremes.

She had to get out of here. Now.

"Come with me," he demanded as he loomed over her. Lucia's hips hit the edge of the bed. She had no more space in her favor, but she needed to keep moving. She needed to run.

Lucia dashed, barely dodging the man's figure before he reached out and grabbed her arm. His tight grip pulled her towards him as he tried to contain the woman.

"No! Let me go!" she screamed, fighting with all her might to break free from his grasp. However, Valentino was too strong. He easily overpowered her, throwing her onto the floor with a force that left her winded.

Her lungs ached for air, her spine radiating pain. But despite the odds, the queen refused to give up.

She continued to fight back, arms outstretched in an attempt to push him away. He chuckled, finding amusement in her struggle. "Stop fighting. You will only wear yourself out."

Lucia did not listen, nor did she care for the consequences of fighting against a superior male. She squirmed. She pushed. She hit. She scratched. Only when she lifted her knee to kick the man in the groin did she stop with widened eyes.

Realization had hit. Valentino was aroused.

She panicked.

"No! No! Get off of me!" Lucia shouted, hoping that someone would hear her wails. A wave of disgust washed over her. This man was planning to assault her sexually. A cycle repeating itself.

"You stupid woman, no one can hear you," he snickered, a smile plastered on his face. He moved to pin her wrists together above her head with only one hand. "On the day you fell and injured yourself, did you know I was there? Watching you bathe? All naked and for show?"

She gasped.

An unworthy, perverted man.

"And since I already got a peek at what your body looks like, I wonder what it feels like."

"No! Please, no!" she begged, but Valentino was relentless. His hand reached out to slither underneath the wrinkled, velvet red dress, his digits trailing upwards from her calf, knee, and close to her inner thigh. He was inches from her most intimate areas, and she was not going to allow it to be easy for him.

Lucia jolted and then insulted. "Wandought!"

She rolled her hips, using the side of her knee to push the man off balance. It was not enough for him to fall face-first, but it got his hand off her leg.

"You puterelle!" Valentino hissed.

"Help! Help!"

"Shhh—"

"Somebody help me!"

Valentino clamped her mouth shut, silencing her calls. "Stop screaming! I told you, nobody is near! You are only hurting my ears!"

The queen scuffled, refusing to stop despite the warning. She was not allowing this man to control her without a fight, no matter how hopeless the situation seemed.

She whipped her head side to side to try to loosen the hand. A hard bite of a few fingers would be plenty to falter in his hold. However, he had had enough with the resistance and decided to take a much more drastic measure, moving his hand downwards and grabbing the woman's delicate throat. He squeezed tightly on her trachea to cut off her air supply.

If he could make the queen pass out, she would not be able to fight back, and he could have his way with her.

Oh, how he had fantasized this for days.

His smile returned to his face as he watched her chest flutter. Redness quickly tainted her skin, and her hands instinctively grasped his arm while he released her wrists. The sound of her heart drowned out her surroundings, oblivious to the sound of his trousers unbuttoning. Oblivious of her gargle. Oblivious to the rushing footsteps vibrating the stone.

The conclusion that she might not survive this encounter daunted her.

This was the end.

For her. For Charlotte.

Who would care for h—?

BANG

The bedchamber door almost flew off its hinges. The chair barrier stood no chance.

Lucia could barely turn her head, the corners of her vision fading into darkness. She was so weak, so helpless, so vulnerable. She tried to fight—she really did—but it was not enough.

The hand that held her throat released. She inhaled sharply.

"Alaric, hel—," she tried to sputter, but she did not finish her sentence before Alaric grabbed Valentino by the collar and threw him. The advisor stumbled for balance. He already tried to scurry off the queen, but the king was just too quick.

"I-It's not what it looks like!" Valentino stammered, trying to explain the situation falsely. "This whore tempted me with her spell of—!"

Alaric wasn't interested in excuses as he did not hesitate to ball his fist and strike his advisor directly in the face. The older man had no time to dodge. Blood splattered on the king's knuckles.

He did not give a second thought to swing at Valentino again. The blow gouged his eye, and the king did not doubt that the man could go blind.

But he did not care. He did not care one bit.

No man was going to take advantage of the women under his castle roof, especially the woman forced to be his wife by law. Her rights may be taken away, but not her body, her soul. That was sacred; it must be given by her, and only her.

The older man crumpled to the ground, face bruised and swollen. Nadia had drawn her sword, the cold metal mere inches from the man's chest. Alaric wiped the blood off his hands. "Imprison him."

"B-But, Your Majesty, I am your advisor! You need me—!"

"You will be publicly hanged for your crime," Alaric interrupted, his tone brutally cold.

Valentino tensed up. "No."

"No? Would you rather spill your blood by Nadia's sword? It is an option, but I do not wish to clean the mess."

Valentino's mouth opened, but he did not object. That was enough of an answer.

With her sword still pointed, Nadia grabbed him roughly by the tunic and pulled him upwards. Although she was small, her body was rippled with muscle from the labor of her position. She pushed him out the door, her blade pointed at his back, as she led him. Valentino remained quiet.

A sob broke out.

Alaric twirled, noting Lucia leaned against the sturdy bed frame, still settled on the floor. She tried to wipe away her falling tears, but even with all her best efforts to control her emotions, she seemed to fail. The tears just kept coming.

Alaric sat down by Lucia's side. "Lucia?"

When Nadia and he returned, the king was suspicious of her absence. Seconds later, her cries and pleas for help immediately reached their ears, springing them into action. He ran like his life depended on it, trailed by Nadia, as the two leaped after each step. He nearly tripped on the third floor.

What Alaric did not expect was to find his appointed advisor on top of his wife, strangling her while he reached for his trousers. And when she looked at him and called out his name for the first time in desperation, it shattered him.

"Lucia?" he repeated.

The queen's breathing became increasingly erratic. She frantically grasped her disheveled blonde hair and drew it into a tight ball atop her head. Her legs instinctively drew up towards her chest, and a gut-wrenching sob tore its way from her throat.

Why did men, with their insatiable hunger for power and control, have to be so predatory and uncivilized? They parade around as if they were untouchable aristocrats, yet their actions belied their true nature: that of wild, unruly dogs.

The memories of her past returned. The relentless beatings, the vile name-calling, and the suffocating control that her ex-spouse had exerted over her life. She only wished for control over her life, not others, as men genuinely desired. She clenched her fists and tore. Alaric recognized the behavior.

"Lucia? My Queen?" He tried to offer comfort, to place a hand on her shoulder, but he was unexpectedly met with aggression.

"Do not touch me!"

Alaric recoiled, but he was not offended. He recognized the manifestation of the immense stress. Despite his discomfort at witnessing her self-harm, he tried once more, his voice soft and soothing like honey. "Lucia, you are safe now. He is gone."

But Lucia's words betrayed a deep-seated fear. "He is not! He will come back! He always does!"

The king was left confused as to who she was referring to, but he chose not to probe the matter. "He will never set foot on this palace floor again, I promise. As long as I rule, I will make sure of it."

Lucia sniffled, accompanied by a hiccup that racked her body. The side of her cheek had started to swell. Alaric was going to murder the man ruthlessly.

He brushed the hair from her face, pulling out his handkerchief from his pocket to gently wipe away the tears and snot that clung to her skin. "I can promise you that he will never be in your sight again."

She allowed him to tend to her, releasing her grip on her hair and submitting to his care. Her eyes were puffy and red, but Alaric's gentle touch helped to soothe her. She whispered, "I am sorry. I am so sorry for my disrespect."

"There is nothing to apologize for. I did not see you do wrong. Please focus on taking deep breaths."

Following Alaric's instructions, Lucia monitored her breathing, trying to calm her racing heart and ease the ache in her throat, which she knew would likely result in a bruise. The two of them sat in silence, recollecting themselves. Minutes had passed.

After what felt like an eternity of mutual silence, Lucia spoke softly, her voice hoarse from crying. "Thank you." Her eyes barely met Alaric's. "Thank you for helping me, for staying with me."

Alaric smiled ever so slightly, his chest swelling with affection for the woman sitting beside him. "Of course, Lucia," he replied. "What he did was entirely wrong. You are a living being with boundaries, emotions, and thoughts. It was wrong of him to disrespect you in that way. It was more so disgusting, and I am sorry that I was not there sooner."

Lucia nodded, more at ease. "Like you had just said, I did not see you do wrong."

Alaric huffed through his nose and fought the urge to shake his head at her re-usage of chosen words. She carried on, "And, you are very kind."

This time, Alaric could not hold back his chuckle. "You have already told me that before."

A sniffle. "I know. I am ensuring that you remember."

"Are you implying that I am old?"

"Never. I am simply stating the fact of your character, and you mustn't forget."

A cheeky thing she is.

Lucia sniffled again, and Alaric placed the handkerchief into her hands. She used it to wipe.

"Where will he go?"

"Valentino?"

Lucia nodded.

"Behind bars, before I will send him to Hell."

18

Stormy Revelation

The ominous, labyrinthine hallway that sent shivers down the spines of all who dared venture near was none other than the palace's dungeon. An iron spiral staircase wedged between the cobblestone walls led to the cells. It was the lowest level, barely lit by the flickering light of the torches. It was rare for a prisoner to be locked away in this silent isolation, but Valentino was not the first.

The king took his slow and steady steps down into the ghastly seclusion, the keys jingling behind him as Nadia followed. They were set to converse with the imprisoned man.

Though Alaric could not shake off the feeling of negligence that gnawed at his conscience. He should have heeded the warnings from his servants and the knight about his advisor's malevolent intentions sooner, but his denial of the hatred lust the advisor had towards Lucia had blinded him to the danger that lurked in the shadows. He took the blame for the inappropriate encounter, although he was consulted not to.

Valentino perked up to the sounds of footsteps approaching him. His face had swollen, the damaged eye closed shut and bruised to a dark shade of purple. Serosanguinous fluid leaked from the outer wrinkled crevice. The scratches done by the queen had scabbed on his flawed neck and hands.

The older man was undeniably sore. When Alaric and his knight stood before him, separated by a row of metal rods that began to show signs of rusting, he slowly rose to his feet. He hissed under his breath from the pain. Truthfully, the man never thought he would be man-handled like a criminal in his lifetime of service.

"What is wrong with you?" Alaric coldly asked, his eyes observing every detail of the man.

Valentino groaned as he proceeded forward, a subtle limp in his walk. "Do not tell me you were serious. You are going to hang a man over a misinterpretation? She tempted me by flashing her pretty, new dress up—"

"She was screaming for help, and you were on top of her; that speaks differently to me."

"She was merely meeting the consequences of her actions."

"Are you calling her a liar and that my eyes deceived me?" The king's voice was laced with disgust, and his eyes narrowed as he took in the sight of the man who sought pleasure in hurting others.

"Your Majesty, I am stating that every story has two sides."

"I would have her testify if it pleased you, but I promised her that she would never lay her sights on you again."

Valentino shook his head as he mocked. "I cannot believe you. Never would I ever think a king would fall so low to a bitch."

"Watch your tongue," Alaric threatened.

"I am simply speaking the truth. You have become increasingly in-fatuated with her; it is truly pathetic."

The king maintained his displeased, reserved face, but one eye-brow began to climb towards his hairline. The advisor gave him a wry smile. "I can tell by the look in your eyes of the denial you think of. Do not try to be fatuous. All of your court can see your attempts at benevolence towards her."

Alaric released a deep exhale. "Your opinion on my court holds no meaning while you reside in this dark cavern."

"It may, or it may not, I do not care, but it does not hide the truth," Valentino said, pausing momentarily. He contemplated his next move. "You know, I saw her naked body not too long ago; how squirmish she was, pale skin down to her breasts that bounced with each step, soft curly, peach fuzz protecting her delicate—"

Alaric slammed his fist against the steel, startling the advisor and rattling the stone walls. The sound echoed through the dark chamber. His nerves screamed in protest from the pain, but his mind was a jumble of unanswered questions and unwanted thoughts.

"It is a weak display for a king to get overly emotional," Valentino huffed. "As I have previously said, you may think you are a king, but she will be your downfall."

Nadia tightly squeezed her wrists behind her back to contain the rage simmering beneath her composed exterior. She felt like she, too, was partially to blame. Her vow was to protect her people, and she was unsuccessful in doing so, even with the king's own wife.

"Unlock the door."

Nadia tensed, but she obeyed. The ring of keys chimed in her hands.

Valentino's face wavered as he watched the cell door creak open.

There was no longer a barrier. No physical protection. Danger consumed the damp air of the prison.

In a heartbeat, Alaric had lunged at Valentino, pounding his fists into the man. The advisor tried to defend himself, but from all the relentless blows, the pain became too unbearable to focus. Blood splattered on surfaces as Valentino's nose was crushed, his lips split, and his cheekbone shattered.

"King Alaric—"

He wasn't listening. His ears rang loudly in his head as all his energy was directed at the evil man.

The advisor had already fallen to the floor, face already swelling beyond recognition, twisted with agony. Blackness faded in and out. He was barely conscious.

"Snap out of it!" Nadia shouted, grabbing Alaric's shoulder. But the king nudged her hand off, staring down at the quivering, wounded man below him. He delivered a kick in the abdomen, and his next kick was aimed at the neck.

Nadia forcefully intervened with a shove, as she could see the king's next blow was fatal. "You are about to kill the man!"

"And there would be plenty more dead if I find others like him!"

Murder was in Alaric's eyes. Nadia could see it. It was the same look he had planted on his face when he faced the ex-Ironwood king, seconds before he plunged the sword into the tyrant's chest; raw and primal.

Valentino coughed as he choked on his blood. It trailed down the side of his puffed face and onto the stone. Alaric finally took a step back, his chest heaving with exertion, as he rolled his neck. Crimson and sweat painted his skin. The knight challenged, "Do you want me to hang him or not?"

The king studied at Valentino. He did not care if he caused any fractures or internal bleeding. The man deserved to die.

"Starve him instead," Alaric commanded before he sharply turned away. Nadia glanced at the advisor for a split second before she followed.

"Your Majesty?"

"Do not heal him, give him food, or spare water. Allow him to soil in his own filth and blood."

Nadia locked the cell door. Alaric was almost at the spiral stairs, but his voice boomed from the vibrations of the stone walls. "Appoint a guard outside the door. I will check on him in two days."

The sensation of the old man's hands caused her to gag internally, almost retching in her mouth. As anticipated, a faint imprint of his fingertips appeared on her neck, adding to her growing collection of injuries.

To express her gratitude, the queen concocted a tray of nougat in the hearth. She infused the sweet treat with aromatic spices like cinnamon and cloves, enhancing its nutty flavor. The servants had praised its taste when they sampled it, and she carefully arranged the nougats on a small steel plate.

She stealthily entered the king's chambers, carrying a hot kettle filled with a new blend of tea, filled with new, fresh ingredients from the market. She then placed the plate of nougat and the cup on the nightstand. Smiling to herself, she hoped it would be pleasurable to his tastes.

Closing the bedchamber door behind her, she nearly bumped into the head servant. The older woman's hands were folded together, and she smiled gently at Lucia. The queen wondered what the servant had in mind, unconsciously picking at a fingernail.

"My Queen, are you doing all right?"

"Yes, I am doing fine."

Rose squinted her eyes. She was not convinced.

"Really, there is no need to worry," Lucia added, but it did not help her case.

The head servant knew from personal experience that such events took time to recover from, and she did not want Lucia to face it alone. Without warning, Rose embraced Lucia, wrapping her arms around the petite woman. The queen was caught off guard, but she slowly returned the gesture, feeling as if she could dissolve into Rose's warmth.

"I know a lie when I sense it."

Lucia only sighed with relief. The head servant was too wise for her own good. "If you need to confide in someone, I will always be here to listen. All you have to do is find me," Rose offered as she patted the queen's back.

"Yes, of course."

Rose broke away, giving Lucia a tender smile before she excused herself with slow, steady steps.

To have that unshielded support.

To have security.

These needs were undoubtedly neglected for years.

Lost in thought, Lucia's feet began to move on their own, guiding her down the levels of the grand staircase steps and through the palace hallways. It was quiet, despite the faint roll of thunder echoing from the distance. A storm was on the move. Rain was set to come.

Eventually, she came across two double doors that had been locked since her and her daughter's arrival. She never dared tug on unknown doors, but she felt rather curious. So, the queen gave it a long stare before she reached for one of the metal handles on the door. With a nudge, and to her surprise, it was unlocked.

Lucia's eyes widened in awe at the sight before her.

Rows upon rows of literature lined the walls, each unique in color, shape, and age. The shelves were intricately engraved, filled to the brim with countless volumes. A ladder was present but coated in a thick layer of dust from its lack of use.

In the center of the room, a vibrant red rug with blossoming white flower stitching beckoned invitingly. On top were tables and chairs, arranged neatly in the middle of the space. Unlit candles were set around.

Above, a second balcony stretched out, filled with even more books nestled within the shelves. A small seating area, complete with two cushioned chairs, sat at the center of the balcony, offering a panoramic view of the center tables below. The room was a sight to behold, untouched and waiting for its treasures to be discovered. Although it was overall small, that did not disappoint her.

From a young age, Michael had the privilege of a private tutor, hand-picked by Father to provide him with a comprehensive education. He learned

to read and write fluently, delving into various subjects each day. For Lucia, however, it was strictly forbidden.

Intrigued, Lucia crept up to the slightly ajar door of the massive library, eager to listen in on the conversations between her twin brother and his tutor. She knew it was wrong for a princess to eavesdrop, but she could not resist the temptation. Despite her belief that she was hidden well behind the wooden door, the tutor, a tall, slender man with white hair, caught sight of her.

"Princess Lucia, you can not be in here."

She jumped, but there was no point in running. She was caught.

Lucia nervously fiddled with her little fingers as she stepped out, dressed in a cute gown adorned with sparkling jewels. Her long yellow hair was braided. She felt ashamed and apologized, "I am sorry."

Michael stared at his sister, and the tutor continued his scolding. "Leave before I tell your father. You do not need to get in trouble for this."

"Please, no," Michael said. The objection caught the tutor by surprise.

"Prince Michael?"

"Can she join us?"

The tutor shook his head. "My Prince, Lucia can not join us. It is not for a princess to learn what I am teaching you."

Before Lucia could add, an arm reached out and yanked her out of her father's library. A young servant, barely old enough to work, dragged her down the empty hallway. Lucia's little legs struggled to keep up, and she winced in pain, "Ow!"

The servant hissed at her, "Shut it! Do not get caught in there, do you hear me?" Her eyes glared angrily, and the princess nodded frantically. She did not want to get in trouble.

The servant stared her down for a few more seconds before she released Lucia to resume her duties. The blonde princess watched her, left alone in the nearly empty hallway.

The twins had never had a motherly figure in their lives. Their biological mother had passed away shortly after childbirth, so they were raised mainly by the midwives and servants around the castle. It was only them in this big world, following their father's command when he was in their proximity with utter strict obedience.

A few days passed before the princess was assigned to her royal bride tutor. It was unexpected for her, but it was the right time for the kingdom to start preparing. Father went out of his way to introduce the new member in his court to his daughter. "Consider her as your mother from now on," Father said. "She will teach you traditional role standards and shape you into a proper wife for your future husband, understood?"

Lucia was unsure of what to say. The woman, an older lady with strands of grey in her black hair, pulled into a bun, stared at her with a stoic expression. Her knuckles were large, her nails long and sharp, and her face was devoid of any emotion. It was clear that she had never smiled a day in her life.

When Lucia did not respond immediately, Father cleared his throat. "Do you understand?"

"Yes, Father," Lucia replied.

"Good. Make her feel welcome. She will be staying in my court until the day you marry."

The woman attempted to smile at Lucia, but it was a fake, wicked smile. And that day forward, Lucia knew her life would become a living hell.

The royal bride tutor was merciless and harsh in her teachings. Her lessons were demanding, often leaving the princess in tears. She was forced to learn how to clean and tidy rooms, memorize verbal recipes, and cook for the servants day after day. She also had to practice walking with perfect balance and elegant postures, as well as learn how to follow orders and maintain complete silence in the presence of powerful, noble men. If she failed to obey or did not achieve the desired outcome, she was punished with cruel words and a sharp slap on the wrist from a flat stick. The slaps were painful, but it never broke the skin.

The servants felt pity for her, and Michael watched with sadness. One day, he asked Father why their lessons were so different. The king replied, "Lucia's destiny in life will always be different from yours. You are meant to conquer lands and influence political gatherings. Your sister is expected to be a breeder for a royal man, to create a strong family."

"But Father, as I may, why not teach Lucia at least the basic mathematics, english, and science? She expressed interest—"

"Your teachings are dangerous to her. It will give her ideas and opinions. A bride can not be educated. It challenges the future spouse."

Frustrated by this contradiction, Michael decided to take matters into his own hands.

The young prince smuggled old literature materials to his room prior to nightfall. And once the palace was quiet and sound asleep, he snuck into his sister's bedchamber every night. The books were gifts for his sister.

He taught her how to read and write, addition and subtraction, and the fundamentals of science. The moonlight streaming through the windows provided enough light for their nightly lessons. And when Lucia finished the books, Michael would bring more, ensuring she never ran out of material to learn from.

Lucia was a quick learner, eager, and intelligent. Through her words and gestures, she expressed her gratitude to Michael and appreciated his efforts. They continued this secret for several years, the books hidden under her bed, until she was caught at the age of eleven.

"What the hell do you think you were doing!?" her father bellowed as he swung his arm, striking Lucia across the face. She fell painfully to the floor of her bedchamber, stunned, not aware that her own father would hit her.

"Father, I-I-I—," she stammered.

"Shut it! I do not want your excuses!" he shouted. "How long have you been learning?!"

Lucia was too terrified to answer, her tiny body shaking with pure fear. Father's shadow loomed over her. "How long?!" he roared.

She whimpered, "A couple of years."

"Years?!"

The bride tutor chimed in. "This is probably why I have been having trouble enforcing my teachings on her recently."

The wicked woman was correct in her statement. For the past year, Lucia had given up absorbing her lessons and maintained focus on an unknown distraction. This undeniably led to the princess's constant red wrists.

Father was fuming. He grabbed her by the biceps, pulled her up, and shook her. "No prince wants a sharp bride! It threatens their status and the kingdom! It dooms the people around him!"

Lucia began to cry, feeling saliva hit her face. Her arms were being painfully squeezed. "F-Fath—"

"Do not say my name! I give you life, try to make you prepared for a long-fulfilled marriage, and you dare to oppose me and your tutor!"

Tears rolled down her face, pain seared from Father's tight grip. But before she could even attempt to offer an apology, his iron grip tightened, pulling her out of her bedchamber with a harsh jerk. Her calves scraped against the rough rug, the friction burning her tender skin as she struggled to keep up with his relentless pace. "Father, please, you are hurting me!"

Father ignored her plea, followed by the tutor with a monstrous smirk on her face. "If you dare pick up a book again, I will blind your eyes. A bride who cannot see is still more desirable than a smartass."

With that, he shoved her into one of the hallway storage closets, the darkness swallowing her whole. Her heart raced as the door slammed shut behind her. Only a thin sliver of light seeped through the bottom of the door, taunting her.

"You will stay in there until you have learned that what you did was highly unacceptable," he growled before his footsteps faded into the distance, leaving her alone in the suffocating darkness.

She pounded on the wood, her fists aching. "Father, please!" she screamed, but her calls fell on deaf ears.

The small, cramped closet was a living nightmare, a pitch-black prison that fueled her every fear. Lucia's imagination ran wild, conjuring up all sorts of terrifying monsters lurking in the shadows.

She had no idea how long she'd been trapped, but it felt like an eternity. Her throat was parched, her stomach growled with hunger, and her bladder ached with the need for relief. She tried to call out for help as servants passed the door, her voice hoarse from crying, but no one seemed to care. All she could do was sob, weakly knocking on the door in the hopes someone would finally hear her and set her free.

As the hours dragged on, Lucia's hope began to fade. She was alone, abandoned, helpless.

It wasn't until two days later that the door finally creaked open. A servant, acting on King Johnathan's orders, helped carry the broken princess back to her bedchamber. She was given clean clothes, a warm bath, food, and water, but she felt utterly shattered. She sat in a chair, staring blankly at the tiny portion on her plate, her mind reeling with despair. In that moment, she came to a devastating realization: to be loved by a man, she had to be an ignorant toy to him.

Michael knocked on her bedchamber door before he entered, having returned from a political trip with King Johnathan's advisor. He had heard the rumors as soon as he stepped through the castle gates. "I am so sorry, Lucia," he said softly as he approached.

Her eyes, once bright and full of life, now seemed lifeless, her soul crushed beneath the weight of Father's cruelty. "Do not dread. It is not your fault. I was being careless and did not cover my tracks well enough."

"It still does not make it right to be locked away in a dark closet for days," he continued, trying to reach her, but he could tell his efforts were in vain when she replied with flat words.

"It is fine."

Michael bit his bottom lip in defeat. Since then, the princess had thrown all her time into her training, excelling at every task set before her. She had transformed into one of the most skilled and obedient women the wicked tutor had ever seen, as the old lady had so proudly proclaimed.

It had made Father proud. And he excitedly waited until the day she had ripened with her first period.

Thunder cracked from above. The storm had arrived.

The leather of the leather-bound book tickled the sensors on her fingertips as she ran over the cover. Although she felt compelled to open it, she only examined the front and back, sensing that it hailed from a distant kingdom, perhaps a gift from a former alliance or the people.

Alaric silently observed her from behind. She seemed intrigued, and he wondered if she was educated. He cleared his throat.

Lucia jumped and quickly slid the book back into its place. "I apologize terribly for my lack of self-control. I should not be in here."

He scoffed with disbelief. "Pardon? What kind of silly rule is that?"

Lucia blinked at him with confusion. Alaric wondered if his remark was too harsh. "Do you know how to read and write?"

"I do."

Alaric looked around. "Then, I suppose these books have a dedicated reader now. I feared the neglect that I have shown them."

Lucia almost gasped. "Are you sure?"

"Do I seem uncertain?" The king gestured at the vast collections of books that surrounded them. "This library is as much yours as it is mine. Feel free to explore and take whatever your heart desires."

Lucia was trying to comprehend her newfound freedom in the library. A place she had been banned, forbidden to set foot in, was now within grasp whenever she pleased. Adrenaline filled her veins. "Thank you."

The corner of his lip curled. Questions came to mind about her past and how she learned the basic language, but then the context of the previous day crept in like a heavy rock barreling down a pond. His chest tightened. "How are you feeling?"

"About yesterday?"

"Yes. Is there anything I could do to help you? Anything to elevate the stress?"

She sighed, not out of frustration, but in appreciation. She gave it some thought, looking down at her fingers, before she responded. "I was anxious earlier in the day, but as of now, I feel more at ease."

The king acknowledged, but he wanted more. He raised his hand, wanting to touch her, to feel the bruises that parched her delicate skin, but his eyes studied the queen's face for an answer.

Permission.

He was waiting for permission.

She met his gaze: another man's hand, this one with the purpose of gentleness, not violence.

This was a proper nobleman.

A powerful being who bows down and cares for the weak he swore to protect. It was the true heart of a knight. And so she trusted him, turning her head to allow a better view.

Alaric's callous fingers, laced with the murder of other past souls, were so humane. Her epidermis tingled, and she fought the urge to shiver as he slowly moved from her throat to her jawline, his thumb caressing her feminine chin. He whispered, "Are you sure?"

"Do I look uncertain?" she shot back, which made him chuckle. He withdrew his hand.

"Thank you again for being there to stop it. I do not want to know what would have happened if you had not intervened."

He inclined his head. "Please, tell me right away when a member of my court makes you uncomfortable. I do not care if they have just been appointed or are long-term members; I will not allow anything like that to happen on my castle grounds again."

Lucia was appreciative.

19

Kingston

Another stunt. Another stunt done by that bastard prince.

On the western edge of Alaric's land, a large grove of ever-green pines clustered together as the shadowy Mariana Forest, their dark needles reaching towards the sky like skeletal fingers. Amidst this eerie backdrop, a crude hay doll lay discarded, stripped bare of any clothing, its pale surface exposed to the elements. The doll's face, however, bore a faint, unsettling smile, carefully etched into its coarse fabric with black charcoal. Positioned on its back, a rusted sword pro-truded from its chest, the blade piercing deep into the Earth.

The sight left a bitter taste in Alaric's mouth—a clear and ominous threat from Kingdom Ironwood.

To make matters worse, his prisoner had escaped. An incompetent guard was struck unconscious by a stone, and under the cover of the darkness, the advisor fled with nothing but the clothes on his back and his infected injuries.

Alaric launched an investigation, learning that Valentino desper-ately clawed a loose stone off the dungeon walls, leaving behind the color of his blood on the surrounding rocks. He then bent the cell door lock out of place, cracking the bars just enough for his slender frame to slip through the narrow opening.

It was out of desperation—for survival. The older man wanted to live despite his fatal fate laid upon him.

An urgent manhunt was ordered.

Alaric could not allow the older man's attempt at escape to be successful, so he appointed Nadia and her most trusted knights to search for the prisoner's tracks. The orders were clear and direct: Valentino had to be found, and Nadia was given explicit permission to kill him on sight.

After the king finished his furious letter to send to Kingdom Ironwood again, he descended, seeking respite from the confines of his study room. The crash of the day's events had left him mentally drained. At first, he aimed to smell the fresh air that the winds carried from the north, but once his feet met the bottom floor, echoes of laughter and chatter greeted his ears.

He followed the sounds towards the split doors of the library.

There she was, sitting across from her daughter, engrossed in a world of books and imagination. Picture books lay open before them, filled with colorful illustrations and simple stories, while textbooks and blank sheets of paper served as tools for practicing the alphabet.

Lucia patiently guided Charlotte through the letters, her face alight with a warm smile as she watched her child's eyes light up with each new discovery. Alaric unconsciously slipped in and quietly took the stairs to the second balcony. He did not want to intrude, to distract them from this moment.

So he leaned up against the railing from above and watched, a big grin on his face as the two below were lost in their own little world of wonder. The turmoil from earlier had faded as if it had never happened, his mind consumed by this simple joy.

Alaric was so captivated that he failed to notice the approach of the head servant from behind. She also found interest in the laughter and chuckles that rang out of the library doors. She appeared at his side like a ghost. Alaric flinched. "Pardon, you startled me."

Rose let out a soft titter, her eyes twinkling with amusement. "You are falling in love," she whispered, her voice barely audible over the distant laughter from Lucia and Charlotte.

Alaric's brow furrowed. "Come again?" he asked.

Rose leaned in closer. "You can not seem to take your eyes off her. And the more she opens up, the more excited you become."

He stood there, silently observing the pair below; his heart warmed, but his mind deep in battle. He could not deny the truth behind her words, but there was still a faint patch of denial. Lucia was forced to be his wife, and he was scared that she was only participating for the sake of her and her daughter's survival in the castle. But all his previous ideas of allowing her to become a working member of his court to withstand the marriage were fading so ghastly out of reality.

"You are not wrong," the king muttered. "I find myself unable to stop thinking about her."

"And her daughter?"

Alaric's gaze softened as he thought of Charlotte. "A very cherishable girl. I never knew I would find myself fond of children, and she is quite a charmer if she managed to befriend our lovely, so sweet, horse farrier, as I've heard."

"She is a natural."

The king began reminiscing, and he chuckled to himself. "Yesterday, I was granted the privilege to play with Charlotte for the very first time. We tore through the hallways, and when she shrieked with pure joy, I felt an overwhelming sense of jubilation."

Rose's wrinkled eyes pinched together with happiness. "Young children are a fountain of life, and we continue to learn about ourselves, even in our elder stages," she explained.

The two fell silent briefly as they returned their attention to Lucia and Charlotte, who were now singing to commit the letters to memory. The harmonious notes filled the air. "I think I will take her out tomorrow. I want her to see the kingdom, and my people want to see her. They are becoming worried by her absence."

"She might enjoy that, especially since she hasn't left the castle since her arrival," Rose added. Alaric's eyes lit up at the thought.

The head servant was right; Lucia and Charlotte had been cooped up within the castle walls this entire time. He was proud of his people; without them, he would not be here today. He wanted Lucia to see what they had accomplished.

Alaric turned abruptly, catching Rose off guard. "Where are you suddenly going?"

He replied, "To purchase a gift."

"Keep your eyes closed."

"I am trying, but it makes it difficult to move around when I have no sight. I am afraid I might fall," Lucia argued.

Alaric chuckled, the sound rumbling in his chest. "Fear not, Lucia," he reassured her, his thumb brushing against her knuckles as he guided her with a hold of her hand. "I will be here to catch you if you manage to stumble."

She mumbled, "You are quite reassuring." The king could not tell if it was sarcasm or a simple statement, but nonetheless, it made him smile bigger like a fool.

As she continued her small and cautious steps towards the palace's back entrance, the bright sunlight from the clear skies shocked the queen's system. The warmth of the rays caressed her light skin, and she winced. "I did not expect that we were going outside. I wonder what you have in store for me." Her eyes squinted even tighter.

"You will see," Alaric replied, trying to contain his overwhelming enthusiasm. He positioned her and took a few selfish seconds to marvel at how the sunlight danced across her face and blonde hair, highlighting the beautiful features he had grown to love over a short period of knowing her. "Now, open your eyes."

Lucia's eyelids fluttered open, and her gaze widened as she took in the breathtaking creature before her. Alaric's words followed. "I do not want you to feel trapped in the palace. You have every right to leave and meet the people as you wish."

It was a majestic horse, held by the reins by the once-in-a-lifetime clean, grumpy horse farrier. A floral saddle was already equipped on the mare as she waited patiently to be mounted.

"I searched the lands for the most beautiful horse bred by a prosperous breeder yesterday. She is a Gypsy Vanner, a gorgeous horse breed with a kind temperament. Her blue eyes reminded me of you," Alaric added. The queen stepped forward, her fingers instinctively reaching out to pet the animal's silky white mane, as well as getting a closer look at the grey pinto stripes. Not a single speck of dirt marred its coat from impeccable grooming.

This was a gift unlike any she had ever received, a far cry from the dresses, jewelry, and other necessities that had been her only indulgences in the past. "You are very generous, but..."

"Hmm?"

"I do not know how to ride."

"Oh, I did not know."

Her hand continued stroking the horse's mane. Plans were already coming to mind to braid the white hair. "No, it is all right. The horse is magnificent, thank you."

Alaric was too stubborn of a man, and so he extended his hand and asked, "Do you want to go on your first ride?"

Lucia's head whipped around. "Pardon?"

"I can teach you," he said. "We will take her out and see the town."

She smiled.

She smiled at *him*.

A gift to the king. A gift so precious, it took him by surprise. His heart swelled, and he forgot how to breathe.

She questioned, "You would do that?"

Alaric had to swallow to break free from his trance. "Absolutely, it will be much fun," he answered. His eyes gleamed as he grabbed the reins from Hank and flipped them over the horse's head. He lent his hand, aiding Lucia to settle on the side of the saddle, slow and gentle, allowing her to adjust comfortably on the animal. She awkwardly gripped the horn, her fear of sliding off evident as she clung to it for support.

However, Alaric's enthusiasm was infectious, and she smiled again at him; her apprehension had melted away. As he mounted behind her, his arms encased, he reached to grab the reins, making her feel more secure. "Comfortable?" he asked, his breath tickling her ear.

"Yes," she quietly replied.

This was all new.

Excitement coursed through her veins like a potent tonic. She tried hard to keep her hands from trembling, her fingers white-knuckled as she clung to the horn.

With a gentle nudge from his heels, the mare began to walk forward, and Lucia felt herself swaying slightly with each step, her body moving in perfect rhythm with the animal's gait. She had no idea where Alaric was leading the enormous creature, but she started to get a sense of their destination when they left the castle courtyard and ventured onto the open, winding gravel road, towards the homes ahead.

Alaric patiently taught her how to use the reins, the subtle body language required to communicate with the horse, and how to slow down and come to a complete stop. Lucia absorbed every detail and knowledge like sweet nectar. Her horse was responsive and well-trained, and although the pace was leisurely, she thoroughly enjoyed listening to Alaric's soothing voice and observing her surroundings.

The lush greenery of the trees lining the road was a sight to behold during this time of year, their leaves rustling gently in the warm breeze. Tiny wildflowers bloomed along the outskirts of the path. The gravel crunched satisfyingly under her horse's hooves as they approached the bustling marketplace.

The people, men, women, and even children, stopped to watch their king and queen pass by, their faces breaking into broad, genuine smiles. A handful of adolescents ran up to the horse, followed by a younger girl, and Alaric returned their hellos and touched their hands. The little girl rejoiced and then waved to Lucia.

The people did not hide their overjoyed nature to see their beloved queen, and she could feel their eyes watching her—not menacingly, but lovingly, admiring her. Alaric could sense it, too. He leaned in to whisper, "My people are happy to see you."

The queen was too overwhelmed to respond, her eyes taking in every detail of the charming town. It was clean and well-maintained, with homes close together, made of sturdy stone. It was a tight-knit community. The residents seemed to know one another. Alaric added, "They have built this kingdom, not me. I would not be here today without them." His words were filled with gratitude and respect.

Alaric urged the horse to speed up, and the soft wind whipped through Lucia's hair, causing it to flow behind her like a golden river. She could not hold back her soft, melodic laughter as the fresh breeze tickled her face, the sun baking her face tenderly. The king swore his heart skipped a beat, maybe even fluttered, at the sound of her joy.

As they exited the town, Alaric pulled the horse to venture into the countryside. The landscape opened up to rolling fields of vibrant colors—pink, white, red, and yellow. Wildflowers had overtaken the meadow, and Lucia was stunned by the breathtaking scenery. She had moved her hands onto the horse's neck to get a closer look. "This is gorgeous. What is this place?"

"Gentle Meadows. It is a sight to behold. The way the flowers bloom every year in the spring and summer is like a painting. It is within our kingdom borders, so this is all for you to enjoy."

"I love flowers," Lucia purred. "Something about their delicate beauty speaks to the soul."

Just like her, Alaric thought.

"Allow me to help you down," the king said, halting the mare amid the fields. He dismounted fluidly before he helped her down from the saddle, his hands cradling her waist as she stepped onto the soft grass.

Despite her sprain being fully healed, the new position on the saddle left her thighs feeling stiff, and she nearly lost her balance.

Alaric's hands instinctively gripped her hips, steadying her as she regained her footing. "Takes time for the body to adjust to a saddle," he said nonchalantly, hoping Lucia did not feel embarrassed about her stumble.

"I see. I must take baby steps again."

Alaric chuckled. It took Lucia a few steps to adjust, but once the stiffness dissipated, she immediately dropped to her knees to observe the wildflowers up close. Her fascination intrigued the king, holding onto the mare's reins as he watched her become engrossed in a task.

She plucked the flowers, her fingers deftly selecting the most vibrant petals and leaves. Her nose twitched as she inhaled their sweet fragrance. She carefully weaved the stems together, creating a crown that she placed atop the mare's head.

She stepped back to admire her handiwork, a satisfied grin spreading across her face. The mare was now adorned with the colorful creation. "That is adorable," Alaric commented.

"Would you like one?"

"Please."

Lucia's eyes sparkled as she set to work on another flower crown. She finished it within a minute, and Alaric bowed his head to her creation, which was placed upon his hair. The petals and leaves tickled his skin as she secured it in place.

The two did not take long to settle down within the grass, the mare grazing peacefully beside them. Lucia conversed freely and effortlessly. Alaric listened to every word, not daring to interrupt her, his gaze never wavering from her radiant face. He was captivated by her beauty, her laughter, her unleashed, hidden carefree spirit.

He felt like the luckiest man to be given so many smiles and the privilege of her laughter all in one day.

A very lucky man.

The sun was soon to set, casting a warm orange glow over the horizon. The two had been sitting together in endless chatting tranquility. That was when the king's remaining faith in denial had faded away.

He was lost in her. Under her mercy, her thoughts and feelings. She was now the centerpiece of his life, and he could no longer object to it.

The king was in love.

20

Death of the Wolf

A crack of a whip echoed through the dimly lit chambers, and a cry of pain followed. The older man's head hung low as he endured the humiliation. The cobblestone beneath him was now stained with a crimson hue.

"You fool!" the voice boomed. "You were supposed to provide me with information from inside the castle walls, not go undomesticated on his wife!"

The leather lash fell once more, Valentino's body jerking violently as the pain coursed through him. His arms were bound by metal chains, rendering him immobile, merciful to the shadows of men before him.

"Cain, please," Valentino pleaded, sweat trickling down his forehead. His chest heaved with ragged breaths.

Cain's back straightened, his eyes fixed on Valentino with a cold, calculating gaze. Behind him were the princes of Ironwood and Shadowmere, watching. Staring. "You bewitched yourself by used cunt."

"No, she did this to me."

"Liar!" Cain spat, not holding back to spray more blood from the older man. Prince Victor laughed. Valentino was at the brink of unconsciousness, his body already battered and broken by King Alaric's relentless beating. Every muscle ached and burned, bones screamed, and fatigue crushed him. When he fled back to Kingdom Ironwood, he expected solace and protection. Instead, he was placed into a dungeon once more, surrounded by real criminals who wanted to pick on his previously opened wounds.

Cain continued, "You think you can seek coverage here after your foolish mistake?! Are you mad?!"

"My two children live within your castle walls—"

"Excuses! If you cared for your children, you would have thought twice before acting. Now you cannot go back. You are a failure at your one mission."

"I will make it up to you," Valentino moaned, the lashes on his skin burning with intense fiery. It was hard for him to focus, the pain making his vision blur.

Cain glanced over his shoulder, awaiting instruction from Prince Alexander. The prince stared long and hard. He could order the man's death right here, right now, but it would not be enough to satisfy his anger. Valentino was his only source of information directly from Kingdom Hartfelt, and he had failed. "Yes, you will make it up," Alexander said.

One of Cain's eyebrows arched in response, Victor holding his breath in anticipation. Alexander's order was clear: "Castrate him."

Cain's lips curled into a massive grin. With a flick of his finger, a few more knights burst into the caged chamber, their hands grasping metal tools and a large knife. The last scraps of Valentino's pants were dropped, leaving him exposed in the open.

"No! No! Stop!" Valentino shouted as he resisted, but his attempts were futile. The knights held him down, their grip unyielding as they began their gruesome task.

Alexander explained, "If you can not control your male tendencies, then we must eliminate the source."

Valentino answered with a blood-curdling scream.

Screams of torture.

It bleached the other criminals' ears, but they dared not take a peek. Most were cowardly turned away in their own cells, trying to block out the agony.

This was entertainment to Victor. He inspected every cut and pull of the man's organs, but Alexander pulled him to the side within minutes, farther from the commotion of the wailing man, away from prying ears. Victor pouted. "You don't know how to have fun."

"Cease your petty play," Alexander hissed, his tone low.

"Do you mean my doll displays? I think he is quite enjoying himself going mad over them."

"I do not care. He is up my ass for things I did not do. He might be sending letters now, but it could lead to sending knights instead."

Victor whined in protest. "All right, all right, but I do have another in mind."

"Save it. We have much to discuss before our travel to Kingdom Morningstar."

The torch in the hall flickered, nearing its end. The older man's screams had stopped, blood running down to his ankles, pooling between his legs. He was already unconscious by the time the job was done.

Nadia could not find King Alaric's most wanted prisoner, tracking his trail across the border into the land of his demise. He had fled to Kingdom Ironwood.

She reported back, and although disappointed, Alaric reminded Nadia not to bear fault, praising her unwavering dedication and loyalty throughout the pursuit. The king's words lifted her spirits.

In the weeks that followed, the queen and her daughter swore they were blessed. An overflow of fabric clothing, showers of glittering jewels that sparked in the light, and an array of toys designed to bring endless joy. Each gift came with a heartfelt note penned in Alaric's handwriting. With the addition of the unlimited library materials, the bedchamber was becoming limited in space.

The king, resplendent in his attire, stepped out into the bustling courtyard, the air thick with anticipation for the grand event that was set in the upcoming days. Servants scurried about like ants, hands full of supplies and ingredients. Amidst the flurry, Charlotte darted across the grass, chasing the butterflies that fluttered around, their wings a kaleidoscope of colors. Her giggles of delight pierced the air.

Alaric approached the small girl, the grass crunching underneath his weight. "Where is mommy?"

Charlotte smiled, jumping excitedly as she pointed towards the direction of the horse barn. "In there!"

"Is she with her new horse?"

"Yes, she tells me she really loves her horse. She let me pet her earlier."

"That makes me overjoyed. Thank you, my sweet princess," he said, ruffling her hair before he departed.

Hank worked at his station outside the barn, under the open shed, where the wood was stained black from the collective ash. He struck the hot metal against the anvil with a rhythmic clang, soon to be freshly sculpted horseshoes, only stopping to bow his head to Alaric's approach. The horse farrier and his men kept a watchful eye on the queen's safety.

Lucia tended alone in the barn, brushing her mare's mane and braiding its hair. She had already placed small flowers into the twisted braids, the ones considered as weeds as they grew overgrown in the courtyard. Alaric had made his way in quietly, watching the queen work passionately on her horse. Her horse was in a large, well-kept stall, situated directly across from his black stallion. He patted his horse's face before clearing his throat, drawing her attention.

She turned, then smiled.

That damn smile. It was so captivating.

"Alaric, what a delightful surprise," Lucia purred. Her casual, emerald green dress, with the corset pulled taut, accentuated her newly filled-out figure compared to the months when she first arrived. She also began to address him by his name, which made him feel lightheaded and intoxicated, as though he were basking in the warm glow of her attention.

He entered the stall. "Have you thought of a name yet?"

"Devona," she said as she finished up one of the braids on the mare. "I have never asked for your stallion's name. He is a very large horse, with a coat as black as the midnight sky. I would be lying to myself if I stated that I did not fear him."

"Emris."

"How lovely. What made you choose a sophisticated name?"

"The ex-king of Kingdom Ironwood promised me the best horse. He delivered, and when I laid my eyes on him for the first time, he radiated power," Alaric said, petting Devona. "Have you gone out on a ride on your own yet?"

"No, but I plan to do so with my daughter soon."

"She would love that, and probably never want to come down."

Lucia chuckled. "You might be right."

Alaric grinned, extending his hand. "Take a walk with me."

Lucia looked down at his outstretched hand, and without the slightest hesitation, took it into her own. Small, enveloped by his warm, strong grip. It felt more intimate than a simple lead of direction. And more than she cared to admit, her thoughts tinged with affection when he was within her proximity.

"Where do you plan to take me?" she asked. He closed the stall behind her.

"Take you? Are you suggesting that I whisked you away?" Alaric replied, his eyes twinkling.

"Maybe. I was in the middle of tending my horse."

He led her out of the barn, into the open sun. "I only asked for a walk, and you willingly took my hand, so I believe otherwise."

Lucia's face could not hide the playful smirk and frolicsome intention. "Hmm, although you state that you did not, why must you whisk me away, Alaric?"

The king fought back a shiver and shook his head. "I have something to ask."

"Oh?"

Out in the open courtyard, Charlotte conversed with Axel, dirt already marked upon her lightweight dress. The servant was hanging linen up to dry.

The king and queen began their slow stroll along the neatly trimmed shrubs near the stone walls. "A festival is coming up. The celebration of summer."

"Your kingdom celebrates the seasons?"

"It is simple, maybe silly to others from the outside, but it brings joy to my people's faces. It is small, filled with music and flowers," he explained.

"That must be why the servants are so busy baking that I cannot find my way into the kitchen."

Alaric chortled. "Yes, the castle provides the majority of the food." They turned, circling around the track of knights preparing for their next patrol. "The festival takes place in two days, and I wanted to ask you and Charlotte to join me."

Delight consumed Lucia.

A festival. The first for her to experience.

She had attended balls—the music, the food, the people. She was not granted the privilege to mingle and dance with the noblemen or partake in the lavish feasts. However, she found solace in the harmonious tunes that filled the air as she stood motionless beside King Johnathan and Prince Michael, blissfully unaware of her role as a mere visual spectacle due to her tender age. She wondered if she was expected to do the same by King Alaric's side.

"How should I present myself?" Lucia asked.

"What do you mean?"

The queen shrugged. "Should I stand by your side? Do you want me to sit and watch your people celebrate? Do you wish for me to be mute through the entire event?"

Alaric scoffed. "What awful rules you say. No, I want you and Charlotte to join me to dance and feast."

"Dance and feast?" She looked up at him to see if there was a flicker of tease or joke on his face, but there was none. Alaric was serious.

They had turned again, returning back to where the princess was. Charlotte was now helping Axel with hanging the linens. "Yes. I want you and Charlotte to have fun at the festival and enjoy yourselves. You know how to have fun, or am I wrong?" Alaric teased.

"You are a jester of a man," Lucia replied, rolling her eyes.

"How rude." Their hands were still interlocked with one another, and Lucia was becoming increasingly aware of the hold. He had never held her hand this long before. "If I may ask again, would you two care to join me when the festival starts?"

Lucia never had the freedom to dance. It would be overwhelming, but also interesting—something new, something exciting. She agreed before she could convince herself otherwise. "Yes. We'll accompany you."

"That makes me very pleased."

The night had settled, and Lucia was excited about the upcoming festival. A cocktail of emotions swirled within her—anxiety, trepidation, elation, and ebullience all melded together. She shared the news with her daughter, and not to her surprise, the little girl was thrilled to be part of a large gathering. Her response aided in the queen's relief.

Together, they made their way towards the communal washroom for a bath, and upon opening the door, Victoria, Caroline, and Mia were gathered around the large basin, in the process of removing their uniforms. They chatted animatedly, folding their clothes as they stripped, but the arrival of the queen and her child, with Alaric's robe draped over her arm and her daughter's little hand in her other, paused at their unannounced arrival. "My Queen, is something troubling you?" Victoria asked.

"No, nothing at all. Charlotte and I came to bathe," Lucia replied. Charlotte's yellow hair was covered in glades of grass.

"With all due respect, My Queen, you both must not bathe here," Victoria insisted. "This is a washroom for the other members of the court, and it is not appropriate for you and your daughter to use it."

"But we washed here before," the princess chimed innocently. She wiggled her hand free and raced over to the racks of towels. Lucia followed to place the robe down.

Caroline questioned, "You have washed here before? Does Alaric know this?"

"I am not sure, but I cannot burden Alaric by intruding into his space and accompanying his private washroom," Lucia protested, beginning to undo the laces of her dress. "Water is simply water. I do not mind."

Mia quickly excused herself, mumbling about forgetting some clothing as she exited. Victoria stepped forward and gripped the queen's hands. "My Queen, I cannot allow this."

"Why does it bother you so?"

"You and your daughter are devaluing yourselves as lowly as a servant, and Alaric would not approve of this."

"But my past union commended my daughter and I to share in the communal wash."

"No, and if those highly bastards had any honor of your grace, they should have—"

The door flung open with a ripple.

Alaric barged in.

Lucia whipped around to the man stalking towards her.

"Speak of the Devil," Caroline murmured, and Victoria stepped back as the king swooped down and picked up the princess with one arm effortlessly, resulting in Charlotte squealing. He used his other arm to wrap around Lucia's waist, and with a firm grip on her frame, he pulled her out of the washroom. Mia slipped past them as they left.

"Alaric!" Lucia shrieked, nearly stumbling to keep up. He spoke no objection as he led them down the hall to his private washroom. With her body pressed against his, she felt every muscle moving underneath his attire. Charlotte kept laughing, dangling like a helpless puppy as the king pushed them through the threshold.

"If you wish to bathe, please use this washroom."

"But, Alaric, this is yours."

"No, this is ours. Use it as much as you please."

"And Charlotte?"

He placed the princess down onto her feet, and she pouted from her ending play. "She must bathe here too, nowhere else," he said firmly, and without another word, the king took his leave and closed the door behind him. Of all the days the queen assisted his baths, he was not going to limit theirs in the servant washroom.

It took time for Lucia and Charlotte to settle in and undress, slowly sinking into the warm water that kept the air humid. But soon, the hallways were filled with the sounds of songs and laughter. It was sweet to Alaric's ears, and he took it upon himself to grab his robe that Lucia had left behind and fold it neatly behind the door, awaiting use once they were done. It flustered him to know that she still used it.

Momma,

I hope you are doing well and tending to your flower garden. I would love for you to visit again soon. I'd like to hear about your plans for expanding your homemade meadow. If you wish to open a flower stand in the town market, let me know. I will always fulfill your wishes.

Lucia has become more open with me as the days pass. She is so kind and intelligent, even surprising me with her knowledge of how to read and write. Her interest in literature excites me as I watch her take textbooks to her bedchamber to read in the evenings or when the weather is gloomy. Charlotte shows the same enthusiasm regarding her lessons in the library with her mother. Her imaginative games never cease to amaze me, and I find myself having a delight playing with her. She always seems to surprise me!

For better news, Lucia agreed to my invitation to join me at the summer festival. I know Charlotte will have a magical time, especially when she meets with other children in the kingdom. I feel a pang of pity for her being alone, so I have purchased additional toys to support her growth. The servants are so sweet to play with her as well.

I have also been seeking new members for my court, particularly a new royal advisor. Valentino was stripped of his title and announced as a criminal wanted in my state. I hope to find an individual who has similar skill sets. I might ask my allies for assistance, as they may have a candidate to suit the role.

Anyways, I shall see you at the festival. It brings me much excitement!

Your son,
Alaric

21

A Promise

King Johnathan coughed.

A cough that rattled his lungs and shook his body.

He clutched a silk handkerchief to his mouth, hiding the crimson droplets that stained the once-white fabric. He had been fighting these fits for the past month, and the increasing fatigue and his dwindling appetite had prompted unfavorable news from the physicians.

Across from the ailing king, Prince Alexander sat, his perfectly groomed eyebrow arched in concern as he waited for the coughing fit to subside. "Your Majesty, are you unwell?"

"No," he lied. "Continue, please."

The political meeting table was a veritable gathering of the kingdom's elite—knights, barons, dukes, and even the enigmatic Morningstar prince. None of the Morningstar's court dared to make eye contact with their sickly king, their gazes fixated instead on the intruding Prince Alexander, his Knight of the Body, and a few of their loyal men. Prince Victor was not present; his insubordination months prior, when he spat at the Morningstar's name, had resulted in his exclusion in regards of safety.

Dressed in his finest clothing, draped with a fur cape around his neck fastened by a golden chain, King Johnathan looked, and felt, powerful in the large room despite his weakened state. His crown gleamed brilliantly beneath the candle chandelier hanging above, its trim reflecting the light that danced across the room's opulent furnishings. Michael, too, was clad in a similar fashion, sitting beside his father.

Prince Alexander cleared his throat, gathering his thoughts before addressing the room. "Kingdom Shadowmere and my kingdom desire this alliance with your realm, Your Majesty. It will fortify the powers of the southern civilizations and—"

King Johnathan raised his hand, a command to silence. All eyes turned to him. "Does this *proposed* allegiance have anything to do with the squawking trouble between land disputes?"

Alexander sneered. "Land disputes? There is no such conflict between territorial lines. It is only a spectacle that northern kingdoms seem to pick about."

The king, however, was not convinced. He glanced towards his trusted advisor, who promptly rose from his seat, a sheaf of crumpled papers in hand.

The advisor, a short and portly man, flipped through the pages until he found the information he sought. The sound of the rustling paper echoed throughout the room of men. "According to multiple reports gathered and analyzed by verified members of the court," he began, his voice carrying the weight of his findings, "there have been several unsatisfactory meetings between Kingdom Ironwood and Kingdom Hartfelt. Furthermore, there have been alterations to the established territory lines and increased activity and construction in the disputed areas. It is safe to conclude that an official rivalry has been initiated and all outside interactions must be handled cautiously," he finished, resuming his seat. Michael's lips thinned.

Johnathan let out a sigh of displeasure. "You ask for my support, for my power, to aid against your neighboring realms? Over a mere dispute over land?"

"No, we do not seek your assistance over a matter of territory. This alliance is in response to a crime committed against Kingdom Ironwood, and the subsequent actions that have been taken as a result."

"I am not stupid."

Alexander tensed up, his breath caught in his throat. This realm could squish him like a helpless bug.

Johnathan adjusted his position in his ornate chair. "I am well aware that this is about your late father," he said. A flash of sympathy crossed his face. "I offer my condolences, but I am not interested in the history of your feud. I actually commend Alaric Hartfelt's ambition for power. Most royalty are handed power; he seized it."

Alexander's blood boiled at the king's words, but he kept his anger in check, his face a mask of calm. "Does this mean you refuse to offer your support?"

"I do not wish to participate in a fight unless it is absolutely necessary. Your kingdom, alongside Kingdom Shadowmere, are simply itching for it," he said. The assembled men nodded in agreement, murmuring between each other on the king's stance. Cain's eye twitched.

"Your kingdom—"

"I know. My kingdom has a history, including my own, of rushing into battles, conquering enemies, and expanding our territory. I am not clueless as to how my rule and castle got so huge and defined."

"But we cannot allow this injustice to stand."

"And yet, my daughter is married to King Alaric," Johnathan reminded him, fighting against another cough spell. "You would be declaring war indirectly on my kingdom if you were to continue with this whinge. Allow the past to rest; some battles are better left unwon."

Alexander wanted to growl. To curse. To spat. Yell. To throw his anger at the man who saw him as just an infinitesimal in his life. But he held his tongue, knowing that such a display would only hurt his cause. Instead, the prince took a deep breath and tried a different approach. "What if I were to offer you something in return for your support? A proper exchange to unify a relationship?"

"Your attempts to persuade me are growing tiresome. I figure the same for my men." A few nodded, one even yawned.

Ignoring the king's comment, the prince pressed on. "When was the last time you had a female in your bedchambers? A bride, perhaps?"

"No," Johnathan replied curtly.

"She is very obedient," Alexander persevered. "A product of my father's indiscretion with a servant, and she has just reached maturity. A physician had examined her and found her ripe for the taking."

Michael's face twisted with repugnance. A poor attempt of a bribe.

"What do you hope to gain by offering me this girl? She is not of pure royal blood, and her value is minimal at best. I would not even consider her as a suitable bride for my baron's sons," the king said.

"But she is a young girl, willing and able to do your bidding."

Johnathan left out a loud, raspy cough before he spoke again. "And I am loyal to my deceased wife. After years of fruitless attempts, she finally gave me a priceless prince that has exceeded my expectations over and over again, and an alliance-bounding princess true to her duties. What more could I ask for?"

"For a daughter you almost hanged, you talk rather highly of her," Alexander sniggered. The men in the room stared at him, frozen still from the insult. A tawny-skinned, tall man, broad-shouldered and decorated with scars, slowly stood from the other side of the king. Weapons gleamed by his sides from beneath the candlelight. His eyes narrowed down on them.

"You are fortunate that you are a prince. Were you not, I would have my Knight of the Body cut you where you sit, like the insignificant swine you are."

In an instant, Cain was on his feet, his hand resting on the hilt of his sheathed weapon. The Knight of the Body was now fully alert, aware of the danger his prince was facing in this foreign room, surrounded by men who would follow the king's command without question. The chair almost tumbled behind him.

Johnathan flicked his hand in dismissal. "You have insulted me enough for one evening. I will not tolerate your insolence any longer. Please, allow my men to escort your group out."

"Your Majesty, allow me to—"

"This meeting is over. Save your tongue from petty words."

Alexander clamped his mouth, his eyes squinted, but he did not object as he slowly rose from his seat, signaling his men to do the same. Cain casted a dark, threatening glare at the king. A few Morningstar knights trailed behind, ensuring the foreigners' departure would be swift and uneventful.

The king sighed, and that was enough for the remaining members of the court to excuse themselves, emptying out of the room quietly to return to their duties. The king's Knight of the Body remained by his side. "You are dismissed, Remus. I wish to talk to my son privately."

Remus bowed and did as ordered. Michael remained seated by his father's side. He waited until the shutting click of the double doors before he spoke. "What a pitiful and desperate man."

"I know," Johnathan groaned, rubbing a hand across his weary face. "I may have reacted irrationally, but I did not need a reminder of my failures when it comes to Lucia. I still bear the scorn you have given me." He paused, pain hinting in his eyes as he remembered the night his own son had threatened him with a sword, driven to the brink of madness by his decision on punishment against his daughter. Michael scolded himself in the process for only finding out after her marriage. Johnathan resumed, "Now, I can only pray that she is doing well with King Alaric."

"I pray the same, Father."

Another coughing fit seized the king, but it was less severe than the previous one. He dabbed at his mouth with his soiled handkerchief, trying to contain the mess from his lips. "The cough. It is getting worse," Michael said.

"And it will continue to worsen until my death."

"Do not say that."

"My son, it is the truth. I will not be on this Earth much longer, and you must be prepared to take my place when the day arrives. But I have one remaining task I want to do before that happens, but due to my current state, I am afraid I can not achieve it alone."

Michael's expression remained one of worry. "Father?"

"Go to the Kingdom Hartfelt and strengthen our alliance with King Alaric," he instructed, firm but gentle. "You and Lucia have always been fond of each other, which will serve as an advantage. Establish a trade road and supply him with our men and resources. It will not do much good on our part, but while King Alaric can still be influenced, we must foster his growth and make the bond unbreakable."

"Where is this coming from? Do you fear trouble?"

"I am not sure," Father admitted, "but I want to ensure my daughter is safe once I am gone. My anger and adherence to the old ways blinded me to her true needs. I only wish I could apologize to her in person."

Regret was etched on King Johnathan's face, a rare display from the proud king who had never admitted fault.

Michael had never seen it before.

The festival was in full swing, with music filling the air and laughter echoing even through the tightest of alleyways. The common folk, their faces aglow with joy, mingled amongst each other, enjoying the delicious foods that sat beautifully decorated on wooden tables under the warm sun. The smell of grilled meats and sweet breads lingered, mingling with the scent of freshly cut flowers bundled in display. Stray dogs and cats snooped around for a hopeful drop of meat.

Amongst the throng of people, the princess could be seen. Her cheeks flushed as she ran and ran and ran, chasing around with the other children her age. Her laughter rang out above. The servants kept an eye on her.

The king and queen had arrived with their arms interlocked, and had been so for the past hour. They were immediately greeted with warm smiles and kind words. Alaric was dressed in a fine white tunic and black trousers that hugged his muscular legs, looking every inch as the regal figure he was, but his demeanor was the opposite of royal standards. He spoke freely, openly, and the people were relaxed in his presence.

Lucia, on the other hand, was a picture of shyness. Dressed in a flowing embroidered flower dress that did not draw too much attention to herself, she kept her arm wrapped with her husband's, seemingly overwhelmed by the sheer number of new faces. Her grip tightened on his bicep, and that was when Alaric noticed the tension she held as her eyes stared off into the distance. He excused the group they were congregating with and directed her to the tables.

It had given her a breather, and after a couple of minutes of solitude, she got comfortable and tried a few hand-held food dishes. She pointed out which one was her favorite, and Alaric could not resist not to try it—savory beef slow-cooked in honey. Lucia never knew meat could be made sweet, but she did not argue against it. She loved it.

Alaric's mother was present, greeting the two with a motherly smile before showering Lucia with compliments on her appearance. She also noticed how well Charlotte was getting along with the local children; told the queen it was beneficial for the princesses' growth. Lucia agreed.

Suddenly, the soft tones of instruments shifted to a fast-paced rhythm that seemed to match the beating of a heart. A couple of vielle fiddles joined in, followed by the tight strings of a lute. The shawm and sackbut soon chased their lead, and groups of townsfolk quickly cleared a space to allow the brave dancers to showcase their skills.

Lucia watched in awe as the dancers whirled to the music, their movements fluid and effortless. She was anxious but intrigued. Before she could comment on the new attraction, however, Alaric pulled her close. "Care to dance with me?"

"Pardon me?" Lucia scoffed. She could never dance in front of such a large crowd.

Alaric smirked. "You heard me."

"I don't know. I have—ahh!"

Alaric pulled her in.

The music swelled around them as Alaric took Lucia's hands into his own. At first, she was hesitant, her steps stiff and awkward, tripping over his as they twirled and spun. It made Alaric laugh. She gave him a dirty look in exchange.

But quickly, the rhythm of the music took hold of her, and she let go.

Cheers of the people around them filled their ears. Her dress flowed fluently through the air, and her laughter made Alaric grin even bigger as they moved as one. Their hearts beat along with the feet-tapping and the strings. It was a moment of pure bliss.

Then, she was swept away.

Her new dance partner was a young woman in her twenties, but the queen did not seem to care. She danced with her, the two giggling uncontrollably, before she was passed to an elderly man. She only gripped his wrinkled hands, swaying gently to the left and to the right. He chortled as he matched her moves.

She was their queen, and she was dancing with them. She dreamed that the fun would never end.

As Lucia was tossed to switch partners, Alaric snatched her again. He rested a hand on her back, the other holding hers. She moved eloquently now, her eyes never leaving his as they gyrate with the dancing crowd.

The music sped up, and they were spinning.

Their breaths mingled with each other's. The thrill consumed them. Claps of hands joined in to boost as the song soon reached the climax.

And as the band hit the matching, final note, they wrapped around each other, panting as their foreheads touched. The king's eyes were filled with admiration, and she did the same.

Oh, how she was most vibrant now than ever before.

She glowed.

Effulgent.

And without hesitation, and rashly, Alaric tilted his head and kissed her.

His lips brushed against hers in a tender, passionate moment that sent shivers down her spine. The crowd erupted into applause, and the musicians politely bowed.

Lucia quickly melted into his arms despite her shock, returning the kiss with equal fervor. Her desire flared, and she did not want to let go. Only when they needed air did they pull apart.

Alaric leaned in close to her ear. She could feel the heat emanating from his body, his scent enveloping her in a way that made her feel dizzy. He whispered, "I have fallen for you."

But the queen could not respond. Could not think.

Her world was focused on his eyes, entranced by the depth of emotion she found there. His words, though softly spoken, held the weight of a thousand declarations. "My heart sings for your love—aches to uncover the angelic beauty hidden beneath your guarded soul. The simple pleasures, like your laughter and smile, shine brighter than the rising sun and the falling stars. I cannot force myself to think any other way," Alaric paused before the lingering question left his lips, "Lucia, will you have me?"

Lucia's hands, trembling not from fear but from unexplained exhilaration, rose to cup the king's face. She asked, "Have you?"

"To truly be my wife by spirit, not by testament," he clarified. The queen was dazed, and he quickly added. "It would shatter my being if you think otherwise, but I will not force you to be a part of this marriage any longer if you wish to be free."

Lucia chuffed, "This feels like you are asking me to marry you."

Hope glimmered in his eyes. "I am."

"Have you lost your head from the spinning we've done? We are already married."

Alaric struggled to hold in his laugh at her remark. This woman was going to be the death of him. "It was by your father's approval, but I want yours."

A man had never taken her thoughts, wants, and needs into consideration. No man dared to care, except him.

"Will you be my equal? I promise to cherish, to protect, to worship, both you and Charlotte."

He already had, and still is.

Her hands moved to bury around his neck, to pull him closer, to keep his eyes drinking only her. The crowd was invisible to them. From every possibility, from every thought, from any speck of chances, her past self would never have concluded this to be her and her daughter's life.

Without a doubt in her mind, she leaned in. "Yes," she said breathlessly, before she slowly, and carefully, kissed him.

22

Shift of Power

The next day, Lucia rose at the crack of dawn, eager to prepare delectable pastries for the townspeople. She enlisted the assistance of the servants, all of whom were more than happy to aid her in her project. The kitchen was soon filled with the divine aroma of freshly baked goods, which wafted through the open windows and tantalized the senses of anyone passing by.

Before setting out to deliver the pastries, the queen did her usual signature surprise blend of tea for the king. She quietly crept in and placed the kettle and cup on one of his bedside tables, chuckling at the sound of his gentle snores. He was nestled in his blankets.

Yesterday felt like a fever dream. A dream so sweet and unimaginable, like sugar melting from the heat of a palm. She could still feel his lips on her and those tender words that she longed so desired to hear.

A blush crept onto her face. She shook the thoughts away, then hunted down her ecstatic daughter.

The princess brimmed with furor as she climbed onto Devona, on her first-ever ride on a majestic animal. The two set off towards the town with the filled satchel bags attached to the saddle and strapped around the queen's back. It was another bright day.

The queen and princess greeted the people and distributed the pastries, receiving expressions of gratitude from all various ages. Some of the recipients even offered their own goods in exchange, such as intricately sewn rags, fragrant soaps sprinkled from the wildflowers outside, and even dried wild berries and strips of meat. Afterward, Charlotte reconnected with the children she had played with the previous day at the festival. She spent a delightful hour engaging in games and laughter, while Lucia watched from a short distance away, petting Devona.

Upon their return to the castle, Alaric greeted them with a beaming smile that seemed to stretch from ear to ear. Charlotte wrapped her arms around his legs in a warm embrace before darting off to playfully pester the servants. Lucia was curious about Alaric's uncharacteristically jovial demeanor and raised an eyebrow. "What has you grinning like a mischievous jester in the middle of the day?"

"I have something to show you."

"Is that so?"

"Yes," he said. The king's elation was perceptible as he listened to his servants' accounts of his queen and stepdaughter's actions, swelling him with undeniable pride. Yet, there was an additional element that contributed to his euphoria.

"Come, I will show you." Alaric softly placed his hand on Lucia's back, guiding her gracefully along the grand staircase and toward the bedchambers that she and Charlotte had come to call their sanctuary since their arrival at the castle. Right away, the queen noticed the wide-open door, with pieces of old furniture moved into the hallway. It was cluttered, and she was confused. "What must have happened?"

"Take a peek inside, my love."

Lucia gasped in astonishment as she stepped through the threshold and into the room. The chamber had been completely transformed.

A collection of soft, cuddly toys had been carefully arranged in one corner, while a new, more feminine bed frame with elegant curtains now occupied the center of the room. An artist was in the process of painting delicate wildflowers around the window frame, the sunlight casting a warm glow over the scene as he worked diligently with his rows of paints. A luxurious rug made of the finest wool lay on the floor. It would be pleasurable to step onto the soft fur rather than the cold stone when winter arrived.

In addition, the room boasted brand-new blankets and sheets, a small table and carved chair, and a thoughtfully organized bookshelf stocked with an assortment of Charlotte's favorite picture books. It was an ideal room for a little girl.

"Alaric, how did you manage to do all this?" Lucia asked.

"Charlotte is a growing girl, and I figured she would need her own space soon," Alaric replied as he leaned against the threshold. In the past weeks, he had orchestrated a small army of artisans, a plan to create when the right moment arrived to transform the room while Lucia and Charlotte were away for a short period. And it seemed that today was ideal.

As the queen continued to marvel at the makeover, she could not help but be amazed at the speed with which it had all been done. She knew that they had only been gone for a few hours, and yet the room now looked like something straight out of a fairy tale.

"And do not worry about your items. I had your personal belongings moved into my bedchambers," Alaric said as if these tasks had been simple.

Lucia turned to face him, her eyes wide with surprise. "Alaric, this is too much."

"No, it's not," Alaric disagreed, stepping closer to her. "Charlotte needs her own space, just as you need yours. And you don't have to move into my space right away. Take your time to adjust to the changes."

The queen looked around the room again, absorbing the details and the love that had been poured into every corner. "I mustn't," she objected.

"You mustn't what? Do you wish for your own bedchamber instead? I'll do as you please."

Lucia was at a loss for words. She had never shared a bedchamber with anyone other than her daughter, and the prospect of sharing such an intimate space with Alaric was terrifying. She did not know what to say or how to feel about the situation, and her silence spoke volumes.

Alaric, perceptive as ever, reached out and gently took her hands in his own. "Is this about your previous marriage?" he softly inquired.

Lucia bit her lip, and that was enough of an answer for Alaric.

"I may not know the details, but I am not an uneducated and clueless man. I have gathered that your previous marriage was a foul and cruel one to begin with." He raised a hand to leave a soft peck on her smooth skin. "I can promise you, Lucia, that you will be cared for and loved. Do not let these past demons hold you back from embracing new changes in your life, do you understand?"

The queen nodded, a flush painting her cheeks from his gesture. The king added, "Whenever you are ready, you will be welcomed. And if you wish for something else, I will make it happen."

"Well, I do love your rug."

"That old thing?" Alaric scoffed playfully. "A lady gifted it to me when the castle was being built. It had been passed down through her family for generations, and she wanted to give it to me as a symbol of the new era of fairness and equality that was dawning on this kingdom."

"That is incredibly generous of her."

Alaric chuckled.

That night, Lucia slept with her daughter, who was smitten with the newly renovated room. The young girl's eyes sparkled as she eagerly explored every nook and cranny of the spaces. This was undoubtedly the most extravagant and thoughtful gift the princess had ever received.

Alaric could not resist the urge to check in during the late hours, when the candles had burned to wet wax and the nightly creatures sang through the night. He wanted to ensure that the two were comfortable and content.

A quick peek at their sleeping faces was enough.

Michael wasted no time in preparations.

With the help of King Johnathan's entrusted Knight of the Body, Remus, he began assembling a group of men to accompany him on the expedition. A letter had been created and sent immediately after the distasteful political gathering. Father went to retire for the night, and when the morning sun rose, he had gotten too weak to sit up. He was told he had a few days to a week remaining left to live.

The ominous rattling sounds emanating from the royal bedchamber echoed into the gold-trimmed hallways. The physicians, in their relentless efforts, applied various remedies in an attempt to alleviate the king's suffering. However, the severity of his condition was undeniable, and the news of his potential demise was soon to spread like wildfire across the kingdom, infiltrating even the most remote corners and finding its way into the ears of foreigners.

King Johnathan was on his deathbed.

Michael's anticipation of reuniting with his twin sister was tinged with the grim understanding that the king might be no more upon his return to the castle. And with that possibility, the prince approached Father's bedchamber the night before his departure.

He treaded carefully, cautiously, as he stepped foot through the open double doors. Upon his entrance, the physicians turned their heads. They quickly and respectfully took their leave, closing the heavy doors behind them.

A few burning candles around the bed frame kept the darkness at bay. Basins filled with water and towels were cluttered around. It reeked of death.

The king's voice, weak and strained, rang throughout the room. "Who is there?"

"Me, Father."

"Michael," the king managed to pant out, his chest heaving with the effort. He looked pale and diminished, a mere shadow of his former self, dwarfed by the grandeur of his massive bed. Sweat drenched the luxurious grey covers beneath him. He was rapidly deteriorating.

As he reached out to take Father's hand, Michael could feel the cold, clammy skin. The room bore silent witness to the unfolding scene. "I entrust you to continue the Morningstar legacy."

"I will. I promise," Michael said. He watched as the king struggled to clear his throat, coughing painfully. The prince patiently waited, and by the time Father was done with the suffocating coughs, he reached for a towel from one of the basins, squeezed out the excess water, and wiped away the trickling blood from the king's cracked lips.

"Thank you, my son."

Michael dropped the towel back into its basin.

"Are you set to leave tomorrow?"

"Yes, Father. It will be a day's journey, but a letter should be in King Alaric's possession now."

"Good," Father rasped, seemingly satisfied with his son's response. "Take Remus with you. I do not need him here as I rot."

Michael nodded. "As you wish, Father."

As the prince did a slight tug, his goal to separate from the king and order the Knight of the Body, Father tightened his fingers. He did not want his son to leave. Not yet.

"Stay with me awhile. You are the only family I have left."

Michael did not argue, did not object, as he gingerly sat on the edge of the bed, listening intently to the labored breaths that escaped his father's lips. He dared not let go of his hand again until he was certain he was asleep.

Amongst Kingdom Shadowmere, Prince Victor ascended to his title as King Victor after a strategic move to marry the virgin girl that Prince Ironwood tried to offer to King Johnathan the day prior. A new marriage alliance bond that would intertwine the fates of the two ruling families.

News flooded the lands.

23

The Tree's Secret

Two muscular horses, their coats glistening with sweat, trotted in unison, flank to flank. Their riders, seeking solitude from the inquisitive ears of others, had ventured to the fringe of Baysor Grove. The woodland teemed with life, and they were a stone's throw away from the small, meandering river, its waters sourced from the distant, snow-capped mountains.

A letter had arrived at the castle just as dawn broke through the night clouds, delivered by one of his kingdom's knights tasked with the solemn duty of patrolling the borders. The missive had been passed to him by a messenger, the emblem of Morningstar—a radiant star shadowing smaller ones—proudly displayed on his clothing and the saddle of his steed.

It was in regard to Prince Morningstar's arrival, and Alaric immediately ordered his men to seek their approaching ally. The king had also notified Lucia, who was electrified that her twin brother would soon arrive. She explained that he had always been kind to her, and was the one who taught her how to read and write when others followed her Father's rule to forbid it.

However, at that very moment, Alaric's attention was not on the joyous reunion that was to come, but on the baron who rode beside him.

The baron, a man of noble lineage, had relinquished his luxurious residence from Kingdom Cinderhaven at the request of his king. It was in favor of the mounting unrest simmering in the territories, and a strategic move to bolster forces. In a letter expressing his gratitude to Kingdom Cinderhaven, Alaric had welcomed the baron, recognizing the valuable addition in numbers that the baron would bring to the population.

The baron was a tall, wiry man, his skin adorned with a multitude of moles, and his eyes a deep, dark brown. At first glance, he appeared to be just another man, indistinguishable from the masses. But his attire was an ostentatious display of his status, a riot of colors and fabrics that, while appropriate for his rank, made Alaric's stomach churn in silent protest.

Alaric could never comprehend the need for such extravagance in a man's attire. A flamboyant proclamation of status seemed unnecessary to him. Despite the king's distaste for the baron's sartorial choices, he couldn't deny the man's influence. The baron had the allegiance of a sizable group of men, who were content to follow him as long as he provided for their basic needs: food, shelter, and protection.

"All I require is land and some resources, and my men and I will pledge our loyalty," the baron stated.

"I can promise you land, but resources are scarce." That was not a lie. Alaric had been strict on usage to maintain kingdom stability, given its small size.

The baron was unfazed by this potential setback. He sighed. "That is all right. I can draft a proposal to my king, and I am confident that he will provide without consulting his court. He has been particularly preoccupied with the affairs of his third heir to care so little for minor conflicts."

"How is the queen?" Alaric asked.

"About the same as with the previous pregnancies. There's been a lot of screaming, midwives running, towels flying on the floors. But she delivered another healthy son."

"Another son?"

"Yes, she will be quite occupied with three boys now, but I always say, the more sons, the better for the kingdom."

Alaric's smile broadened. "That is splendid news. Please convey my congratulations to the king and queen."

"I will." The gelding the baron was mounted on grunted. The latter was in the midst of shedding its coat, a natural process, but rather a sign of the animal's lack of immediate hygiene. An hour of brushing was what the gelding needed.

In regard to marital status, the baron asked a daring question. "I have heard that you've managed to secure a tainted pure-bred royal bride for yourself. Given all the unaccounted for adultery that goes on behind closed doors with royalty, it is quite a delight to find and have a pure-bred. How did you manage that?"

Alaric shrugged nonchalantly. "Luck, I suppose. My name was cursed, so it was a challenge no matter what," he explained. He did not like the direction this conversation was heading.

"Have you forcefully impregnated her yet?"

"Pardon?" Taken aback by the question, Alaric instinctively pulled Emris to a halt, his expression a mixture of horror and disbelief. The baron's own horse, following its rider's cue, also stopped, its rider wearing an expression of confusion, as if unable to comprehend Alaric's reaction.

"Is something the matter?"

"You are asking if I... If I had forced myself on my wife?"

The baron sniggered, more annoyed with the fact that he had to explain himself. "It is more than just forcing yourself, Your Majesty. It is about building your family, strengthening your kingdom. You are the first king of Kingdom Hartfelt, for heaven's sake. You need plentiful heirs."

Alaric stared at the man, his fingers turning white from his tight hold on the reins. His nostrils flared. Hatred could not describe the seething, righteous fury that dared to pull him in a churning sea, wanting to drown him in its depths. He could incinerate the baron for these lousy words.

The baron, oblivious to Alaric's turmoil, shrugged and spurred his horse onward, and Emris followed suit. "You will understand someday that I am right. Heirs are born to serve you, to conquer land, to woo other kingdoms' brides, and so forth."

Alaric remained quiet.

"I am jealous of your wedded position, but oddly excited like a pathetic, poor child receiving stale bread. I cannot wait to get my own bride. I need a beautiful virgin to bear my seed and pamper me. She shall be flawless."

The king was still reeling from the baron's earlier words, his ears seemingly ringing. The baron pressed on: "Do you think the girl who came with your bride could be a potential match when she comes of age? It would certainly strengthen the bond between our two kingdoms if she were to become my bride."

"She's four years old!" It was getting harder and harder for him to control his temper. It was abhorrent to have a thought of child marriage being acceptable.

"Good, she is young. It is never too early to start her training to become a suitable bride," the baron said, unperturbed by the king's outburst.

Alaric's jaw clenched tightly. His mind was a whirlwind, his anger now a living, breathing entity within him.

A beast, a wild, untamed creature, ready to pounce.

He was finding it increasingly difficult to hold it back.

After several quiet minutes, with only the sound of their horses' steps between them, the baron took notice. "Your Majesty?"

The king's strained voice managed to respond. "Hmm?"

"You went silent, like your tongue fell off."

"Oh. Please, forgive me. My mind is elsewhere."

The baron, ever the diplomat, smiled. "It is no trouble, Your Majesty. I have been doing all the talking, after all. I get too excited discussing about young, ignorant women, it is humiliating!"

Alaric had snapped.

And the laughing fool had no weapon.

Without warning, the king leaned forward and shot out his hand to grasp the baron by the back of his ostentatious collar. He used his brute strength to yank the man off his horse, the momentum causing them both to tumble, colliding onto the grass. The baron's horse, startled by the sudden violence, squealed in fear, its hooves skidding on the soft Earth as it backed away from the fallen men.

Alaric wasted no time climbing on top of the baron in an instant, the man's face a mask of fright as he struggled to breathe, the wind knocked out of him. Terror was in his eyes. Murder was in Alaric's.

But the king did not care.

He was beyond reasoning, beyond diplomacy.

The desperate baron clawed at anything he could reach—his clothing, his arms, his hair—anything to try and free himself from the king's grasp. In a sudden burst of adrenaline, he managed to land a kick to Alaric's stomach, causing him to grunt in pain.

But that was not enough. They were locked in a deadly struggle as they rolled down a muddy incline towards the river. Their clothes were now caked with layers of wet dirt.

"What are you doing!?" the baron gaped. His face was dirtied, his vision blurry.

Alaric spat, "To make sure you never retake a breath again!"

"No—!"

Alaric threw a few punches directly on the baron's face, weakening his struggles enough to yank him towards the riverbank on his knees. The baron was nearly limp, the pain becoming too unbearable on his face to sustain until he felt the icy water consume him. Then, his strength from pure instinct and adrenaline returned.

The baron's hands flailed, desperately trying to push himself off the muddy ground and loosen Alaric's iron grip. But his attempts were in vain, the water churning and frothing as he struggled for air, not water, to fill his lungs. The king kept his hold on the back of the man's head. His face was a snarl of determination, fingers aching with the effort.

Nothing could stop his motive. He was beyond caring, beyond remorse.

No one was going to disrespect *his family*, not ever again. Valentino had been the first, but he would not be the last to feel Alaric's wrath.

The baron's struggles slowly ceased, his body still underneath Alaric's hand. Only then did he let go, staring down at the murder he had just committed, his feelings a strange mix of relief and indifference. He was more concerned about the state of his soiled clothing and bruised knuckles than the lifeless body on the riverbank.

He looked up at the sky.

It was cloudless, beautiful, without a known notice of the life taken beneath the blanket of blue. Pity was nowhere near on his mind. He may go to Hell for all the death he had left behind, year after year of it, but it was for a purpose. He would not waste the energy to convince himself otherwise.

So, with a deep inhale that expanded his bronchioles, Alaric rose to his feet and stumbled into the water to wash off the mud.

Alaric had dried by the time he returned to the castle, with the baron's horse held by the reins following his stallion. The sun had vanished, leaving behind a trail of gold that would, too, fade in a matter of time. The stars were beginning to emerge from the field of darkness.

Nadia strode up to him, immediately sensing that something was amiss. The baron's neatly folded clothing sat atop his horse's saddle. An unexplainable scent of smoke clung to the king. He had been gone much longer than expected, a fact that did not escape the knight's notice.

"I will write a letter to Kingdom Cinderhaven regarding his acceptance here on my lands and the need for additional resources he will require to settle," Alaric stated, his voice weary but resolute as he grabbed the folded clothing and dismounted from Emris. Several stable boys quickly took the reins of both stallions and led them to the barn. The new gelding would suit well for a knight.

Nadia whispered, "Where is he?"

"Dead." Alaric placed the clothing into her hands. He wanted to burn the ugly fabrics, but it would be futile if Alaric needed evidence of the baron's arrival.

"The body?"

"If I am challenged before the arrival of his people, then I will explain in writing that the baron's body was burned to prevent the spread of disease. I will have a physician support my claim," Alaric said softly, not wanting to please uninvited listeners. He began his walk towards the castle doors. Nadia followed, not pressing for specific details regarding the actual death of the baron. He had his reasons, and she would stand by him regardless. "And when his people arrive and his king is not suspicious beforehand, I will personally explain the unforeseen circumstances: falling ill and passing while awaiting their presence. That is when you present the new baron."

"You entrust me with this responsibility, Your Majesty?" Nadia questioned, surprised by the honor he had just given her.

Alaric, his hand on the intricate carvings of the castle door handles, paused. "Yes, I want you to promote one of your most faithful senior knights for the position of baron. He or she will be granted land in the north. I trust your judgment."

This, she could do. She would not disappoint.

Alaric entered through the threshold, and immediately, Lucia rushed up to greet him. She began to help him remove his outerwear, the scent of smoke clinging to the fabric. She smelled it right away. "Did you start a campfire? You smell like ash," she said, her voice light as she teased him. A small, radiant smile was on her lips.

Seeing her smile was a gift he would only ask from her.

He watched her every movement, studying until the evil ideas consumed and taunted his mind from the baron's sour tongue. How could any man, especially one in a position of power, even entertain such a vile act? How could one do such things?

It was all about *power*.

Power to take from someone.

Power to control: physically and emotionally.

A game to feel enriched.

His demon-enraged thoughts were interrupted by Lucia's sweet, melodic voice. Her voice could break any spell he was in. "I made a meal for the first time in a while. Let me know when you are ready and I will warm it up by the hearth."

Alaric took in a deep inhale and slowly exhaled to control himself. He shook his head. "No, allow the servants to do that."

"The servants?"

He reached out and took the clothing from Lucia's hands, placing it neatly on a nearby chair before he pulled her close by her waist. She was touching him. He was touching her. It fueled her greed for him.

"Let us go eat together, my love," Alaric suggested, softly into Lucia's ear. She did not object as he led her to the dining hall. Charlotte later joined them, and the three of them ate their evening meal together.

His family. Together.

"Cain, what do you want?" Prince Alexander groaned. He leaned his head on his hand, propping his elbow on the wooden table that separated him from King Victor. The king casually nibbled on a small, sun-dried morsel of beef. To the right of him, his newlywed bride sat quietly, not daring to move a muscle, her posture rigid.

They were gathered in Alexander's private study. Books were strewn about chaotically—on the table, on the floor, and even outside the room, by the door, creating a labyrinth of knowledge that only Alexander could navigate. It was a mess, a beautiful, chaotic mess that the prince cherished and refused to let his servants touch.

"A legion of Morningstar men have been sighted traveling towards the borders of Kingdom Hartfelt," Cain announced. The warm glow of the candles highlighted his features, the wax pooling around them like lava.

"And?" Victor retorted nonchalantly, his broad shoulders shrugging carelessly. He couldn not care less about the potential implications this could have.

"Are you certain?"

"I am not blind," Cain hissed, his patience wearing thin. He was not in the mood for useless banter.

Alexander ran a hand through his hair in frustration. "Do you comprehend the gravity of this situation?" he asked, directing his question towards Victor. He shrugged again. "It means that our covert attempt to gain an ally has failed. We have not only failed to secure an alliance, but have also alerted Kingdom Morningstar."

"Who could have predicted this?" Victor mused.

"You are insufferable," Cain said. There were times when he wished he could take the king's face and smash it into the castle's cold, unforgiving stone walls.

Alexander thought long and hard as he considered their options. Victor was not helpful in the situation and continued to chew loudly. His bride was still as frozen as a statue.

After what felt like an eternity, Alexander shook his head, his hands slamming onto the table in a gesture of defeat. "Our only course of action now is to avoid further antagonizing Kingdom Morningstar. Since we cannot have them as allies, we must tread a fine line of neutrality. King Johnathan's power is too formidable for us to challenge."

"I wish we still had a spy."

"As do I," Alexander sighed, his eyes feeling heavy with the weight of their predicament. "But what's done is done. We must deal with the consequences of our actions and move forward."

24

The Rise of the Star

L ucia admired the rug, her mind drifting back to the day she had first arrived. She remembered how beautiful it had been, and still is, the vibrant tapestry of colors and patterns. It had caught her eye and become a symbol of the new life that awaited her—a life she was eager to embrace now. A life she had not known would be so kind to her.

Then, she fell asleep.

A midday nap, in Alaric's bedchamber, *their* bedchamber. Her clothes from her previously shared bedchamber had been carefully folded and placed next to his, and her books added to his collection.

Witnessing her nap made Alaric swell. It meant she felt safe enough to adapt to his space.

Their space.

Alaric leaned forward, his fingers gently brushing a stray lock of hair from her face. He marveled at her alluring beauty, even in her sleep. He had brought her a gift, a collection of new novels he hoped she would enjoy. But for now, sleep was the priority, and he placed the novels on the bedside table for her to discover when she awoke.

With a tender kiss to her forehead, Alaric quietly left the room.

His feet rhythmically tapped against the steps as he descended to his study room. The task that awaited him was far from appealing, and the thought of tackling it alone filled him with dread.

Lucia had become more present around him, wanting to be within his proximity. What had initially started as leisurely afternoons spent together in the solar room, indulging in shared reading sessions with their novels from the library, had slowly evolved into something more. Now, it was not uncommon for them to work side by side in his study, their minds and ideas intertwining as they tackled the responsibilities of ruling a kingdom.

She was quick-witted and longed to learn, and her new interest in political matters was a refreshing change. When she read the new compensation agreement for Prince Alexander, she was astonished to learn that he had refused even to acknowledge it. The proposition would have brought mutual peace, but it was now too late.

The rising tension between their kingdoms was a great cause for concern.

After enduring lengthy, taxing hours of business, when the queen needed a moment of mental rest, she would collapse onto his lap and lay her head against his chest. The dark aroma and the beating of his heart calmed her frayed nerves. If she were lucky, he would occasionally glide through her hair. It was a simple pleasure she came to enjoy and a challenge not to succumb to sleep.

To Alaric, he felt like the most blessed and spoiled man across the lands.

And at other times, Charlotte would barge in with boredom, which was a better excuse to leave the study room. A session of play was more appealing than layers of drudgery.

Prince Michael arrived.

The news traveled quickly as the band of Morningstar men marched to the castle grounds in their resplendent armor, escorted by Hartfelt's knights. It stirred the townsfolk as they watched.

Now, a hive of activity, the servants scurried to and fro to provide water, food, and other necessities to aid them from their arrival. The stable boys, their faces smeared with sweat and grime, led the weary horses away to the stables, the animals' hooves stomping on the soft grass. Rose barked orders, while Charlotte played with her wrinkled hands as she watched the swarm of newcomers. She was fascinated by the sight of so many unfamiliar faces at once.

Alaric greeted the newcomers with a nod of his head, his keen eyes taking in the procession of knights as they passed by. Each man, clad in gleaming armor and bearing the crest of the Morningstar family, offered a slight bow in return. As the crowd parted, the king's gaze fell upon Prince Michael, who was easily identifiable due to his striking resemblance to his wife. The only thing changed were his cut hair.

With a graceful leap, Michael dismounted from his majestic steed. "Greetings, King Alaric," he said as he offered a courteous bow. His attire was immaculate, and the rich fabric of his tunic, along with the carefully brushed strands of his hair, gave the impression that he had just stepped out of a royal portrait. It did not look like he had spent a day outside.

"It is a pleasure to have your presence. I hope your travels went smoothly," Alaric said.

"It was uneventful, so I say it went as planned."

Another figure detached himself from the group and approached, tall and muscular, with a series of faint scars tracing a map of past battles across his tawny skin. His black hair was pulled back into a messy ponytail. As he drew closer, Alaric could not help but feel a frisson of apprehension at the man's imposing presence.

"This is my father's Knight of the Body, Remus," Michael introduced, gesturing towards the figure at his side. Remus drew his sword and embedded the blade into the soft, flowery Earth; the petals of the flowers crushed beneath the knight's weight as he dropped to one knee, head bowed. This was the first time Alaric had been acknowledged honorably by a knight, a status similar to his past. His heart was touched.

"A pleasure to meet you, too, Remus. My Knight of the Body, Nadia, is on a patrol at the southern border. You will meet her soon."

"I remember her. Small woman with dark brown hair?" Michael asked.

Before the king agreed, a squeal of the prince's name erupted into the air. The princess had caught sight of her uncle.

Charlotte sprinted, her skirts billowing around her as she threw herself into Michael's arms. He broke out into a warm smile as he knelt to hug his niece, his strong hands gently patting her back as he whispered sweet words into her ear. She giggled in return.

Remus rose to his feet and tousled Charlotte's hair playfully, his fingers grazing her delicate locks. He had a special place in his heart for the girl.

He had been present at Lucia's birth, not long after he had been appointed to his position. He was a young, violent man back then, but he had watched her mother grow and eventually marry, only to return to her father's castle with a child of her own. Now, it was his turn to watch over the little princess. To watch her grow.

As the group entered the castle's doors, Lucia raced down the grand staircase with her dress skirts held high. She was already aware of their arrival, roused from her nap by Alaric when he was notified by his servants. She could hardly contain her excitement as she leaped out of bed, hastily shooed the king out of the bedchamber, and donned a rich, velvety gold dress. The fabric caught the light and gave it a luxurious sheen.

"Michael!" She outstretched her arms and threw herself into her brother's hold. Her enthusiasm took him aback, and his eyes were wide with surprise at the transformation of the woman he had last seen months ago. She had been mute and shy and had offered only a bow in greeting upon his arrivals. Now, she was a whirlwind of energy. What must have happened?

"Lucia?"

The queen pulled away, clueless to her brother's questioning thoughts. "It is so good to see you."

"You as well," he replied. "Though, I must say, you appear different." He studied her carefully, his eyes taking in the changes in her appearance and demeanor. "You seem...happier."

"That is only because you have not seen me in a while. And you should examine yourself at a mirror," Lucia protested. The short hair looked good on him.

"No, I don't think so."

Alaric tried not to laugh as he watched, an arm on Charlotte's back, keeping her from being restless.

Then, Lucia turned her attention to Remus, who stood a foot away. She was not at all intimidated by his scarred appearance and greeted him as if they were old friends. "Greetings, Remus. How have you been?"

"Lucia," Remus acknowledged, his voice gruff but not unfriendly. "And as well as I can be."

"That makes me very pleased to hear," Lucia replied, her smile still in place. She turned back to Michael and Alaric, her blue eyes shining. "I must not hold your time. I will be in the solar room, so please, come find me afterward, Michael. I wish to talk to you more."

This was the most Lucia had ever said in an open space filled with men, especially noble men. Michael did not know what to say, but Alaric chimed in. "No, come with us. I want you to be part of this as well."

"I can establish a road here, following along the slope to give coverage from the open plains," Michael stated confidently as his finger drew an invisible line on the ink-drawn map that lay spread out on the polished wooden desk. Alaric took in every detail, standing beside the prince as he considered the proposed route. Lucia sat in the king's plush, cushioned chair, listening to the two men discuss the plans for the new road.

The three of them were in the study room, as Remus and Nadia stood on either side of the colorful glass pane doors outside, their faces impassive as they carried out their duties as guards. They were not supposed to glance at each other, but it was becoming rather difficult to maintain their serious demeanor when faced with the antics of the young blonde princess. Charlotte was relentless in her array of useless questions, and it was clear that the two would soon give in to her innocent charm.

"I will have it constructed and completed in a few weeks by my men, so we will be able to supply you with the necessities you need." Michael reached for a feather that rested on the desk and dipped it into the inkwell. He drew a few figures along the planned pathway. "And to avoid crime, designated outposts will also be established alongside the road. The knights would rotate once a week in rounds."

"Why?"

Michael scoffed. "Do you wish for rogue people to steal supplies? You cannot be that naive."

"No, why go all this way?" Alaric clarified. "Your letter only mentioned strengthening our bonded support. I assumed it was only a private visit to discuss domestic topics, not various continental construction plans, trade disclosures, and an unlimited supply of men. So, I must ask for details: Why?"

Michael straightened his back, his face suddenly hardening. "Kingdom Shadowmere and Ironwood are plotting against your realm," he revealed, his voice low. "The two came to King Johnathan requesting assistance and his support without disclosing any plans in their drafts, other than revenge for the fallen Ironwood king."

The atmosphere in the room suddenly shifted.

The construction of the road, the establishment of the outposts, the rotation of the knights—it all made sense now. This was not just a visit from a friendly ally but a preemptive defensive measure against a potential threat.

Lucia's body tensed, and her face paled.

Michael added, "And the prince of Shadowmere married one of Ironwood's brides. They are now in an official allegiance to one another."

Alaric sighed loudly. "I offered propositions for peace," he said, his voice rising in frustration as he held out his arms. "I tried to negotiate with them to avoid conflict and bloodshed."

"I am afraid that does not matter anymore. These royals worried our father, so he sent me in his place due to his inability to travel in his weakened state."

"Weak?" The questionable word came across softly. Alaric turned to his wife.

"He is sick with a cough that rattles his body. He is now on his deathbed. Once I return home, I might be crowned."

A wave of dizziness washed over the queen. She wished she had made some tea before they started, something to help her keep her grounded in the face of such shocking news. She leaned her elbow on the armchair, her head resting in her palm as she tried to steady herself. Alaric reached out and rubbed her back in a soothing gesture.

"Lucia, I am sorry," Michael whispered. Although she was never close to Father, he still gave her life. The world was changing, shifts of power were being created, and there was nothing that could be done to stop it. "But war is truly brewing, and I am here to help in every way possible. And, I suggest reaching out to other former allies on this matter."

Alaric did not respond immediately; his eyes clouded with thoughts as he considered the prince's words. After a moment of silence, he nodded, his expression grave. "I have much appreciation for

Kingdom Morningstar, even though I...disagreed with some of the methods."

"I understand. King Johnathan rules with a heavy hand, and I am expected to do the same by him."

"Do you plan to?" asked Lucia. Her voice was still so soft, so small.

Michael shook his head. He had always promised himself to be a different ruler. A ruler who had what Father had lacked—to be softer to the people who ran the castle, to be more present in his future heirs' lives, to be more forgiving. He also wanted to be more involved with his sibling since he had been forbidden to do so throughout childhood.

Alaric queried, "What do you anticipate our foes' initial move will be?"

"Does it really matter?" Lucia countered with indifference. She proceeded to rest her head on her hands, which were now propped up on her knees. "If there is a potential threat, our primary focus should be safeguarding our people, irrespective of their first strategy."

Michael gaped at his sister's response. She had indeed changed, and Alaric seemed to have played a part in this.

"So, what course of action do you propose?" Alaric asked, seeking her opinion.

"I suggest we establish a patrol route around the town for the security of our people," Lucia elaborated. "Although this would require more men, I am not inclined to compel participation from our people if they are unwilling to contribute. It is not their fault that we are in this predicament."

"Indeed," the king affirmed. "We must exhaust all measures to ensure the safety of our people."

Michael vowed. "Consider that done too, as I will send in men for that purpose. Allow your advisor to give mine an estimate of the men needed. I suppose more housing can be built, too, to house them."

"I do not have an advisor anymore."

"Why so?"

"He had committed an unspeakable crime, and I have been handling all of this on my own with Lucia by my side. I would be behind on matters without her," Alaric said.

"Would you like me to procure a suitable candidate for the required role? I assure you, I can provide the most competent man."

Alaric replied, "If a woman, I will still accept her."

Michael blinked, but then he grinned, shaking his head in amusement. "The rumors do not lie about your unconventional beliefs. I witnessed it firsthand when I encountered your Knight of the Body several months ago, but that only scratched the surface."

"And I am not ashamed of it."

"I value a man who stays true to his beliefs. It is no surprise that you rose to power swiftly," said Michael.

"People appreciate being treated fairly," Alaric stated coolly.

Fairness fosters contentment among the populace.

More discussion was underway, but a break was needed. The weight of it all was taking its toll.

The siblings settled in the solar room, across from each other, with a freshly brewed tea kettle awaiting in the center of the small table, the steam curling upwards the wood beams and stone. It was something Michael had missed during his sister's absence. No tea could compare to anyone else's in the castle they grew up in.

The sun breaching through the windows warmed their skin as Charlotte played nearby with her wooden toys. Remus was stationed right outside the threshold, eyes alert. Nadia stayed with Alaric.

"You have become a different person," Michael said, his eyes studying his sister carefully.

Lucia took a sip of her tea, savoring the taste, before replying, "What do you mean?"

"You have become more lively, more joyful, more confident. And you speak in everyone's presence with no fear in your tone of voice."

"Alaric wanted my voice to be heard, and he said he enjoyed it when I spoke to him instead of my quiet gestures."

"It gave you freedom," Michael concluded.

Freedom?

A word she had not considered. *Freedom.*

How did she fail to realize this until now?

Freedom to choose. Freedom to speak. Freedom to teach. Freedom to learn. Freedom to explore. And freedom to love.

She chose to love Alaric Hartfelt, and he allowed her to have that choice since the day of their joined union.

Oh, how this made her want to chase him down and kiss him.

"You are dazed." Michael chuckled. He then took a sip from his teacup.

She blinked, not recalling how long she had been lost in thought, but the slight embarrassment on her face betrayed her. "My apologies."

He waved his hand dismissively. "No need to apologize. Though I have to ask, is bride training planned for Charlotte? She is about the age you started, isn't she?"

"Alaric never mentioned the subject and never expressed interest in such strict royal customs. He stated that he found my actions, learned specifically from my bride training, displeasing, and I assume he would never force Charlotte to endure the same."

"Is that so?" Michael questioned, leaning forward with his elbows on the table. He was intrigued more by Alaric's odd ways.

Lucia nodded. "I find myself very appreciative of his disinterest in such things. It makes me less worried about Charlotte's future. I don't know how I would react if I saw her forced to do such horrid things by a bride tutor." She glanced at her daughter, who was still engrossed in her imaginative play. The thought of reliving her own traumatic experiences through her daughter was unbearable. To be taught to be a silent slave to please men.

"Well, that makes me pleased to hear," Michael said, a small smile tugging on his lips. "As long as you and Charlotte are treated well and happy, that makes me less anxious of the distance between each other."

Lucia looked down at her teacup shyly. "Yes, and Charlotte and I feel blessed every day."

The smile on her brother's lips slowly faded away, replaced by a glum frown. It unsettled Lucia. "What is it?"

"Father wanted to apologize to you," Michael revealed, "but it's not for me to give."

Lucia gasped. "Apologize?"

She was in disbelief.

"For his neglect of you."

She could not believe it. A prideful tyrant, known for his powerful and cruel tactics, wanted to apologize to the daughter he barely acknowledged? Was this a desperate attempt to make amends before his possible, inevitable demise?

"I can see it in your eyes that you don't believe a word of it."

She grimaced in emotional pain. "How could I?" she said, her voice cracking. "You were his proud trophy, the golden heir. I was nothing more than a speck of dust to him."

Michael's eyes clouded. "You've heard that?"

"I was destined to be *hanged*. No father would hang his daughter if he truly loved her," Lucia said, trying so hard not to spill her tears. She may be troubled by his sickness, since he had given her life, but he was never a father to her.

"I am sorry. If I had known earlier about his punishment, I would have advocated for you more urgently."

Lucia looked at him reassuringly, her eyes softening with gratitude despite the complex array of emotions she was experiencing. "You already had, and I could not thank you enough for trying."

Michael remained somber, his thoughts a tangled web of past experiences and the unexpected revelation of their father's guilt. He could not form an opinion on the matter, as it was not for him to hold judgment on the relationship between Father and Lucia.

"How much longer do you believe Father has? Do you think he will recover?"

Michael sighed. "He was bedridden when I left. If he does pass, I imagine it will happen within a week. But I do not believe he can overcome this."

"You think so?"

"I know so."

Lucia accepted her brother's words.

Unknowingly to them, King Johnathan had passed hours after Michael's departure. The news was concealed for the unreined kingdom's safety, the fallen king rotting in his bedchambers, awaiting for the prince's return.

25

Onyx Falls

Preparations for the decided actions were put into motion.

Nadia bestowed the prestigious title of baron upon one of her most loyal and seasoned knights, Rayne, who had been an unwavering pillar of support since the beginning of Kingdom Hartfelt. Rayne was honored, and he awaited for the throng from Kingdom Cinderhaven to make their arrival.

A motley crew of men, interspersed with women and children. Some were skeptical, but with the persuasive eloquence from King Alaric and the uncompromising decorum from Nadia and Rayne, they assuaged the people's doubts. Consequently, the ranks of supporters swelled significantly.

With the prince's promised assistance, a new advisor was ushered into the fold for Alaric's burgeoning kingdom. The individual, Baelyn, was the youngest son of a duke hailing from Kingdom Morningstar. Despite his tender years and a physique that was far from imposing, puny and scrawny to be exact, and with a crown of unruly, curly russet hair atop his head, Baelyn proved to be a prodigious intellect.

His youthful visage belied the insatiable curiosity and a razor-sharp mind, already diving into the study of Hartfelt's politics and penning letters to allies in a bid to rally support. Lucia's additional assistance expedited the process and eased the burden on the young advisor.

The queen rose from the floor of the study room, her lithe form unfurling with a feline grace. Baelyn, however, ignored her, his attention engrossed by the mountain of documents that lay before him, spread out and divided by purpose. Even his cramping knees would not stop his work.

Alaric paced around the desk, his hands full of papers. He glanced at his wife. "Tired?"

She nodded. "Let's take a ride. If I stay in this room any longer, I will throw a childish tantrum."

Alaric gave her a lazy smile, his eyes crinkling with mirth. "I suppose a break would be nice."

"Indeed," Lucia affirmed, her own eyes sparkling with mischief. "Do you have any thoughts on where we could indulge in a race?"

"A race?"

"I need a thrill since I am bored out of my mind right now," Lucia said with a wink.

"Oh, my lovely lady is—"

"Pardon my rudeness," Baelyn hissed as he whipped his head with a glare, trying hard to keep his tone in check, "but go be coquettish elsewhere, Your Majesties. I have work to finish and I do not need a distraction."

Alaric chuckled, which made the advisor scuff before returning to his documents.

The Onyx Falls owed its name to the dark, almost black stones that had been shaped and smoothed over centuries by the relentless flow of water, nestled in a secluded area far from the hustle of civilization, and surrounded by a forest of towering pine trees. The water cascaded into a pond, its surface dotted with cattail weeds, and the banks occupied by soft, verdant grass. Dragonflies danced through the air.

The king and queen raced to the stunning waterfall on their horses. The animals galloped as fast as they possibly could, and Lucia laughed as her hands gripped hard on the reins, leaning forward for momentum. The wind whipping through her hair felt phenomenal, as the blonde strands had grown slightly past her shoulders. In just a month's time, she would be able to create those beautiful braids she had missed, with flowers pecked in.

As the couple nudged their horses closer to the serene shores of the pond, the thunderous roar of the waterfall filled their senses.

It was breathtaking.

"I stumbled upon this place by chance when Nadia and I were establishing ourselves with our people. It was a sanctuary I did not realize I needed as I grappled with the reality and new responsibilities of being a leader. I had never been accountable for so many lives before."

Lucia was still at a loss for words, her eyes drinking in every detail of the scene before her. This was the first time she had seen a remarkable sight from nature, and she had to bring Charlotte here next time.

The sun was at its peak, the summer heat baking down on them. Although they had only been still for a handful of moments, it was enough time for the king to feel the sweat forming on his skin. The breeze from the race kept them cooler than he expected. He turned to his awestruck wife. "Do you wish to return?"

"No, this is gorgeous!"

"But it is getting hot."

"Are you afraid of the water? We can cool off here," Lucia teased as she dismounted Devona. She secured the mare to a nearby tree branch.

Alaric did the same with Emris. "From the number of baths you have seen me take, do you honestly believe that I possibly could be afraid of water?"

"You never can be too sure," she replied as she walked to the water's edge.

To the king's surprise, Lucia began to undress, her nimble fingers deftly untying the simple dress she wore and slipping it off with ease. She then grabbed onto her undergarments and pulled. Even though Alaric had seen her bare before, her body was still a sight to behold. She always took his breath away.

"Join me!" Lucia called out, her laughter ringing across the water as she stepped into the pond. Alaric struggled to maintain his composure in the face of his growing arousal, shedding his own clothing and carefully laying it beside Lucia's before wading into the water after her. The cool water, a welcome respite from the sun's relentless heat, sent a shiver down his spine as he immersed himself in its refreshing embrace.

The queen was fully submerged to her neck, the water lapping gently at her skin. She watched Alaric with an infectious smile, and without warning, she playfully splashed him. He flinched. "How could you?"

He did not wait for an answer from her before he retaliated with a splash of his own, this one larger and more impactful. Lucia shrieked, her hair now soaked by the cold water. She cursed, "You sheep-biting scut!"

Alaric roared with laughter. He splashed her again for the playful insult, the two now engaged in a water fight. The fish in the pond swam hastily away from the commotion, and the birds in the trees above sang their sweet melodies, oblivious to the antics below.

By the time the two were tired and panting hard, Lucia clung to Alaric. Her eyes were full of affection when she looked up at him. It pierced the king's heart.

There was only him and her. Alone together in the water.

Her eyes trailed to his chest, to the jagged scar that marred his skin. She had been curious about it before, particularly when she bathed him for the first time shortly after moving into his domain, but she was submissive and acquiescent. It was not her place to ask. Now, however, she felt as if she could conquer the world by his side.

"How did you get this scar?" she asked, her fingers gently tracing the raised line of the injury, causing Alaric to shudder.

"I got it on the day I murdered the Ironwood king," he admitted. "I fought like a rabid dog when his men tried to capture me and bring me to his mercy at his throne. This was the result of the fight." He watched her intently as she kept touching his scar, trying not to stare at her small breasts, which were barely submerged in the water.

Oh, how badly he wanted to touch them.

Hold them.

Fondle them.

The temptation was overbearing.

But he barely managed to restrain himself. He had gone so long without a touch from a woman, and though he had been with many women in his past, none of them had ever made him feel the way Lucia did.

She was his wife. He could forever treasure her without the need to touch her. All Lucia had to do was give him the command.

Lucia asked, "Did it hurt?"

"Very much so. But the rage that consumed me was so all-encompassing that I did not feel the pain until I had fled. I might as well have bled to death if it were not for a man in the group who stitched my skin."

Lucia studied the scar more closely, retracing its outline. Her fingertips were so soft on his skin. And without giving him caution, she leaned in and pressed her lips against the healed injury. "I am sorry this happened to you," she whispered.

Alaric was falling in love all over again. He did not deserve this woman.

"You are a very brave man. To face the odds, to challenge a king, and to come out alive, stronger than ever. You have built a safe place for people who believed in you, as you believed in them. You are a remarkable king."

He really did not deserve this precious woman.

Alaric leaned in, his lips brushing against the side of Lucia's cheek in a tender, affectionate kiss. He whispered into her ear, his breath warm and ticklish. "And to be shunned by the outsiders and other kingdoms of these lands, I somehow landed a shining woman that my heart cannot stop beating for."

He wanted to love her more.

To make her feel cherished.

To be desired.

But it all depended on her.

"Your heart stops beating once you die," Lucia said, nearly breathless.

"Yes, you are correct, but I hope it never stops so I can admire you for as long as I can." Alaric leaned in once more, his lips gently caressing the delicate skin of her neck. He watched her closely, gauging her reactions. He did not want to make her uncomfortable with his advances. Yet to his surprise, Lucia seemed to melt into him.

"I am burning up," she whimpered, her voice barely audible as he continued to shower her with love. Another kiss on her neck, right below her earlobe. Uncharted territory, lips on her skin. Her core was hot; she could not breathe.

New feelings, new desires.

Alaric pulled away, his arms wrapped around her waist beneath the water. "Do you wish for me to stop?"

Lucia shook her head, her eyes locked on his. "No, I feel all right."

"Good." His lips brushed against her jawline, cheek, and nose before finally finding her lips. This woman, who had stolen his heart and made him feel things he had never thought were possible, was now willingly exploring this new level of intimacy.

As their lips grew more passionate, Alaric moved one hand behind Lucia's head, burying it in her hair as he deepened. The scent of her, fresh, floral, intoxicating, enveloped him. It was clear that she was enjoying this as much as he was, and the knowledge that she trusted him to let him take the lead was reassuring.

When they finally broke apart for air, Alaric took the opportunity to trail his lips to her collarbone. Her skin was hot to the touch, and he could feel her lust for more. "Alaric…".

"Have I gone too far, my love?"

"No. Is it bad that I crave more of this?"

Alaric's chest swelled with gratification. "Never." He cupped her face. "Allow me to worship you, to deliver your soul to the Gates of Heaven."

Lucia's voice was so small as she answered. "What have I gotten myself into?"

His low chuckle rumbled in his throat. "May I? May I uphold my word and worship my woman?"

A whisper of air. "Yes."

Alaric began to explore her body, his hands moving with reverence and awe as he touched her neck, shoulders, and gently caressed her breasts. He marveled at the feel of her, the way her small breasts fit perfectly in his hands, and the way her nipples hardened beneath his touch. Lucia gasped.

Each touch, each grab.

Hands continued to roam, touching her backside, thighs, and abdomen. Lucia was lost in the sensation of it all, holding onto him with dear life. She felt as if she were dreaming, and before she knew it, she was picked up and laid on the soft grass of the bank, with Alaric hovering over her. Although he was aroused, his attention stayed focused on her.

Alaric braced himself on his forearms, water droplets dripping on her, as he continued to explore. He touched and savored the stretch marks that spoke of her motherhood, from her abdomen to her thighs. He devoured the pretty view of the soft fuzz on her pubic mons, and the way her chest rose and fell with each breath.

He anchored one arm beneath her head, providing a soft cushion as his other hand slid down her abdomen and between her thighs, stopping just short of delving deeper. His breath was hot against her ear as he asked, "Allow me?"

He was a hungry man.

Ready to devour.

But he needed permission.

Her breathless *yes* escaped her lips, her eyes dazed. She was truly in Heaven, as her husband had promised.

He slightly parted her thighs before callous fingertips grazed into her sex, touching her labia before finding her already swollen clitoris. Just the slight pressure of his touch made her hips jerk. The hum of pleasure she released brought satisfaction to the king's ears. He did not want the new sounds to stop.

No man had made her feel this way, made her feel so good. She did not know she could feel this good.

She barely heard Alaric's chuckle as he watched her, refusing to stop as he stimulated with his hand, slickness coating his digits and palm. He adored how much her body responded to his touch, the sweet noises that escaped from her lips, the tight grip she had on one of his biceps. The soft dirt was messily shuffled around them.

"You are doing so well," Alaric praised. He left trails of kisses on her neck as he sped up his movements. He wanted to sink his fingers inside her, to feel and stretch, but he did not want to take all of her at once. They had all the time in the world, and that was a treasure for the future.

As she came to the edge of an orgasm, her body tightened and squirmed beneath him. Her thighs clasped together on his arm. That did not stop him.

He sensed her peak, continuing the pace on her clit until she was screaming. "Alaric! Alaric!"

How beautiful. His name on her tongue.

The crashing wave of her orgasm slammed into her as she arched her back and shook with the intensity.

An extraordinary display.

"Keep going, keep going," Alaric urged as he milked her pleasure. She cried out, engulfed in her high for a few more seconds before he slowed his movements. Words of praise and affection were whispered after.

But he was not done. He was far from done.

Alaric barely waited for Lucia to catch her breath before he gently moved lower, adjusting her head as his lips kissed her breasts, abdomen, and finally down to her pelvis. His hands gripped the back of her knees as he positioned himself between her thighs. He was ready to take her to a higher level of ecstasy.

"Alaric?" Lucia questioned with a hoarse voice, unsure what his next move was as she felt her thighs part widely. She was floating in her mind, lightweight and tingling from the aftermath. A few aftershocks rocked her body.

Without an answer and a warning, his hot tongue lapped at her sex. Lucia's hips jolted from the overstimulation, a loud moan following. She did not object as his lips were on her folds, sucking and tugging as he tasted her. It was not long before he targeted her clit again.

Before Lucia knew it, she shook with the force of another approaching orgasm.

The high volumes of Morningstar men did not go unnoticed by the other kingdoms. In response, both Kingdom Shadowmere and Ironwood decided to take action. They sent spies, ordinary commoners, to observe the construction projects, the movement of troops, and gather any other information that would be helpful to the prince and king. These spies reported back.

Neutrality did nothing, another enemy amidst. A sign that the recently crowned young prince of Morningstar was not to be trusted.

Disappointment flooded the people.

"Why are you so worked up?" Victor asked.

Alexander snapped.

The prince grabbed the edge of his work desk and flipped it over, sending books and papers flying through the air. A few candles tumbled on the floor, luckily blown out. It added to the already-formed mess in his study room.

Cain, and Victor's newly appointed Knight of the Body, Tobias, wisely stayed out of the range of fire, their hands clasped behind their backs as they watched the scene unfold from the threshold. Victor, who was now sitting on the only standing furniture in the room, tensed at the outburst. Maybe he shouldn't have asked that ridiculous question.

"What are we supposed to do now?" Alexander demanded, his voice full of frustration. "Prince Michael is kissing Hartfelt's ass!"

Victor stared at Alexander's volatile state. He cautiously answered, "I know, I know. It was unexpected, but not unrealistic. Maybe staying neutral was not the key move to make?"

Alexander unexpectedly jumped and stomped onto the flipped desk, causing the wood to groan and splinter beneath his weight. The furniture was soon crushed into pieces. It did nothing to calm his rage.

Victor debated whether or not to take cover alongside Cain and Tobias. "But—"

"But what!?"

The king winced and bit his bottom lip. "I might have an idea?"

I am sorry, momma.

I hope this letter finds you well. The kingdom, as you may well be aware, is currently in a state of political unrest. I am doing everything in my power to maintain peace and avoid a declaration of war, which is a course of action I wish to avoid at all costs.

For precaution, I am condoning additional knight training and patrols. Sign-ups for voluntary assistance surprisingly got filled with occupants. While this show of support heartens me, I cannot help but feel a sense of responsibility for the lives that might fall under my name. These people do not deserve this trouble. This is a conflict between two leaders and I. If only Prince Alexander would listen and read my proposal, but that is now in the past.

Please come to my castle for temporary housing. This would provide me with peace of mind knowing that you are safe and well within my court. I have taken the liberty of preparing a room for you on the second floor, and I assure you that every effort will be made to ensure your comfort and well-being during your stay. Ask and I will always fulfill your needs and wishes.

I eagerly await your response, and I love you.
Alaric

26

Wasp Nest

"We have been dealing with some rather persistent pests," Donovan elaborated, his voice raspy from the constant dust and debris kicked up by the ongoing construction. As the overseer appointed by Prince Michael, he was tasked with managing the road and outposts, with his hands stained with dirt and brown hair sticking out in odd directions. Despite the conditions, he seemed content, even proud of the work his men were doing.

Alaric questioned, "Pests?"

"Yes. Our theory is that they are outcasts, likely driven to thievery out of desperation. But curiously enough, they do not seem to take much, if anything at all. It's quite baffling, really."

"Interesting."

The two strolled along the newly laid gravel road, surveying the nearly completed outpost, one of many such projects in progress. Nadia trailed behind them in quiet, graceful steps as she observed as well. The construction was progressing swiftly and smoothly, thanks to the resources and manpower provided by the Kingdom Morningstar. "Do you think this could be the work of your rivals? Trouble does not go unprovoked," Donovan questioned.

"It is hard to say, but I would not be surprised. They have been known to pull childish tricks just to arouse me."

"Should I request knights?"

They paused in front of the outpost, men using various tools to build. Alaric nodded. "It would be unwise not to."

With a swift hand gesture, Donovan flagged a young man. He looked barely in his teens, his skin bronzed by the sun and coated with dust. The remaining thread barely held together the fabrics on his back from the ruthless hours of hard work. "Soran, take a horse and request knights from Prince Michael, and add that King Alaric supports the demand."

"Is it about the outcasts?"

"That is none of your concern."

"But we can handle these outcasts ourselves," Soran protested, his voice tinged with defiance. He stood with foolhardiness.

Donovan snapped. "Do as I say, boy. You caused enough trouble as it is lately."

There was a moment of hesitation in the boy's eyes before he begrudgingly took off, his youthful stubbornness evident in every step. Alaric could not help but chuckle at the display. "These men," Donovan grumbled. "I swear."

"He is barely old enough to be a man."

"True, but his balls have dropped, so according to the laws of nature, he is a man."

Alaric made a brief detour at the meadows to pluck a variety of wildflowers.

Two colorful bouquets in each hand, one for his beloved wife and the other for his cherished stepdaughter. By the time he rode back to the castle, commotion was about when he spotted his mother's horse, laden with all her belongings. She must have received his letter and come immediately. Immersed relief washed over him.

Not to his surprise, his mother brought her treasured seeds and seedlings, already envisioning a plot behind the castle walls where she could create a breathtaking garden. He kindly asked her to propose Lucia's joining, since, due to her secluded upbringing, reading was currently her only delightful distraction. She was pleased to hear that her daughter-in-law had slowed down her chores. It was the purpose of the servants.

The bundle of wildflowers was placed in a decorative clay vase in their bedchamber. Lucia sat in a chair by the bookshelf, engrossed in a book, dressed in a soft, flowing nightgown. The sun had already settled, and the room was bathed in a warm glow from the lit candles scattered throughout.

The queen was lost in the pages of her book when she failed to notice Alaric's entrance, his footsteps muffled by the tiring rug. He cleared his throat, and she looked up, her eyes meeting his. "What book are you reading this time?"

"The Song of Roland," Lucia answered, placing a hold on the page before settling the book aside.

"A classic."

"You've read it?"

"Indeed, one of my favorites."

Lucia rose to her feet. "I assume that you can relate to the conflict between personal honor and duty, fighting on the thin line of treachery and treason. Loyalty is challenged, selflessness provoked. A responsibility to protect the people and their beliefs." She winked at him.

Alaric shook his head. She had grown with a wily tongue, and soon, she would be too clever to read along the lines of people. He glanced at the vase to hide his flustered self. "A lovely place for the wildflowers."

"I know," Lucia purred, reaching for his outerwear, her fingers deftly undoing the buttons. "I placed them there."

Alaric chuckled at her cocky remark. He shifted his shoulders as she pulled the fabric from his body. "How is the construction going?"

"The construction is going as planned, although we've had a few minor incidents with some uncivilized individuals causing trouble."

"Are these troublemakers driven by selfish desires, or are they desperate souls in need of help?" Lucia asked, neatly folding his clothing. Alaric took control to undress the rest.

"Why does that matter?"

"I would not want punishment placed on the people trying to meet their needs. If they need help, help shall be given."

"I wish it were the case so it can be resolved immediately, but these riots do not steal."

"That is odd," Lucia said as she took the other clothing from his hands and folded them as well. Her eyes narrowed as she considered the situation. "There must be a reason behind their actions. People do not act without purpose. Could it be a ploy to get a closer look at the layout and defenses before launching a larger attack? Could this be related to our foes?"

Alaric shrugged. "If that is the probable cause, then our foes are doing it messily."

"Messy, but fast results, don't you think? Why bother smuggling a spy when he or she has to gain their peers' trust months prior? Would it be easier to do quick sweeps dressed as thieves?"

"How did you become so wise? What happened?" Alaric teased, his voice warm and affectionate.

"You happened," she whispered as she leaned and pressed her lips against his. The kiss was sweet and lingering, her fingers digging into his bare chest. Desire flared in Alaric's veins.

He pulled her closer, fingers tangling in her hair. For a moment, the world seemed to fade away. He wondered if she realized just how much power she held over him.

Her presence, her touch, her very essence.

Nothing in this world could do this to him.

A letter, stamped by the emblems of Kingdom Ironwood and Kingdom Shadowmere, had arrived—a rare one of its kind.

Baelyn quickly rushed to warn the king of the news, the envelope flapping in his hands. Yet, of all his duties taught from the moment he was a small child and his lack of manners from his pumping adrenaline, spotting a bare naked king was not what he had expected in his career.

Based on Alaric's suggestion, Lucia practiced in the spacious courtyard of the palace, in underarmour clothing borrowed from Nadia, luckily being a close fit. Nadia braced her hands on the queen's body, guiding her to maintain correct balance and posture to distribute weight evenly for adequate defense. Then, it was how to anchor her body by bending her knees slightly and engaging her core muscles.

Lucia had never wielded a weapon before. She was anxious, shaking like a startled pup, as she rambled to Nadia helplessly as she worked through her nerves. It took several minutes before the knight convinced her, shoving a wooden weapon into her hands.

To prevent potential injuries from the queen's clumsiness and inexperience, she was given wooden daggers and swords to practice with first, similar to those used by novice knights during their initial training. While the wooden weapons were easier to handle and master, Nadia warned her that transitioning to metal weaponry would be a different story. The weight and resistance of the metal would strain her muscles for several days.

With her wooden sword poised, Lucia watched as Nadia unsheathed her own sword. The metal gleamed in the sunlight, momentarily blinding their eyes. "Remember," Nadia advised, "the sword is an extension of your arm. You do not want to hold it too tightly or too loosely."

Lucia nodded, attempting to mimic Nadia's stance. Gradually, she swung the wooden sword in front of her, the wind brushing past her face as she followed her instructor's movements. They practiced a series of thrusts, parries, and feints, each move more intricate than the last. She began growing confident.

She relished the idea of not being defenseless, like her previous cowardly self would be. When Alaric suggested the idea, she did not reject. In fact, she was eager to commence her training immediately. And the next day, she was promised that when Nadia fetched for her.

"You are doing swell."

"You believe so?" Lucia asked between her ragged breaths. Sweat made her face moist.

"I do, but it will still be some time before I allow you to touch a weapon made of metal. You need to work on your balance and posture. You are too loose when you turn, and too open at times. Those crucial seconds are all it takes to strike you down."

"Understood."

Alaric approached, causing the two to whirl around from his soft footsteps. Despite her tired nature, she still smiled at the sight of him.

"Lucia, my love, it is time."

27

The Snake with Fangs

The meeting took place in the vast, unobstructed expanse of the open plains, situated at a reasonable distance from the ongoing construction project. It was a neutral place for all three leaders to be present, devoid of any hiding spots that could be utilized for treacherous ambushes. A sturdy table with chairs arranged around it stood as the focal point of the meeting area. Given the lack of trust among the parties involved, this was the only feasible arrangement.

The tall grass tickled the king and queen's legs as they approached, arms interlocked, to the table with figures already seated. Nadia and Baelyn followed closely behind them, while rows of knights trailed. The opposing side also had its knights in tow, but one crucial figure was conspicuously absent: Prince Alexander of Kingdom Ironwood.

The absence of this individual was a clear violation of the terms outlined in the letter, and it had already simmered Alaric's temper. He could not help but fume at the blatant disregard for the agreed-upon conditions, and he knew that this could only bode ill for the negotiations that were about to ensue.

As they drew nearer to the table, Lucia's heart raced at the sight of King Victor. Their eyes locked, and Victor smirked. "Lord, have mercy on me. I did not expect to see your pretty little face again."

His amused demeanor only heightened Lucia's unease, and she tightened her grip on her husband's arm. Tobias and Prince Alexander's advisor, seated on Victor's left, exchanged bewildered glances, while Cain, positioned on the king's right, was unamused.

"The last time I saw you, your father and you fled with your tails between your legs from my palace floors. I thought that would be the last time I lay my eyes on you. What was your name?" He thought for a few seconds, tapping his chin. "Lucia. Yes, Lucia was your name." His gaze was lustful, and Alaric's jaw flexed.

Before he could defend his wife, however, Lucia spoke for herself. "In your words, I am a snake. Snakes are particular about their food. If a snake consumes bad meat, it regurgitates, allowing it to fester and attract flies. I am particular about my food. After catching a whiff of your putrid stench, I fled from the sour flesh within your soul. My father came to the same conclusion."

A weaving mix of truth and lies.

She refused to let herself be humiliated and stood tall, her eyes piercing into her foe's. Victor bared his teeth in disgust. Alaric admired her.

They took their seats, Alaric pulling out a chair for his wife before sitting beside her. Nadia took Lucia's other side, and the space fell into a brief silence as everyone studied one another. Every clothing, every expression, even every twitch, was closely observed. If someone made one wrong move, one wrong glare, hell will be loose.

Though curiosity got hold of Alaric, particularly of the new men at the table. Victor's eyes followed his, and he knew what was on his mind. "This is my Knight of the Body, Tobias, blessed by Kingdom Ironwood," Victor said, gesturing towards the curly-haired brunette with golden eyes that seemed to glow like the sun. "The other is Ironwood's advisor. His life is so insignificant that I have already forgotten his name, except for his nose. Doesn't it look hilarious?" He laughed as he pointed at the poor advisor, who indeed had a noticeably scrunched nose, likely the result of an accident. Sad to be known as that.

Alaric asked, "Where is Prince Alexander?"

Victor grinned, his laughter dissipating. "Now hold on, introduce your pretty little court."

"It seems you already know who my wife is," Alaric growled. He hated that this man knew.

"Yes, I do, but what about your other woman and man?"

Alaric gave Victor a long, intense stare before he started. "Nadia, my Knight of the Body, and Baelyn, my recently appointed advisor, blessed by Kingdom Morningstar."

Victor gave them a curious look. "Morningstar? Prince Michael gave you a man? Interesting. Interesting how close the two of you became right before King Johnathan's passing. I ponder why."

"That is none of your concern."

"Hmmm, I know, but what a shame for Valentino to miss all this," Victor mused, resting his head on his hand. Alaric's muscles tightened at the mention of his former advisor. How did he know about Valentino?

Alaric questioned, his voice laced with suspicion, "Do you have him within your walls? He fled to Ironwood territory weeks ago. He is a wanted man."

Victor shrugged. "Stop your pondering. He died from an infection. His children—"

"He had children?" Alaric interrupted.

"Whoops, I suppose I spoke too much," Victor snickered.

Alaric's arm hairs rose at the revelation. The fact that his enemies knew this information alarmed him. "Where is Prince Alexander? Where are his men?" he asked once more.

Ironwood's advisor coughed, drawing everyone's attention to him. "Prince Alexander has other urgent matters to attend to that have come unexpectedly. I am here to discuss the proposition on his behalf."

Alaric scowled. "No, Prince Alexander is supposed to be in your place, not you. This was agreed upon between letters."

Victor rolled his eyes. "King Alaric, we can still discuss the proposition with your court."

"How can I when one leader is absent?"

Lucia chimed in. "That is accurate. If political matters are to be discussed and agreements are to be made, Prince Alexander has to be present to represent his people properly; unless he purposefully made this gathering a chaff?"

"It would not be the first time," Alaric grumbled.

"And, what does he expect to gain from his absence? Avoidance of the issues? Or is it simply immaturity to conclude the need to work with his people? Yet worse, is he allowing himself more time to build his forces against his foes? Are you, King Victor, merely a distraction?" Lucia challenged.

Victor was amused. "I am impressed, the snake has fangs," he said, then sighed dramatically. "It is sad that one with such beauty has been soiled by rotten ideas by a crazed king. Years of training and obedience, down the dirty drain."

"That is not relevant," Alaric opposed.

"It is not? I keep getting spoken to by a *female*. The first time she opened her mouth, it was entertaining. The second was infuriating. Now, this is downright unacceptable as she jumps to uneducated conclusions."

Alaric bristled, jaw clenched. Victor continued, "Why bother to bring her in the first place? She should have stayed within your pathetic palace walls, taking care of her offspring conceived by another man."

Victor's words were like a spark to a flame. Alaric was having none of it.

An abrupt move, the chair suddenly in the air. Kingdom Ironwood's advisor was struck, letting out a yowl as he fell to the ground. Tobias managed to dodge.

Victor howled, pointing his finger, "You missed!"

"I wasn't aiming at you."

A truth, but he wanted so badly to hit the laughing king.

Alaric helped his wife to her feet and wrapped an arm around her. Lucia did not object. She was actually amused at her husband's excellent aim.

"We shall take our leave now."

"Ha! You are more of a child than I have ever imagined!" Victor sniggered.

"Maybe, but I will not waste my court's time and allow my wife and stepchild to be continuously insulted. If I truly had my way, I would have slit your tongue from your throat instead of throwing that lightweight chair."

Cain and Tobias drew their swords, but Alaric's court had already begun their leave.

The journey back to the castle was a quiet one. As evening came to an end and darkness enveloped, Lucia entered their bedchambers with an air of quiet contemplation. Alaric followed closely behind. "My love, is something the matter? You are awfully quiet."

"My mind is in turmoil, that is all." She began to unfasten the ties on the back of her dress.

Alaric stepped forward and gently pushed her hands away, taking over the task of removing her garments. His large, gentle hands slid the fabric off her body, revealing her delicate form beneath.

"My mind does too, but let tomorrow deal with those burdens," Alaric murmured, burying his nose in her hair to inhale her sweet scent. His hands moved to her undergarment dress, settling on her hips, causing her to shiver.

"You want to push the tasks away."

Alaric chuckled softly. "I do. I do not want to think more about it tonight." He kissed the side of her neck, and Lucia leaned into his touch. "I do, however, have a jealous question."

Lucia chortled. "Jealous? The mighty king of Kingdom Hartfelt, jealous? What has aroused such emotion in you?"

"How did King Victor's tongue know your name?"

"Pardon?"

Alaric's voice grew more insistent. "Answer my childish question."

She wasn't sure whether to be scared or excited by his demand. Swallowing nervously, she explained, "Father proposed me to the man as an unwed, widowed bride before my marriage to you, but I did not meet his expectations, mainly because I was not a virgin. He then spoke inappropriate words before he drenched me in wine."

Alaric's hands tightened around the fabric of Lucia's clothing. He was deadly silent, but Lucia did not need to turn around to see the anger seething from him. She tried to brush it off. "It is not a problem now. It happened a while ago. I am honestly surprised he still remembered the interaction after all."

"You should kill him."

Lucia turned to catch Alaric's possessive glare, her heart racing in her chest. She had never heard such demonic words come from her husband's mouth before, but it made her instinctively squeeze her thighs together, feeling the heat radiating from her core.

"I will catch him one day, drag him to his knees in front of you, as a gift to take his life," Alaric stated. Her breath was taken away as she envisioned King Victor on his knees, battered and bruised by her husband's hand, with a sword in her own.

The control in her dream. It was enough to be intoxicating. She felt powerful.

She understood why noblemen craved it.

"Alaric," Lucia whispered.

"Hmm?"

"You would do that for me?"

"I will do anything that your heart desires. You should have learned by now that I am an obedient dog to your will," Alaric growled. She felt the vibration, alongside the surge of power and desire. A tug of a smile pulled on her lips.

"Good," she said, leaning upwards to kiss him. The word alone made Alaric aroused, and her hands trailing upwards from his chest to his face, holding him, made him feel like putty from bliss.

Passion consumed them both as their lips interlocked, clothing pooling onto the floor one after the other. It was only a matter of seconds before they were bare. "You are exquisite," he breathed, his large hands roaming his wife's form. He was touching her everywhere, hot like fire to her skin. He cupped her breasts, kissing the back of her neck as she whined out with pleasure.

She loved it.

These hands were the only man's hands ever allowed to touch her. She vowed.

With her back pinned against his chest, the king's right hand trailed from her breast and down to her abdomen. She eagerly parted her thighs; an invitation, and he accepted it as he sank his fingers between her folds. He squeezed her breast while performing lazily, gentle circles on her clitoris. She was already soaked, and it drove him wild.

"Alaric," Lucia panted. She could feel his arousal twitching against her backside.

"Do you want me to stop?"

"Never."

"Then what can I do for you, my love?" Alaric whispered. He could feel her trembling, but he did not stop his hands.

"I want you to take me to the Gates of Heaven again."

"I will do as your heart desires." But there was nothing to warn the king of her outreach, giving his erection a few strokes. He tried not to buckle his knees helplessly as a groan rumbled from his throat. "Lucia..." His voice was so pathetic.

She giggled. "I want you to come with me so we can arrive at the Gates together."

He looked up, searching for a hint of sarcasm or a tease, or even a flicker of a shifted expression, but there was not one. She was serious, and as she guided him between her labia, the doubt of her words dissipated. He understood what she wanted.

"Yes, My Queen," he murmured, clutching her hips. He proceeded with a deliberate slowness as he gradually immersed himself in her warmth. He barely managed to push an inch or two inside before his wife let out a loud gasp that echoed through the room. His initial impulse was to halt, but the same thought seemed to be mirrored in her mind, and she quickly reached back, her fingers digging into his muscular thigh.

Encouragement to continue. He obeyed.

A long, searing, sharp pain spiked her body, a testament to her years of abstinence. Each inch felt intense, yet she was far from regretting it. This was what she had yearned for, what she had dreamt of.

She desired this, and only this, with the man who had set her free, who had given her the power to make her own choices, the freedom to pursue her desires without the constraints of societal norms.

This was the man she loved. The only man she would love.

Alaric was in pure ecstasy, his mind clouded with pleasure as her walls clenched around him. He tried hard not to fall to the mercy of his body, but it was a challenge as the sensation consumed him. He was barely holding on to his control.

His wife. His woman. Allowed him in.

The king's arms wrapped around his wife's body, fondling her breasts as they stood still, both settling into the new experiences. Breathing was only heard between the two until Alaric asked, "Are you all right?"

"Be quiet."

Alaric chuckled and then performed a set of slow, experimental thrusts. Lucia released a few sounds of surprise, adjusting and clinging to her husband, but it did not take long before they were fully engrossed in the passionate act. Her breasts bounced with each movement, and Alaric cupped them, his face buried in the nape of her neck.

His decent and compassionate pace made her moan without a care for who was listening outside the walls. She stretched and tightened around him, the sensation overwhelming her ability to think. But then Alaric's hand moved once more to stimulate Lucia's swollen clit.

The moment his fingers made contact, her mind was blown away. Just a few massages sent her spiraling over the edge, and she cried out in ecstasy as a powerful orgasm tore through her. Her body shook violently, and Alaric held her close, keeping her upright during the intense sensation. He pressed his lips against her shoulder, waiting patiently for her to come down from her high.

When she finally did, she begged, "Down. I need to lie down, please." Her flimsy knees and ankles felt like jelly. She was grateful for his hold as her entire body tingled.

Alaric aided her to the bed, lifting her onto the red soft cushions. She sank onto the fabrics, planting on top of the pillows. He climbed on top of her.

As he looked down at her, Lucia could see the lingering question in his eyes. "If you ask me if I am all right again, I will make you sleep on the floor once we are done."

Alaric laughed. "Why are you being so cruel now?"

"I may be a delicate flower, but do not convince yourself that you have somehow hurt me at every moment we touch."

Alaric huffed with amusement before he kissed a path down her neck to her breasts. Lucia moaned again as he took a nipple into his mouth, suckling greedily. "Alaric," she gasped, her fingers tangled in his messy hair. She arched her back, turning into a blabbering, moaning mess.

The king does the same with the other breast before he pulled away and drank at the sight of her, his cock throbbing with need. She must have noticed the hunger in his gaze as she opened her legs, inviting him to continue. That really made him hungry.

Alaric's hands moved lower, caressing the stretch marks on her hips and abdomen before he did a teasing stroke on her swollen clit. She jerked her hips. "Why must you play with me?"

He chuckled and positioned himself between her thighs, his erection nudging against her entrance. With a low growl, he thrust forward, burying himself deep inside his wife's wet heat. They both groaned out in response, their bodies joining in a dance of passion once again.

A slow, deep rhythm. Sounds filled the room as the bed rocked back and forth. He buried his face in her neck, breathing her.

It felt so, so, so good. She swore she was going to orgasm again at any moment.

As they moved together, their bodies slick with sweat, Alaric knew his mind was slipping away, consumed by primal urge. He sped up, hooking his arms underneath his wife for better leverage. Then, he began to pound against her hips.

Lucia cried out. His thrusts were erratic.

She was at his mercy, unable to think or form proper words. Skin slapped on skin. She gripped onto anything she could, mainly the skin on the king's back, as her body writhed in pleasure.

"I love you, I love you," Alaric whimpered before he succumbed to his mercy.

With a hoarse moan, he gave in, his body spasming as he emptied himself inside. She clung to him, her own release cresting as she felt him fill her.

The two panted. A long moment of recollection before Alaric pressed his forehead against Lucia's, feeling her aftershocks as she slowly came back to reality alongside him. Her little giggle was enough of an answer that she was all right.

"Allow me to carry you to the bath."

Lucia brushed back the messy ginger strands from his face. "Bare naked?"

"Do you oppose? I assume our court is asleep about now," Alaric said with a mischievous glint in his eye.

"What would happen if we are spotted?"

"Now it is bound to happen since you've mentioned it."

Lucia laughed. "Even if we are caught, I know you would not be embarrassed one bit."

"Absolutely not. I will use my backside to keep you shielded."

"A pair of cheeks for the unexpected viewer?"

"That is correct."

"How romantic."

28

Glass, then Blood

As the days went by, Lucia spent hours on her knees, planting and tending to the soil alongside her mother-in-law. Dirt caked under her fingernails as she laid the seeds. Elizabeth shared her vast knowledge, and the queen eagerly listened. She enjoyed the older woman's company, especially when she shared stories about Alaric's childhood.

Before the winter breeze approached from the mountains, the garden would sprout and grow. Elizabeth explained what she should expect, and the queen was thrilled.

When Lucia's time wasn't occupied by the desire to read, care for her daughter, and work alongside her husband, she was out in the courtyard training with Nadia. The sessions continued to be intense and challenging, pushing her physical limits to the brink, but she persevered through.

Strength and endurance built, and Nadia soon felt confident enough to allow her to train with her entrusted professional fighters with blunted swords. However, the Knight of the Body was clear not to cause harm, threatening their lives if they even left a scratch on the queen's body with a blade. And so they obeyed, cautious as they fought her.

"How is she doing with her training?" Alaric asked. The king and his knight stood at the edge of the courtyard, watching from a distance at the dancing queen. Sweat soaked her borrowed clothing, yielding her weapon against a tall male opponent. Metal clashed together.

"She is doing exceptionally well," Nadia replied. "With every session, she surprises me with her dedication. I do not doubt that she can defend herself."

Alaric glowed. "This is pleasing to hear." He paused, a sly smile spreading across his face, before he continued, "She has been following your suggestions quite diligently. I was quite astonished to discover a dagger strapped to her thigh several nights ago."

"Did she use it against you?"

"I would not have objected if she wanted to," he said, his mind drifting back to the night he had pinned her against the bed, his hands gripping her thighs as he positioned her just so. As he slid his hands underneath her dress, the sharp blade nearly sliced his skin. Lucia apologized, but it only heightened his arousal. He was startled to come to the conclusion of a new proclaimed desire himself.

Nadia playfully shoved his shoulder, which only made the king laugh. She did not press for details as they watched several more minutes of Lucia's training before they turned away.

Today was the day to inspect the progress of the road construction. Donovan was waiting for them.

Donovan coughed, scratching at his caked scalp. Alaric approached the grizzled man with a warm smile. "Donovan, my friend, how have you been?"

"Better," he replied, clasping his grimy hands together in an attempt to rid himself of the dirt. Dust puffed from his fingers. "My men and I could use some rain. The heat is unbearable."

"Any new trouble regarding the thieves?"

"No, it has been a peaceful few days, not a single distraction to speak of. We also received a few more men, alongside the additional knights, to help speed up the progress."

"Excellent, excellent," Alaric said, pleased with the update.

Horses neighed in the distance, shirtless men at work. Several men in armor stood about. Nadia trailed behind her king and the construction overseer as they walked towards the beginning project of another outpost. The road was more than halfway complete.

One man, whom she noticed amongst the sea of moving bodies, stood still. He stared, a glass bottle in hand. His expression was unreadable, eyes glazed and unfocused. One would assume that he was intoxicated.

"Is there any way I can lend a hand?"

Donovan nodded. "Yes, would you be able to provide some clothing? We are in dire need of it, as my men's garments are straining from the days of hard labor."

"I can make that happen. I'll gather some seamstresses and make a delivery within about a week's time. Would that be doable?"

"That would be fine," Donovan replied, his shoulders relaxed. "I know I could ask Prince Michael for help, but it would likely take two weeks, given the longer journey to his kingdom now." The progress was closer to Kingdom Hartfelt's side.

"I will expedite the process as much as possible."

The drunk man's eyes, once hazy with the perception of alcohol, now burned with a piercing emotion that stabbed like a sharpened dagger; his jaw tightened. This sudden change did not go unnoticed by the knight's vigilance.

Nadia quickly pulled the king to a halt, her firm grip and intense eyes enough to warn him of the impending danger. One glance at the still man was enough for the king to know. Donovan slowed his pace. "Your Majesty?"

Alaric did not answer, his hand slowly sliding down his side towards his sheathed weapon. She, too, reached for her's. The working men around them were oblivious, alongside Donovan, until he spotted the drunken man himself. He hissed under his breath as he excused himself and marched towards the inebriated man.

"No drinking at this hour!" Donovan bellowed, his voice booming through the crowded space. Some of the men stopped and turned to look at him, but the drunken man merely shifted his gaze to Donovan.

Nadia whispered urgently, "We shall take our leave now."

Alaric did not object.

"Are you deaf!?" Donovan challenged, his red face blistering and spit flying. The drunken man did not respond as he lifted his bottle. One could assume he was to strike, but then a blinding light and intense heat enveloped them all.

The air crackled with energy. Red was spilled everywhere. Bodies littered the ground. The scent of blood and smoke hung heavy in the air, tingeing the once vibrant skies with a somber hue.

Sounds of agony pulled Nadia to her consciousness, weakly blinking at the unfolding carnage. She struggled to stay awake, barely comprehending the sword plunging into Donovan's chest by an armored man, his face too blurry to make out. Donovan let out a guttural cry, blood pooling beneath him as he slowly met his end. He was only a few feet away from her, his face burned and lifeless.

Nadia blinked again.

Flakes of ash danced across her face. Flames licked at the edges of her vision. Smoke choked the air from her lungs. Her ears rang with high tunes.

She coughed, warmth from her nose tracing a path down her cheek to the grass below. More armored men rushed past, their focus on their steeds as they retreated. Death had come to claim its victims, and in its wake, it left a haunting silence mixed with the crackles of fire.

Nadia thought of death. The lush grass on her face was comforting, and she wanted so badly to fall asleep and accept death's invitation. She yearned for the release the darkness promised, but one thought kept her from surrendering to the void—one person who anchored her to the world of the living.

Alaric.

Where was Alaric?

Her king. Her best friend. A man she could call her brother.

Where was he?

The world spun as she sat up, her face grimacing tightly as her left arm kept her upright. She tried to feel for her right arm, to wiggle her fingers, to use the extremity as balance alongside its opposite companion, but her body did not respond. Only intense pain consumed her shoulder.

She dared to look down.

Sliced and mangled by the attackers, with clumps of tendons and a protruding, broken bone. Blood still dripped, the right side of her body soaked in it. Her breathing quickened, her heart in her throat.

Instantly, she touched the dirt-coated wound with her remaining hand. Denial consumed her. She tried to wiggle her right fingers again, to flick her wrist, to bend her elbow and raise her hand; but nothing happened in return. There was no response, other than the subtle movements of her glenohumeral joint.

She could not cry or scream, despite the need to. Her mind was still fixated on one thing alone: her king.

The Knight of the Body struggled to her feet, swaying unsteadily from the blood loss. She scanned the area around her. Black smoke billowed above, obscuring the sun. The grass was now crimson red with the blood of the fallen. Most of the bodies were Donovan's men. It had happened so fast that none of them saw it coming. All she could do now was wish these men had a quick death.

Nadia called out his name, her voice hoarse and weak. She wandered the burning field.

There was no response. Her heart continued to pound.

She called out again, helplessly looking around.

There was still no response.

Where could he be?

Where?

He had to be near her.

She tried again. But despite her endless calls and search, Alaric was nowhere to be found.

29

Shuttered Earth

The king and his entrusted Knight of the Body had gone missing. Lucia anxiously nudged for their well-being. She stood outside the courtyard, watching the sun move as she waited and waited and waited. A simple task deemed only to consume a subtle amount of sunlight was extending into the approaching evening.

The servants occasionally assessed her. Rose offered a stool for her legs, and Mia presented fruit in a decorative bowl, but Lucia refused their advanced kindness. Charlotte joined her mother with the same concern, holding hands. Rayne organized a group of his men, alongside a few of Alaric's knights for protection, to follow the trail and locate the kingdom's leader and valued knight. By the time the group left, then the queen and her child returned to the palace.

What was thought to be a minor delay to the king's meeting was instead a shock to the men's systems at the sight of the catastrophic destruction.

The area was littered with debris and corpses; construction outposts and wagons were smothered, black, dark ground, and weapons lay about. The fires that scorched the land had died to a white smoke. The only figure that stood in the middle of the demolition was the Knight of the Body.

Nadia barely clung to life, had wandered the battlefield for some time, and her vertigo momentarily overcame her mind. Using the last vestiges of strength in her left arm, she turned over the lifeless bodies in a desperate attempt to identify her king. Her heart sank as she feared that amongst the charred remains and human ashes were those of Alaric. The possible conclusion was almost too much to bear, her stomach threatening to churn.

And now she sat on a horse, bound around the chest and the remainder of her right arm with whatever cloth the group of men could find on the cold bodies. It smelled of smoke, but it did not bother her. It was a miracle she was alive, but the weight of her failure pressed down on her like an inexorable force.

Alaric.

Alaric was not by her side.

The horse she rode was pulled to a stop by leather reins from the leading knight. The sun had sunk halfway into the horizon, and the blanket of stars now appeared. The pacing queen burst out of the large wooden doors. "Alaric! Nadia!"

The pitch of the queen's voice reached Nadia's ears, but her eyes refused to rise to the running figure, the servants chasing after her. Her hands were on the skirts of her dress as she ran as fast as she could.

Two men helped the wounded knight to her feet. Her knees wobbled, her strength ebbing away.

"Alaric? Where is Alaric?" Lucia asked, fear coaxed with each word. She searched for the answers on the men's weathered faces, but mourning was only engraved.

The Knight of the Body kept her head lowered, unable to meet the queen's eyes with such cowardice. She did not have the stomach to tell her. To tell her about her failure to keep her husband safe.

Lucia's voice cracked. "Nadia?" She nudged the knight on her left shoulder.

No one dared to speak. It frightened the queen more. "Say something! Where is Alaric!?" she demanded, shaking her harder. Her eyes stung with tears. "Please."

The desperation in her tone rattled Nadia enough to finally look up at the queen's watery expression. The face of defeat was all Lucia needed to know. Her face paled. "No... No. No."

A plea of denial. "Tell me he is all right. Just tell me," Lucia whimpered. Nadia did not respond, resuming her gaze downwards. Her silence told the queen otherwise. "Nadia, please... Tell me he's alive."

Nothing again. The silence was deafening.

One valiant man spoke, overcome by her pleas. "We could not find the body—"

"No!" Lucia recoiled as the words pierced her very being, a knife of despair that cut through her soul. Her fragile heart felt like it was going to burst from the sheer weight of her anguish. "It cannot be true!"

Rose reached out and grabbed her arm firmly. "My Queen, let us go insid—"

Lucia shoved the older woman away with a snarl. "Get off me, wench!" she spat venomously. Rose was unfazed by the cruel rebuke.

Her world had just *stopped*.

Lucia stumbled a few steps, her reality spiraling out of control as she buried her hands in her hair, trying desperately to hold herself together as hot tears streamed down her face. But when her blurry vision landed upon Nadia, disgust flared up at the pitiful sight of the knight. Rage quickly overtook her body.

Her heart pounding, Lucia took off at a frantic pace, startling the servants as they tried to reach for her again. They attempted to restrain her, but she fought them off with a strength fueled by her raw anger. And without warning, the queen's elbow quickly collided with the knight's face with a sickening crack.

Nadia's world exploded in a kaleidoscope of painful colors as she fell sprawled onto her backside. "You were supposed to protect him! You were his best knight!" Lucia yelled, spit flying from her lips. "But you failed! You failed to be his guard!"

Blood gushed from the knight's nose. Darkness threatened to close around her, tunneling down to the figure standing right over her.

"You killed him!" Lucia screamed, her voice becoming hoarse. "You killed him! You allowed him to die!"

Victoria and Axel clung to her forearms, desperately trying to restrain her to prevent more harm. Caroline raised her voice. "Stop this!"

But the queen's wrath propelled her forward.

The servants were overpowered as Lucia twisted her body, her hand snaking under her dress to retrieve her dagger strapped to her thigh. The sound of metal ringing out drew the attention of the incompetent men surrounding them, their eyes widening. Only then did they interfere, grabbing their queen and pulling her away.

Lucia could not challenge the men's strength. "Release me!" she ordered, thrashing her body side to side, but the men refused to let go. The knights attended to their captain.

Nadia could not hear her trained men's words. She could barely focus, her eyes glossy, her body limp and unresponsive. Her world had been irrevocably shattered, and she was no longer able to comprehend the reality that was crumbling around her.

Her king was gone. Alaric Hartfelt was gone.

The man who sought her out of the kitchen when he noticed her talents. The man who trained her and believed that she was much more than a kitchen girl. The man who entrusted his life in her hands, who shared his secrets and followed her advice. The man, who believed that she could always protect him, was gone.

She wished for that strike of the dagger. A shame it never touched her skin.

Lucia's screams echoed through the castle halls as she was whisked away. "He's dead! He's dead!" she wailed, her words punctuated by sobs and gasps for breath. She had lost her dagger in the scuffle outside, so she lashed out with her fists and nails, beating and scratching at the men who held her.

She tripped and fell onto the stone floor, the impact jolting through her body. The men tried to pick her off the ground, but Rose shooed them out the doors. The rest had to be handled by the privacy of the court.

The pair of lungs inside the queen burned from the force of her sobs. She wanted to tear the floor apart beneath her, to rip it to rubble with her bare hands. She wanted to kill those men who held her, all of them, to inflict the same pain she felt as they dragged her away. She wanted Nadia hanged for her unqualified fit as Knight of the Body; for the crime of her husband's death.

And without warning, Lucia released a scream that was almost in-human in its intensity, an agonized, animalistic howl of pain and rage. But she did not care how it would make her look. She did not care about anything except for the searing emptiness inside her.

She had just lost her king, her love, her everything. And now, she was left with nothing but this burning, all-consuming grief.

Rose dropped to her knees. She whispered soft words, but all was muted by the cries Lucia released. She waved to the other servants to help the queen up. "There was no use being on the floor," Rose said, using her strength to uphold her. She was dead weight in their arms. "To the bedchamber."

Luckily, Charlotte was already tucked in her bed, not to bear wit-ness to her mother's agony. But breaking the details to the young princess would shatter the head servant's heart all over again.

30

A Star to Shooting Stars

Lucia lay on the floor of the grand hallway, her body wracked with sobs as she clutched at Alaric's clothing. She inhaled the fading scent that barely clung to the fabric.

He was gone. He was truly gone.

She looked up at the new oil painting that now hung beside the one of Alaric's and his mother's canvas. It was a massive portrait, every brushstroke meticulously crafted to capture the beauty and love that radiated from the three subjects. Alaric stood tall and mighty, embracing Lucia around the waist with his eyes fixed on her. Despite the painter's initial instructions to keep looking forward, he had given up and painted the eyes that adored the queen. Lucia was drawn so beautifully in her most eloquent dress. A bouquet of flowers was in her hands as she looked forward. Charlotte stood before them, her stubbornness evident as she clung to her toys.

It was a gorgeous collection. It was completed not too long ago.

The queen wailed out again. Her voice echoed throughout the halls.

It took the notice of the head servant, as she hurried to the crying woman, who was settled on the floor. "My Queen." Lucia was helplessly lifted off the ground, supported by Rose's strength. "You must not be on the floor."

Lucia groaned, her face soaked with tears. She clenched the clothing to her chest.

With some gentle coaxing, Rose had finally managed to convince the queen to leave Charlotte's bed after days, weeks, of adamantly refusing to budge. It was too much for the queen to enter the cold, empty bedchamber she shared with her husband. Her daughter willingly invited her, embraced her, and the two cried together.

Today was the first day the queen found the strength to step away from the sanctuary of Charlotte's bedchamber. The head servant, however, should have anticipated that this progress would not be without its challenges.

Nevertheless, this was a marked improvement from the tempest of fury that had swept through the queen the day after receiving the devastating news. Lucia had unleashed a torrent of destruction upon the library, her wrath scattering the cherished books like leaves before a storm. The garden she had lovingly nurtured with her mother-in-law had borne the brunt of her anger, its once-vibrant tiny growths now trampled. Even the sanctity of the kitchen had not been spared; cooking utensils turned into weapons of chaos.

"Why must one care that I lay on the floor, dreaming of the life I barely tasted?"

"None of that sorrow talk. Allow me to aid you outside," Rose said, beginning the lead. "You have not touched the sun's rays in some time."

"No," Lucia whispered.

"No?"

"I wish to see a physician."

"I imagine. You have been relieving yourself and picking at your meals more lately. Could you believe something is wrong?"

Lucia did not answer.

Nadia's messengers have been vanishing without a trace.

No responses. No signs. No spottings.

Letters could not travel past or through the kingdom's borders. Men were being hunted. Kingdom Hartfelt was left in the dark, secluded from the outside world.

It had been ongoing for weeks since the announcement of King Alaric's death. It was Baelyn's advance to seek direction and order for the grieving kingdom. However, due to the repeated failures to reach out, particularly to Prince Michael, political unrest brewed. The citizens of Kingdom Hartfelt lived in constant fear.

Some townsfolk have already fled, the rumors overcoming as the kingdom was on the brink of collapse. Trades had halted. The economy suffered. With no leader, Nadia tried everything in her power to maintain order and stability, navigating through treacherous rumors and problems to prevent the looming threat of an all-out uprising.

Although the Knight of the Body struggled to keep the threads of the kingdom together, her wound had healed closed with jagged skin. It was a miracle that no infection threatened to claim her life, pleasing the physicians. Only layers of scabbing were present around the stitching, soon to crumble away to intriguing scars.

But her nose, with careful examination, was permanently crooked.

Despite the healing progress, she now had to navigate her world with an empty right sleeve dangling by her side. Relearning tasks was arduous, but the mere thought of seeking a replacement was a dreadful notion she wanted to avoid at all costs. She had placed her faith in Rayne to assist her in the tasks she could no longer perform with just one arm, biding her time until the day came that proper leadership replaced her.

"Nadia?"

The Knight of the Body shook her head, snapping out of her reverie. Baelyn sat in the cushioned chair that once occupied the king, his brows furrowed upon the tired woman. The room was filled with the scent of ink and parchment, the remnants of their long session of paperwork and strategizing.

She rubbed her forehead as she fought a yawn. "My apologies, it seems I need a break."

"This is my work; you do not have to force yourself to be involved," the advisor said, setting aside his inked quill.

"I must."

Baelyn frowned. "If you wish so. I can not force you not to help."

"Good. I am already forced to do things that I wish not to do for the sake of the kingdom's well-being," she retorted, her voice bitter.

They both fell silent, passing through for a few seconds before Baelyn broke it. "This burden is unfair for all of us. I still grieve every day, every hour, every minute. It adds hardship and challenge to the tasks that have previously been easy to handle."

Nadia hummed in agreement. She had grieved, but she also had to stand tall for her people, whom Alaric had promised to protect and provide sanctuary for. If she didn't, who would?

"However, the only thing we can do now is push through. Keep pushing and hope for relief soon."

"That can only be doable if Queen Lucia stopped hiding in her daughter's bedchamber and be present in this mess," Nadia said.

"But she has. The servants were glowing with joy."

Nadia perked up instantly. She nearly fell off the chair she sat in. "You lie?"

Baelyn shook his head. "I have no reason to lie."

A corner of the knight's mouth curled upwards. This was splendid news. News that she feared to admit she desperately awaited for.

A step in the right direction, a chance to regain the trust of the common folk.

"Where is she now?"

"I do not know. See if you can find her," Baelyn replied.

And before the advisor could add anything else, the Knight of the Body exited the glass-stained doors urgently. At the perfect time, she nearly collided with Victoria. That smile was still gracing Nadia's lips.

It was a blessing that the servants kept the castle in order while commotion and rumors rattled throughout the kingdom. She was certain the fall of Kingdom Hartfelt would happen much sooner without them. "Victoria, I have just heard favorable news."

"Huh?"

"Queen Lucia has finally emerged from her daughter's bedchambers. Do you think she is stable enough to address the unrest that plagues our land?" Nadia asked. "It tires me much to juggle these issues when they are not my priority focus years prior."

Victoria hesitated before answering, "Indeed, but...".

Nadia held her breath.

"Queen Lucia had consulted a physician and now adamantly refuses to abandon her daughter's bedside again. Rose is attending to her right now."

Nadia's expression quickly morphed into one of disbelief. "You must be fooling with me," she exclaimed. Victoria stayed silent, not wanting to upset the knight further.

Wasting no time, Nadia instantly turned and raced up the grand, ornate staircase, leaving Victoria to watch her vanish from view. A whirlwind of anger, frustration, and even betrayal stabbed into her all at once. She had lost her dominant arm, nearly bled to death, and stepped up to aid the leaderless kingdom with Baelyn. The thought of Lucia lying around in her daughter's bedchamber for days while the kingdom teetered on the brink of disaster infuriated the knight.

How could she be so selfish?

The people were anxious, families packing in preparation to flee. Chaos was in the brick of happening. A proper leader was needed.

As Nadia stormed onto the floor, Rose cautiously stepped out of the princess's bedchamber, shaking her head in dismay. Her gentle attempts to reason had become dull to the queen. Axel and Mia wore expressions of defeat and sadness, further igniting Nadia's anger.

The knight forcefully pushed her way through the gathered servants, followed by loud gasps, and burst into the bedchamber. Her
body shook. "Your Majesty!"

Lucia was perched on the edge of the bed, idly picking at her fingers, her eyes devoid of emotion as they followed the destruction of
her own nails. Her gown was wrinkled from days of wear. As Nadia
stood before her, she refused to acknowledge the knight's presence.
"You cannot just sit here and twiddle your thumbs! There is chaos
unfolding in the streets! These people—*your people*—are relying on
you, waiting for you, and you are just sitting here without any regard towards them!" Her voice boomed through the room, the servants watching by the threshold helplessly.

The queen did not respond.

"Your absence has sown fear and madness! And when you finally
deign to show your face, you feign illness as an excuse?"

Lucia's jaw tightened, and her hands started to quiver.

Nadia continued, "You think you have it hard? Alaric's mother has
lost her last living child, and can barely leave her bed or eat! She's the
one who needs a physician, not you!"

In an instant, Lucia leaped to her feet in the blink of an eye, and
before Nadia could react, one of Charlotte's desk chairs was flung
through the air. Wood smacked into the knight, stumbling and nearly
colliding with the wall as pain erupted in her side.

"You think I want attention?!" Lucia's voice rang out, her eyes
shining with unshed tears as she stood, defiant and furious, in the
center of the room. "You are a pottle-deep pignut for thinking such
foolish thoughts!"

"I am only extinguishing the damages due to your lack of awareness! How do you think this palace still stands?!" Nadia shouted back.
The servants were too scared to interfere.

"How can I be there when my husband, without warning, was
murdered due to your incompetence as a knight!?"

"Do you think I don't blame myself for this!?"

"You certainly intend to blame me! My husband is dead! *Alaric* is dead."

Before Nadia could spit her next forming insult, Lucia quickly interjected, "And I am with child!"

Nadia's eyes widened in shock, her breath hitching in her throat as she stared at the queen as if she were some abomination. A heavy silence descended upon the room, thick with tension and unspoken secrets.

"*His* child," Lucia whispered, a tear racing down her face. She tried to keep herself from breaking down completely, biting her lip to hold back any sobs or whimpers that threatened to escape.

"Child?" Nadia finally managed to choke out, her face draining of color. "You... You are pregnant with his child?"

"I begged the physician not to discuss it, but it seems that to keep me from being insulted by my own court, I have to expose the truth."

Nadia's anger dissipated instantaneously, replaced by a deep sadness that threatened to suffocate and clog her chest.

Her best friend, her brother, had wooed his wife. His legacy was still alive.

Alaric had never mentioned his thoughts of having children. He had always seemed more focused on others than himself. Still, from the months of watching him interact with Charlotte, running and playing, caring and feeding, adopting her as a daughter against the laws of shame of caring for another man's spawn, Nadia had no doubt he would have been over the moon if he were alive now, learning that his wife now bears his child. He would be an excellent father.

Actually, he already was.

Nadia reached out for the queen's hand. Lucia looked down at the offered hand, hesitated, but seeing the sadness in Nadia's eyes, she placed her hand into hers. The knight led her back to her spot, settling beside Lucia on the edge of the bed. She waved the servants away.

A few heartbeats of silence passed, making sure they were out of earshot of the servants, before Nadia spoke. "I must apologize," she said, her voice choked with emotion. "I know how much you loved him."

Lucia squeezed the knight's hand.

"And I want you to know that he loved you and Charlotte deeply. He thought of you both every day, speaking highly when I was not present to witness the scene. You were the highlight of his life."

The tears no longer threatened to escape the queen's eyes. These words brought her comfort.

Nadia continued, "I have never seen him so happy. You and Charlotte gave him so much purpose and fulfillment," she took a deep breath to muster up her courage, "and, again, I apologize for my cruel statements and shouting. It was out of line."

"I will accept your apology for this fight, but I will never offer you forgiveness for his death."

"I know. It is the greatest sin I must carry for the remainder of my life. I have failed the kingdom with my negligence."

Lucia did not reply. In the grand tapestry of life, every thread, every soul, was tainted with some form of sin. She was no exception; cursed to raise her children alone, and then be called a whore for being widowed. She had accepted this bitter reality.

For what felt like an eternity, Nadia slowly rose from the bed, releasing the queen's hand as she did so. "Choose a successor for my title. I have been honored to serve under King Alaric, but now, find a worthy person who will serve you and provide the protection you need."

Pain sparked in her chest. "Nadia? What are you saying?"

"I can no longer fulfill my duties as a knight," Nadia confessed. "Announce your decision soon. Your people are waiting." With those final words, the knight turned on her heel and strode towards the open doorway, her figure vanishing as quickly as a gust of wind.

Lucia remained seated on the edge of the bed, her mind reeling with the knight's words.

No explanation. No details of plans.

Her people?

She had no people. The people within the kingdom were her husbands. They followed him, not her. She would not be able to rule a marked land. She was a woman, after all.

Rose appeared around the threshold seconds after Nadia's departure. The head servant stood outside the doorframe to await the queen, but as she stepped into the room, Lucia dismissed her with a wave of her hand. Rose froze, stalled, but then bowed before she left. The wooden door clicked closed.

The queen did not need another in the room while she grieved again.

A firm knock on the door before it opened seconds after.

No waiting for reply. No permission. Only a simple warning of entry as the advisor emerged.

Evening had begun to settle, the sun fading through the window. Charlotte was being cared for by the servants. The little princess had her moments after Alaric's death, sunken in grief as she tried to comprehend her stepfather never returning home. There were days she would wait by the castle doors, clutching his toys in her arms, to the point her legs began to ache. Other times, she would call out his name as she wandered the halls, all in denial.

Lucia laid on her side, facing the now-opened threshold, at the smaller man. She had not moved since the incident, only to rest as she patiently awaited her daughter's arrival from her evening meal.

Baelyn stepped forward, his voice barely above a whisper as he said, "My Queen." He held a steaming kettle in one hand and an empty porcelain teacup in the other. A gesture suggested by Rose, regardless of his lack of knowledge about brewing tea.

Lucia ignored him.

He repeated, "My Queen?" in a more insistent tone as the refreshments were placed on the bedside table.

"Am I even a queen?" Lucia murmured. Her distant eyes glanced upwards.

Nothing but emptiness and despair lay within those pupils. She had fallen deep into a pit of grief.

With a child.

"The people of this kingdom need you, so I condemn so."

"By law, I cannot rule. I am only a pure-bred royalty woman, handed away to serve only one purpose in this life."

Baelyn frowned, watching the woman carefully, listening intently.

"Besides, no kingdom would recognize me. I would be deemed a woman of Hell if I stray away from the structures of society."

He scoffed. "No kingdom recognized King Alaric." A pause as he uninvitedly seated himself at the foot of the bed. "And when did His Majesty ever follow the laws of society, too?"

The advisor had a point, and Lucia could not help but weakly smile at his words. She shifted and sat up in bed, facing him fully. He was so young, but yet so stubborn. Michael had chosen well. "There might not be recorded history of a woman leading a kingdom, but it certainly did not fear His Majesty from being the first outlawed knight to do it."

The queen looked down, absentmindedly picking at her fingers again. She knew what the advisor was implying. The kingdom needed a leader, and with all odds stacked against her, she was the only hope left. She sighed. "I am in no state to rule."

The advisor's voice was firm, yet gentle. "Absolutely not, but you will never truly be prepared for the roles we are thrown into suddenly. But pick yourself up and do it anyway." Lucia's lips thinned as he continued, "At least you would not be doing this alone."

"My, your advisor is wise despite his lack of years on Earth."

Lucia snapped her head up to spot her mother-in-law standing in the threshold, her face pale and hair disheveled from the hours of lying in her own bedchamber. Her figure had become alarmingly thin, and dark circles coated under her eyes.

She looked so, so tired.

The older woman studied the two of them as she approached the other side of the queen. Her wrinkled dress rustled as she sat delicately, barely a weight on the bed. Her hands reached out and grasped Lucia's. "My, you look awful."

Lucia snorted with a chuckle. "You do too."

The corners of Elizabeth's mouth curled ever so slightly, pleased to see her son's wife after a long period of solitude. The two women had endured their pain in silence, but before Elizabeth could utter another word, Lucia hastily whispered, "I am so sorry."

That tiny smile faded away as she thought about the loss of her last child. The memories of him running around the open yard naked without a care in the world, tending to the feisty chickens, working the fields with his father, and caring for her and his sister as he aged into a fine man. A man that deserved to live a long and prosperous life; not to be cut short in a painful death.

She gently squeezed the queen's delicate, soft hands. "I am sorry, too. I had dreamed of you and my son living a long and happy life together, watching your kingdom grow and flourish, and seeing our beloved Charlotte become a strong and fierce princess." She shook her head. "My, how I have dreamt for the past days. But now, I must make room in my dreams for the grandchild growing in your womb."

"You have heard?"

"News travels fast like wildfire, my dear, especially when it concerns an heir," Elizabeth explained. "It won't be long before the people of this kingdom find out. I do not know what they will do with that information, but I do know this: You carry my second grandchild, and soon, you will nurse the babe with your bosom. Please, continue my son's legacy. Do not let his work be in vain—for him, for your children, and for the people who need you."

A tear slid down Lucia's cheek, and Elizabeth quickly reached out to wipe it away with her thumb. Her motherly words and touch comforted the queen. Baelyn added, "I would be honored to follow you, and I can promise others would be too. Rattle the bonds of the old laws and be a leader that inspires the weak."

"Inspire the weak....," Lucia mumbled before a sob broke from her lips. Her mother-in-law pulled her into a warm embrace, arms wrapped around each other. Her body shuddered.

Elizabeth tried her hardest to hold back her own tears, while Baelyn looked on, a small smile gracing his lips at the scene. This was a start.

A start of a new rein.

31

The First Woman

The seamstress's deft fingers meticulously finished the last golden buttons on the crimson tunic, carefully maneuvering in and out to avoid pricking. The sleek black trousers, with her dagger secured at her thigh with designed bounds of leather, clung to her curvaceous figure, adorned with gold trim along the black and red fabric.

With a black shoulder cape that draped down to her waist, Lucia exuded intimidation. Outsiders and enemies would deem her mad for donning men's garb, but it allowed her greater mobility and readiness compared to a cumbersome dress.

"When do you expect our guests to arrive?" Lucia asked, as still as possible, as the seamstress worked around her.

They were in Alaric's study. Despite his absence, the queen left it as he had originally decorated it. His handwriting on his work remained.

"Hopefully soon, Your Majesty. I have arranged for them to meet at the northern border to evade the raids," Baelyn said, seated at the desk, organizing papers. The desk and chair were more so the advisors now, since Lucia had lost interest in writing letters. Her focus was mainly elsewhere. Although she wouldn't admit it to anyone, it brought her sadness from the memories of spending hours working alongside her husband on the tasks now purely for Baelyn.

Lucia replied, "Good."

Troops of allies from Kingdom Zuiphate were on their way, having traveled for a day. Though reluctant to get entangled in the serious bickering between kingdoms, and now ruled primarily by a woman, the king hesitantly dispatched a small contingent of his knights—the last addition to the growing army encamped just outside of Kingdom Hartfelt's small town.

The men from the kingdoms of Ironwood and Shadowmere had been relentlessly taunting and provoking the patrols, spreading rumors of missing messenger men who had vanished a month prior under Nadia's command. Approaching the construction site was nearly impossible without facing harassment. But with a bit of luck and a captured knight from Kingdom Shadowmere, alongside hours of brutal torture inflicted by Rayne, the court learned that the two rival kingdoms were responsible for the attack and death of King Alaric.

It started as an attempt to distract with small raids, men dressed in disguise, to pave the way for the final, large-scale attack. This sparked outrage among Hartfelt's townsfolk, who now followed her lead.

To make matters worse, letters from the two foe kingdoms were thrown over the borders, threatening assault to claim land and resources of the "unnoble" realm, even setting a date for their proposition to arrive and claim the land within the next month.

It was an act of war.

Revenge burned in her people's veins, even in herself, but foolishly jumping in without their allies directly involved was a death sentence. Everything had to be planned out, precise, for their survival. Even her clothing today was meticulously chosen—black for mourning, red for her husband.

Kingdom Cinderhaven had dispatched most of its forces, followed by Ojore, unwilling to risk losing a cherished trading partner and thrilled at the prospect of allying with a kingdom ruled by a woman. The Kingdom Zuiphate army was en route. The only drawback was the severed communication with her brother's kingdom. With an empire as vast as Kingdom Morningstar, the shift in direction could drastically alter the outcome of the conflict.

Their final hope for reaching communication was through Nadia.

A letter penned by Baelyn and Lucia herself, a desperate last resort to reach out for her brother's aid. The Knight of the Body understood the perilous nature of her mission but was prepared to face the potential consequences head-on. She donned her armor, secured the letter in her satchel, and mounted her horse, ready to ride into hostile territory.

"Nadia, wait."

The knight, her only hand on the reins, turned her head at the sound of the queen's voice. The sun had already set, and the darkness served as a cloak, concealing her figure in her dark attire. "Your Majesty?"

Lucia gestured for Nadia to lean downwards, and when she did, soft lips pecked her cheek. It was a gesture of appreciation, a blessing from the kingdom's ruler. The fate of their kingdom rested on the knight's shoulders.

With a kick to her horse's flanks, Nadia galloped into the unknown. Uncertain if she would encounter her foes. Uncertain if she would even achieve her task alive. However, she was certain that this would be the redemption of her character.

Now, it had been several days since the queen last saw the knight. Rayne had taken Nadia's position, from baron, to temporary placement for Knight of the Body. He followed the queen like a tall, dark shadow, observing with his eyes but never speaking a word. The man was quiet and reserved. She had yet to hear him utter a single word.

He stood by the study room glass doors, as still as a statue, until the little princess came running towards him from the grand staircase, dressed in a vibrant purple sundress. She, too, tried to speak and befriend Rayne, but she only managed a smile from the senior man. He grasped the handles of the glass-planned doors and held them open. Charlotte beamed with delight. "Thank you."

Lucia turned her head at the sight of her daughter. The seamstress, finally finished with her task, excused herself and left the study room. "Mommy! You look so different," Charlotte exclaimed.

"Do I at least look good?" Lucia asked, bending down to her knees to hold her daughter's hands. In the upcoming months, she will be unable to bend her legs or reach her toes, as her belly will become swollen.

"You always look good. The most beautiful woman in the world."

Lucia booped her nose. "I can say the same for you, princess."

Charlotte giggled. "Do you think daddy would like the purple?"

The queen's heart sank a little. Although he was no longer present, he was still on her daughter's mind as much as he was in hers. She brushed a golden hair strand behind her daughter's ear. "I do believe he would love it. He was the one who purchased it, so he must have thought you would look pretty in it."

"I wish he could see you in your new outfit."

"I do, too," Lucia replied, sighing, "I do, too."

She knew he would become ravished at the sight of her.

Vibrant flags of colors danced in the crisp autumn breeze, their hues representing the diverse kingdoms from which the men hailed, proudly displayed on their tents. The local townsfolk eagerly emerged each day, mingling with the knights, sharing food, music, and conversation, as they all awaited the impending moves.

Her head held high, the queen surveyed the scene with delight on horseback. The encampments circled the small town, with the more vulnerable inhabitants protected at the center by the skilled knights on guard against potential threats. Accompanied by her temporary Knight of the Body and a few members of her court, they journeyed to one of the nearby mountain rivers at the suggestion of Baelyn, who rode alongside them on a slender mare. His discomfort was evident throughout the ride.

The autumn leaves were just beginning to change color, not yet dry enough to crunch underfoot, creating a stunning display of reds, oranges, and yellows. The ride to the meeting spot was nothing short of breathtaking.

As the royal entourage approached after a half-day's journey, Queen Lucia's cheerful expression gradually transformed into one of stoic composure. Though her eyes betrayed a flicker of surprise at the sight of the Kingdom Zuiphate's men already assembled on the banks of the shallow river. Their horses' legs were wet from wading through the water, and their riders stood patiently in anticipation of the royal party's arrival. All heads turned to the sound of approaching hooves.

A handful of men, a few carriages of supplies, not as much as Lucia had hoped. She had grown accustomed to Kingdom Cinderhaven's generous provisions. A disappointment, but she remained impassive to conceal it.

A middle-aged man approached them instantly upon their arrival. He wore layers of metal on his body, torn leather underneath. His right eye was missing, likely the result of a brutal knife wound, and his dark brown skin bore numerous scars, telling the tale of many battles fought and won. His curly grey hair hung loose around his face, framing his tired features. He studied the queen, squinting his eyes for a few uncomfortable seconds before he cleared his throat. "I am Mael, senior knight of Kingdom Zuiphate, blessed by the king himself to lead his men in service for your cause," he declared, his voice firm and commanding. "I have personally selected the finest warriors for this endeavor."

"Queen Lucia, first woman of Kingdom Hartfelt, and this is my court. Advisor Baelyn," she gestured with her head to the right, "is the man who inquired for this pleasant arrangement."

Baelyn acknowledged Mael with a wave, but the knight remained silent and still. Lucia then gestured to her left, "And this is Rayne, one of my most trusted knights, temporarily promoted to Knight of the Body. He oversees the daily operations and maintenance of the grounds. If you have any concerns after settling in, please direct them to him."

Mael's gaze lingered on Lucia for a moment longer before turning to survey the smaller contingent of Hartfelt's forces, his expression unreadable. The tension between the two groups was palpable. She tried to ease it as she continued, "Besides, how was your travel, Mael?"

"I do not wish to uselessly converse. Save those pleasures for the courtesans."

An ignorant man, that's what he was. A very arrogant, ignorant man.

She retorted sharply, "My court does not seek the relief of prostitutes. You'll find yourself quite disappointed if it was expected during your stay on my kingdom grounds."

Instead of dissatisfaction, Mael left out a roar of laughter, his arms outstretched. A few of his men chuckled from behind. "We will seek ourselves to make our own prostitutes, then."

Lucia stood her ground. "You are welcome to make your own, but it will remain only among your group of men."

"I will not make a male harlot out of my finest—"

"Oh, I believe you will. You will not force yourself upon my people. You will find it quite challenging to handle a sword again without all your fingers. I'll ensure Rayne upholds that if you go against my orders. The same goes with your men."

Mael and Rayne locked eyes. He sought invalidation of the queen's foolish words, but Rayne only nodded along with the statement.

Mael flashed his teeth, but instead of arguing further, he gestured his men to ready their steeds. Before he vanished into his crowd, Lucia said, "Please, allow my court to lead. We can discuss more about my kingdom's arrangements while we ride."

She pulled on Devona's reins. The mare neighed and turned to begin the journey again.

It never came to mind in the past years of her life that Lucia would own a kingdom, passed down from a man she loved so dearly.

She slowly undressed, neatly folding her clothing and releasing a deep sigh. It was so empty, so quiet.

So cold. So dark.

Each night alone in the big, empty bedchamber that she once shared with her deceased husband amplified the sorrow that haunted her. And with this private time, away from pitiful eyes, she wept freely. Wept until she fell asleep, burying her face into his scent that threatened to fade.

Lucia placed the clothing aside on the corner chair, glancing at the flowers that still sat on the mantel of the unlit fireplace. The same flowers Alaric had given her, now wilted and dry. Petals and leaves had already fallen from the slightest breeze of air. She could not force herself to throw them away; it brought her so much joy.

And so it sat there, in the same vase, same dirty brown water, with the same dead flowers in it.

Her eyes dared to water. It was not the time to cry. Not yet.

She looked at that rug beneath her. That lovely rug she loved so much. It was a symbol of her past happy life, in which she sometimes dared herself to toss it out of the room. But then, she thought about how Alaric would not like that. It was a gift after all, from an old lady who believed in him.

She wondered: Was that lady even still alive? Does she know that this simple donation was one of the greatest gifts that Alaric, and herself, had ever enjoyed?

She hoped that the lady knew. She really hoped she knew.

Lucia crawled underneath the soft, red blankets, inhaling his scent as she wrapped herself. She felt too lazy to change into her sleepwear, so she went bare instead, as if he would have cared anyway. He loved every part of her, and she knew he loved it when she slept bare beside him.

His rough, but gentle, hands would roam all over her body. Her skin tingled from the sensation. Sometimes, he dared himself to massage her breasts, and she, too, loved it very much.

She inhaled his scent again, dreaming it was his embrace. Salty tears formed in the corners of her eyes. Now it was time to weep—to weep for hours, quietly, until she soaked the fabric underneath her.

These quiet moments, every night, were what made her realize—he was really gone.

Dreams. Only dreams and jolts of pain filled the desolate expanse of the injured man's mind.

Dreams of an agitated horse, the smaller body he leaned on from behind, the air on his face. Everything was hazy, as if seen through a foggy lens. Wet warmth filled his belly.

A hiss emanated from the smaller body. A boy, so young. His voice was laden with urgency, though the exact words were unintelligible. The man wanted to respond, to comfort the boy, but his body refused to cooperate.

He could not move, could not blink. His vision began to darken, the blackness encroaching from the periphery, swallowing his sight entirely.

Then excruciating pain, like a searing fire that threatened to consume him.

Pain racked his body. He tried to scream, to call out, to fight, but his strength had completely abandoned him. He felt as though he were made of jelly, devoid of all rigidity.

A stab wound, they said. A concussion, they said. Lucky to be breathing, they said.

He couldn't give a damn. He needed to fight.

Hands touched him, prodding and poking. He didn't want those hands on him.

More pain came, a fresh wave of agony that left him breathless.

He wanted to cry now.

He wanted to open his eyes, to see the faces of those who continued to inflict the pain on his skin.

Pain.

Pain.

Pain.

More voices, more hands, more pain.

Pain.

And then, finally, a blissful nothingness.

32

Leader's Table

"From my scouts," Ojore said as he pointed on the map, Kingdom Cinderhaven's senior knight entrusted with his troops, "have counted, and the number of men present has doubled. More trees have come down and flags have been attached to the branches."

Lucia studied hard on the inked-drawn map of the lands, which lay on a large, wooden, rounded table. It narrowed down to the finger laid upon the Neemere Forest. "At this point, the forest barely exists," she replied.

"It would assume so at this rate," Ojore confirmed. The broad man stepped back, his light grey hair shimmering from the candlelight. Due to the deforestation committed by Prince Alexander's men, only a thin tree line seemed to remain as a border between the kingdoms.

King Alaric's effort to secure the forest went in vain. As of a week ago, the kingdom's knights on the previous border were slain to pieces; there was not one survivor. Once the next set of knights arrived for their rotation, the mess was discovered. The border wall was destroyed, and the outposts were burned to ash. While this was a fall and a reduction in territory, it did not shatter the queen's spirits.

Mael, on the other hand, argued that the infestation of the invading men should be attacked immediately. He yelled, slammed his fists on all present tables, kicked up dirt, but no matter how much fear he tried to instill in the queen, she disagreed. Trades had only just resumed, and more people who could influence the conflict were still crossing the borders from the allied kingdoms; a brash reaction could lead to early defeat.

This angered the senior knight—*a fool*, he called her—but she only gave him a warning glare. The two have not spoken since.

That was broken today as Ojore, Mael, Rayne, and Lucia gathered around one of the large rooms on the castle's third floor, away from prying ears. The dreadful month was approaching.

Following a deep sigh, Lucia concluded, "Hold firm on what we have left on the border. Keep a distance so our foes are not provoked, but maintain your scouts' careful watch, Ojore. No more men need to be lost at this time."

Mael's nostrils flared. "I doubt that would work in our favor." Rayne stiffened as Mael tapped his finger on the map. "You have allowed our foes to think that the forest ambush was acceptable, which, in reality, it was not. More ambushes would now be sure to come. Hard and fast, to pick off the little things before the final blow."

"There are limitations on what we can do then, and still now. Our army is still building itself," Lucia objected. Food and supplies were still being collected and stockpiled on wagons. Skilled healers and their families were being recruited and counted, given money for their services. Specialized blacksmiths had begun focusing on armor creation. An exceptionally skilled artisan from Kingdom Cinderhaven took precise measurements, designing armor explicitly tailored to the queen's figure.

It was made with the finest iron, polished to a brilliant shine. Intricate plates were carved and molded beautifully to fit the feminine body. Lucia was stunned at its quality when she first laid eyes on it.

"But we can fight in arranged waves. Instead of Ojore's scouts only watching, he should command his men to begin picking at our foes. Then, a few hours after his initial move, we'll send another wave to follow suit. This does not allow our foe's army a moment to rest."

"But give them a reason to come to this castle's doorstep sooner?" Ojore said before he took a sip from his porcelain cup. The steam from the kettle wafted a sweet aroma that the knight particularly enjoyed during their political meetings. His stern face always eased from whatever blend Lucia made. This time, she prepared a special berry tea blend to tingle the tongue with the aftertaste of sweetness.

Mael's annoyance was evident when he crossed his arms. "You have to slam the army with an iron fist as fast and as hard as we possibly can. That way, as our numbers continue to grow, we are not sitting here like waiting ducks."

Lucia replied, "Reckless strategies will only lead to death and destruction. Arrogance leads to failure."

"Your plans are too safe," Mael growled, stepping forward. His breath hit the queen's face. She tried to stand as tall as possible to meet the man's stare and challenge his intimidation.

"Mael."

"I have been in war. How many have you been present at?"

A snarl formed on her lips. "Why must you still express your displeasure with my final decision a week ago?"

"Because of your weak leadership, I might not see my kingdom again. I am coming to terms with the fact that I will be lying dead in the middle of a field somewhere instead."

"We all could be lying in a field next week, cut up piece by piece, but at least my death was in the best efforts of my people."

"Enough of this," Ojore interjected, but his words fell on deaf ears.

Mael laughed, a sinister sound that sent shivers down everyone's spines. "You are truly a crazed, womanly fool! You are with child! You really believe you can lead us into battle?"

"I carry the blood-related heir of my kingdom. I have every right to do as I please!" Lucia shouted, using both hands to shove the man away. His breath was too foul, and she could no longer stand it.

Mael stumbled, surprised by her boldness, but before he could react in a gesture that he would later regret, Rayne stepped in between them. He shook his head with a fierce stare. Ojore tried to wrap an arm around the queen to guide her away, but she smacked his hand away. Instead, she twisted around Rayne and gave Mael her final word. "I will lead, whether you like it or not."

Rayne gave his queen an uneasy glance. He had never imagined she would be so adamant about leading the army. He shouldn't have assumed that he would be the one to take charge.

"Queen Lucia?" Ojore questioned, confused by her decision.

"I have made up my mind," she replied. "I am leading our men, and you cannot convince me otherwise. You all can be by my side while I do it, or stay behind to protect the town."

Mael tsked. "Then you have damned your precious, little kingdom to Hell." He stomped out of the room and slammed the doors behind him. The sound of his departure echoed through the halls.

Lucia did not flinch.

The world felt like a dream; everything seemed unreal and detached.

The explosion, the fire, the scent of iron in the air—these memories returned to his unconscious mind as foreign nightmares.

He twisted and turned, sweat soaking the fabrics beneath him. Strangers' hands touched him, forcefully fed him, cleaned him, their actions as foreign as they were intrusive.

From a lack of awareness, he was scared. Utterly terrified.

Yet amidst the chaos, one figure stood out—a man with golden hair and piercing blue eyes. Though the stranger's lips moved, uttering words that should have been clear as day, he could not hear them. He simply stared at the golden-haired figure, uncomprehending, before drifting off to sleep mere moments later.

What felt like years of slumber were only days.

As the second month dawned, the man's consciousness slowly began to return, like a flickering flame in the darkness. He weakly blinked against the blinding light that leaked through the large windows. Everything around him was a blur, but he was able to note the gold trimming and oil paintings on the walls. An unknown figure moved in his peripheral view.

He did not dare make a sound. He did not know where he was. He remained still, unsure of his surroundings and whether he was in danger.

But despite his efforts to stay quiet, the man's tongue stuck to the roof of his mouth, and his lips were cracked, leaving him parched. He tried to swallow, but it felt like sandpaper scraping against his throat. He fell to the weakness of his basic needs.

"Water," he rasped out, his voice barely audible. Pain spiked in his rough throat.

The figure in the room stopped moving and turned towards the man on the bed. He could feel the heat of their stare as they assessed his condition. He tried again. "Water."

The figure gasped, then quickly disappeared from view. The click of the doors signaled their leave.

Well, that went according to plan. If he was not going to be given the simple pleasures of water, he was going to do it himself.

He wiggled his fingers, stiffness aching in every joint, every muscle, before he dared to move his arms. His extremities felt foreign as he gathered his fragile strength to hoist himself up from the sheets.

Pain shocked his system. He whimpered and fell back onto the soft mountains.

Large pillows, to be exact. He lay on a luxurious bed with enough room for two more people.

As he lay there, defeated and overwhelmed by the random pain that repeatedly stunned his nerves, he could not help but notice the outline shape of a water basin on the bedside table. It seemed so far from within reach.

He lifted his head to his bare chest, only in his undergarments. An injury was present across his abdomen. He blinked a few times, enough for his eyes to begin to focus. Enough to make out the stitching.

The wound throbbed. A row of stitches held the sensitive, red skin tightly. He did not remember when it was done, or how it was there, but it was guaranteed to leave a nasty scar, a sibling to the one on his chest.

A groan escaped his lips as he lay his head back down in defeat, trying to lick his lips desperately. He turned his head towards the water basin once more. It was so close yet so far away again. He could almost taste the cool, refreshing liquid on his tongue.

He was going to be dried out to death. He swore by it.

Then, the doors swung open. Several individuals entered, their faces etched with shock as they looked down at him as he lay still on the bed. Among them was the same golden-haired man from his dreams, his smile lighting up his face.

And from that smile alone, in that exact moment, everything came rushing back.

The explosion.

The fire.

The blood.

The horse.

It all came flooding back, and with it, the realization that he had been gone.

Gone for a long time.

"You are truly awake!" Michael hollered, his voice filled with excitement. He turned to the two women who had accompanied him, servants. "Get him fresh food and water. Find my physician."

The women bowed and hurried out of the bedchamber. He watched as the prince moved to grab a nearby wooden chair and sat down beside the bed. "Oh, King Alaric, welcome back to the living."

33

The Acceptance to Fate

"You had such an undeniably high fever that you soaked the sheets and became fidgety. My court and I were afraid you were going to succumb to infection."

"Where is Lucia? Where is my wife?"

Those were the first questions that came out of the king's mouth. The topic of infection was not his priority. A servant nudged the edge of a cup of water against his lips, but he shook his head. If he took another sip of water, he was going to drown from the inside.

"She remains in your palace."

"Is she well?"

"I cannot give you that specific answer, but she is all right from what I've collected," Michael answered, still sitting in the wooden chair, a leg propped up over his other knee. The physician had just finished assessing the condition of the king's stitched wound, applying soothing salves to ease the pain that allowed him to sit upright in bed, layers of pillows behind him. He excused himself to prepare a special drink blend to aid in the healing process.

Not an answer that Alaric desired, but it was enough to bring comfort, to know that she was alive. He had spent too much time trapped by the same four walls of the glorious castle. "I need to see her."

Michael's expression softened. "You need to rest. You are in no fit to travel, and it is too much of a risk to do so."

"I can travel with caution," Alaric countered.

"It is not about your wound, Your Majesty," Michael replied, exhaling a deep, weary sigh. "It is the war."

Alaric's face had faded of all color. He remembered being in the middle of an impending conflict, bickering between the two kingdoms insatiable demands for peace. It had finally led to war?

Michael continued, "The war has taken its toll on our infrastructure, disrupting our construction efforts. I am unsure of the condition of the progress. My kingdom has been isolated since your arrival. I have tried to send letters to your kingdom, to my sister, but my men have been intercepted and executed by the forces of Kingdoms Ironwood and Shadowmere, who have seized control of the roads."

Alaric swore he needed that cup of water again. The news had dried his mouth similarly to the desert sands. "Pardon?"

"The sudden ambush and your disappearance instigated it all. I had my suspicions when Donovan first spoke of random raids by unknown pests." A flicker of sadness overcame the prince.

"How did I even survive?" Alaric questioned, gesturing to his salved-leathered wound. The aching pain had already dramatically faded.

"Soran managed to pull you on horseback and raced you here. I was not sure you were going to survive. You were as pale as a specter, and the gash was so deep that my physicians were not sure if the wound had possibly punctured an organ. I do not know how you pulled through, but I am overjoyed to see you conscious," Michael confessed.

"I have to express my gratitude. My life is in debt to him."

Michael smiled, a hint of pride in his eyes. "No need. He is a wealthy boy now. Your debt has been paid."

"That puts me in an obligation to pay you the debt."

"No. You married my sister and made her and my niece very happy. It is more than I can ask for. Your kingdom does not owe mine."

"Then you have my gratitude. You are a better man than your father."

The prince's chest swelled from the compliment.

A knock vibrated the bedchamber doors. Michael did not get a chance to ask who it was before the doors swung open. The news of the king's awakening traveled quickly.

There stood Nadia, her face marred by a crooked nose and a missing arm. She took a cautious step forward, unsure if her eyes were fooling her. The man looked alive. He was breathing and staring right back at her. He, too, seemed unsure if his eyes were playing tricks.

"Alaric?"

The king blinked. "Nadia?"

The knight gasped and dashed, lunging her arm out, nearly knocking the king to his side with the force of her embrace. Bed covers swooshed from her speed.

"Oof!"

"My lord, my prayers have been answered!" She melted into his grasp and inhaled him deeply without hesitation, savoring the scent she had longed for from her brother.

He was *alive*. He had survived the surgery, the fever, the cruel darkness.

A true blessing indeed.

Michael stood to retrieve a chair as Alaric pulled away to study her face, clamped between his hands. There were new changes. "What happened to you?"

Nadia wiped away a tear that threatened to spill down her cheek. "The ambush," she replied, her voice trembling. "I lost my arm in the ambush."

"And your nose?" Alaric inquired.

"Your wife gave me that honor."

"Then you must have deserved it."

Nadia gaped and slapped his arm. "All this time, I thought you were dead," she admitted, shaking her head. Michael placed the chair for her to sit down, and she did as she reached out with her only hand and gripped the king's. "Poor Lucia, she thinks the same."

Alaric frowned. The stress he must have inflicted on his wife and stepdaughter. They did not deserve that at all. Guilt fluttered inside him.

"She went mad, so, so mad, that she tried to kill me," she said, but then chuckled right after. "But she is now a queen leading your people. She arranged an army from our allies, aided in training men with Rayne, and enforced kingdom law. Now, she is working alongside senior knights provided by our allies on a counterattack for the upcoming days. That is the reason she sent me—a last resort to reach for Prince Michael in aid."

"Counterattack?" Alaric's brows creased.

"Kingdom Ironwood and Shadowmere are launching to overtake your kingdom in one swoop. Lucia is set on the defense," Michael answered.

"And she is settled on leading it; the whole army. She did not tell me herself, but in the letter that Prince Michael graciously allowed me to read, she stated so." Nadia's face turned to one of disappointment, pulling away from Alaric's hold. Michael was also in disbelief.

"My wife is going to lead an army?"

Nadia replied, "Yes."

Alaric's face contorted into a visage of utter horror, following a maelstrom of emotions swirling within him. A potent concoction of pride and fear, a lethal recipe that threatened to consume him whole.

"If I were still present at the castle, I would have tried to convince her otherwise, take her place instead, for the well-being and care of her children."

"Even with you not present, Rayne should have—." Alaric froze, as if his own mind had slapped him. Then, in a tone so soft, as if speaking the word out loud would shatter the fragile reality he was clinging to, he questioned, "Children?"

Nadia nodded solemnly, her eyes reflecting the same horror that was etched on the king's face.

"She is with your child, Your Majesty."

The words hung heavy in the air, a death knell for the life Alaric had previously known.

The woman who had his heart and soul.

His goddess.

Pregnant.

He was going to be a father to another child.

Alaric shot up, to take action, to be the protector he had sworn to be, but he only managed to swing his legs over the edge before Michael was in front of him, gently pushing him back down onto the pillows. "You are in no condition to stand."

"She is with child and is going to lead people in battle! I cannot allow this!" Alaric exclaimed, his voice echoing the desperation that clawed at his heart. He needed to be there, to protect his family, to save his people. Now.

He tried again to rise, his head pounding with the effort and his stitches screaming in protest, but Nadia joined in Michael's efforts, her hand firm as she nudged the king back down. "I cannot allow this either, but it is already too late," Nadia hissed.

"What do you plan to do? You cannot even reach her from the road blockage," Michael added, his voice strained. "Even with my own displeasure in her choices, there is nothing I can directly do."

Alaric struggled, trying to shove the two away to try and stand again, wincing in pain as the movement pulled at his stitches. Nadia had enough. "You are going to rip your stitches if you don't stop right now! You are worse than a babe!"

His head pounded as he snapped back. "This is my wife! My children! I will not sit here and wait helplessly as war rages on, praying that she somehow survives!" He was more frustrated with himself. His whole world could be ripped away from him in the blink of an eye. War was unpredictable.

"There are sacrifices to be made," Michael stated.

Alaric sent a glare, flashing with barely contained rage that could kill a man. If the prince were a commoner, he would be smacked into unconsciousness, probably stomped on until his ribcage caved in. "What is your command on the situation?"

"My army moves out tomorrow. Remus will lead my army to try and push forward to your kingdom's aid. I will stay behind to protect my people here, to hold defenses."

Nadia added, "I plan to join Remus's side."

Alaric huffed. "No, I will join him."

"Your Majesty?"

"You will stay by Michael's side on the defenses."

"With all due respect, again, Alaric, even my physician cannot clear you fit enough to travel," Michael firmly repeated.

"There will be blood on my lands, death on my hands. If I hear you mention that again, you impertinent, ill-nurtured inchworm, I will throw that pathetic wooden chair at you."

Michael mumbled under his breath, "I like to see you try," but Alaric ignored it.

Even if it damned him to reopen his stitches. "My *pregnant* wife will be on the battlefield; I will stop at nothing to be there."

Lucia stood upon the oil painting of her family again, reminiscing about her fallen husband. His scent had long gone stale, even in the bedchamber. Clothes and belongings that were his still remained untouched, except one.

She wore his elegant burgundy houppelande with intricate gold thread patterns woven into the sleeves—the one she had eyed and was astonished by its precise beauty. She even wore similar black trousers tailored to her body measurements to honor him before battle.

Barely entering into her second trimester, the queen now presented a small belly bump. A little unusual by Elizabeth's experience, but Lucia paid no heed as her hands constantly touched her abdomen.

She was going to be a mother of two—her second child.

She had already decided on names. If the babe came out as a boy, he would be named after her husband, and if a girl, after her mother-in-law. Father did not deserve the honor of having his name passed on through her, regardless of his death.

"Mommy?"

Lucia's head snapped towards the sound of her daughter's voice. She saw Charlotte clinging to the plush horse her husband had gifted her so long ago. Sadness and fear were etched across the little girl's face.

"Don't go," she said, her voice crackling. Her eyes were already puffy and wet.

Lucia dropped to her knees, opening her arms in an invitation. The little princess rushed into her embrace, inhaling her mother's scent, feeling her warmth. This was a lot for a child to take in.

Truthfully, unfair as well.

"I have to go," Lucia whispered, angling her head to kiss her cheek.

Charlotte sniffled, burying herself completely into her mother's chest. "I-I know."

The two held each other for long minutes, not daring to let go. "I will come back," Lucia said, though she wasn't sure if she'd make it out of the battle alive tomorrow. It was a gamble with her life, her unborn's, but to make her daughter feel better, she said, "I promise."

A truth, or a lie.

The princess seemed to melt in her arms in a sense of relief. "I love you."

"I love you, too. Never forget that."

"How can I when you say it every day?"

That made Lucia chuckle, kissing her daughter's face again.

Victoria, concealed behind a distant wall, clutched a handkerchief to her face to stifle the sobs that wracked her body. The looming fear casted a shadow that was too much for others to bear.

Rose tried to stand tall, her face a mask of strength, trying to be strong for the other fellow servants. But when night fell, she could only pray and wipe away her tears before slumber claimed her. Axel was less cheery, Caroline more tamed, and Hank alone had remained more isolated and quiet, even around the princess. But no matter how hard the servants tried, even with the royal advisors' support, Lucia had been set to lead.

"Charlotte, I have a task for you." The princess pulled away to meet her mother's eyes. She patiently waited.

Lucia continued, "I need you to look after the court while I am away tomorrow. They would need guidance, comfort, and I entrust you to take care of them. You are so brave. You are so, so brave with a big caring heart, I can't think of anyone else that can do the task." A distraction for her, to keep her mind elsewhere and not fixated on her fears. "Could you do that for me, princess?"

Charlotte did not hesitate as she nodded her head. She loved to help. "I won't let you down."

"Good."

A held-back sob broke through from Victoria. It caught the royals' attention. Lucia stood. "Come."

Victoria slowly moved around the corner of the wall, but once she saw the queen's face, she dashed towards her. She wrapped tightly around Lucia's neck and tears flowed uncontrollably. The fear of losing another great leader shook her to her core. She hiccuped, her voice weak and fragile, "I apologize, Your Majesty."

"Don't be sorry. Charlotte will look after you all tomorrow," Lucia said, rubbing the servant's back in a comforting manner. A smaller army of knights, as well as Baelyn, were to be stationed in the town and castle for tomorrow's raid, as a defense in case her offensive army got overwhelmed.

She prayed it never came to that.

The sounds of the night were peaceful, to be savored before the massacre of cries tomorrow. Under the blanket of scars, Prince Alexander watched outwards from the border. He knew hidden scouts were out there, watching his men's every move. They were well hidden, he gave credit to that, but although he could not spot them, he knew they were watching him.

Behind him, his combined army slept soundly. A definite outnumber to Kingdom Hartfelt's numbers, if the kingdom even possessed an army. Tomorrow was the day to see.

A sudden crunch of grass alerted the prince to the approaching king. King Victor was now by his side, the two fixated at the distance while men snored. Despite having no experience in war, Alexander had been generous in his aid and teachings, grateful that the king's plan had succeeded in King Alaric's death. He was basically showered with gifts.

After a week of celebration and their upcoming plans, the final takeover was here to take. "Are you afraid?"

Victor side-glanced at Alexander before he shook his head. "No, you?"

"Never."

A pause of silence. A question lingered in the king's mind.

"Are we to kill her?" Victor asked softly, referring to the queen of Kingdom Hartfelt.

"Yes," Alexander replied without a second of reconsideration. "Even if she is with child, that commoner's bloodline must be wiped out for my father's honor. I will do the kill."

Victor scoffed, a dark smile playing at the corners of his mouth. "That is monstrous, even for you."

"I suppose you had much more deranged ideas for her?"

"I do. You can do the killing blow, I do not care, but leave her body as tidy as possible."

Alexander sighed. He knew the king would find a way to have cruel fun with his enemy's spouse. And to his surprise, the king hadn't killed his wife yet. It was a matter of time, however. "I do not want to know."

"Good, I wasn't going to tell you," Victor said, patting Alexander's back before excusing himself. A deep chuckle left his lips as he walked to his bedroll. The man's mind was twisted.

Alexander remained where he was. He still had a few things to clear in his head before he could properly rest.

34

The Arrow

Each step was like fire.

Metal clanged as men, dressed in their armor, some bearing family heirlooms, prepared for the march. Young farriers scurried about, saddling the hundreds of colorful, decorated horses as fast as they could. Wagon loads of supplies and provisions were set to trail behind, and flags fluttered atop poles, destined to be borne by the standard-bearers.

As the men readied themselves, some knew they would not walk the road with their lives. Perils and uncertainties lay in wait, but no fear was instilled in them as the king trotted through the crowd on his borrowed steed. A display of bravery and confidence, especially from the months of incapacitation.

Alaric's knees buckled when he arose from that recovery bed. It was arduous, as he nearly toppled two servants who aided him. Searing pain coursed through his body, but after several walks around Morningstar's large palace, he coalesced the strength to ready himself to ride out with Remus.

The Knight of the Body bowed his head respectfully and offered a subtle smile that hinted at his relief to see Alaric. He was already on his finest horse, waiting and watching his army's assembly. The king returned the gesture, stopping the horse at the knight's side. "Remus, it is a pleasure to see you again."

"You as well, Your Majesty. It is an honor to march by your side. The army is almost ready to march."

"Splendid. My nerves are choking me."

"You fear war?"

Alaric's hold on his reins tightened, trying to keep himself grounded and steady. "War is every living being's fear, but my nerves are for my wife and children."

Remus understood. He, too, was worried sick for them. Alaric continued, "The sooner we leave, the sooner we are there to aid."

Nearly consumed by darkness, and already in their armor and swords at their sides, the two remained waiting. Only the nearby faint light from the fire torches touched their faces.

From within the castle, Nadia planned by Michael's side. Routes for emergencies were drawn, and knights ordered to stay behind were placed in positions throughout the massive town. Anxious folks bickered with each other. Some were kind enough to offer food and water for the patrolling knights.

Despite not knowing if he would survive to see her again, Alaric knew that Nadia was the best place to be if a siege were to occur.

The first rays of dawn had barely kissed the horizon when Queen Lucia May Hartfelt, wife of the deceased king, King Alaric Ricard Hartfelt, led her forces into battle, softly singing to help calm her men's anxiety. They approached the enemy camp situated south of the battered Neemere Forest.

Rather than waiting for their foes to attack, the queen devised a cunning plan to catch them off guard. She would lead the initial charge, much to the surprise of her adversaries, halting their initial plans to overtake her kingdom. This was the only strategy that she and Mael could come to an agreement on.

Flanking Lucia were the two senior knights—Mael on her right and Ojore on her left. Both men were astride their finest warhorses, positioned at the forefront of the army. Lucia herself rode Emris, her blonde hair pulled back in a tight bun with her sword at her side. Her dagger remained strapped to her thigh, barely concealed beneath her armor. A tight fit, alongside her abdomen.

Rayne held the rear of the army, to oversee the fallen, to ensure that any injured knights received aid from the small contingent of people that followed them. He carried his large bow and sword.

Flags of the three kingdoms fluttered gently in the soft breeze, a breathtaking sight to behold. Their numbers were enough in hand for the offensive move, consisting of swordsmen and archers. The archers positioned themselves near the rear, strategically moving slower and slower behind into the green foliage, to hide from prying eyes.

Not a single bird chirped or a creature stirred, as if Mother Nature held her breath in anticipation of the impending carnage. Lucia felt it in herself.

She prayed for her kingdom's men, her allies' men, and those waiting for her return to the castle.

She prayed for the safety of her children and that if she fell, it would not be in vain.

She stopped once she saw the tree line from a distance.

"Victor!"

The king groaned and twisted his body in the bedroll, too early in the morning to be woken from the warmth of his tent and the comfort of his sheets. "Victor! Get your ass up!" Alexander shouted. The prince then gave the king a hard shove with his boot, jolting the man awake.

"Ugh, if I wanted a wake-up call, I would have told you last night," Victor grumbled, his voice thick with sleep as he grudgingly emerged his head from the warmth of his bedroll. The cold morning air slapped him in the face, and he shivered. The leaves outside had begun to fall.

"Cain reported back!"

"So?"

"So? That widowed bitch mustered an army and is marching down to us right this moment! They are going to ambush us!" Alexander exclaimed, his face red from either a lack of oxygen or anger, perhaps a mixture of both.

Victor's eyes widened, and he squirmed out of the bedroll, his bare feet tangling in the fabric. He was only in his luxurious undergarments as he stumbled. "Are you certain?"

Alexander grabbed Victor's arm, yanking him upwards as he watched the king fumble and nearly fall. "Do I look uncertain?" he challenged as he pulled Victor outside the tent. The king had little protection against the soft breeze, but reality sank in.

The camp was in chaos—men shouting, horses neighing, and a general sense of pandemonium reigning supreme as the sun had barely risen. Panic was everywhere.

Knights scrambled to get ready, to assemble, to ride out. Any moment now, the army led by the queen of Hartfelt would be in sight, and their own forces were woefully unprepared.

And just as their army managed to get assembled in the shortest time possible, Alexander felt his blood run cold as he glanced at the sea of men ahead of them. At the forefront of the opposing army stood the queen, her delicate features illuminated by the rising sun and flickering fire touches. He had only heard rumored descriptions of her, never having laid eyes on her himself, but it was a shame that the beautiful woman had to die today.

On both sides of her were two men, armed to the teeth and bulky in size. Their warhorses were massive creatures that overshadowed the widow. She looked like a tiny speck between them.

Her own Knights of the Body? He did not know.

The space between them was vast, the pale yellow grass swaying gently as an eerie silence was broken only by the swishing of horse tails. They had barely made it out of the forest before the queen's army greeted them from a distance.

Disorganized. Their army was disorganized.

All previous plans of their own ambush had been thrown out.

Victor, resplendent in his finest armor, sat on his steed beside Alexander. He leaned in close and whispered, "There are more than I anticipated."

Alexander cleared his throat, trying to project confidence. "Our numbers will hold." A flicker of worry crossed Victor's face, but it did not go unnoticed. "We advance and claim what is ours," he added, and only then did Victor nod in agreement, his eyes returning to the horizon.

The prince urged his horse forward a few feet, in clear view of his enemies. Cain trotted his horse in his leader's place, his face serious and ready to draw blood. He had been in enough battles to know better than to underestimate their enemy, assigning Tobias to manage the kingdom's defenses. Just like now, this unexpected turn of events had caught him off guard.

Alexander licked his lips before he shouted, "The Kingdom of Hartfelt has fallen. King Alaric is dead. My ally and I have come to collect the wealth owed for my father's murder and burn it to the ground."

Lucia glanced at the knight at her left, mumbling under her breath, before she nudged her stallion in sync. She looked small atop that majestic, black beast. He wondered how she even managed to mount it.

"No. I rule this land, this kingdom," Lucia shouted back, her grip on the reins white-knuckled. The wind carried her voice.

"A widowed woman cannot rule; it is the law of the people."

"This one can, regardless," she declared.

He lifted his brows. The bravery of this woman. He gave her credit for that.

Victor, on the other hand, howled out in laughter as he nudged his horse back to Alexander's side. "She is mad! Listen to her!"

A few knights from behind snickered in agreement.

Lucia remained unamused, her face unchanging. "I bring an army of men from kingdoms across the lands to protect the one you sought for." She gestured behind her to the rows of knights, flags of different kingdoms fluttering with different colors. "And with these kingdoms' support, it concludes that Kingdom Hartfelt has not fallen."

"You can spew nonsense as much as you desire, but that will not change the laws that have been set hundreds of years ago," Alexander retorted.

"Laws can change."

"Not this one."

Lucia grunted, "I think you and your ally cannot fathom a woman in a position like yours. It makes you *afraid*."

Victor sent out another roar, but Cain had had enough. Bickering was a women's talent and a waste of time. He approached beside Alexander's other side, "End this right n–!"

A loud *WHOOSH* and an arrow shot into the side of his chest, his body jerking from the impact. His horse bucked and kicked. Gasps from the crowds, then the rush of hooves as the foe's army charged.

It had happened too fast. There was not a spared second for Alexander and Victor to think as they reacted in toll and charged as well.

Cain lay on the ground, choking on his own blood.

Rayne's arrow had hit him.

35

Death's Call

Lucia had found herself surrounded by a sea of chaos and violence. The clashing of swords and the thunderous roars of men filled the air, punctuated by the rhythmic pounding of hooves and the sickening sound of flesh being torn apart. Blood spattered the ground, staining it a dark crimson hue as the battle took its toll on both sides. Despite the carnage, she remained unremarkably focused.

She swung her sword in a flurry of motion, blocking blows and striking back with deadly precision on foot. The adrenaline coursing through her veins drowned out any thoughts of regret as she took her first lives, leaving only the primal instinct to survive and protect those around her. However, she knew when she recollected herself, she would become nauseous and irrational about the murders she had committed.

She could never go back to her old self if she survived today. She would be forever changed.

But even amidst the fighting, Lucia could not help but notice the tide of the battle turning against them. One by one, her allies fell, their bodies littering the ground like discarded pawns in a twisted game of chess. Ojore tried his best to stay by her side, but was soon torn away to engage a larger foe.

Sweat dripped down her face, stinging her eyes as she fought on. Arrows occasionally rained in the air, hitting unsuspecting targets unmercifully. She dodged them with ease, watching a few of her armies own fly into the opposite direction, until a bigger body un-knowingly slammed onto her from behind. Her hands braced her fall.

The dirt, mixed with blood and other bodily fluids, crunched un-der her palms. She focused on reintroducing air back into her lungs before she sat on her knees. With a glance at her surroundings, it all came crashing down.

The army she had built over the past two months had begun to waver. Men—her men, her allies' men—followed her order and were then chopped into pieces.

Fire had alighted and spread across the withered grass, lighting up the skies with smoke and heat. More horses buckled from the flames, galloping and trampling clueless men. It was quick to spread.

Rayne was nowhere to be found. Ojore had fallen not too far, wounded, a hand clasped over his hip as blood seeped through his fin-gers. In the corner of her eye, Mael glanced over his shoulder and fled, swinging his sword against enemies.

Hopelessness grew on her face.

Screams and shouts echoed in her ears. The blood of her enemies and her men stained her armor and skin. Her chest felt heavy.

More than half of her army was gone. It was not enough men after all.

Was this it? The end of her beloved kingdom?

Charlotte's face came to mind. Then her husband, followed by her brother. She wondered what her unborn child would look like. Would he be as daring as his father, but just as gentle? Or beautiful as she is, but with determination in her heart? She would only know if she somehow, by miracle, survived this battle.

But from the turn of events, even a miracle would not be enough.

She had failed.

Failed her allies.

Failed her people.

Failed herself.

The queen closed her eyes and inhaled deeply.

This was it—the end.

Unknowingly to her, she was watched from a distance. Prince Alexander had kept his eye on her, tracking every move, much like a hawk stalking its prey. He awaited this moment, only defending himself from the knights who dared to challenge him. He had already lost his steed to the chaos, but approaching on foot would make him nearly invisible amongst the crowd.

And so, he drew his bloodied sword, eyes cold and focused, as he began his lethal advance.

His heart raced with anticipation. The thought of spilling her blood sent shivers of excitement down his spine, orgasmic to the mind. Revenge for his father would finally be commended.

Rayne's voice echoed faintly in the distance, calling out to her, but it was drowned out by the cacophony of battle. He saw what was unraveling. His queen was in danger.

He kicked his horse into a gallop, stepping on bodies and dodging men to reach her, but it was not fast enough. The prince's sword had already risen from behind, building his momentum for a swing that would slice her neck. He was going to decapitate her.

Panic shook his voice as he called out again, "Lucia!!"

She opened her eyes and twisted her body to the shadow of her assailant. Alexander smirked, his sword raised, ready to strike. She tried to move for her blade on the grass, but she was too slow. Not even a second was enough.

"ARGH!"

A sloppy slice of the underarm, the sword dropping onto the crunchy grass.

Ojore, baring his teeth, braced the pain in his hip as he hovered over the queen. Darkness threatened to overcome him, balance swaying. But despite his odds, he had somehow swung with enough accuracy.

"Fuck!!" Alexander hissed as he clutched his armpit, staggering away. Blood gushed and gushed and gushed.

But before he could seek refuge, the ground began to rattle. His body vibrated, and his men screamed.

"Move! Move! Move!"

"Brace yourselves!"

"Run!"

"Look out!"

Lucia felt like she could not breathe.

This was greater than an omen.

Rows and rows of colorful horses, dressed in fine fabrics, raced through the flames. Their riders, clad in vibrant and intricately designed armor proudly displaying the Morningstar emblem, charged forward with a fierce determination that immediately panicked the enemy.

Alexander cursed under his breath as he fled from the ambush.

Damn the queen. Damn his men. He needed to get away now.

The air was thick with the scent of sweat, blood, and fear as the Morningstar army clashed in a violent dance of death. Foes were mowed down, the front lines standing strong.

A surge of triumph coursed through Lucia's veins.

This was her brother's army.

Her brother had gotten her letter.

Nadia must have survived.

Kingdom Ironwood and Shadowmere's forces were caught off guard by the sudden onslaught.

King Alaric rode alongside Remus, his sword drawn from its sheath as he roared for war. The pain from his wounded abdomen burned with each swing of his blade, but he gritted his teeth and prayed the stitches would hold.

Due to the foes' weak defense on the unfinished road, the men left present were easily sliced down by the front lines. Only a few knights were injured on their side; no casualties. However, when the army neared the territory lines of his beloved kingdom, the charred bones littering the ground made the king's stomach churn with pity and dread. Just by a miracle, he managed not to lie amongst the massive graves that marked the conflict two months ago. He made mental plans to return to show proper respect.

The initial plan was to reach the palace, but it was quickly abandoned as dark smoke was spotted from the horizon, changing the army's course. With a heavy heart, they headed towards the smoke, and Alaric prayed he was not too late for his kingdom and his family.

Bodies dropped one by one by Alaric's sword.

The crackling flames engulfing the grass created a thick, choking smoke that obscured his vision. Men were trapped in the inferno, their screams echoing through the air. Horses ran wildly, their burning pelts flapping in the heat as they fled in pain. The fire was quickly becoming uncontainable, spreading rapidly across the battlefield.

Alaric scanned the field desperately, his eyes straining to spot the golden queen amidst the mayhem.

His queen. His wife. She was out there, fighting valiantly, and he had to find her.

The thought of her in harm's way ignited fiery within him. He charged his horse forward, his sword slicing through the smoke, his armor clanking against the steel of his enemies.

He had to find her. He had to protect her. The thought of losing her was a fate worse than death itself.

Alaric pressed on, his arm growing weary but his resolve unwavering. His eyes studied the field again for a glimpse of her golden hair. But instead, through the haze, he caught a glimpse of Prince Alexander dashing towards the tree line, grasping his underarm.

He was fleeing.

Fleeing.

From all this death. All this sorrow, and pain and selfish vengeance—-all due to him, by his lead.

Retreat was not optional. He had to *die*.

Alaric wasted no time, sheathing his sword and kicking his horse into a gallop towards him.

36

A Woman's Rage

A pair of hooves grew steadily louder, and Alexander dared to glance over his shoulder. A gasp escaped his lips.

It was not possible.

How?

How?

Was he being chased by a ghost? Sent by Hell to torment him?

The prince tried to run faster, but his legs gave out from the blood loss. He could not go any faster as the animal's steps were right behind him.

Without warning, Alaric leaped off his mount and tackled the prince. Their bodies rolled across the ground, armor clanging and flying, until they were separated by mere feet. Mud caked onto their skin, stirred up from the campgrounds of men who were likely sprawled out dead in the field somewhere.

Alexander looked up and gasped. Shock etched on his face. The ghost of his enemy was not a ghost, sent from Hell to plague him, but alive in flesh and blood. This did not make sense.

"How are you alive?!" he hollered, struggling to stand from the slick ground. His wound had nearly stopped bleeding, but he lacked the energy and strength to keep his arm upright. He reached for his dagger with his good arm, the metal slinging out of its sheath around his waist.

"Your attempt at assassination was pathetic," Alaric said, rising to his feet as well. He drew his sword. An unfair fight, he thought, but the prince did not deserve fairness.

Alexander snarled. "No, it is the grace of God that you walk again."

"Then my time was not due."

Alexander laughed and lunged, swinging his dagger with all possible might with his good arm. Alaric weaved the sharp, clean blade that whistled past him. Never once had it touched his skin. The prince continued, "Your time may not, but I cannot promise that pretty little wife of yours would be as blessed as you."

Heat rushed Alaric's face, ears ringing, nares flared. "Watch your tongue," he growled, raising his sword to swing. Alexander used the last remaining strength in his injured arm to hold the dagger sideways to parry the blow. A spark ignited.

Alexander hid the pain that pierced his hand from his own dagger, groaning to keep the weapon at bay. "Do not fret, she managed to escape my clutches, but my ally knows very well to capture her for my killing blow."

Alaric cursed and did an under-swing, knocking the dagger from the prince's hold. Before Alexander could defend himself, the king was already a blur of motion towards him. "You have threatened my home."

Alexander yelped from a slice to the side.

"You have threatened my people."

Another slice on the injured arm, more blood staining.

"And you have threatened my wife," Alaric stated as he carved at his foe's knee. Alexander howled in pain as he stumbled backward on his ass. The king hovered like the grim reaper. "And your life can only pay for those words and actions." He raised his sword.

Alexander grunted as he rolled away from Alaric's swing, the sword burying into the mud beside him. He grabbed at his dagger that lay not too far. "I would like to see you try!"

Sparks lightened the air. Their bodies danced around. Alaric huffed through the pain, but kept going despite knowing well that a few stitches had popped open. He felt the warmth pool on his abdomen.

What felt like a dance of eternity, came to an end as the prince faltered in his balance from his wounded knee and could not evade Alaric's weapon.

Metal contacted skin.

Air escaped Alexander's lungs as Alaric's blade sank into his midsection. It was agonizingly deep, inch by inch, driven by the king's strength. Pain that felt like fire ignited and shook his body. He looked down in horror as blood quickly spread and soaked his under armor. "What have you done?!"

In one swipe, the blade exited his body. Blood flung in the air.

A scream left Alexander's lips, tasting iron as he fell to his knees. The wound narrowly missed his rib cage. He met Alaric's eyes, his own watering. "You...You demon. You have cursed my family name by your commoner blood. Took my father and now, you stand before me to claim what is left of him."

Alaric did not say a word.

"I curse you and your kingdom to Hell. And I curse your mad bastard of a wife to birth stillborn heirs for the remainder of her life!"

The king continued to stare. The prince was a dead man talking.

Instead, he simply turned and walked out of view.

Alexander took this as a chance to get back on his feet, but it was unbearable. He panted hard, the blood in his mouth trying to clog his throat. The pain made him shake violently.

He cried out in misery.

Everything around him waved and faded from view.

He was not sure if he could be saved. The terms of dying in the forest alone were becoming a reality.

But then, Alaric approached with his hands full.

A rope.

The same one that hung the hay doll from the tree branch for many months prior. He recognized it.

With his iron boots planted firmly on the ground, the king's shadow casted a dark silhouette over the bent figure of the prince. Alexander whimpered, "What do you have in mind now, *king?* I did not take you as a sadist."

Alaric could have already left the man to die from blood loss. To be eaten by animals. Allow the mud to swallow him whole.

No.

Death by sword was too merciful. He had to *suffer.*

A nasty cut-off gag followed as Alaric fought to secure the rope around Alexander's neck, using his weight as he pulled it taut. The noose dug into the prince's neck. He was too weak to prevent the inevitable.

"You talk too much," Alaric said as he watched Alexander's eyes bulge, his face turning red as he choked, spittle flying from his lips. His hands reached for his neck, fingers weakly digging for the rope. It was a beautiful display for the king, but not enough to satisfy him.

Bracing the pain in his abdomen, Alaric hauled the prince by the rope's end until he found a sturdy branch. Alexander produced more awful sounds as he was dragged through the mud, meeting his approaching end as Alaric lashed the rope around it. With a firm grip, he pulled.

Alexander's body jerked and convulsed, now turning blue, then purple, using whatever remained in his body to fight. A face of agony, limbs flailing uselessly. Alaric watched as his foes' struggles grew weaker, not a hint of empathy for the man.

He deserved none of it.

And if he did end up in Hell by his curse, he would have no regret. This was repayment for all the pain he had caused to his kingdom and family.

It only took a handful of minutes for the prince's body to go limp, hanging lifelessly from the branch. His underarmor clothing reeked of blood and bodily fluids. Soon, it would attract flies.

Alaric did not even consider cutting him down, leaving the dead prince as a final spectacle of his own fallen kingdom. He was unsure what would happen to the remaining townsfolk who followed him, but that was a worrisome problem for later.

As he emerged from the dying forest, his hand applying pressure against his open stitching, his foot slipped, and he fell on his knees. His arms and legs felt so, so weak, and his head was spinning.

He sighed in annoyance and forced himself upwards, grinding his teeth from all the pressures and aches in his body. Just as he looked outwards, a flash of gold caught his eye.

Far from the distance, blended in amongst the flames, his wife fought.

Kingdom Morningstar had arrived.

Ojore, bloodied and battered, helped the queen back onto her feet, nearly stumbling as he stood hunched over. "You need aid," Lucia said.

"Queen Lucia, I can manage."

Lucia scoffed. "Our chances of victory have shifted to our favor. My brother's army is here. I need you alive."

Before Ojore could protest further, Rayne reared his horse in front of them, relief painted on his face. He had finally caught up.

"Rayne, take him. He needs aid," Lucia ordered.

Rayne reached down and, with Lucia's help, managed to pull the husky man onto his steed. His blood stained their hands. With a nod to the queen, Rayne flapped the reins and charged, veering away from the enemy lines while carrying Ojore to safety towards the back of the army.

Ojore groaned, resting his forehead against the knight's shoulder. Rayne did not mind, as he was to make sure this man stayed alive. He swore to owe him a life debt for defending his queen.

Lucia whistled, and Emris raced across the flames with bravery in his heart. The two had been separated earlier, but the queen allowed the intelligent steed to create distance for his safety.

She gathered the momentum and mounted him, kicking him into a gallop to resume her fighting alongside her brother's army. Her sword flashed like a warm firelight as she cut down foe after foe. Numbers dropped drastically.

She searched for her brother while she fought. She was unsure if he was actually present since she did not see who led the army, but she hoped he was all right. She doubted Nadia would be present because of her reduced ability to fight. Nonetheless, with each swing, she prayed for her fallen men and pushed forward to victory.

A familiar yelling voice caught Lucia's attention. There, from a distance, stood Remus, engaged in a fight against an unidentified foe. It wasn't until the foe turned that she recognized who it was.

King Victor.

The clash of swords echoed through the air, and flames engulfed the grass around them. Determined to help Remus, Lucia urged Emris forward, galloping towards the confrontation.

But before she could help, Victor managed to overpower Remus, causing the knight to lose some of his armor plates and tumble to the ground. The king then stabbed his sword into Remus's exposed shoulder, causing a sickening crunch and shattering of bones. Remus hollered a painful cry.

"No!" Lucia shouted, kicking Emris faster. The horse neighed loudly, his saliva drooling from his bit mouthpiece.

A few words were exchanged, but the queen could not hear from the pounding of her ears as she drew her sword and, in a flash, carved into Victor's exposed backside. Superficial, but enough to sting.

Victor hissed and whipped around.

A devilish smile enlightened his face when he saw the assailant.

Lucia had no fear as she stopped Emris, turning him to face her foe. The king pulled his weapon out of Remus, blood dripping from its tip. "Look who it is," he said with a deep chuckle, flicking his sword. Dark crimson splattered the dry grass.

Remus' eyes widened, glazed over in pain. "Do not...," he pleaded. Fresh wounds marred his face as he struggled to maintain consciousness. He could not dare to see the girl who grew up before his eyes, be ended as well. He would not be able to bear it.

As Lucia hopped off her husband's steed, she asked, "Where is your ass-kisser?"

"Prince Alexander?" Victor shrugged. "I do not know." Truthfully, he had not seen his ally in a while, but all he could do was hope he had not fallen. "But it does not stop me from having you for myself. I just won't kill you, though."

Lucia spat, "Shut it! That is, very well, a lie!"

Victor laughed wickedly and raised his sword, pointing directly at her. "I was told by your father that you were an obedient bitch. All this time, I believe he lied."

Lucifer remained silent, but her eyes spoke volumes of anger. She clenched her fists tightly around the hilt of her sword.

"You were always a corrupted female, an *actual* venomous snake in disguise, but he was too prideful of his throne that he had you dressed like a doll and lied about. From what I have gathered from your past, I believe you are solely responsible for your first husband's death."

They began to circle, swords ready.

"How did you do it? Did you poison him? Choke him in his sleep? Stabbed him through the heart? It would not be hard to believe, since you seem to think you can be a leader, drunk on seeking the ultimate power," Victor taunted.

Lucia sniggered, "You truly believe I murdered my first husband?"

"I have no doubt, seeing how you are right now."

"He is scared," Remus murmured, applying pressure on his seeping wound with his good arm. He still lay on the grass.

"I do not need your erroneous opinion!" Victor snapped. "Besides, let's end this make-believe play. You have no place to be here, regardless, *man-killer*."

"You can believe in any delusions that feed into your ego, but I have every right to be here to honor my husband and protect his kingdom, you disgraceful chicken shit!" And she lunged.

CLANG

Metal vibrated.

Victor deflected her strike easily before countering with a swift jab at her side. She dodged it, feeling the wind of his sword whistle past her ear.

Their eyes locked in a fierce gaze as their weapons clashed again and again and again, each strike more powerful than the last. Sweat beaded on their foreheads as they circled each other warily again. "I cannot believe I am fighting a pregnant bitch!" Victor sneered. The fire around them intensified.

"Cockered-clotpole!"

Victor roared and charged. Their blades met once more, sparks flying in all directions. Lucia's breath came in ragged gasps as she fought with all her might against the stronger opponent. She could feel the heat of the flames licking at her skin, but she refused to back down.

The final dance.

Death vs. Life.

One wrong move, and either opponent was the winner.

The smile never once left the king's face. This was entertaining. Remus tried to move, to help in any way he could, but unconsciousness quickly took over. Lucia was on her own, fighting against a foe that wished to see her destroyed.

With a swift riposte, Victor's sword sliced across her cheek, drawing blood. "There goes that beauty of yours!"

Lucia did not cry, did not falter or whine as her skin burned, the blood trickling down her face. She did not care if she emerged from the battle carved up beyond beauty. She only cared if her kingdom survived. She swept forward and thrust her pointed sword, but Victor managed to underswipe her weapon, causing it to fly from her grip.

A triumph for the king.

She was defenseless and up for the taking, just as long as she was kept alive for Prince Alexander. Beginning with slices behind the knees would subdue.

But then a flash of light hit his eyes—next, a sudden sharp pain in his chest.

A feint.

It was all a feint.

She had allowed him to swipe her weapon. And in exchange, a dagger was plunged into the side of the king's chest, right behind his chest plate.

Her dagger. Marked between ribs, piercing a lung.

Blood immediately spewed out of Victor's nose and mouth, painting his chin and neck red. He could not breathe. No air could go in. He was drowning, a lung filling up and choking the other.

The sound of his gargling filled the air, a satisfying music to her ears as she watched in disbelief.

He was dying.

He was truly dying.

She had *won.*

Victor took a step back, his sword clattering to the ground as he fell backward, the dagger still lodged deep. More gargling sounds followed as he stared upwards to the smoky sky.

The king was finished.

Nothing could save him.

She glanced at Remus, noting his chest moving up and down as he lay on the ground. She wanted to approach him, to shake him awake, and tell him the news, but her feet refused to move. There were too many complications of emotions swarming her. Her hands trembled uncontrollably.

She felt mad.

So, so mad, and confused, and frustrated.

All this war, all this fighting.

There was still Prince Alexander to deal with. But did it matter now?

The air in her lungs sped up, and her surroundings moved and waved around her, dizzying her vision. She collapsed to her knees, and the prickly dry grass tickled her hands.

Fire continued to burn. Men still fought in the distance. Piles and piles of bodies surrounded her.

So many lives lost. So many. And, at what cost?

She released a wail of frustration. Spit flew everywhere. Tears swelled in her eyes.

Nothing could bring her life back to what it was months ago. Nothing at all.

She looked up at the darkened sky, the sun covered from the layers of smoke. She had to keep going, to pick herself up and keep going. But she was so tired.

Her bloodied hands moved to her abdomen, feeling for her unborn child.

She was so, so tired.

Without warning, arms wrapped around her from behind. She thrashed, using her elbows to jab her unknown enemy. "I will kill you! I will kill you! Let me go!"

"My love–!"

A familiar scent hit her nostrils, the gentle voice to her ears.

This could not be *real.*

It can't be.

Lucia turned and gasped. "Alaric–!"

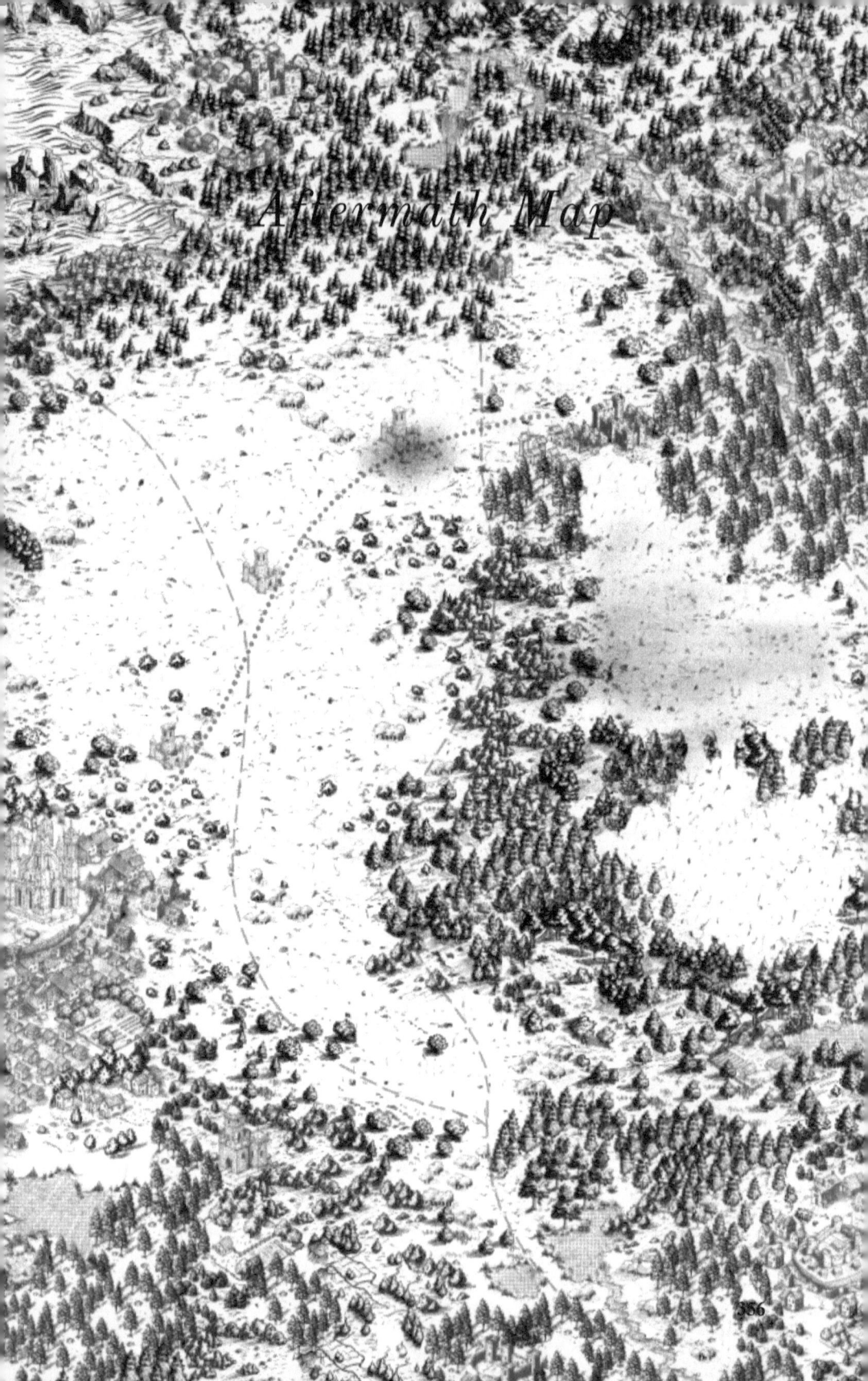

Aftermath Map

Acknowledgements

So, this is my first ever published work. I never dreamed of ever publishing a novel, but with encouragement from my family, I'm like, "fuck it," and I don't think I'll plan on stopping soon. I had too much fun writing, and the idea of sharing with readers out there in the world just gave me too much joy and excitement. I was looking forward to the brainstorming, the art, the cover, the editing, and so much more when creating this world.

I am unsure when I will publish another novel, but I have so many incomplete drafts written that I've abandoned on my Google Drive. I think I will steal one of those and see if I can expand into a new world with lovely characters.

I want to thank my family for being my number one supporter and pushing me to do this. My sister, specifically, told me not to hold back and express the details, even if it was morally uncomfortable or explicit. My mom and dad told me not to hold back my imagination. And to my best friend, Jacky, for always being there to listen to my rambling, creative ideas. You have never told me to stop or that I couldn't do it. Instead, you read some of my work and believed it was achievable. And for that, I will forever hold in memory. Not every day can you randomly announce you'll write and publish a book without a hint of criticism or disbelief.

This story was brainstormed in June 2024, officially finished in October 2025.

This novel was previously published as an uncompleted fanfiction online. The characters have been altered to avoid copyright, but the writing is original and revised. The online username and author of this book are the same individual.

Born and raised in Texas, Anya Mamaeva is a solid tumor & hematology on-cology nurse while part-time in school for acute care nurse practitioner. On her days off, she enjoys allowing her imagination to run wild, having an in-terest and passion for writing since middle school; however, it wasn't until 2024 that she found the courage to share her stories. When she's not im-mersed in her work or lost in the pages of a book, she's either reading or cre-ating other forms of art, constantly sipping on a Dr. Pepper. Her only child is her enigmatic black cat, Rune.

For comments or concerns, feel free to contact us at our website or email:
www.mamaevabooks.com
amamaevabooks@gmail.com

www.ingramcontent.com/pod-product-compliance
Lightning Source LLC
Chambersburg PA
CBHW030230120726
47903CB00005B/1429